Emily Harvale lives in East Sussex, in the UK – although she would prefer to live in the French Alps…or Canada…or anywhere that has several months of snow. Emily loves snow almost as much as she loves Christmas.

Having worked in the City (London) for several years, Emily returned to her home town of Hastings where she spends her days writing. And wondering if it will snow.

You can contact her via her website, Twitter, Facebook or Instagram.

There is also a Facebook group where fans can chat with Emily about her books, her writing day and life in general. Details are on the 'For You' page of Emily's website.

Author contacts:
www.emilyharvale.com
www.twitter.com/emilyharvale
www.facebook.com/emilyharvalewriter
www.instagram.com/emilyharvale

***

Scan the code above to see all Emily's books on Amazon

Also by this author

Highland Fling
Lizzie Marshall's Wedding
The Golf Widows' Club
Sailing Solo
Carole Singer's Christmas
Christmas Wishes
A Slippery Slope
The Perfect Christmas Plan
Be Mine
It Takes Two
Bells and Bows on Mistletoe Row

The Goldebury Bay series:
Ninety Days of Summer – book 1
Ninety Steps to Summerhill – book 2
Ninety Days to Christmas – book 3

The Hideaway Down series:
A Christmas Hideaway – book 1
Catch A Falling Star – book 2
Walking on Sunshine – book 3
Dancing in the Rain – book 4

Hall's Cross series
Deck the Halls – book 1
The Starlight Ball – book 2

Michaelmas Bay series
Christmas Secrets in Snowflake Cove – book 1
Blame it on the Moonlight – book 2

Lily Pond Lane series
The Cottage on Lily Pond Lane –
Part One – New beginnings and Summer secrets
Part Two – Autumn leaves and Trick or treat
Christmas on Lily Pond Lane
Return to Lily Pond Lane
A Wedding on Lily Pond Lane
Secret Wishes and Summer Kisses on Lily Pond Lane

Wyntersleap series
Christmas at Wynter House – book 1

Merriment Bay series
Coming Home to Merriment Bay – book 1

Coming Home

to

Merriment Bay

Emily Harvale

ISBN 978-1-909917-52-1

Published by Crescent Gate Publishing

Print edition published worldwide 2019
E-edition published worldwide 2019

Editor Christina Harkness

Cover design by JR and Emily Harvale

In loving memory of my grandmother, May,
who encouraged me to tell stories.

Chapter One

'There's a letter for you, Mum. And it's postmarked Merriment Bay.'

Cat Devon recognised the writing on the stark white envelope the moment her daughter, Kyra placed it in front of her on the kitchen table. Even after eighteen years, the sight of those sharp angular capitals, three times the size of the rest of the spidery scrawl, brought back that last day in Merriment Bay, so long ago now that Cat rarely thought of it, or what she'd left behind.

Until now.

At least that's what she told herself.

She met Kyra's concerned stare and forced a smile.

'Perhaps it's a birthday card. It is your eighteenth, after all.'

Kyra snorted derisively, tossing a lock of long, unruly ginger curls over her shoulder. She dropped her colourful canvas bag – bearing an image of one of Cat's paintings – on the floor, pulled out a wooden chair, twisted it around and swung her long legs over the cushioned seat, resting her arms on the top of the back rail.

'Yeah right. And what would it say? "Happy eighteenth from your gran and great-gran in Merriment Bay. Sorry we haven't been in touch for eighteen years but there was a bit of a falling out and all the Devon women are far too stubborn to make the first move and apologise." If it was a birthday card, it would be addressed to me, not you. Are you going to open it?' Despite the acerbic tone, Kyra grinned.

Cat shrugged and nonchalantly pushed it away, but her heart pounded and a lump formed in her throat, making it difficult to swallow. She forced down several swigs of coffee and gave another laboured smile.

'Maybe later.' She stood up, the feet of her chair scraping against the tiled floor as she did so, and on jelly-like legs, walked to the fridge. 'Is it too early to open the champagne?' She grabbed the bottle and wiggled it in her hand.

Kyra laughed. 'It's never too early for champagne. It may be 8.00 a.m. in Bonniemount, but somewhere in the world, it's cocktail hour. And it *is* my eighteenth. One glass won't hurt.'

'I can add some orange juice.'

'God, no. That's murdering two perfectly good drinks, in my opinion.'

Cat closed the fridge door and Kyra got up and grabbed two glasses.

'Get a couple of plates, too, please.' Cat opened the cupboard next to the fridge and, putting the bottle on the worktop she quickly did the necessary before turning around; a birthday cake set on a glittery cake stand in her hand, with lit candles and a sparkler sticking out of the top of the purple and white iced numbers, one and eight. 'Ta dah. Happy birthday to you. Happy birthday, dearest, darling, wonderful daughter. Happy birthday to you!'

'Aww, Mum. That's gorgeous. Thank you.'

Kyra beamed at her, put the glasses and plates on the table and dashed towards Cat. She took the cake from her and placed that on the table too, before giving her mum a massive hug, towering over Cat's five-feet-five frame by at least four inches.

A few seconds later, Cat took her daughter by the arm and swivelled her around, grabbing the champagne again. 'Don't forget to make a wish.' She stepped away, popped the cork and filled the glasses.

Kyra closed her eyes, blew out the candles and the sparkler, bit her lower lip, as she often did whilst thinking, and after a little while, reopened her eyes and smiled.

'All done. And if that comes true, I'll believe in miracles.'

'I truly hope this year brings you nothing but miracles and magic, happiness and good health, warmth and wealth, love and laughter, shelter and safety. May all your dreams come true and your wishes be granted.' Cat handed Kyra a glass and raised hers in the air. 'To you, Kyra. The best

3

daughter any mum could ever hope for. Happy birthday, sweetheart.'

'Aww, thanks. And to the best mum in the world. Are we really having cake and champagne for breakfast?'

'Absolutely. We can have a fry-up for lunch. You'll need something substantial inside you if you're going out with your friends tonight.'

Cat cut the number one of the cake and they sat down again, munching on the layers of melt-in-the-mouth sponge, homemade raspberry jam, together with the cream filling and soft, thick icing, sipping champagne between mouthfuls.

'This cake's delicious, as always. I wish I could bake even half as good as you.' Kyra licked off a dollop of jam that had oozed out on to her finger. 'So are you going to open it?'

Cat shot a look at the envelope but quickly looked away, taking a gulp of champagne.

'Not yet. It's been eighteen years. They can wait a little longer. You've got presents to open before you dash off to get your results. And you should check your emails. The university may have emailed you.'

Kyra raised her expressive green eyes heavenwards. 'Thanks for reminding me. They'll only email if my results are good and I get in. At least if they're bad, I can postpone my plans and retake the exams.'

Cat tutted. 'They'll be brilliant. Because you're brilliant. You may not have inherited my baking

4

skills, but luckily for you, you didn't inherit my abysmal intelligence either. You take after your dad in the brains department.'

A momentary wave of sadness swept over Kyra's freckled face. 'I wish I'd met him.' She let out a small sigh. 'But don't keep avoiding the subject, Mum. Why won't you open the letter?'

Cat flinched. 'I wish you'd met him too. And that's another reason why I don't want to open it yet. Besides, this is a special day. I've got a feeling that letter may ruin it and I don't want that. They ruined quite enough. They're not going to spoil this day. We'll open it together tomorrow. Deal?'

Kyra tilted her head to one side and bit her lower lip again but after a second or two, she nodded. 'Deal. But let me just say this and then I'll shut up about it. Eighteen years is a long time, Mum. That letter could be telling you that something has happened to Granny Viola. Or to your mum.'

Cat sucked in a long breath and nodded. 'I know. And that's also why I don't want to open it today. That's Mum's writing on the envelope, so the only thing she'd be telling me is that Granny Viola has passed away. If that's the case, another day's not going to change that.'

'Or one of them could've had an accident. A day could change that. A day could make all the difference in the world. All I'm saying is, no matter what that letter says, it won't ruin today. We won't let it. And there's not much point in delaying it. You know as well as me that you're going to be worrying about it all day. It's going to be like a thorn in a dog's paw, festering away and you'll keep chewing at it until it comes out.' Kyra tapped Cat's fingers with her own. 'And we've got champagne today. At least we can drown any sorrows it might bring. Or celebrate if it's good news.'

A slow smile spread across Cat's face, pushing the scar running the length of her left cheek into tiny ridges of pale skin. For years she wore her long, dark chocolate-coloured hair down, to hide the scar on her face as much as possible, and high-necked blouses or dresses to hide the scars on her neck and shoulder, but now, here in Bonniemount at least, and especially at home with Kyra, her scars didn't bother her. Although they did seem to bother some people.

'It can't be good news, sweetheart. Unless they've both decided they were wrong and they're finally asking to see us again. And I'm pretty sure it won't be that. But OK. You're right. We'll open it after you've opened your presents. And once you've checked your emails.'

'Open it before. Then if it is bad news, we'll still both have something good to look forward to. Possibly two good things if I get into uni.'

Cat gave a little laugh. 'You're so stubborn and bossy. But as it's your birthday, we'll do as you say.'

Kyra laughed too. 'I'm a Devon and Devon women are all bossy. And stubborn to the core.

That's one of the first things you told me when you explained about Merriment Bay.'

Cat's insides were like a washing machine but outside she smiled as Kyra slid the envelope back to her across the table.

The one thing Kyra hadn't asked – and what was puzzling Cat the most – was how Mary Devon had found them.

Chapter Two

Amias Wells inhaled a deep breath, narrowed his dark eyes beneath his Raybans, and prayed. Not to God. He lost any faith he may have had in such an entity long ago. Now he prayed to the Universe, or anything out there that might be inclined to listen. Not that he really believed there was anyone or anything out there, listening. But he did believe in will power and inner strength. And this kid had both of those, in spades.

'Come on, Marcus,' he whispered between clenched teeth and a tight jaw. 'You can do it.'

And for a couple of seconds, Marcus did.

So the splash when the kid fell in didn't bother Amias as much as it clearly did, Marcus' grandparents.

'I don't know what's the matter with the boy.' George Lester tutted and looked away.

Sybil Lester snorted in derision. 'I told you it was a complete and utter waste of money. But would you listen? Oh no. George Lester always knows best. Well, clearly he doesn't, does he?'

'You were the one who said you were glad he was spending the summer here and perhaps he could try again at sailing, windsurfing, and the like.'

'But did you have to buy the bloody windsurf board thing and all the kit and caboodle? Just because Lucas is good at sports, it doesn't mean Marcus ever will be. They're cousins, not brothers. You could've just rented it. Amias suggested that was the best thing to do. He even said not all kids take to water sports. And let's face it, when has Marcus ever shown any interest in anything other than that bloody computer of his and those stupid model aeroplanes he and Lucas build?'

That was it. Amias had had enough.

'Sybil. George. Will you please take your bickering elsewhere. What Marcus needs is confidence. Self-belief. And frankly, you two don't inspire either.

Sybil's mouth dropped open and George's face resembled a pot about to boil over – a big, red, cast iron pot.

'You may want to take that back, Amias Wells,' George said, his eyes forming tiny slits. 'Are you forgetting who my son is, and that I was also on the Merriment Bay Council? I could have your licence revoked just like that.' He clicked his fat fingers together and sneered.

'As you remind me and everyone else at every opportunity, George, I could hardly forget the heady heights you reached. But I think you'll find you overestimate your power. It's Will who's the elected Mayor of Merriment Bay. And I know I don't have to remind *you*, he's a very good friend of mine.'

'You think my own son will side with you, rather than me?'

A slow grin spread across Amias' face. 'You're welcome to ask him and see. But for now, please leave Marcus here with me and go and enjoy an afternoon at The Hope and Anchor. I know that's where you'd both much rather be. I'll drop him home later.'

George briefly met Amias' gaze before lowering his eyes. 'I'm not paying for the whole afternoon.'

Amias turned away with barely veiled disdain. 'That's fine. Marcus can help me pack things away later in return for an extended lesson.'

Without waiting for their reply, he walked towards the edge of Wyntersleap Reservoir where the water gently lapped at the sand-coloured concrete and towards which, Marcus was paddling his windsurfer and sunken sail with a huge smile on his face. Amias smiled back and gave Marcus a thumbs up.

He shouldn't have taken his bad mood out on Sybil and George, even if they were a pair of jerks, but when he glanced over his shoulder, they were marching towards their car. They weren't even going to wait to tell Marcus what was happening. Or to give him the slightest iota of encouragement. They really were complete gits.

But they were also customers and he was running a business. Alienating the Lesters wasn't one of his better moves, even if his business was highly successful and extremely profitable. George was all bluster and his son, Will shared Amias' opinion of his parents, but George had friends. Well, one or two cronies really, at the Merriment Bay Golf Club. But word got around, especially once Sybil's mouth started flapping at the Women's Institute meetings, the hairdresser's or the pub. He probably should apologise.

But he wouldn't.

These two weeks in August were always bad for him, even after all these years, and this year it was worse. He was furious with Lorna for telling Mary Devon where her daughter was, but he was angrier with himself for being stupid enough to tell Lorna in the first place. If he hadn't had so many beers followed by at least half a bottle of whisky, he wouldn't have been drunk and loose-tongued enough to do so. But then if he hadn't been foolish enough to agree to see Lorna on the eighteenth anniversary of Kyle's death two weeks ago, he wouldn't have been telling anyone other than his drunken self that he was still so angry about it. That time hadn't lessened the guilt, or diminished the pain. And it definitely hadn't healed the hole in his heart that seemed to get bigger with every passing year; not mend so that he could move on with his life and put the past behind him.

Eighteen years. Where had they all gone?

If he let himself, he could see his best friend as if the eighteen-year-old Kyle stood before him. The wild, ginger curls, those huge hazel eyes so full of life and laughter and plans for the future. So full of love for Cat sodding Devon.

But he wouldn't do that. He couldn't. Especially not this week.

And yet, only this morning he'd woken up wondering what she'd look like. Kyra. The daughter of his best friend. And Cat. Bloody Cat. If only she had never come into their lives. If only she'd stayed on her side of River Wynter. The posh side of Merriment Bay. If only she hadn't wandered down to the bay every day that summer, looking far too sexy for a sixteen-year-old without even trying. And being far too friendly for someone like Kyle to resist. And exactly one year later, Kyle was dead. All because of Cat bloody Devon and her bitchy, snooty, hypocritical mum and gran.

'I did it, Amias!' Marcus tumbled off the board and splashed his way to the shore, dragging the windsurfer behind him. 'I stayed upright. At least, for a minute or two. Oh. Where're Nan and Granddad?' He glanced around, the triumphant smile fading and a look of dejection taking its place.

'They had to go.' Amias took Marcus by the shoulders. 'But they said to say they thought you did brilliantly. They were so pleased, in fact, they wanted you to stay and build on your success. So come on, kid. Back on this board and let's see what you've really got in here.' He gently poked a finger at Marcus' chest and turned him back towards the water.

'I'm not a kid, Amias.' Marcus twisted his head to look at Amias, and threw him a smile. 'I'll be eighteen next week. I'm a man. And I've been having sex for the last two years. Ever since I hit the legal age. Mustn't break the law. Granddad would kill me.' He gave a nervous little laugh.

'Don't be in too much of a hurry to grow up, Marcus. Adulthood isn't all it's cracked up to be. And if you're having sex, I assume you're taking precautions. Believe me, the last thing you want or need at your age is to get some girl pregnant. It'll change your entire future. It might even be the death of you.'

'Hey, man. What's that supposed to mean? Don't get all serious. I get enough of that from Granddad. And yes. I'm taking precautions. I'm not an idiot. Despite what Granddad thinks.' He hung his head and kicked at a loose chipping of concrete with his brand-new surf shoes.

Amias ruffled the blond waves that dripped on the shoulders of the equally new wetsuit, which made Marcus look like a stick of liquorice.

'Come on then, young man. Show me what you've got. And I'll make you a deal. Stay upright for five minutes this afternoon, and tomorrow I'll let you have a go on the Spitfire simulator for free.'

Marcus' blue eyes opened wide and his jaw dropped. 'Are you serious?'

Amias stood beside Marcus and nudged his arm. 'Deadly. So go and do your stuff.'

If anything could spur Marcus on, it was the

promise of half an hour at the controls of the Spitfire simulator in the Merriment Bay World War II Museum. Two of his passions rolled into one: computers and vintage planes. It cost thirty pounds a time for the privilege but that was a small price to pay to see even the tiniest hint of pride in their grandson on George and Sybil Lester's faces – if Marcus could learn to windsurf.

Besides, Amias didn't need to pay. Not only had he helped out at the museum for most of his life, he was now one of the owners which meant he could basically do anything he wanted as far as the museum went. But he would pay because it was the right thing to do. All profits from the simulator went to the RAF Benevolent Fund. He never had and never would, take advantage of his position. Unlike George Lester.

And he liked Marcus. Even if the kid did tell lies. Whoppers, in fact. If Marcus Lester was having sex – or ever had – Amias would eat his wetsuit. Now Marcus' cousin Lucas, on the other hand was definitely having sex. He was just a few months older than Marcus and they had the same shoulder-length blond wavy hair and the same passion for planes. They were both good kids too. But the similarities ended there. Marcus was clumsy, loose limbed and all pale skin and bone. Lucas was agile, tight-muscled, broad shouldered and the colour of builder's tea. Girls didn't notice Marcus; they spotted Lucas the second he walked on to the sand or rode like some Greek God across the waves on his kiteboard. And they fell at his feet like adoring slaves.

The same way Kyle had fallen at Cat Devon's feet, from the very first day he had met her.

Chapter Three

'Have you got everything?' Cat bundled suitcases and bags into the boot and glanced towards Kyra.

'Everything but the kitchen sink. Give me a sec and I'll go back and grab it.' Kyra laughed and when she shook her head, the gold locket Cat had given her for her birthday, bounced around her swan-like neck. 'Anyone would think we're moving to Merriment Bay, not just going for a visit.'

She was wearing the floaty, white cotton dress with purple flowers dotted over it; another of the presents Cat had given her. She looked remarkably grown up, as if she had blossomed overnight from a bud into a flower, and yet she retained a youthful innocence as though she wasn't quite ready to be a woman.

'But we don't know how long we'll be staying, do we, sweetheart? It's better to take everything we may need, rather than wish later that we'd brought it.'

'I think we may need a bigger car, Mum.'

Kyra had two holdalls slung across her body and was dragging two suitcases down the path from their cottage to the gravel area amongst the trees. It was just large enough to fit two cars, but that was more than adequate. Bonniemount Cottage, Cat and Kyra's home for the last eighteen years, rarely had many visitors.

It was hidden in a copse on the outskirts of Bonniemount, a tiny hamlet a few miles from Berwick-upon-Tweed and within earshot of the flowing waters of the River Tweed, and Cat still thanked her lucky stars for Isla Presley, the elderly woman who had owned it.

Eighteen years ago, on the very spot, Isla Presley had tapped on the window of Cat's car which had groaned to a halt, having run out of petrol.

'Are you lost, dear? Oh my Lord, you're crying.' Without another word, she had yanked open the car door and flung her arms around Cat's shoulders, dropping her torch on the grass in the process. This was long before the grass was replaced with gravel. 'What's the matter, child? Are you ill? Are you – Oh my Lord. Is that your baby? You don't look old enough.'

'I'm seventeen,' Cat said, unable to think of anything else. She swiped at her cheek with the tear-soaked sleeve of her jumper and turned to check on Kyra, who was sound asleep in her white, wicker bassinet, strapped safely on the rear seat. 'I took a wrong turn in the dark and now I've run out of petrol. And yes. This is Kyra. She's almost three months old.'

'Three months! Oh my Lord. Come inside and

have a cup of tea. I'll call Alastair. He'll have you sorted out in a jiffy and you can be on your way. Where are you off to? Visiting relatives? I can tell by your accent you're not from around these parts. I'd know a Northumberland accent anywhere and you don't have one. A southerner, I'd say.'

Cat nodded. 'The south-east coast. Um. Who's Alastair?'

'He owns Bonniemount Farm, but he's always got a can of petrol handy. And what he doesn't know about cars isn't worth knowing. Where did you say you were going?'

'Scotland.'

'Scotland's a big place, dear. Whereabouts?'

Cat shrugged. 'Edinburgh. If you'll give me Alastair's number, I can call him from my mobile.'

'No need for that. Come inside and get warm. It's chilly out here. We may be having an Indian Summer but late October nights come with a chill no matter what the weather. And rightly so. It's been far too warm for the time of year.'

Cat hesitated, glancing again at Kyra. She was tired and cold and could murder a cup of tea but this woman was a total stranger and they seemed to be in the middle of nowhere.

Isla Presley laughed. It was a warm and cheerful sound. 'I won't bite, dear. I promise. I'm Mrs Presley. No relation, and no, Elvis doesn't live here.' She chuckled at a joke Cat didn't really understand. 'But you can call me Isla. Of course you're wary. And rightly so. You never know these days, do you? I'm not sure what I can say to make you feel at ease. But I give you my word that you and Kyra will be perfectly safe with me. Much safer than you might be sitting all alone out here in the dark in this car. Oh, not that there's anyone around here to be afraid of. Quite the contrary. We're all a friendly bunch in Bonniemount. But one or two lorries come this way by mistake, just as you did, and when one of those juggernauts tears by, you certainly know about it.'

Cat decided to trust Isla Presley and it was one of the best decisions she had ever made. When it transpired that Cat's car hadn't just run out of petrol but the engine had died due to lack of oil, Isla had been Cat's saviour.

In the warmth and comfort of Bonniemount Cottage, Cat had told Isla the truth: that Kyra was just ten weeks old. She'd also told the truth about her unsightly scars. The truth about Kyle. Even the truth about how she, her mum and her gran had had the row to end all rows, and that she'd run away from home, as she and Kyle had planned, and was determined not to return to Merriment Bay.

From that day, Isla had been a surrogate mum and grandmother until the day she had died two years ago. Even after she died, in fact, because she left Bonniemount Cottage to Cat in her will, and a few thousand pounds to Kyra. And although, from time to time over the years, Isla had suggested that perhaps Cat might consider getting back in touch with the family she had left behind, when Cat refused, Isla dropped the subject.

Cat and Kyra managed to fit everything in the car and by 8.00 a.m. the morning after Kyra's eighteenth birthday and the arrival of the letter from Merriment Bay, they turned on to the A1 and followed the signs to 'The South'.

Cat had often wondered over the last eighteen years, when – not if – she would make this journey. Despite telling Isla she didn't want to get back in touch with her mum and her gran, Cat had always been certain she would, one day. Although she had no idea why. Or when. Merriment Bay held too many memories. Some good. Some bad. Some horrendous. But the moment she read the letter out loud to Kyra, she knew it was a journey she had to take as soon as possible. And Kyra agreed. Yet they both did so reluctantly.

With the help of Isla Presley, her warm welcome, her comfort and support, not to mention her love and generosity, Cat had been able to make a good life for herself and Kyra. And as crazy as it seemed, some instinct told her that if she went back to Merriment Bay, she wouldn't return to Bonniemount.

She'd had some money of her own when she had left Merriment Bay on that warm, late October day, and her intention had been to go to Edinburgh. She would find a place to live; she had enough for several months' rent; then she'd find a job and child care. Once that was sorted, she'd apply to study art, hopefully part-time, at the Edinburgh College of

Art, which was now under the umbrella of the University of Edinburgh where her own daughter would be going in September. But as Cat neared the border and darkness crept over the horizon, her petrol gauge flashed and the engine sputtered. Instead of continuing ahead, she had turned off the A1 and remained on the English side of the border. Her car broke down just a few minutes later and when she told Isla Presley the full story, Isla was convinced it was Fate.

'How long will the journey take?' Kyra asked. They had hardly said a word since leaving the cottage half an hour or so earlier.

Cat smiled and tried to sound more cheerful than she felt. 'Is this the grown-up version of "Are we there yet?" sweetheart, because if it is, I'm sorry to say there's an awfully long way to go. We'll be lucky if we arrive before nightfall.'

'We'll stop a few times on the way though, won't we? My bladder can't last for more than a few hours, let alone yours.' Kyra threw her a cheeky grin.

'I told you to pee before we left,' Cat joked.

Kyra rolled her eyes. 'I'm eighteen, Mum, not eight. I peed. Rather a lot, as it happens.'

'Too much information.'

'You're lucky that's all I did. What with cake and champers for breakfast yesterday, a fry-up for lunch together with more champers, thanks to getting the confirmation email and then my fab results, followed by several glasses of Prosecco with my mates, and finally a Vindaloo, I thought my head would be down the loo for most of today. Even though, after we read the letter, I was being careful and not drinking as much as originally intended.'

'I'm exceedingly grateful for your restraint. You were certainly home earlier than I'd expected. I didn't even hear you come in.'

'I did poke my head around your door just before midnight but you were snoring like an old tug boat and thrashing about.' Kyra gave a loud demonstration, pulling faces and wildly waving her arms around. 'Like that.'

Cat laughed. 'Thanks. I didn't think I'd sleep a wink and yet by ten, I was nodding off on the sofa so I went to bed.'

'Old age, Mum. It comes to us all.'

'It won't come to you if I have much more of your cheek, young lady. Oh God. I didn't mean that. I shouldn't have said it.'

'Hey. Calm down.' Kyra placed a comforting hand on Cat's arm. 'I know you were joking. This month is always bad for you but it's worse this year, isn't it? Is it because I'm the same age as my dad was when he died? The letter's made it worse, hasn't it?'

Cat nodded. 'It definitely feels different this year. I don't know why. Perhaps it's because of the age. I don't honestly know. And yes. The letter's made it worse.' Cat forced a grin. 'And by the way, thirty-five is not old. Even if it feels it sometimes.'

Kyra grinned back but a moment later she let

out a melancholy sigh. 'I'm not sure what I expected, but I think I expected more than it said: "Catherine, Your grandmother has had a fall and is in a coma in Eastbourne District General Hospital. You may or may not wish to see her but this might possibly be your last chance. You can stay here, if you do decide to come. Your room is as it was when you ran away eighteen years ago. Mum." I mean, it's not exactly love you, miss you, please come home because we're longing to see you, is it?'

Cat blinked at her. 'You remembered it word for word?'

Kyra shrugged. 'I can do that. You know I can.'

That was true. Kyra had what was called an eidetic memory, or photographic memory, or maybe just a damn good memory, because Kyra had only heard the contents when Cat had read the letter out over cake and champagne at breakfast yesterday, whereas Cat read it several times over and still couldn't remember what it said. Just what it didn't say.

It hadn't mentioned Kyra. It hadn't even acknowledged her existence. That had angered Cat far more than the lack of warmth or feeling.

'I can't even remember my own mobile phone number. You don't know how glad I am that you take after your dad in so many more ways than you take after me. All you've got from me are your stubbornness, bossiness, and love of art.'

'That's not all. I've got your optimism. Your generous nature. Your gorgeous green eyes.' She

23

fluttered her long lashes. 'Your smile. Everyone loves your smile and mine too. Your strength and determination. But what you've also given me is my freedom. Freedom to choose my own path, no matter what. And the knowledge that you'll love me whatever I do and whether you agree with it or not. Basically, you've given me the things that are truly important. Things you never got from your mum, or from Granny Viola. I still can't believe that letter. I don't know how your mum stays alive because she clearly doesn't have a heart. I'm not really sure I want to meet her. Can't we stay somewhere else?'

'Don't get upset, sweetheart. We've got this. You and me together can deal with anything. Remember? After we agreed we'd go, I did try everywhere I could think of. Merriment Bay is small and it's still only got a couple of B&Bs according to those hotel booking sites, but I did try farther afield. The problem is, it's August. There wasn't one room available anywhere, at least for the next two weeks. We'll probably be coming home by then. But if we're not, or if it's really too bad, I promise you we'll find something. The one good thing about my mum though, is she's so wrapped up in herself that she'll leave us to ourselves most of the time. I dated your father for months before she even noticed I wasn't in the house most evenings.'

'But once she did realise, she made your life hell. Both your lives.'

'It wasn't so bad. It was only when we discovered I was three months pregnant with you that things really went downhill.' Cat smiled and reached out and gave Kyra's hand a quick squeeze. 'And you were worth every second of it. Your dad thought so too. The odd thing is, despite everything that happened, and as painful as it's going to be to be back in my room again with all those memories, it would feel really strange to be in Merriment Bay or anywhere close by, and not stay in that house. It's still my home in many ways. And I think it always will be.'

'Was it really just because Dad came from the wrong side of the river that they didn't like him? Just because he was from a poor family? It's so Victorian. And so wrong.'

'I think there was a lot more to it all than just that, sweetheart, as I've always said. But yes, the fact that his family was poor was a big part of it. His father was unemployed with no prospect of finding work because he had no skills and he drank like a fish. He was hardly ever sober enough to get up in the mornings. His mother wasn't much better, sadly. It's a miracle your dad turned out the way he did. And where his intelligence came from will always remain a mystery. Although it was probably from his granddad. Your dad left school at sixteen and got a job just to help support the family but he should've gone to uni. Perhaps, if he hadn't met me, he would have. When I met him, he had such grand plans. The main one was to save some money so that he could go back to college and study to become an architect. But of course, that didn't happen.'

'You can't blame yourself for that, Mum. Or for his death. Which I know you sometimes do even though you always say you don't.'

'I know. But … well, we never know what life has in store for us and perhaps that's just as well. We might all do things so differently if we did.'

'What would you have done differently if you'd known how things would turn out?'

Cat darted a look at Kyra. There was only one thing she would have done differently. But if she'd done that, she wouldn't have had Kyra. And Kyra was the one thing in her life that she was really glad she had.

'Nothing, sweetheart. Nothing at all. Look. There's a service station ahead. I'm hungry. Are you? Shall we stop for breakfast? I know you said you couldn't face food earlier but maybe a coffee and a slice of toast?' She raised her eyebrows and grinned.

'I could do with a pee. And yeah. Coffee and toast sound good. Or maybe I could stomach a Full English now. But Mum?'

'Yes, sweetheart.' Cat indicated to exit left – and held her breath.

'You have told me the whole story, haven't you? About Dad and everything, I mean. Only I'm getting a very strange feeling that there may be something you haven't told me. Something that you think I might not want to hear. Something you're worried may upset me. It wouldn't. And I'd rather know. No secrets, remember. That's what we've always said. If there was something bad about Dad, I can handle it.'

'There was nothing bad about your dad, Kyra. Not one thing. That much I can promise you. And I've told you everything you need to know. Everything.'

'That sounds as if there's something you think I don't need to know. Mum, what is it? You've never mentioned this before. But there is something, isn't there?'

Kyra fiddled with the metal strap of the watch Cat had also given her yesterday. It was far too big and it slid around Kyra's slim wrist like a loose bracelet. It had been Kyle's and it was the only thing of his that Cat had. It had a small square and compass and the letter G, the well-known Freemason's symbol on the white face, and of course, the symbols for architects. On the back was etched: 'To Kyle. With all my love. Now and Forever. Cat.' She'd found it in an antique jewellery store on a day trip to London and she'd had it engraved and given it to him for his eighteenth birthday. He'd been so excited he'd insisted they show it to his best friend, immediately. Oddly enough, it had been that very same person who had returned it to her as she lay in the hospital bed a few days after the fatal car crash. Kyle's body had been broken, but his 'new' watch had survived intact. Irony at its worst. Or simply Fate, perhaps.

Cat let out a sigh. She pulled up in a parking

27

space and turned in her seat to face her daughter. 'It's nothing really. And yet it is. But remember this. I was sixteen when I met your dad. Old enough to legally have sex, but far too young and foolish to fully understand what I was doing, or how to deal with my emotions. I'm worried you're going to be shocked, and hate me if I tell you this, and I couldn't bear that, sweetheart. I really couldn't. But I know you love me so I'm being silly–'

'Just tell me, Mum. I'll never, ever hate you, no matter what. You know that. Say it. Please.' Kyra took Cat's hands in hers and smiled.

Cat took a deep breath and smiled back, but rather wanly.

'OK. The day I met your dad, I was already in love with someone else. Madly in love as it happens. I only went to the bay that day because I knew this guy would be there. I'd been going every day for a couple of weeks, but he couldn't stand the sight of me and he made that very clear on more than one occasion. That day your dad was there, and he, on the other hand, made it very clear the moment we met that he had fallen in love with me at first sight. I'm ashamed to say this. Truly ashamed. But when I first dated your dad it was because he was the best friend of the man I loved. And I did it because I hoped it would annoy him. The best friend, I mean. Not your dad. But I wasn't a complete idiot even then, and I soon realised how lucky I was to have Kyle. I fell in love with him. And the best friend was history as far as I was concerned.'

'Wow! Is that what you feel guilty about? That you started dating Dad under false pretences? Because that's just silly. As you said yourself, Mum, you were sixteen. I think I was in love with at least three guys when I was sixteen. Don't look so worried. I didn't have sex with all of them. None of them, actually. I still haven't. I told you I'd tell you when I do. And I will. I think your generation was more relaxed about it than we are. Now we're all so aware of all the awful things that can happen, and I don't mean getting pregnant. I mean all the STDs, the sex-shaming on social media etc. I just don't think it's worth it unless you believe you've met the right guy. Or at the very least, a guy who's really important to you.'

'I'm so proud of you, sweetheart. You're wise beyond your years. Sex-shaming sounds horrendous. Do they really do that on social media?' Cat pulled a face. 'That makes me even more pleased that I'm not on any of it and extremely grateful that the gallery handles all that stuff for me.' She looked Kyra in the eye. 'So, you're not upset about what I've just told you? We're good?'

Kyra laughed. 'Of course we're good. And no. I'm not upset in the least. I am glad you told me though and I don't know why you haven't done so before. We can't choose who we fall in love with, Mum. Even if, sometimes, we wish we could. Let's go and eat. I'm starving.'

'Me too. And I had toast before we left.'

Cat shoved the door open and Kyra came and linked her arm through Cat's as they walked towards the glass doors of the services.

'Is that how your mum got your address, do you think? Via the gallery.'

'I have no idea. I called Carrie yesterday morning after you went to get your exam results and she said no one had asked for my details recently. If anyone does, she simply tells them I like my privacy and if that's a deal breaker on purchasing my art, that's tough. She says it isn't. Thankfully.'

'How did she get it then?'

'I don't know. But it's certainly something I'm going to ask her.'

They grabbed a couple of trays at one of the restaurants and ordered Full English breakfasts, coffee and orange juice, along with toast, and two coffees to take away afterwards.

Kyra sat at one of the tables by the window and stared out into the baking sunshine. Cat sat opposite and studied her daughter's face for a second or two before Kyra looked at her and smiled.

'Do you think that guy you mentioned still lives in Merriment Bay? What was his name, by the way?'

Cat glanced down at her plate and didn't answer right away.

'Mum?' Kyra persisted.

Cat managed a smile. 'Knowing him, I think he probably does. He loved the place. And his name was Amias. Amias Wells.'

'Amias Wells. I like the sound of that.'

Kyra rested her chin on her hands, and her elbows on the table. There was a faraway look in her eyes as if she were trying to picture him.

'Don't let your breakfast get cold.' Cat picked up her cutlery and stabbed her egg yolk with her knife. 'If he's anything like he was, you probably won't like him. He was sarcastic, rude, opinionated and arrogant. And yet he had the biggest chip on his shoulder imaginable. A complete tearaway. Although he did help out at the WWII Museum, oddly enough. He was fascinated by vintage planes.'

'What did he look like?' Kyra cut her rasher of bacon into bite-sized pieces. 'Was he anything like Dad?'

Cat shook her head. 'No. Apart from in height. He was tall, broad shouldered, fit beyond belief, with hair the colour of black treacle and eyes as dark as midnight, yet sometimes, when he smiled, it looked as if those eyes were filled with golden stardust. And his smile. Wow. It was often slow to take hold, as if he really didn't want to look happy, but when it did, it was as though there was nothing else in the world except that smile. Basically, he was so damn gorgeous that the first time I saw him he actually took my breath away.' She inhaled deeply and let it out in a sigh. 'The last time I saw him, I wanted to strangle him.'

Chapter Four

Amias shoved the front door open and let it slam shut behind him.

'Hey gorgeous. Something smells good. I'm starving. I've brought wine but I expect you've already got a bottle open.'

He strolled into the kitchen and put the bottle on the worktop. Natalia had the phone pressed to her cheek and, pointing to it, silently mouthed, 'Lorna.'

Amias frowned and shook his head. He kissed her on the other cheek, grabbed a wooden spoon and took a mouthful of chilli, grinning when she slapped him on the hand and glowered at him.

'No, Lorna. That wasn't Amias. I haven't seen him since last Sunday but when I do, I'll let him know you're worried and I'll definitely ask him to call you.' She placed her hand over the mouthpiece and added, 'Even if I have to dial the number for him because his fingers must be broken or I'm sure he'd call.'

He flicked his eyes heavenwards and tutted.

Natalia sighed. 'No, Lorna. All I said was I'll definitely ask him to call. I must go because I think there's someone at the door. Take care now. And don't worry about Amias. He's probably just been busy. Bye.' She hung up and, still glaring at Amias, stretched out her arm and the phone. 'Call her. Call her now.'

He frowned again, took the phone and put it back in its cradle on the wall.

'Just because I love you it doesn't mean you can tell me what to do. It may work with your husband but it doesn't work with me. Why are we having chilli? It's the middle of August and there's a bit of a heatwave, in case you haven't noticed.'

'And just because I love you it doesn't mean I'm going to lie to your girlfriends for you.'

'I've never asked you to. And Lorna's not my girlfriend. She's just someone I'm seeing.'

Natalia let out an exasperated sigh. 'You asked me to just now when you refused to speak to her. So what do you expect me to do when they call here because they haven't heard from you for days and they're worried sick about you?'

'Tell them I'm a grown man and you have no control over my actions. And tell them not to worry. Worrying never helps anyone.'

'Why won't you just speak to her?'

'You know why.' He threw her an irritated look. 'Because apart from the fact that I'm annoyed with her for blabbing to Mary Devon, I'm also annoyed with myself. And when I'm annoyed, I'm not nice to be around. I may say something to her that she might not want to hear.'

'Who told you you were nice to be around when you're not annoyed?' She tossed a tea towel at him. 'Make yourself useful and wipe the glasses on the drainer. And don't break them because they're irreplaceable. They were Mum's.'

He gave a sad little smile and did as she asked. 'What's the special occasion? These only come out on high days and holidays. Are we celebrating something?'

Natalia poured him a glass of wine from the open bottle by the cooker. A large glass.

'Drink this. You're going to need it.'

'Oh? Why?'

She raised her brows and nodded towards the glass. 'Drink.'

'Jesus, you're getting bossy. I could really go off you, you know. Wait. Is that why we're having chilli? Because it's my favourite and you're trying to feed me comfort food as well as alcohol.'

'Give the man a gold star. Ready or not, here it is. Our firm has got the sale instructions for Devon Villa.'

Amias choked on the gulp of wine he'd just taken and Natalia slapped him on the back. More times than were actually necessary.

'Thanks, sis.'

'You're welcome. Do you need a top-up?'

She grabbed the bottle and waved it in front of him. He took it from her and filled his glass to the brim.

'When?'

'When what?' She shot him a confused look as she stirred the chilli.

'When did you get the sale instructions?'

'Yesterday. Shortly before I called to invite you round for dinner. And I was as surprised as you are. I don't know when it'll go to the market yet though. She said she may do it up a bit first to get a better price. She's going to let me know in a few days or so but either way, I've got the instruction. You're not going to sulk about it all evening, are you? I know how you feel about the Devons but this is a huge deal for me. I've always wanted to sell that house and if I do get a sale. No. *When* I get a sale, the commission will be fantastic.'

He took a deep breath, shook his head and forced a smile. 'Nope. It was a shock, I'll admit, but I'm fine now and it's nothing a few glasses of this won't cure.' He took another gulp of wine. 'Who gave you the instruction?'

'Who do you think? Viola's in a coma at Eastbourne District General, haven't you heard?' She rolled her eyes at him and added more pepper to the chilli. 'That only leaves Mary. She's got power of attorney. She's had it for a while now. But I couldn't believe it when she came in yesterday. I mean, talk about not wasting any time. Viola only had her accident a few days ago.' She turned and shot a look at him. 'Oh wait. Did you think that maybe the one who can't be named had come home?'

'Funny.' He smirked at her. 'I've never said

she can't be named. I've simply said I'd rather not talk about her, that's all.'

'And yet here we are again. Talking about Cat Devon as we always do at this time every year. I know Kyle was your best friend, Amias. And I know how much you loved him, but it's been eighteen years. Can't you ever let it go? Mum's been dead for ten years now and you loved her far more than you loved Kyle, yet you don't get anywhere near so maudlin on the anniversary of her death as you do on the anniversary of his.'

'That's because it wasn't my fault Mum died. I did everything I could for her but if the surgeons couldn't remove the brain tumour, then I definitely couldn't.'

'Kyle's death wasn't your fault either. You can't stop cars from crashing.'

'No. But I could've tried to stop him. I could've tried to talk him out of it. I could've made him stay.'

'What? Talk him out of running away with the girl he loved? The girl who was having his child. I think you overestimate both your charms and your powers, brother dear. Not even God could've talked Kyle Morris out of taking what he saw as the only chance to be with the girl he adored. And you were nineteen, Amias. Nineteen. Why do we have to go through this every single year? Let it go, for Heaven's sake. You deal with it for the rest of the year. Why do these two weeks always have to turn you almost feral? I just don't get it. I really don't.'

He banged his wine glass on the counter. 'You don't have to go through this. I'll leave.'

He turned to go but she grabbed his arm. 'Don't you dare. Don't you bloody dare. And don't have one of your moods. This is a special day for me and you're going to sit down and have dinner with me and my husband like a civilised human being. OK? I mean it, Amias. I'm so glad Dad's away so I don't have to deal with his reaction too. Now smile. And be grateful that glass you almost smashed wasn't one of Mum's because if it had been, we'd be mourning you in August every year, too. You bloody moron.' She smiled and gave him a hard shove which took him by surprise and nearly knocked him off his feet. 'Go and sit outside and cool down. I don't want you being like this when Josh gets home.'

He ran a hand through his hair, sucked in a long slow breath and forced a smile.

'I'm sorry, sis. I don't know why it does this to me. Perhaps I do need to see someone about it, like you've often said. It's crazy. You're right. I know it is. But this year it feels worse somehow. It feels as if something's going to happen. I can't explain it. But you know Lorna told Mary Devon where Cat lives. And you know that Mary will now get hold of Cat. Because as weird as that bloody family is, they'll still tell one another if something bad happens.'

'And you're worried Cat might come back? Is that it?'

Amias shrugged. 'It's stupid. It doesn't matter to me if she does or doesn't. It's Kyra I've been thinking about. When I saw her all those years ago she looked the spitting image of Kyle. She's eighteen this year. Yesterday, in fact. The same age he was when he died. To be honest, I'm not sure if I'm eager to see her or terrified at the prospect. Do I tell her I promised her dad the night he died that I'd look after them? Cat and his then unborn child. A promise I couldn't keep because, first, Cat suddenly refused to see me and then just a few weeks later, once again, the bloody woman decided her best option was to run away.'

'I don't think you need to tell her that. Although you did track them down. It took you years, not to mention a good deal of money, but you did it. And you discovered they were safe and loved and thriving. So you did fulfil your promise. We have this conversation every single year and each time I tell you the same thing. When will it finally sink in?'

He shook his head despondently. 'I'm not sure it ever will.'

'The only bit I'll never understand, is that having found them, you walked away without even saying a word to Cat or to Kyra. But hey. That was your choice and I won't question it. What I do question though, is why, having done that, you still feel so bloody guilty about the whole thing. And as for Lorna telling Mary. Well, considering what happened to Viola just a day or two later, I'd say that it was Fate.'

'Fate? Seriously?'

Natalia nodded. 'Seriously. You've known where Cat and Kyra were for more than fourteen years and I know you've been drunk more than once in all that time. And yet never have you ever mentioned Cat's whereabouts to anyone. Not a soul. Not even to me. Until this year. And you pick Lorna to blab to. A woman who, however stunning she may be, is not known for her discretion. I think, perhaps the Universe decided it was time.'

'The Universe? Really? Time for what? Time for more wine, I think.' He grabbed the bottle he'd brought and opened it.

'Time to put the past to rest. Time to heal. Time for the Devons to do the same. Time you met your best friend's child face to face. And this time, actually said hello to her. And maybe it's also time you forgave yourself. And Cat. Neither of you did anything wrong. Life's just shitty sometimes.'

'Thank you, oh great one.' He bowed his head. 'It's time we changed the subject.' He poured them both more wine. 'Marcus Lester managed to stay upright on a windsurfer today for a whole six minutes.'

'He did? Really? Wow. That is something to celebrate. I feel so sorry for that kid. Imagine having George for a grandfather and Lucas for a cousin. Always being compared to the paragon that is Lucas must be tough.'

'Yeah. But Lucas is great with Marcus. And

Will's a fantastic uncle. It's just the grandparents who are jerks.'

'Ah yes. I heard about your little disagreement with George and Sybil. Not content with telling them to behave, you called them alcoholics.'

'I didn't.'

'You said you knew they'd rather spend the afternoon in the pub. Or did Sybil make that up?'

Amias grinned. 'No. I did say that. But it's true.'

'We all know it's true. But some people don't like to hear the truth. You should understand that better than anyone.' She threw him a sarcastic look. 'Now if you've calmed down and don't need to go outside, make yourself useful again and set the table. Josh will be home any minute. Oh. Maybe I should text him and ask him to bring more wine. I've a feeling we're going to need it.'

Chapter Five

'So this is Merriment Bay?'

Kyra darted looks from side to side and Cat gave her a sardonic smile.

'Yep. A buzzing metropolis, it isn't. And so far, it hasn't changed. This road has as many potholes as it always had, the grass either side of it needs cutting, the sign to Merriment Farm's exactly the same, as are the signs to the WWII Museum. They looked as if they could've done with a lick of paint back then, and they look like that tonight. The Hope and Anchor pub hasn't changed at all, nor has the Spitfire Café.'

She didn't mention the sign to Bay Water Sports, the business Amias Wells had just started on the beach when she first met him. That sign had definitely changed. Back then it was just three words, hand painted by Amias on to a piece of driftwood. Now the sign was huge. Another driftwood one over an actual surfboard, brightly painted by an obviously talented artist. There was also a life-size cut-out figure with a brightly smiling face, colourful shorts and a surfboard under his arm, seemingly walking towards the beach, with

'*Everything good happens on the water*' written on his board.

'Look at that view, Mum!' Kyra sat upright and peered through the window. 'Can we stop for just one minute? I must get a photo of that full moon over the bay. I'd love to paint this view. Look how the dark sapphire of the sky melts into the indigo sea on the horizon. And that long trail of silver sparkles across the water. The sand in the bay looks almost black from here, except for the moonlight and the few flashes of lights reflected from the pub and those houses over there. And the stars. I thought we only got night skies like this in Bonniemount. The water gives it all a completely different perspective.'

Cat smiled and glanced in the rear-view mirror before indicating and pulling over to the side of Coast Road, at the top of the hill leading down to the bridge, the river and the village. The view from here was just as Kyra had described it. The bay sat to their left and the English Channel swept out before them, a shimmering dark sapphire blue, flat-calm, with the trail of moonlight angled across it leading directly towards the centre of the bay.

Kyra leapt out of the car but it took Cat a second or two to catch her breath. She and Kyle and Amias had sat on that sand on nights like this, staring out to sea, each deep in thought, and in her and Kyle's case, silently planning their future together.

Memories would come back; of course they

would. But she hadn't expected so many conflicting ones to hit her all at once, like a Tsunami. She took a few deep breaths and finally got out.

Music and laughter from the pub, drifted through the sultry night air but there was no breeze at all to carry it. They'd had the air conditioning on in the car and the heat of the night settled around Cat like a warm, damp towel. Unless anything had changed, her old bedroom would be like sleeping in a sauna tonight. Why hadn't she thought about that and brought a fan? Not that it mattered. She probably wouldn't get much sleep anyway, even though she was shattered after such a long journey.

'Oh, Mum. I know you told me this place was beautiful, but I hadn't expected this. It must've been so hard to leave. Although, of course, under the circumstances, it probably wasn't. I don't suppose we can go down to the beach, can we?'

Cat shook her head. 'Not tonight, sweetheart. It's gone 10 and Mum doesn't know we're coming, remember. If we don't get there soon, she'll have gone to bed and we'll have to spend the night in the car. I told you. Everything is fully booked.'

'I'd be happy to sleep in the car. Or on the beach on a night like this. The sand as my bed and the stars as my blanket.'

Not only did Kyra look like Kyle, she sounded just like him too. That was exactly the sort of thing he would've said if he were here tonight.

'You might not feel that way if it rains. Wet sand isn't quite as comfortable.'

43

'It's not going to rain, Mum. Look.' She swept her arm out in front of her. 'See all those stars? There's not a cloud in the sky.'

'Maybe not. But I'm too old and too tired to risk it. I need a proper bed. Sorry, sweetheart.'

Kyra shrugged. 'That's OK. I'll do it another night.'

'Not on your own, please. This place used to be safe at night but it might've changed in eighteen years.'

Kyra threw her a mischievous grin. 'You said it hadn't changed a bit. But don't worry. I'll find someone to go with me. I know you said this village isn't huge but there must be people of my age here and I'm pretty good at making friends.'

'Another thing you got from your dad.'

The grin grew wider. 'Who knows. I may even find a boy I like. I was going to say man but that'd probably give you palpitations, wouldn't it? Even though, strictly speaking I'm now a woman.'

'Everything gives a mother palpitations. That's something you'll find out for yourself one day. But hopefully not too soon.' Cat's smile faded. 'Oh God. Why did I need to add that bit? I've only been here for five minutes and I'm already sounding like my mother. Next time you hear me say anything like that, give me a good whack, will you? It's your life. You can have kids whenever you want, and with whomever you choose. Although I hope you won't mind if I give you my thoughts and feelings on the subject.'

44

Kyra laughed as she walked back to the car. 'I'll discuss everything with you before I make any major decisions in my life. You know that. And I'll always welcome your thoughts and feelings on anything I do, or don't do. Just as I know you always welcome mine. Let's go and face our doom, shall we?'

Cat laughed too. 'I expect it'll be more than a little unpleasant arriving at Granny Viola's, but doom is hopefully a bit strong. Although with my family, anything is possible.'

They drove down the hill, across the bridge separating the village and continued past shops, restaurants and offices until Cat turned left into Channel View Lane.

Kyra gasped when Cat pulled up outside Devon Villa.

'Bloody hell, Mum! You said it was a big, Edwardian villa. You didn't say it was five storeys of grandeur overlooking the sea. Wow! This is really something. It makes Bonniemount Cottage look like a garden shed.'

'It's grand. And it's just as amazing inside too. But Bonniemount Cottage was twice the home Devon Villa was. Grand isn't necessarily better, sweetheart.'

'Oh, I know. I didn't mean anything against the cottage. I love it there. But this place is impressive. And you said it still feels like home, so it can't have been all bad.'

'It wasn't. My childhood was good. And very

happy. Granny Viola was wonderful, if a little prim and proper at times. Mum was kind and caring, amazingly. She wasn't around as much as Granny but when she was, she was great. It was only once I turned sixteen that things suddenly went downhill. Granny was getting aches and pains and grumbling all the time. Mum was panicking about getting old and dying alone, for some reason, and decided she needed to find a man to share her life with. Even though she'd always said – and so had Granny Viola – that the only luck Devon women have with men is bad luck.'

'What?' Kyra shot her a worried look. 'You've never told me that.'

'Haven't I? Well, it's probably because it's nonsense and not worth mentioning.'

'Really? Um. Granny Viola's marriage was brief and ended badly, so you said. So badly that she changed her surname back to Devon, and she never married again. Your mum had you and you don't know who your dad is. She never married either, as far as we're aware. Unless she did so in the last eighteen years. And – I know this is horrible to say, but you and Dad weren't exactly lucky, were you? Plus you've had only one relationship since, and that's always been more platonic than romantic. Based on the facts, I think they may be right. Devon women are unlucky in love. I might as well give up right now.'

Cat frowned. 'Don't say that. Although, when you look at our experiences, I suppose I can see what you mean. But please don't take it to heart. Life is what we make it, sweetheart. Yes, bad things happen, but good things happen too. I'm happy with my life the way it is. I don't want a husband. Neither did Granny Viola. She said one was one too many for her. And I feel very lucky indeed to have met your dad. Although we weren't together long, and we were very young, I'll be grateful for him my entire life. Especially as he gave you to me. And because of that, I'll always have a part of him in my life. Besides, everything comes in threes, so the old superstition goes. That means Granny Viola, Mum and me, have had the bad luck. So you'll have only good. Now do you want to stay in the car while I go and see if Mum's still up? The house seems to be in complete darkness. She may've gone to bed.'

Kyra smiled. 'So we might be sleeping on the beach, after all.'

'You take the beach. I'll have the car.'

Cat gave her a playful tap on her leg and got out of the car, breathing deeply as she walked towards the sage green front door, telling herself repeatedly to stay calm, no matter what. She pressed the doorbell hard and closed her eyes for a second, not sure whether she wanted the door to be opened or not. She was about to give up and return to Kyra when the hall light came on and the front door was held ajar.

'Hi. It's Cat. Catherine.'

The door burst open and Mary Devon, looking like she'd stepped off the cover of a magazine, in her silk pyjamas and matching dressing gown, almost seemed pleased to see Cat, for a second. Just one tiny second. But the brief smile and light in Mary's eyes were quickly gone and were replaced with a granite-like expression.

'You came then?'

'Did you think we wouldn't?'

'We?'

Unbelievable. She was truly unbelievable.

'Me and my daughter, Kyra. Please don't expect me to believe you don't remember Kyra.'

'Of course I remember her. How could I possibly forget? But I'm surprised she'd want to come. I assumed she'd stay with friends or something. Although I didn't know what to think. How could I? I haven't seen you for eighteen years. Not since that night you ran away.'

'It was the morning. Early morning that's true. But I left in the morning, not in the night. The second time, anyway.'

'Ah yes. I'd almost forgotten you ran away twice.'

'Forgotten! Bloody hell, Mum. How could you have forgotten? That's really something. Even for you. And of course Kyra wanted to come. Although no one could blame her if she didn't. But can we not start the unpleasantness right away, please? It's been a very long day and we're both tired. It was Kyra's eighteenth birthday yesterday and I'm telling you now, be nice. Or we'll be gone and you'll never see either of us again. Not that that would bother you, of course. But that's the deal. One nasty comment about her dad and we're out of here. Is that clear?'

'Crystal clear. Does that mean you'll be staying here?'

'Your brief letter said we could. It said I could, to be precise, but Kyra can share my bed.'

'There's no need for that. You're well aware of how many rooms there are in this house. She can have the room next to yours. We don't use it so I'll have to air it and make up a bed.'

'I can do that. Thank you. My room will need some airing too after all this time.'

'It won't. We keep that aired, in case. Well, you'd better come in then. I suppose you want a cup of tea. And maybe something to eat.'

Cat blinked. Had she just heard that right? Had her mum said they kept her room aired, in case. In case she came home? That was a surprise Cat hadn't expected.

'Er. Tea would be good. But we've eaten, thanks. We stopped on the motorway.' She turned and waved at Kyra and Kyra got out of the car. 'Try and pretend you're pleased to see her, Mum. Please. If not for me, then for her. She is your granddaughter, after all.'

Chapter Six

'You're tall.' Mary Devon scanned Kyra from head to toe and a hint of a smile crept on to her lips.

Cat flashed her mum a warning look. 'Mum. This is Kyra. Kyra, say hello to your gran.'

'Hi,' Kyra said, smiling as she reached out her hand.

Mary looked at it as if she wasn't sure what to do but to Cat's astonishment, she pulled Kyra into an awkward and very brief hug. But it was a hug.

Kyra darted a startled look at Cat and Cat gave her a reassuring smile. Once she'd got over the shock.

'It's good to see you again after all these years, Kyra. Come in. I'll put the kettle on. I think there's probably some fizzy drinks somewhere if you'd prefer. We keep them for the gardener.'

'Tea's fine, thanks.'

Cat smiled. 'We'll just go and get our bags, Mum. We'll be back in a sec.'

'I'll be in the kitchen. Leave your bags in the hall for now and join me there. I assume you remember where it is.'

'Unless you've moved it, yes. I remember.'

Mary ignored the quip and turned and walked away, leaving the front door wide open. Cat and Kyra gave one another surprised smiles before linking arms and walking back to the car.

'That was a bit of a shock,' Kyra said, as soon as they were away from the door.

'You're not kidding. And for just a nanosecond, I could've sworn she was also quite pleased to see me. Perhaps this won't be as bad as either of us thought. She didn't even yell at me for getting her out of bed.'

'This'll sound strange, but she doesn't look like I thought my gran would look. The only photo I've seen is the one you showed me years ago and she just looked like a mum, then. But I thought my gran would be plump and warm and sort of cosy-looking, even though I knew she probably wouldn't from what you've told me over the years. Does that make sense?'

'Completely. You expected her to look something like Isla. Warm and loving, in a long, brushed cotton nightgown, a thick fluffy dressing gown and furry slippers, with glasses sitting on the end of her nose, soft grey curls bouncing around her face, a huge smile on her lips and her rosy cheeks aglow. Not tall, slim and perfectly tanned, with painted nails, an immaculate bob the colour of mahogany, and wearing silk pyjamas and a matching silk dressing gown. I was a bit taken aback myself, but only because I think she looked exactly the same that last night I saw her. She doesn't seem to have aged much at all. But then she's only in her fifties.'

'What's Granny Viola like?'

'Last time I saw her, an older version of Mum, only not as tall. And much older, of course. I suppose you'll have to ask Mum what she wants you to call her. You've never called her gran. You've always referred to her as 'your mum'.'

They took the luggage inside and left it in the hall as Mary had instructed.

'It's this way.' Cat led the way to the kitchen but Kyra stopped and peered into each room they passed.

'How many rooms are there on this floor, Mum?'

Cat smiled. 'Sitting room, dining room, TV room, a small library, study, cloakroom, utility room, kitchen and conservatory. So I suppose nine if you count them all. Upstairs there are three large bedrooms and a bathroom on each floor, apart from the attic. There's just one large room up there. Or at least, that's how it all was eighteen years ago. They might've changed things since then. I used to sit in the attic and watch the ships. There's a telescope up there and you can see for miles. You can see the stars too. And the moon looks incredible through its lens. You can also see the bay. And the airstrip of the museum, but you can't quite see the museum itself because it's hidden by the edge of the bay.'

'What's hidden by the bay?' Mary asked. She was seated at a large, round, kitchen table with a crisp, linen table cloth of summer flowers and butterflies. In front of Mary sat a matching, porcelain teapot and cups and saucers on a silver tray, together with porcelain tea plates and a cake stand with an impressive display of small cakes.

'The WWII Museum. This looks lovely.'

Mary sniffed but in a very dignified fashion. 'I know you said you'd eaten, but you never used to say no to a cake with a cup of tea. Please sit down and help yourselves. Shall I be mother?'

Cat bit back a laugh and a sarcastic retort.

'Yes please. Er. Before I ask how Granny Viola is and exactly what happened, what would you like Kyra to call you?'

Mary hesitated as she poured the tea and threw them a confused look.

'Gran or Granny, I suppose. Or Mary, if you prefer. It may take me a while to adjust to being called Gran. But I'm sure I could become used to it. I really don't mind. You can decide, Kyra.' She resumed her task and, having filled three cups, she passed a matching porcelain milk jug and sugar bowl towards Cat and Kyra.

'I'll call you Gran, or maybe Granny Mary, if that's OK?' Kyra reached out and took a mini battenberg.

'That's fine.' Mary passed her a plate.

'So, Granny Viola then?' Cat asked, giving Kyra a quick smile. 'What happened and what's the prognosis?'

'She's in a coma. She fell down the stairs and

was lucky she didn't break her neck. She did break a bone or two, but nothing overly serious. It's the coma, of course, that's the worry. The doctors told me yesterday she's a six on the coma scale. I had no idea there was such a thing but apparently there is. It's called the Glasgow Coma Scale and it's a tool used by them to assess a person's level of consciousness based on three things – eye opening, verbal response and voluntary movement. They each have various thresholds and are added together to get the total score. The lower the score the less likely the person is to recover due to more severe brain damage. I believe they said eight was the high score for most coma patients, so six isn't too bad, all things considered. Based on that, there's a possibility she may recover, but they're monitoring her and we'll have to wait and see. It could go either way, especially due to her age.'

'How old is she?' Kyra asked.

Mary looked at Cat and frowned before replying. 'Didn't your mother tell you? She's ninety-five.'

'Ninety-five! Sorry. I didn't mean to shout. Gosh. That's old. Do they really think she'll recover?'

'Why shouldn't she? She's fit and healthy for her age. And she's strong. And of course, she's a Devon.'

Cat rolled her eyes. 'Like that's going to make a difference.'

'It will,' Mary said. 'We Devon women are

made of sterner stuff.'

Cat couldn't disagree with that.

Kyra helped herself to a second cake. 'I hope she does. I'd like to meet her.'

The tiniest of smiles settled on Mary's lips. 'She'd like to meet you too. I'm sure. You'll go to visit her tomorrow, I assume?' She turned her attention back to Cat.

'Yes. Are the visiting hours still …' Her voice trailed off.

'Yes.' Mary obviously realised Cat was referring to the time when she herself was in the hospital recovering from her injuries and having a caesarean to deliver Kyra one month earlier than she was due. 'From 2 until 9, except in special circumstances. She's in the ICU.'

Cat almost choked on her cake. The Intensive Care Unit where Kyle had died.

Chapter Seven

The smell of coffee hit Cat's nostrils shortly after the tappity-tap on her bedroom door sent the final remnants of sleep scurrying away.

'Good morning, Catherine. Did you sleep well?'

Cat shuffled upright, stretched and yawned. 'Like a log, surprisingly.'

Mary flinched and made the tiniest gasp as her gaze flickered from Cat's face to her neck and shoulder, but she appeared to quickly recover herself and she put the cup of coffee on the bedside table.

'It's the sea air. And the long drive yesterday, no doubt. I wasn't sure whether to wake you or not, but it's 8.30 and I have to pop out.'

'You're kidding? It's 8.30 already? I don't think I've ever slept so late. Sorry. I'll get up right now. Is Kyra awake?'

'Stay where you are and drink your coffee. There's no rush to get up and Kyra's still fast asleep. I popped my head around her door and she's dead to the world. I only came up to tell you so that you didn't come downstairs and find me gone. I know from experience how worrying that can be.'

Cat gave a small sigh but bit her tongue. Better to ignore remarks like that. She picked up the coffee and took a sip. Mary still ground her own by the taste of it and Cat closed her eyes for a second to enjoy the sensation of its mellow flavour.

'I think it's going to be another hot day. Perhaps you and Kyra might like to go for a swim. The water's been so warm thanks to this heatwave. A swim might be the very thing you need this morning.'

'Kyra might. I'll see how busy the beach is this morning.'

'Because of the scars? Do you have any pain, or are they just cosmetic?'

Cat nearly spilt her coffee. Mary still didn't pull her punches.

'Yes, because of the scars and no. No pain at all. Well, not from the scars anyway.'

'I wouldn't have expected you to care what people think. And they're not horrendous. I didn't even notice the scar on your cheek, last night, although I suppose that's because your hair hides most of it and you had your right cheek towards me. I was just surprised to see them in this bright morning light. I assumed they would've faded long ago.'

'Time may heal most wounds, but some, it doesn't. I don't care what people think. Most of the time. But I do care when they start asking questions, as they often do. I'm not some circus sideshow. I find it's easier just to cover them up and get on with my life.'

'Have you got on with your life?'

Cat furrowed her brows. 'Yes. Thanks to a very special and wonderfully kind woman up in Bonniemount, Kyra and I were able to build a good life. A very good life. And Kyra's extremely bright. Just like her dad. Don't pull that face. I meant what I said about not saying anything bad about Kyle. That extends to looks, too.'

Mary replaced the sneer with a small smile. 'You were saying Kyra's bright. I assume she's just got her A level results. Did she get the grades you wanted?'

Cat sighed. 'She got the grades *she* wanted. Better than she wanted, in fact. I didn't mind what she got as long as she was happy with them.'

'I see. Is she going to university?'

'Yes. Edinburgh. Her place has been confirmed and she'll start in September. She's taking Fine Arts.'

'Oh? She's keen on art, as you were?'

'We both are. This may surprise you, Mum, but I earn my living as an artist. And several people seem to think I'm rather good. Kyra's even better.'

'An artist? You … you followed your dream then. Eventually. I'm glad of that, at least. And of course you're a good artist. You always were. That's one of the reasons we …' Mary cleared her throat. 'Well. That doesn't matter now. I'm pleased you're doing something good with your life.'

'I followed all my dreams. One didn't turn out quite as I had hoped though. I want Kyra to follow all of hers. No matter what they are or who they involve.'

Mary turned towards the door. 'I believe that's put me firmly in my place. I'll leave you to it. I'll be back by lunchtime. Your old key is in the bowl on the large coat stand in the hall. Come and go as you please.' She stopped at the door and glanced back. 'But this time if you decide to leave, perhaps you'd be good enough to tell me you're going. And I need to talk with you about this house. But we can do that over dinner tonight. Unless you have plans.'

'Nope. No plans. Other than to go and visit Granny this afternoon. Is there anything you need me to do today?'

'Why would there be anything I need you to do? We've coped perfectly well without you for eighteen years.'

'Mum,' Cat said as Mary closed the door. But it didn't reopen and there was no way Cat was running after her, so she yelled, 'Thanks for the coffee. Have a lovely day.'

There was no reply, but a few seconds later the door slowly opened and Kyra poked her head around it, yawning and rubbing her eyes. Her hair was a tangled mess and she padded across the floor like a zombie in a movie.

'Good morning, sweetheart. Did you sleep well?'

Kyra collapsed on the bed, and Cat had to hold

her coffee cup steady so as not to spill any.

'I think I'm still asleep. Did Gran put something in that tea or those cakes last night? I feel like I've been drugged.'

Cat laughed. 'As strange as Mum is, I don't think she'd do that. I feel the same. It's probably all the excitement of your results, your uni acceptance, your birthday celebrations, the letter and the long drive. We're both in desperate need of sleep.'

'I'm in desperate need of coffee. May I have some of that, please?'

Cat smiled and handed her the cup. Kyra drank two long gulps.

'God, that's good. That's even better than ours.'

'I know. And I suspect there's a pot of it downstairs. You stay here, I'll go and get us some more.'

Kyra shook her head and struggled off the bed. 'I'll come downstairs. I'm starving and in equally desperate need of toast and coffee.'

Cat climbed out of bed and they went downstairs.

'Oh. You're still here.'

Mary glanced at Cat. 'I'm just about to go. Good morning, Kyra. You look exhausted. Are you unwell?'

'Just tired. Morning, Gran. You look nice.'

'Oh.' Mary brushed a hand over her floral summer dress and smiled. 'Thank you. There's a pot of coffee on the go and there's bread in the breadbin. Help yourselves to anything you want. Bacon, eggs, whatever. I'll see you both later. Enjoy your first day in Merriment Bay, Kyra. I was saying to Catherine that it's a perfect morning for a swim. The beach opposite isn't as sandy as the bay and it is a little rocky in parts but it's still a lovely place to swim and it's nowhere near as crowded. The bay will be packed with tourists and locals alike even at this hour. This isn't a private road, sadly, but we don't get as many tourists or even locals here because, unless you live here, there's a restriction on parking.'

'That's sounds good.' Kyra flopped on to a chair. 'I'd get the mugs, Mum, but I don't know where anything is.' She grinned at Cat.

'I'm not sure I do. Can we just look around, Mum?'

'Of course,' Mary said. 'But everything's exactly where it was when you left. Nothing much changes in Merriment Bay. Oh. I suppose that's not entirely true. That's one of the things I need to discuss with you later. But I've a feeling several things may be about to change, now that you've come home. Now that you're both home.'

She turned to the door and marched down the hall. Cat glanced at Kyra before running after her.

'Mum? May I ask you a question?'

Mary's entire body stiffened but she nodded. 'Yes.'

'How did you know where to send the letter?'

'Oh that. Lorna Carlton told me. Just a day or

two before your gran had her accident. It was as if it was Fate.'

'Lorna Carlton?' Cat frowned. 'Oh, I remember her.' The frown deepened. 'But how the hell did Lorna Carlton know where we were?'

'Apparently, Amias Wells told her. He was drunk, so Lorna said, and she didn't think he'd meant to let it slip. But he did and she thought I had a right to know. Which is more than some people seemed to think.'

Cat ignored the dig at her. She was too confused. Amias Wells told Lorna Carlton and Lorna told Mary? That made no sense at all.

'Wait. What? Amias Wells told her? Who on earth told him?'

'Does it matter?'

'It does to me, yes.'

Mary sighed and glanced at her watch before opening the front door.

'According to Lorna, he found out for himself. He's known for years, he told her. It seems he made some sort of promise to … his friend. That's all I know. If you feel the need to find out more, I can only suggest you ask him. He's still got that place on the beach at the bay and now also one at the reservoir. But he no longer lives in that awful place where he grew up. He's got one of the fancy new homes on the hill overlooking the bay. It seems he's done rather well for himself. Who on earth would've expected that?'

'I did, Mum,' Cat said, after a few seconds as

she tried to take in what she'd heard. But Mary had already closed the door.

Amias Wells had known for years where she and Kyra lived and yet he hadn't so much as sent a card, or a note? But why would he? She hadn't sent anything to him. She hadn't told him where they were.

And yet, he'd gone to all the trouble of finding out. Why would he have done that? And what was that about a promise to a friend? Kyle, obviously. But this was the first she'd heard of any promise. When Amias had visited her in hospital and given her Kyle's watch, all he'd said was that he thought she should have it because it had been her present to Kyle.

'It's something to remember him by,' he'd said. 'Not that you'll need anything to remember him. Neither of us is ever likely to forget.' And then he'd given her the strangest look and turned and walked away.

He'd visited her in hospital a few times after that, but he always seemed to be trying to avoid having a conversation and the last time she'd seen him, they'd almost had a row. And then the visits stopped and when she returned to Devon Villa to continue her recovery, he hadn't called round once. Not even to see Kyra. Or even sent a card or note. Nothing.

But what had she expected? He'd never liked her. The only reason he'd been friends with her was because of Kyle. After Kyle died, it seemed Amias didn't want to be her friend anymore. And that was another reason why she had to run away. She had no one to turn to and no one to support her in her ongoing battle with her mum and gran.

And yet at some stage during the last eighteen years, Amias Wells had gone to the trouble of finding her and Kyra. Yet he hadn't got in touch. It simply made no sense. But one thing was certain. There was no way she was ever going to ask him about it.

In fact, while they were in Merriment Bay, she would go out of her way to try to avoid him.

Chapter Eight

Cat and Kyra spent the morning exploring the house before heading to Eastbourne for lunch. It was twenty miles away so it was a bit of a drive but it was where the hospital was.

Cat was dreading going to that place. How would she feel walking through those doors? Going into that ward? The place where Kyle died in the hospital in which she had had their baby. All morning, she had thought of little else but she hadn't mentioned it to Kyra. The last thing she wanted was for her to be upset.

Eastbourne shopping centre had changed since the last time she had visited. Some shops had gone and new ones had replaced them but just as she always had when she went to Eastbourne all those years ago, she managed to spend far more than she'd intended. Although most of it was on Kyra. But she did buy herself one or two pretty, summer dresses and crocheted lace bolero-type cardigans. Just something to give a bit of cover to her scars.

They'd had lunch in a little restaurant that definitely hadn't been there the last time she had, and afterwards she drove the mile or so to the outskirts of town and parked in the hospital car park.

'Do you want to go in alone at first?' Kyra asked as they walked inside.

Cat shook her head. 'No. Unless you'd rather not go in. From memory, there's a waiting room within the Critical Care Unit and then two sections. One for ICU patients and one for HDU, or high dependency. There was coffee and tea in the waiting room, so you can wait in there if you like. I don't expect it's the most pleasant experience to see someone in a coma.'

'No. I'm fine.' Kyra seemed hesitant. 'Mum? Is this where Dad died?'

So there it was.

'Yes. And where you were born.'

'A month early.'

'Yes.'

Cat took Kyra's hand and rang the bell on the door to the entrance to Critical Care. A nurse came to greet them and Cat said they were relatives of Viola Devon.

'Please follow me,' the nurse said, with a smile. 'I see you're not wearing any outdoor garments today, but if you're coming again, jackets and coats can be left in the waiting room or on the hooks at the unit doors, but please take any valuables with you. Use the hand gel here before entering, and again at the bed, and also when you leave.' She waited while they did so then handed them white plastic aprons. 'These need to be worn at the bedside and removed and placed in the bin

before leaving. Please don't sit or lie on the bed. Viola is connected to a monitor that provides us with
 detailed information, and she has a facemask to help her breathe. You may find this distressing, but it's completely normal. At times you may hear or see flashing alarms. Don't worry. These are also normal but if you're concerned, just ask. Feel free to ask me anything. There's tea, coffee and cold drinks available in the waiting room. Do you have any questions before we go in?' She ended with a smile.

'No,' Cat said.

'Then please follow me.'

'She sounds like she's learnt that by heart,' Kyra whispered, as they walked into the ICU. 'Is it awful coming back here?'

'No. I thought it would be. But strangely enough, it's not.'

But the sight of Granny Viola lying with her eyes closed in a bed surrounded by tubes and machines was. It was truly awful. The last time Cat had seen her she was full of life and looked so much younger than her years. Now, she looked like a frail old woman at death's door and it upset Cat far more than she had expected. So much in fact, that when she sat by Viola's bed and took her slender hand in hers, she burst into tears.

Chapter Nine

'I don't know what I expected, but it was a far greater shock than I thought,' Cat said, as she and Kyra sat at the dinner table with Mary that evening.

Mary nodded. 'I probably should've prepared you, but frankly I didn't think about it. I was shocked too when I saw her. Just the morning of the fall, she'd been smiling and singing and making plans for the future. Which is what I need to talk with you about.'

'Oh? Um. Look, Mum. I'm here. And I want to do everything I can to help Granny, but Kyra and I will be returning to Bonniemount sometime soon. And Kyra's off to uni in September. Which reminds me, sweetheart. We must finalise things on that score, like accommodation, supplies, etc.' Cat smiled at Kyra before returning her attention to Mary. 'And I've got commissions to finish, Mum. What I'm saying is, whatever plans you and Granny had shouldn't include me and Kyra.'

Mary stiffened. 'Well, they do. In a roundabout way, so you may as well listen. Don't worry, I'm not going to ask you to stay and help look after her when she comes home from hospital. These plans were made before the fall. But obviously now she may need long-term care, so they may have to change to account for that. We'll have to wait and see, I suppose. The thing is, I've had power of attorney for her for a few years now. She'd been getting forgetful and we agreed it was for the best. So I can carry out her plans no matter what.' Mary took a sip of her wine and continued eating.

'OK. So what are these plans? And why do they affect us, in a roundabout way or otherwise?'

'We're putting Devon Villa on the market and moving somewhere smaller.'

'What!' Cat couldn't believe her ears. Both her mum and Granny Viola had always said the only way they'd ever leave Devon Villa was in their coffins.

'But I thought you both love this place.'

'We do. But we're not getting any younger and this house is far too large for just the two of us. The only thing I'm trying to decide is whether to market the house as is or to spend some money doing it up a bit and then try to get a better price.'

'So how does that affect us?' Kyra asked. 'Do you need financial help?'

A spurt of laughter erupted from Mary. 'Good heavens, no. It affects you both because, God forbid, if the worst happens, Granny Viola made a provision for you in her will.'

'What?' Cat and Kyra exchanged looks of surprise.

'So it's a good thing Lorna told me where you

were because at least now if things don't turn out as hoped, I won't have to employ lawyers and private detectives to track you down. It won't be huge sums of money so don't get too excited. But you'll each receive ten percent of her estate. If the worst does happen, you'll be paid from the sale proceeds once the house is sold and probate is finalised.'

'I don't expect anything,' Cat said. 'But has she really named Kyra in the will? I'm so happy about that if that's the case.'

'Of course she has. You may have run off and cut all ties with us but you're still a Devon and you always will be. And so is Kyra. You're provided for in my will too. Don't look so shocked. Who else am I going to leave my money to?'

'Anyone but me, I would've thought, in all honesty.'

Mary fixed Cat with a stare and then a sudden smile crept across her face. 'Well. That just proves how little you really know me or your granny, doesn't it? When I die, you and Kyra get the lot. Once taxes and costs are paid, of course. And that will be a tidy sum because you'll effectively be getting the other eighty per cent share of this house, plus our savings.'

'I don't know what to say. But I must say this. As lovely and as thoughtful as that is, it still wouldn't change our plans, Mum. You do know that, don't you?'

'You mean you're not going to come back here to live on the promise of money in the future? Of course I know that. We made the provisions half believing we would never see you again, so I'm hardly likely to insist you come back here or I'll cut you out of my will.'

'Well then. Thank you. That's very kind, but it's really not necessary. I'd rather you sell the house and enjoy the money doing things you've always wanted to.'

'And that's what I want to discuss. If I do decide to put the house on the market now, I'd like to know if there's anything here you want. If not, I'll sell what I can at auction, give some of it to charity, and throw out anything beyond hope. I don't need to know right now. But before you go would be good. And, although I had intended to do it all myself, now that you're both here and staying possibly for a week or two, is there any chance that you'd help me to sort things out? Go through the photos and albums, Granny Viola's papers, all the cupboards etc. I'd like to get as organised as possible. We were going to start it the day she had her fall. It would be a great help to both of us, whatever happens.'

'Of course we'll help, Mum.'

Without thinking, Cat reached out and touched Mary's hand and to her astonishment, Mary took Cat's in hers and squeezed it for a few seconds before releasing it and continuing to eat her dinner.

Chapter Ten

'I'm glad you finally called me,' Lorna said, leaning across the table towards Amias and provocatively but gently scraping her false, multi-coloured nails along the back of his hand.

He let go of his wine glass, moved his hand from the table and leant back against the high, padded seat. This was a mistake. He should've done this in the pub. Better yet, at her place. Agreeing to meet her at Bella Vista, her favourite Italian restaurant, wasn't a wise move. But it seemed he wasn't making any wise moves lately.

He cleared his throat. 'Yeah. About that, Lorna. I like you, you know I do. And we've had some fun, but I think it's best if we call it a day, don't you?'

She couldn't have looked more shocked if he'd punched her in the face. Not that he would ever do that. He'd never hit a woman in his life. Although once or twice in his youth he'd been really tempted to grab Cat Devon by the arm and … and what? Shake some sense into her? Make her change her mind?

Lorna was talking and he hadn't heard a word

she'd said.

'Sorry. What?'

She gasped and blinked several times. 'Sorry, what! Is that all you've got to say? I knew you could be a bit of a bastard, Amias, but I never thought you'd treat me like this.'

'Like what? I honestly didn't hear what you said. My mind was miles away.'

'Thanks. That just makes it worse. I asked if you were seriously breaking up with me?'

He furrowed his brows. Could he have been unclear in any way?

'Um. Yes. But I'm not sure 'breaking up' is the right term, exactly. That implies we had a relationship, and we didn't. We were just seeing one another from time to time and we both knew it wouldn't go anywhere. OK, we could drag it out for a few more weeks and see the summer out, but what's the point?'

'Drag it out? Drag. It. Out. Is that what you'd be doing? I'm so sorry dating me has been such a chore. You didn't seem to feel that way when we were having sex.'

He sighed. 'I'm a guy, Lorna. What can I say? But come on. Don't make me out to be the bad guy here. I think I made it pretty clear the first time we went out that I wasn't looking for a relationship. I told you that when you asked me out. I said I'd love to see you and have some fun, but that's all it would be. Fun. No promises. No commitments. No future. Just two people enjoying one another's company and bodies from time to time. You do remember me saying that, don't you, Lorna?'

She opened her mouth but quickly shut it again and lowered her eyes as she fiddled with her wine glass.

'Lorna? You do, don't you?'

She shrugged her shoulders but didn't meet his eyes.

'I didn't think you meant it. I thought that was just a guy thing.'

'You thought I'd made it up? That I was being reticent or playing hard to get or something? Why would you think that?'

Now she did look at him and she clearly wasn't happy.

'Because I thought you liked me, Amias.'

'I do like you, Lorna. That's why I agreed to meet you here tonight. I'd like us to be friends. We were friends before. We can be so again.'

'Friends? You're dumping me and you expect me to be friends with you? You're unbelievable, Amias Wells. Un-bloody-believable.'

'I don't understand. Why are you so upset? It's not like we were in love or anything.'

'Oh, isn't it? Well, you clearly weren't. But then I don't suppose you know the meaning of the word, do you? You've never been in love and probably never will be. No. Wait. You are in love. With yourself.'

Amias met her angry stare with a quelling look. 'I can assure you of two things, Lorna. One, I'm definitely not, never have been and never will be in love with myself. And two. I have been in love. Once. A long time ago. With the wrong woman. I got my heart broken and I won't be doing that again in a hurry. But that's neither here nor there. I'm sorry if you feel I've misled you in any way, because I never intended to do that. And I'm sorry if I've hurt you because I never intended to do that either. But you must know there's no point in us continuing this. You must realise we'll never be anything more than friends. Friends who've had sex a few times but won't in the future. I'm afraid I was never going to fall in love with you, if that's what you've been hoping.'

'Oh yes. I think you've made that abundantly clear. I'm not in love with you either.'

He frowned. 'Then what's the problem? Am I missing something here?'

'We spend the night together. Have fantastic sex. And then you go for days without calling me. Then you call and we do it all again. That's the pattern for weeks. Suddenly, the calls get further apart. Then you open your heart to me and tell me things I don't think you've told anyone. Things about your friend, Kyle, and about Cat Devon. Then you don't call me for days and I had to resort to calling your sister yesterday to find out if you're still alive.'

Amias bristled. 'You didn't have to do that. And please leave both Kyle and Cat out of this conversation. It works both ways, you know. You could've gone for days without calling me. I wouldn't have minded. Or you could've told me you were busy and to get lost. I wouldn't have minded that either. There were no commitments, remember? And yes. I did tell you things I hadn't told anyone. But I was drunk out of my head and I dearly wish I hadn't done that.'

'Well, as it happens, it was a good thing you did. I wasn't sure whether to tell Mary Devon or not, but I'm really glad I decided to, because just two days later, after Viola had her fall, Mary could get hold of Cat. You should be pleased about that. Perhaps that family will finally patch things up now that Cat's back.'

Amias sat bolt upright. 'Cat's back? When? How do you know?'

'Because Mary popped in for coffee with my mum this morning and she told Mum to thank me. Cat and her daughter, Kyra turned up on her doorstep last night and they'll be staying for a while.'

'Shit.' He ran a hand through his hair and shook his head.

'Is that a problem?' She looked as if she might be enjoying this.

'No. More of a slight irritation.'

'That's good. I'm glad something irritates you. It shows you have some feeling. And you know what, Amias? You asked me earlier what the problem was. I'll tell you what it is. The problem is you, Amias. You're the sodding problem. I'm suddenly not hungry.' She pushed her chair away from the table and glared at him. Then she picked up her glass of wine and threw the contents in his face. 'Thanks for the sex, the fun – and the drink. I won't be calling again.'

After the momentary shock, Amias smirked. He should be thanking her for the drink.

And perhaps she was right. He should be thanking her for a lot of things.

Cat Devon was back in Merriment Bay. That meant he might get a chance to meet Kyle's daughter, face to face, without appearing to be some kind of stalker. That was definitely worth getting a glass of wine in the face for. Even in a packed Italian restaurant on a Saturday night where everyone was staring at him and whispering, and even if the entire village would be talking about this by lunchtime tomorrow.

Chapter Eleven

Cat didn't sleep so well the second night and neither did Kyra. They were both up early and in the kitchen long before Mary. Cat considered taking Mary a cup of coffee but the sun hadn't yet come up and it had been a hot and sticky night. When Kyra suggested a swim, Cat immediately agreed. No one else would be around at 5.30 in the morning, especially on a Sunday.

Twenty minutes later, after going back upstairs to get changed, and having a large cup of coffee each, they were on the shingle and sand beach opposite the house, as dawn broke over the horizon. What a sight that was. The slate blue of twilight turned to a deep red, easing into a soft pink and finally a golden hue. Rays of warm yellow filtered over the land mass of the bay as the sun rose to the east, spreading out until the sea sparkled and glistened as if all the stars from the night sky had fallen into the sea this morning.

The water was warm after weeks of baking sunshine, but still not clear. The English Channel never was apart from in the shallows. Cat remembered where the rocks were and led Kyra around them, before diving into the balmy waters and swimming away from the shore.

A flock of geese flew overhead, maybe getting a head start on migration, and as the world of Merriment Bay began to come to life, the silence was broken by the muffled sound of car engines starting and lorries rumbling along Coast Road to and from the supermarket, perhaps. Gulls squeaked and soared above Cat and Kyra and Cat suddenly became aware of how easily she could get used to this again. She could remember mornings just like this from all those years ago. And the thought of Devon Villa being sold hit her this morning, far harder than it had last night. Somehow she couldn't imagine anyone but a Devon living in Devon Villa. And that thought worried her far more than the thought of coming home to Merriment Bay ever had. Because for a Devon to live in the villa meant that she would have to stay. And that was something she wasn't sure she could do.

'I could get used to this, Mum.' Kyra voiced Cat's thoughts as she swam to her side. 'Waking up every morning and swimming in the sea isn't a bad way to start the day, is it?' She smiled, and she looked so much like Kyle it brought a lump to Cat's throat.

Kyle loved being in the sea. She remembered Amias joking that he was sure Kyle was half fish. And there wasn't a thing Kyle couldn't do both in and out of water. He sailed, surfed, kiteboarded, windsurfed, waterskied; could handle a jet ski like a racing driver, plus boats of any type or size. At school, he'd been in the swim team, the rowing club and the sailing squad. There was talk of him being Olympic material in more than one field, but competition didn't interest Kyle. He was the least competitive person she had ever met.

Apart from, maybe, Amias. Amias was one of those rare people who would let another person win if he thought it would make them feel good. And he always championed the loser; supported the kid who needed an extra boost in self-esteem. And yet, he had a chip on his shoulder the size of the bay when it came to where he was brought up. And he'd been far from pleasant to her.

He called Cat a stuck-up kid the first day they met. And when she'd asked if he could teach anyone to ride the waves like he did, he had told her that he could teach anyone but her. But he would never say why not.

Each day she had gone to the bay to see if he might change his mind – simply to see him. He was so good to look at even as an eighteen-year-old and just the sight of him made her body behave in ways she didn't fully understand and definitely couldn't control.

He made it perfectly clear that the feeling wasn't mutual. When she'd offered to pay him double, treble, even four times his usual price to teach her to windsurf, he'd sneered at her.

'You'll find money can't always buy you what you want, and no amount of money is going to get you on to anything of mine. Ever. So stop coming down here and getting in my way. I'm a busy man and I've got a business to build.'

'By turning away customers who are willing to pay any price for what you have to offer? I don't think that's a good way to build a business.'

'I don't care what you think. It's my business and I'll build it any way I want. Now get lost, kid.'

After weeks of being nice and taking all his insults, she had finally lost her temper with him that day.

'I'm not a kid. I'm sixteen. And I don't know what I've done to you to make you so rude and obnoxious to me. You're not like this with anyone else.'

'How do you know?'

'Because I've watched you.'

A strange smile had spread across his face but he wouldn't let it take hold and he turned it into a sneer as he raised his brows and looked her up and down with sheer contempt.

'You've. Watched. Me. I knew you were weird. Are you sure you're sixteen? You look about twelve to me. And you definitely behave like it.'

'God! If anyone behaves like a twelve-year-old, it's you, Amias Wells.'

She'd turned away and ran along the shore, so annoyed and hurt and heartbroken. Yes, heartbroken. She hadn't looked where she was going as she'd run towards the path leading from the bay up to Coast Road and the bridge and she'd crashed headlong into Kyle. He had been jogging towards the beach by the side of the Spitfire Café, and they'd both gone flying. He'd hurried to his feet, gently lifted her up and when he'd stared into her tear-laden eyes and asked her what was wrong, she'd blurted out that all she'd wanted to do was learn to windsurf. Was that really too much to ask?

'I'll teach you to windsurf,' Kyle had said, smiling as if he was holding several bars of gold in his arms, not a sobbing sixteen-year-old. 'I'll teach you anything you want.'

'You will?'

'With pleasure. I'm Kyle. Kyle Morris.'

Cat sniffed and wiped her runny nose with the back of her hand in a manner that would've made both her mum and Granny Viola shudder.

'I'm Catherine Devon. Do you really mean that? I've got money. I'll pay you anything.'

An idea was forming in her head. If Kyle would teach her to windsurf that would show Amias Wells how determined she was. And if she got really good at it, perhaps then he'd look at her in a different light.

'Hi Catherine. Yes, I mean it. And I don't want your money. I'll make you a deal instead. I'll teach you to windsurf, if you'll agree to go out on a date with me once I get you standing upright on the board. Deal?'

'Oh. Um. Are you seriously asking me to go out with you? We don't know each other from Adam.' She'd tried to laugh and make it sound light-hearted.

'That's what dating's for. To get to know one another. And I already know I've fallen in love with you.'

'What?' She'd shrieked. 'You're kidding, of course.'

He'd fixed his gaze on her and his ginger curls had brushed his freckled cheeks as he'd slowly shaken his head to and fro.

'I'm not. I knew it the minute I touched your hand and looked into those gorgeous green eyes. It's love. No doubt about it.'

'How old are you?'

'Seventeen. You?'

'Sixteen. Don't you think you're a little young to be falling in love?'

What was she saying? She was in love with Amias. And she fell in love with him the first time she saw him. Maybe this guy was telling the truth.

'Does age matter? I can feel it here.' He touched his chest above his heart. 'I'm going to love you all my life. Please say yes, Catherine. Unless you can't stand the idea of dating me. In which case, say so. I'll still teach you to windsurf. And I'll still do it for free. But I'll ask you out every chance I get.'

He'd smiled at her and he looked so kind and caring. Yet so intense and determined that she'd said yes.

And now that she thought about it with the benefit of all the ensuing years, perhaps it wasn't just an attempt to make Amias see what he was missing. There was something about Kyle that made her feel as if she was going to be in good hands. And not just on a windsurfer.

'Mum?' Kyra said. 'You look miles away. I said I'm getting out now. My tummy's rumbling and I'm longing for poached egg on toast. Are you coming?'

'What? Oh yes. My tummy's rumbling too.'

But it wasn't due to longing for egg on toast. It was due to longing for what she'd lost. And also, partly perhaps, for something she had never had.

She'd told Kyra she didn't want to get married and she was happy as she was. But was that really true? Because suddenly all she wanted was to be in someone's arms and to feel loved again. Really loved. Not just in a semi-platonic fashion as Greg in Bonniemount, the friend she dated on and off, loved her. She wanted to be loved whole-heartedly like Kyle had loved her. And passionately. And at that moment, she wanted that so badly it was an actual, physical ache.

Chapter Twelve

Two days drifted into a little over a week and without realising, Cat and Kyra had started settling into life in Merriment Bay.

It was now August bank holiday Monday and each day, including this one, had been spent in a similar fashion. They swam early every morning, even on the one day it rained. Mary had joined them on Saturday, to Cat's complete amazement, and they'd laughed and had a swimming race, just as they had when Cat was young.

The heatwave was still going strong, and in the village market, Cat heard people loudly wishing for the cool breezes of autumn. She and Kyra went on shopping trips with Mary. Just to the supermarket, or the village market where local businesses had stalls twice a week, selling homemade or homegrown produce.

Today was slightly different though. Today there was the Monday Madness Market. It had been held on the August bank holiday Monday for as long as Cat could remember and as usual, it was packed, not just with stalls and shoppers, but also with entertainers of all varieties. There was a makeshift stage in the centre, where in the winter, an ice rink would be set up. Singers, dancers, musicians, poets and all sorts performed to cheering crowds.

It was a pleasant way to spend a couple of hours, but Cat had felt a little restless; anxious even. It was events like this she had thought she would try to avoid. She'd rather not bump into anyone she knew from the past and despite the heat, she wore one of the crocheted bolero cardigans she had bought, and frequently glanced over her shoulder. But Kyra had been keen to come and Cat wouldn't do anything to spoil Kyra's enjoyment.

Since arriving just over a week ago, Cat and Kyra often cooked meals for the three of them, and Mary actually thanked them every time they did, but today they decided to eat out. The three of them went to Bella Vista, one of a couple of restaurants on Coast Road, and just a short stroll from the village market. Cat had been once before – with Kyle, on his eighteenth birthday. It had been Cat's treat and the restaurant was fairly new, back then. Like most things in Merriment Bay, it seemed, it had hardly changed at all.

Sections of the floor were painted to look like canals, and other sections, to look like the cobbled streets of Venice, on which the tables were positioned. The walls were painted with beautiful, pastel Palazzos crammed beneath a radiant sun in an impossibly blue sky. The waiting staff were dressed as Gondoliers: the women in dark blue skirts or trousers and red and white striped tops; the men in black trousers and blue and white striped tops, all with straw hats trimmed with white ribbon on which the Bella Vista logo was written in red.

'Hello, lovelies,' a waitress said, beaming at them as she approached their table, her accent definitely not Italian. 'This must be Catherine and Kyra. Lovely to see you, ladies. You won't remember me, Catherine, but I'm Annie, a friend of Mary's and I babysat you once or twice when you were young.' Her eyes flickered over Cat's face and her smile faltered, but she continued. 'I moved away when I met my second husband. But that one only lasted a few years too, so I came back. Just like you. It seems we all come back to Merriment Bay, way one or another. I was so sorry to hear about that awful accident, but your scars are hardly noticeable in this light, and you're still a pretty woman. Now what can I get you? I can tell you everything's good here.'

Cat was going to respond but she caught the look in Mary's eye and forced herself to ignore the comments.

'Hello, Annie,' Mary returned the greeting, although hers was less exuberant. 'Catherine and Kyra are only here for a visit. Because of Viola, of course. Kyra's off to university in Edinburgh soon, and Catherine's now an artist and has work to get back to. Her art is, of course, in great demand.'

'Aah. That's a shame. Oh, not about you and uni, Kyra.' Annie nudged Kyra with her elbow and giggled like a fifty-year-old child. 'Or about your art, Catherine. What am I like, eh? I meant it's a shame you won't both be staying. Mary could do with some company in that big old house. I keep telling her what she needs is a man. But they're in short supply in Merriment Bay. Well the good ones are. Oooh! But speaking of good ones.' She glanced around and leant forward, hardly taking a breath. 'Amias Wells is back on the market. Not that he was ever off it, despite what Gladys and young Lorna may have hoped. Oh Catherine, love. Let me mop that water up for you. Easy to knock these glasses over. I do it myself all the time.' She giggled again as Cat met Kyra's questioning look.

'I'm sorry,' Cat said, heat burning her neck and cheeks as Annie grabbed several linen napkins from a nearby shelf. 'I'm all fingers and thumbs today. I think it's this heat. It's exhausting.' It wasn't the heat. It was the thought of Amias being on the market that had made Cat spill her water.

'Tell me about it, love.' Annie mopped up the water with the napkins and tossed them on to a passing waiter's tray, beaming at him and winking. 'It's like an inferno in that kitchen. But that might have something to do with Luigi, the chef. He could make my pot boil any time he wants, if you catch my meaning. I've half a mind to make him husband number three.'

'You were saying something about Amias Wells,' Kyra coaxed, ignoring the look Cat shot her.

'Was I? Oh yes. Do you know him? Now don't

you go getting ideas in that direction young lady. He's far too old for you. And sadly, he's a little too young for me. Although I'd be more than happy to make an exception if I thought there was the slightest chance he'd throw me one of his smiles.'

'Really, Annie!' Mary didn't sound pleased. 'Amias Wells?' She tutted loudly as she shook her head in obvious disapproval.

Annie laughed. 'Now don't you get all high and mighty with me, Mary Devon. Don't forget I know about you and …'

'Annie!' Mary glowered at her friend before snapping at Kyra. 'Do we really want to talk about Amias Wells?'

'Yes,' Kyra said, smiling warmly. 'He was a friend of Dad's.'

Cat caught Mary's eye and wondered what Annie had been about to say but Annie continued.

'Well. Amias and Lorna – that's Lorna Carlton, Kyra love. She was his girlfriend until the other night. At least she thought she was. They were sitting at that table next but one and he tells her it's over. So what does Lorna do? She gets up, throws a glass of wine in his face and marches out of here with her head in the air. I saw it with my own eyes. Between us, the poor love's heartbroken. She really thought she had a chance with him. Silly girl.'

'What did Amias do?' Kyra asked, wide eyed and interested. 'Was he embarrassed?'

'Bless you, love,' Annie said, shaking her head and grinning. 'Amias embarrassed? Not on your life. He wiped his face and shirt and ordered chicken arrabbiata. And another glass of wine.'

'Doesn't he treat women well?'

There was a note of disappointment in Kyra's tone as she glanced at Cat, who tried to concentrate on the menu and pretend she wasn't listening.

'Treat women well?' Annie looked thoughtful. 'I suppose that depends what they expect from him. He's never cheated on anyone, from what I've heard. And he's upfront about his feelings. Or perhaps his lack of feelings. Amias likes to date and have fun but he's got his future mapped out and so far he's not found anyone he wants to include in that. But he does care deeply about people. Even Mary will agree with me on that. He's not the sort of man to hurt anyone, or anything, on purpose. Man, woman, or beast. Most women who've dated him, sing his praises. The only time there's ever a problem is when one of them tries to change him. Like Lorna. When Amias says he'll call you, he definitely will. He wouldn't say it otherwise. But you shouldn't sit by the phone and wait. It might be a while until he does. Although from what I've heard, he's worth the wait, if you catch my meaning.'

'May we order, now?' Mary asked, clearly trying once again to get away from the subject of Amias Wells.

Cat was equally keen for the conversation to end. 'Yes. I'm starving.'

'I'm looking forward to meeting him,' Kyra

said. 'And I'll have chicken arrabbiata, please, Annie.'

Chapter Thirteen

There was no change in Granny Viola's condition when they visited her that afternoon, but the doctors remained hopeful.

'The signs are good,' one junior doctor said, clearly exhausted after another long shift. 'To be honest, there's not much we can do other than monitor her and continue to treat her and check the broken bones are healing as they should. Just do what you're doing and stay upbeat. But also be prepared for things taking a turn for the worse. It's really just a waiting game.'

Cat wanted to say it wasn't a game. This was her gran he was talking about. But she knew he didn't mean anything by his comment. Sometimes being a doctor in the ICU must seem like a constant, uphill battle.

On her first visit with Kyra, over a week ago, she had asked what they should do and had been told, 'Tell her who you are when you arrive each day. Speak as you would normally. Tell her about your day. But be aware that she may hear every word you say, so try not to say she looks worse or anything like that within her earshot. Show her your love and support, just as you are doing. Reading to her, playing her favourite music through earbuds, holding her hand, gently brushing her hair, or even stroking her skin can be a huge comfort. Even wearing her favourite perfume might help to stimulate her senses. Coma patients all experience it in a different way. Some people say they can remember things happening around them, and feeling comfort from familiar voices. Others remember nothing. Comas usually only last a few weeks and if she's going to come through it, things should gradually start to progress towards a waking state. She'll remain in ICU for a week or so and then moved into HDU if there's no change after that, but she'll still be in Critical Care.'

Cat asked again on this visit, whether there was anything else they should do.

'No. Just continue doing what you have been doing,' the doctor said. 'We're going to be moving her to HDU this week as her condition is stable and her bones are healing well. If she remains the same and shows no change at all, she may later be moved to a ward, or a private room if one's required, and given supportive treatment until she does recover, or other options are thought appropriate.'

Cat understood what "other options" meant, as did Mary, but it wasn't something either of them wanted to consider at this stage. They would behave as if Granny Viola would be returning home. Although if the house was sold, perhaps not to the home she'd known for her entire life. The house

Viola had been born in.

'I've made a decision about the house, I think,' Mary said that evening during supper.

'Oh?' Cat's heart thumped against her chest. 'Are you still going to sell?'

'Eventually, yes. I don't think there's really much choice. If the worst does happen, which I'm sure it won't, I don't want to be rumbling around in this house all alone and trying to get up and down all these stairs every day. I could have stairlifts put in and such, if it came to it, but I don't see the point. But if Mother does come home, I could get a live-in nurse here. Although I could do that wherever we moved to. Anyway. I think what I've decided is to find a builder to do some work. The roof needs some tiles replacing. The façade could definitely do with a lick of paint and the sash windows are on their last legs and need some love and attention. Living right in front of the sea is a sheer delight, but the salt air plays havoc with houses. Especially old houses such as this. I'll tell the agents though that we're open to offers in the meantime. That way, if anyone comes along and offers a good price, we can stop the work and take it, but if they don't, we'll get it looking its best and have a proper marketing campaign. I think Londoners would happily pay a lot of money for this house, don't you?'

'I'm sure they would,' Cat replied, pleased that there was at least no immediate rush to say goodbye to Devon Villa.

'Do you really want to sell, Gran?' Kyra asked.

'It's huge, I know and I've heard you say that it costs a fortune to heat in winter, especially with the bitter winds rushing straight at it from the sea, but it's such a gorgeous house. The light in every room is incredible. Both Mum and I have thoroughly enjoyed painting and drawing the vistas from these windows over the last week or so. I can imagine myself here in the winter, all wrapped up and sitting by the fire as the wind howls outside and rattles the sash windows and the sea crashes on to the shingle shore. And Christmas would be magical in this house, I'm sure.'

Neither Cat nor Mary replied right away. Cat had to swallow something that had seemingly got stuck in her throat and Mary coughed a couple of times and swiped at her eyes as if she were feeling rather emotional.

'Well,' Mary said eventually, 'we won't find a buyer right away, I don't suppose. And Christmas isn't far off, is it? But aren't you going to Edinburgh in a couple of weeks to take your place at university? And Catherine, I'm sure, is keen to get back to her wonderful life in Bonniemount, aren't you?' She looked at Cat and gave a sad little smile, as if the thought of that upset her.

'I'm in no immediate rush to get back,' Cat said, ignoring the veiled sarcasm about her *wonderful life*. 'Having brought a great deal of my art supplies with me, I can work from here. I can have some blank canvases delivered and then ship my work to the gallery by courier. Carrie knows where I am and how to get hold of me.'

Mary opened her mouth, no doubt about to say something like, 'I'm glad you tell some people where you are and how to get hold of you.' But instead she closed it again and smiled.

'About uni,' Kyra said, fiddling with her wine glass. 'I've been wondering whether to apply for a deferred entry. To start next year instead. I always said I might, didn't I, Mum?'

Cat nodded pensively. 'You did. But I thought you'd decided to go travelling after you graduated.'

Kyra shrugged. 'I had. Sort of. But I don't know. It's a five-year programme and that's a really long time. I know we've only been here for ten full days, but already my art is taking a new direction. It feels like it's given me a fresh perspective. I'm sort of wondering – although this depends on what you decide to do, Mum – but … if you do decide to stay here for a while, I'd like to stay too. If that's OK with you, Gran? Just for a few months. Then I'll go travelling in the New Year. I want to go to Italy, particularly. And the south of France. The light there is sensational apparently. And anywhere else that interests me. I'll take a place on next year's course. If they'll still have me. I'm sure, if I call the uni tomorrow, explain my great-gran's in a coma, and that I feel I need more time, they'll understand and give me some leeway. Unis are really hot on student's health and wellbeing, both physical and mental, these days.' She smiled at Cat and Mary.

'It sounds to me as if you've been giving this

some thought, sweetheart.'

Cat smiled at her daughter, torn between wanting her to stick to her original plans, and delighted that Kyra might want to stay in Merriment Bay for a while and follow a slightly different but not unrelated path.

'I have. In fact, I've been thinking of very little else since that first morning we went swimming in the sea, Mum.'

'Don't be taken in by the serenity and beauty of this place in summer, sweetheart. And I agree with what you said about it being wonderful to see the sea at its wildest, but this house can get like an ice box in the middle of winter and even a roaring fire won't take the chill out of your bones. You could go to uni and come home here for the holidays. That's an option, isn't it? But, of course, as I've always said, it's your life and I will never stop you doing anything you want to do. Provided you really do want to do it. Mum? What have you got to say on the subject? It is your house, after all. Well, yours and Granny Viola's. But as you've got power of attorney, you can speak for her.'

Cat grinned and tried to make Mary realise she mustn't make a big deal out of this. Would Mary start on one of her tirades about youngsters throwing their lives away on a foolish whim?

It took a second or two for Mary to answer and she was giving Cat a very odd look, but she was smiling.

'You called this house "home", Catherine.'

Cat looked from her to Kyra and back again.

'Er. Well, it is. But so is Bonniemount. And I will need to go back there at some stage.'

Mary breathed in a long breath and the smile grew as she turned her gaze to Kyra.

'I can think of nothing better than to have you stay here, Kyra. And as for your plans, well, they're yours and you must pursue whatever course you feel is right for you. As Catherine said, it is your life after all. Granny Viola and I once made the mistake of making your mother choose between what we thought she should do and want she wanted to do. No. Not once. We made that mistake twice. And it brought us nothing but unhappiness and regret. So I say this on behalf of myself and Granny Viola. Do whatever it is you want to do, and we'll support you in any way we can, whether or not we agree with your choice or your decision.'

And for the second time since she'd arrived in Merriment Bay, Cat burst into tears.

Chapter Fourteen

The decision made, Cat and Kyra called the university the following day and reorganised Kyra's future.

Cat was still reeling from her mother's admission that they had made mistakes regarding her and what she had wanted, and although Mary hadn't actually apologised in so many words, she'd come as close to doing so as she was ever likely to. It must've taken a lot for her to say those words. And what she'd said to Kyra astonished Cat even more.

After that night, life at Devon Villa fell into a rather pleasant routine and Cat and Mary seemed to be getting on together with hardly a hint of their former resentment, bitterness and pain.

Cat and Kyra, and often Mary too, continued to swim each day, as the heatwave scorched its way through the first two weeks of September. Granny Viola's condition hadn't changed at all though and she was moved into a private room, one of only a few left in the hospital. They visited her every day and other than that, Cat and Kyra spent most of their free time painting, drawing, shopping, swimming or walking.

Not once did Cat venture down to the bay and if ever she saw a tall man with dark hair and broad shoulders coming her way, she would hastily hang her head and dart into a shop or dive for cover wherever she could. She wanted to avoid Amias Wells for as long as was humanly possible.

And it seemed to her that he was probably doing the same because this was Merriment Bay, after all and there was no doubt in her mind that he would've known of her return by the day after she and Kyra arrived, at the very latest. They had been here for one month now, and they hadn't seen or heard from him.

The one thing that did disappoint her was that he hadn't made even the slightest effort to see Kyra. Kyle was his best friend and Cat was certain that Amias had really loved him. More like a brother than just a friend. Added to that the fact that he had, at some stage, apparently gone out of his way to track them down, and it all seemed very odd, that now that Kyra was here, less than two miles from his business and his new home, he hadn't even dropped a card through the letterbox to say hello.

But perhaps he'd forgotten about Kyle and Kyra. He would no doubt have forgotten Cat. He'd never liked her and he'd only made a valiant effort to be nice to her once she and Kyle had started dating. But she'd seen the hard stares he'd given her once or twice and she knew that if he had had his way, she and Kyle would definitely *not* have been dating.

Thankfully, since that day at Bella Vista, Kyra hadn't mentioned him. Cat had thought she might, after the revelation in the service station car park the day they had driven down. But Kyra hadn't said one word about that conversation since, or the things that Annie had told them over lunch on the August bank holiday Monday. It was almost as if it hadn't happened. For which Cat was extremely thankful.

Although she had never lied to Kyra about anything before or after that conversation, she hadn't told Kyra the entire truth.

The one thing she had kept from her was that although it was true that she had fallen in love with Kyle and definitely was grateful every day that she had met him, Amias Wells didn't become history as far as she was concerned.

She continued to love him all the while she dated Kyle. Even when she discovered she was pregnant, she still loved him. And after Kyle died, she continued to love Amias bloody Wells. It seemed no matter what she did, she could not get over Amias. She could not stop loving him.

Which was more than strange to say the least because she told the truth when she said she loved Kyle with all her heart.

She had.

The problem was she loved Amias with her soul.

She loved him with every inch of her being. And somehow, she thought she probably always would.

And that was another reason why she had run away that day, just ten weeks after Kyra's birth.

Chapter Fifteen

Amias spotted her the moment she walked on to the beach and he watched her saunter towards him although she wasn't looking in his direction; she was looking out to sea, no doubt watching the various people having fun on the water, most of whom were his pupils.

'Hi,' he said, when she got near. 'I haven't seen you around here before. Are you here on holiday?'

He was smiling so hard he probably looked demented but that was preferable to grabbing the kid and giving her a massive hug. Which was what he wanted to do. That would really terrify her.

'Hi. Not a holiday, exactly. Just a visit.'

She smiled back and tugged at several long strands of ginger curls that the warm breeze had blown across her freckled cheeks. A watch that was clearly far too big for her, dangled from her slim wrist. He recognised it right away. Just as he'd recognised her. She was the spitting image of Kyle at eighteen – only female.

'Oh? That almost sounds as if you'd rather not be here.'

'Oh no. I'm glad I'm here. Very glad. Are they

your sons?'

She nodded towards the sea where Lucas flew across the waves on his kiteboard, and Marcus tumbled into them from his windsurfer.

Amias cleared his throat. 'No. I don't have kids. They're pupils of mine. Well, not the one in the air. Not now. He can probably teach me a thing or two. But his cousin, Marcus is still learning the ropes.'

'So I see. It looks difficult. You teach people to do that? Anyone at all?'

She pushed her sunglasses on to the top of her head and gave him a smile so full of hope that his heart thumped against his chest. In that moment, she reminded him so much of Cat it was as if the clock had turned back nineteen years – to the very first day Cat had walked up to him and smiled. Weeks before she had met Kyle, and a year before that terrible day that ruined three people's lives. More than three, if you counted Kyle's parents. But Amias didn't.

Unlike the answer he'd given Cat that day when she'd asked the exact same question, he smiled at Kyra.

'I try. The thing about windsurfing and also kiteboarding is you need to have balance. That sounds weird and you'd think everyone can balance, but they can't. As Marcus is demonstrating, some people find it hard. It's about having a strong core and finding your centre of gravity. To some people it comes naturally. Others have to work at it.'

'That sounds very zen-like. Mum and I do yoga. We've also both done ballet, although now all we ever do is dance around the kitchen. And not altogether gracefully, I might add.'

Her laughter sent warmth rushing through him. Not sexual heat. That would be creepy. It was the kind of warmth he felt when he was at his sister's, or in the company of a loving family. And it was a feeling that unnerved him.

'In that case, you'd probably take to it like a duck to water. I can give you a free taster lesson if you like. As you're eighteen, you won't need parental consent so there's no need to ask your mum.'

'How did you know I'm eighteen?' Her green eyes were wide and her lips slightly apart in surprise.

He shook his head. 'I just assumed. You look eighteen.'

She relaxed and laughed. 'Oh yeah? I'm not sure if that's good or bad. We women usually prefer to be told we don't look our age.'

'Hardly something someone like you needs to worry about, is it?'

A tiny crease formed between her brows, but it was quickly replaced by a cheerful smile that lit up her eyes. She had her mum's smile. She also had her mum's, almond-shaped, cat-like eyes. That was why he had first called Catherine, Cat – a name that seemed to have stuck. At least while she was dating

Kyle. Did she still refer to herself as Cat? Or had she reverted back to Catherine the moment she had left?

Kyra was laughing. That laugh was Kyle's. 'There're only two things I'm worried about right now. One is whether or not I'm going to make a complete idiot of myself in front of everyone. And the other is that I've got to put on one of those wetsuits. Although that guy on the kiteboard isn't wearing one.'

He glanced at Lucas, riding the waves and reaching heights that would terrify most people as the wind filled his sail, lifting him and his kiteboard high into the air.

'Wetsuits are optional. But with your complexion, I'd advise it. Either that or a T-shirt and shorts. You look as if you've caught some sun, but you'd be surprised how quickly you can burn out there on the water. The last thing you want is to be burnt red raw. Especially as you'll be aching enough from the exertion and the fact you'll be using muscles you may not have used before.'

'That's not a very good sales pitch, if you don't mind me saying. Shouldn't you be telling me how fantastic I'll feel riding the waves with just the power of the wind, and flying through the air with the warm breeze on my skin?'

He laughed. 'Need a job? You make it sound exhilarating.'

She laughed too. 'Are you saying it isn't?'

'Not for the first few times. Probably not. Most

people spend several hours falling off the board and climbing back on. That can be exhausting. But as you obviously keep yourself fit, you won't tire so fast. Want a go?'

'Definitely. But I can't today, I'm afraid.' She glanced at her watch. 'I'm meeting Mum for coffee in the market at 10 and I'll be late if I don't get a move on. I could ring her and she'd be fine if I wanted to do this instead, but I don't have a swimsuit with me. Can I come tomorrow?'

He nodded. 'Of course. I'm here every day. Unless I'm at my other site. That's at Wyntersleap Reservoir a couple of miles inland. It's where I take some beginners. But I've got a feeling you'll be fine learning right here.'

She narrowed her eyes slightly. 'I'm only doing the taster lesson. I'm not committing to a course or anything. Yet.'

He shook his head. 'Right. Yes, of course. I know that. What I meant was that you'll be OK doing the taster in the sea. It doesn't matter. We can talk about it tomorrow. I'll definitely be here all morning.'

She smiled. 'I'll see you tomorrow then. Oh. What's your name? Just in case you're not around and I have to ask.'

'My name?' He coughed to clear his throat. He'd sounded like he was being castrated. 'Er. I'll be here. Don't worry.'

She screwed up her eyes. 'You don't want to give me your name? Should I be worried?'

He forced a grin and swallowed hard. 'Absolutely not. You've got nothing to worry about from me. I can promise you that. It's Amias.'

'Amias!' Her eyes opened wide, as did her smile. 'Amias Wells?'

His smile disappeared. 'Y-yes.'

She laughed. 'Now you're the one who looks worried. No need. I assure you. My mum mentioned you, that's all. Her name's Cat. Cat Devon. You knew each other once, many years ago.'

His fists clenched at the mention of her name, and so did his jaw but he tried to look thoughtful. 'Cat Devon. Hmm. The name does ring a bell. Oh yes. I remember. She dated a friend of mine a very long time ago.' He hadn't meant to make it sound quite so casual.

Kyra moved closer to him and looked him in the eye. 'That was my dad. I'm Kyra. Kyra Devon. My dad was Kyle Morris. It's good to meet you, Amias Wells. Very good indeed.'

'I don't think your mum will agree with you on that.' What the hell was wrong with him? He shouldn't have said that.

'I think you might be surprised.'

'I would be. Very. But it's so good to meet you, Kyra.'

She looked at him for a moment and it was as if she was taking stock of him. Then she nodded, reached up for her sunglasses and slid them back in place, glanced over the rims and smiled.

'See you tomorrow, Amias Wells. I'm looking

forward to it.'

She turned and ran along the beach, waving behind her as she went.

Amias was looking forward to tomorrow too. And to spending time with the daughter of his best friend.

The daughter he almost wished, was his.

Chapter Sixteen

'What's in this trunk, Mum?' Kyra tugged at a large leather trunk situated near a chair in Granny Viola's bedroom.

Mary had asked them to help her declutter the house. Regardless of what happened, she was determined to go through Devon Villa from top to bottom to see if there was anything they could sell, give to a charity shop, or possibly throw out. She was beginning her 'downsizing' and although she had left her mother's room until last, she had finally said it was time to make a start. But she had left Cat and Kyra to it and gone to make some coffee.

'I'm not sure, sweetheart,' Cat said. 'But I've always wanted to know. I remember seeing Granny Viola sitting in that chair and the lid of that trunk being open. She was looking at a photo, I think, and there was a pile of letters in her lap. When I came in and asked her about them, she held them to her chest before putting them back in the trunk, closing the lid and telling me that some things were private and that they weren't meant for my eyes.'

'Did you leave it at that?' Kyra looked a little surprised. 'I think that would've made me even keener to know.'

Cat laughed. 'It did me. But every time I asked, she said it didn't concern me and I should learn to respect people's privacy. And the trunk was always locked.' Cat shook her head. 'I'm ashamed to say, I crept in here more than once and tried to open it. I even admit I searched for the key but couldn't find it.'

'This key you mean?' Kyra pointed to the key in the lock.

Cat's eyes grew wide and her mouth dropped open.

'I can't believe that's sitting there like that. She always kept it on her, I'm sure she did.'

'Can we open it?' The thrill of excitement made Kyra's voice rise and her smile was huge as were her eyes.

'I'm not sure we should. As Granny always said, it's private.'

'Yes, but Granny Mary asked us to clear out anything we think we can. It's only right that we take a look and see if there's anything in the trunk we can sell, give to charity or dispose of. Just a quick look. And Granny Viola will never know.'

Cat gave her a look of reprimand but she smiled. 'That doesn't make it better. As keen as I still am to know, it somehow feels wrong, with Granny Viola being in hospital. We'll ask Mum and see what she says. If she says we can, then fine, but if she says no then we shan't. OK?'

'If I say you can or can't what?' Mary appeared

in the doorway with a tray, a plate of chocolate biscuits and three mugs of coffee. She had finally agreed that the posh porcelain didn't need to come out at every hour of the day. And that more coffee could be poured into a mug than a china cup.

'Oh. It's Granny Viola's trunk. The key is in the lock and we were wondering whether or not we should look inside.'

'Really?' Mary hurried over to them, slopping coffee on to the tray in her excitement. 'I've wanted to know what was in that trunk my entire life. But it was always locked and I could never find the key. Oh. I suppose I shouldn't admit that, should I? But if the key's in the lock. Well, I think that's Fate, don't you? It's as if mother is giving us the go-ahead to open it. Do the honours, Kyra as you're there.'

Kyra glanced at Cat before slowly turning the key and lifting the heavy lid.

The three of them peered inside. Amongst some items of clothing, a few bunches of dried flowers and a small pile of photos were a stack of letters, the ink fading and the corners curled as if they'd been handled many times. And yet when Kyra picked them up and turned over the ribbon tied stack, the first envelope was sealed. She flicked through the pile of ten or more letters, all with the same handwriting and all addressed to Miss Viola Devon, Devon House, Channel View Lane, Merriment Bay, Sussex, and not one of them was open.

'How strange,' Cat said.

'They could've been opened and resealed,' Kyra suggested.

Mary shook her head. 'No. If they had they'd be damaged. Even if they'd been steamed open and resealed, there would be some sign of that. You can see that these are as they were the day the sender licked the envelope and sealed it down.'

'And who's this?' Kyra asked, picking up a photograph that had fallen to the floor while she had flicked through the letters. 'It was in amongst them. It's a man. A very handsome man and he's in uniform.'

'Let me look, please.' Mary held out her hand and Kyra passed her the photo. She studied it for a while then handed it to Cat. 'I've never seen that photo before, or that man. He's definitely not someone I ever met. I'd remember a face that handsome.'

Cat shook her head. 'You're right. I'd remember this face too if I'd ever seen it before. I wonder who he is.'

'He must've been someone special for Granny Viola to save his photo and probably his letters and keep them all in a locked trunk. But he also must've done something to hurt her, don't you think? Because why else would she hide the photo amongst the letters and leave the letters unopened?'

'That hadn't even occurred to me.' Cat threw Kyra a smile. 'I've said it before and I'll say it again, I'm glad you got your brains from your dad and not from me.'

'Can we open them?' Kyra asked.

They all looked at one another.

'I'm not sure we should,' Cat said. 'I'm not saying I don't want to because I do. I really do. But as you said, Kyra, Granny Viola left them sealed for a reason. She also kept them locked in this trunk. I'm not certain we should invade her privacy to that extent. Especially given her condition.'

'But, Mum. What if something bad does happen? We'd have to open them then, wouldn't we? To see if we'd need to contact the person to tell them about Granny Viola.'

Cat shook her head. 'Those letters look as if they've been there for years. The sender may have passed away. And if Granny Viola never opened them, I hardly think the sender would be someone she would want us to contact in the event of … of anything happening.'

'Or he may be someone we should definitely contact. Think about it, Mum. You and Granny Viola hadn't been in touch for eighteen years, but as soon as you got Granny Mary's letter, you raced back here. This man clearly meant a lot to Granny Viola. You said you'd seen her hugging a photo and a pile of letters to her chest when you asked her about them. These letters. Perhaps he's a lost love. Perhaps he and Granny Viola wanted to be together but Fate kept them apart. Or maybe she didn't open them because she knew they would ask her to do something she felt she never could. Or perhaps he died in the war and she got these letters afterwards and couldn't open them because she knew they would break her heart even more.'

Mary had been strangely silent but she shot a look at Cat.

'I think we have to open them. Or at least one of them to see who he is and what part he played in my mother's life. She may be furious when she recovers but we'll spend every day wondering about them if we don't.'

'Mum?' Cat placed a hand on Mary's. 'Do you really think we should? Unless I'm mistaken that's an RAF uniform he's wearing and by the looks of that photo, it was taken in the 1940s. Perhaps even during the war. And unless I'm also mistaken that building behind him looks very much like the WWII Museum, only as it was during the war when it was an actual RAF base. If he was stationed there, we might be able to find out who he is before we open the letters. There are lots of photos at the museum and several of them have names and dates. And I know there're records of who was stationed there throughout the war. Even who died, or was reported as missing and such, because I've seen them. I remember Am … being shown them once. I'm not sure if all the records are open to the public, but they definitely exist. It's worth seeing if we can find out, isn't it? I simply don't want us to do something we may regret. And I don't know why, but I have the strangest feeling that we may regret opening these letters. As if all our lives might change. I know that sounds ridiculous. But I do.'

Cat handed the photo back to her and Mary studied it again.

'Well one thing I know for certain is he's not my father. I've got photos of him taken in the early sixties and he couldn't have changed that much in twenty years. Besides, I was born in 1965 and he and my mother were only married for a couple of years before that. This must be someone she knew long before she met my father. I definitely don't know this man. But I would very much like to know who he is.'

'The letters will probably tell us,' Kyra said, waving them enticingly before all three of them.

'I'm sure they will. But perhaps Catherine is right. I'd dearly love to open them but perhaps we should see if we can find out who he is first. Mother has kept them under lock and key for years. She must've had a reason. As enticing as they are, waiting for a week or two to open them won't hurt. She may be awake by then and if so, we can ask her. In the meantime, a trip or two to the WWII Museum might prove fruitful. I haven't been to the place for years. I'm not even sure who works there now. But I do know Amias Wells and William Lester became joint owners a few years ago. Which may prove to be rather handy.'

'Amias owns the WWII Museum? I had no idea.'

'Why would you?' Mary gave Cat a very odd look. 'A lot has happened since you've been away. But as I said, he owns it jointly with William Lester.

You must remember William? And his brother, Stephen? Such lovely young men. Stephen lives in Leeds, I believe. William's a solicitor and also the Mayor of Merriment Bay. But the best thing is, he lives next door but one. We could pop to his house and ask him. Or better still, we could invite them round for dinner. His wife Abigail is about your age, Catherine, and his son Lucas is your age, Kyra, as is Marcus. He's Lucas' cousin. Stephen's son. I'm surprised we haven't bumped into any of them over the last few weeks. Although the boys are always in the bay and both William and Abigail work. Yes. That's what we'll do. We'll invite them round and ask William about the records.'

'We could also invite Amias Wells,' Kyra suggested, looking a little flushed.

'No!' Cat and Mary said in unison.

It seemed that was something they both agreed on.

But then Mary had never liked Amias any more than she had liked Kyle. They were both from 'the wrong side of the river' as far as she was concerned. Although she had neither right nor reason to look down her nose at either of them. As an unmarried mum herself, Mary was in a glass house of her own and should hardly be throwing stones at them, to paraphrase the old adage.

Amias had told Cat the very first day they met that Mary Devon was a liar, a hypocrite and a bitchy, snooty cow. But he would never elaborate or say why he felt that way about her. And that was weeks before Cat had started dating Kyle and long before Mary had tried to put a spoke in that relationship.

Cat had once thought that something must have happened to make Amias feel that way. But as he had also taken an instant dislike to her, she reasoned that, with his huge chip on his shoulder, he possibly felt that way about lots of people.

And yet something was niggling at the back of Cat's mind. It had been doing so since they'd had lunch at Bella Vista on August bank holiday Monday. It was Annie's comment to Mary. What was it she had said? Oh yes. "Now don't you get all high and mighty with me, Mary Devon. Don't forget I know about you and …" But Mary had cut her short and Annie had stopped mid-sentence. She had been talking about Amias at the time, so it must have had something to do with him. Cat had mentioned Annie's remark later that day but Mary had dismissed it as "more of Annie's nonsense" and quickly changed the subject.

But was it nonsense?

Cat shivered as a dim and distant memory took hold.

Perhaps it wasn't about Amias at all.

Perhaps it was about his father, Alwick Wells.

Hadn't someone once told her that Mary Devon and Alwick Wells hadn't always hated one another? That in fact, at one time, they had even been quite close.

Or was Cat now imagining that?

Just how *close* could Mary and Alwick have been?

And was it before, or after he met and married his now deceased wife, Gina?

Cat would have to ask Mary about it again.

But Kyra was arguing, albeit pleasantly. 'Why can't we invite Amias too? What's wrong with him?'

Mary tutted. 'Shall I make a list?'

'Well, I like him.'

'You don't know him.'

'Yes, I do. He's been giving me windsurfing lessons.'

'He's been what!' Once again, Cat and Mary spoke in unison.

Kyra shrugged but she had the decency to look a little contrite. 'I was going to tell you, Mum. But I wanted it to be a surprise.'

'Oh it's a surprise, all right. How long has this been going on?'

Kyra sniggered. 'Just a couple of days. And he's teaching me to windsurf, Mum. We're not having sex or anything. Lighten up for heaven's sake. It's all above board. Oh. Forgive the pun.' She sniggered again. 'What's wrong? Why do you look so cross? I'm paying him. That's what he does. He teaches people to windsurf and stuff. And I've met Lucas and Marcus already, Gran. They've both been showing me a thing or two. Well, say something, will you? Don't just glare at me. I didn't realise it was such a big deal.'

119

Cat didn't know what to say. Kyra and Amias having sex hadn't even occurred to her. Although she was definitely his type. Young, gorgeous-looking with a great body.

No, that was unfair. Back then he'd only dated girls his own age. Somehow, she was sure the grown-up Amias wouldn't go for teenage girls.

But Amias and Kyra had met. That was a big enough shock. And now he was giving Kyra windsurfing lessons? How could this have happened? And without her knowledge? Why had Kyra kept it from her? What had Amias said when she'd told him who she was? *Had* she told him who she was? So many questions and thoughts and fears careered around in Cat's mind, but her lips wouldn't form any words. Not polite ones, anyway.

'Well,' Mary said, throwing Cat a look of both astonishment and anxiety rolled into one. 'I really don't know what to say.'

'You're not the only one,' Cat finally managed. 'I think you have some explaining to do, young lady.'

Now it was Kyra who looked cross. 'Why? I'm eighteen. I'm using my own money. The money Isla left me in her will. I wanted to learn to windsurf. Amias teaches people to do that. I really can't see what the problem is. God, Mum! You're fine with me deferring my place at uni to travel the world. But you're furious with me for walking a mile or so to the bay and paying the local water sports instructor to show me how to windsurf? That's just crazy.

Wait? Is this because of what you told me? Because you were once in love with him? Is that why you're so cross?'

Mary gasped. 'You were in love with Amias Wells? When was this exactly?' She flopped on to the chair beside the trunk. 'Oh dear God. Kyra's not his, is she?'

'No! Of course she's not. She's Kyle's. You've only got to look at her to see that. And nothing happened between me and Amias. Nothing at all. I can promise you.'

'Thank God for that!'

Cat darted looks between Mary and Kyra, uncertain who to deal with first.

Kyra was right. She hadn't done anything wrong. Apart from, perhaps, keeping it to herself. Although that wasn't wrong either. And if she wanted to learn to windsurf, there was no one on the planet whom Cat would rather have teach her than Amias.

'You're right, sweetheart. I'm sorry I was cross. I was just surprised, that's all. Amias is the best teacher you could have. And I'd like to hear all about it, if you're happy to tell me.'

Kyra smiled. 'Of course I am. I was going to tell you anyway. Honestly, I was. But I thought it might be fun to get you to come with me to the bay one day, and I'd get on a windsurfer and ride the waves like a pro. Well, maybe not a pro. But Amias says I'm a natural. Just like my dad.'

So there it was. He did know Kyra was Kyle's

daughter.

'Then that's what we'll do, sweetheart.'

Cat took a deep breath and turned to Mary. 'Mum? Is there something I should know? Something about the past? Something concerning Amias? Or more to the point, something concerning Alwick Wells?'

Mary gasped again; a little more softly this time.

'No.' She got to her feet and marched towards the door. 'There's nothing. Nothing worth discussing, in any event. The past is the past. Let's leave it where it belongs.'

'It's not the past if it still affects the present. And, perhaps the future. Mum? I think I need to know. Especially if it has anything to do with me. I don't know who my father was, remember? And I've suddenly got the most awful feeling the reason you've always refused to tell me is because it may have something to do with Alwick Wells. Please tell me I'm wrong.'

The expression on Mary's face was one of abject horror. As if she had seen the four horsemen of the Apocalypse and they were heading straight for her.

'Mum?' Cat's voice was a shrill cry.

Mary shook her head. 'You're wrong. Alwick Wells is not your father, if that's what you're suggesting. That's one thing *I* can definitely promise you.'

Cat's sigh of relief was substantial and even

Kyra sighed, as if she too, had held her breath.

'You don't know how relieved I am to hear you say that, Mum. But don't you think it's about time I did know who he was?'

Mary gripped the edge of the door as if she were hanging on to it for dear life.

'I suppose I'll have to tell you one day, Catherine. You're a woman now and you do have a right to know. But that day is not today. I need to go and lie down. I have a dreadful headache.'

Cat didn't stop her. She wanted to know, but she'd waited all this time, she could wait a little longer. The important thing was that it wasn't Alwick Wells. That thought had almost ripped Cat's heart out. Amias might have been her half-brother. What a twist of Fate that would've been.

'So do you have any idea who your dad might have been?' Kyra asked as soon as Mary was out of earshot.

'No, sweetheart. No idea at all. Mum and Granny Viola both told me he was dead, which is what I told you. Mum also said it was a whirlwind romance and he was the biggest mistake of her life and one she was determined to forget. She didn't even have a photo of him. We argued about it a lot. Until the day she told me I should give you up and not make the same mistake she had. So basically, telling me she wished she'd given me up. That went down well with me, as you can imagine. But I've told you all this before.'

Kyra threw her a comforting smile. 'Several

times. It's not something you're ever likely to forget, is it? But perhaps you can forgive her one day. Especially once you find out who your father was. Perhaps she kept it from you for a good reason.'

Cat smiled back and pulled Kyra into a hug.

'Then we'll have to wait and see what else she tells me, won't we? I'm sorry I was cross with you.'

'I'm sorry I didn't tell you about Amias and my lessons. I promise I'll tell you everything from now on.' Kyra eased herself out of the hug. 'But in the meantime, Mum, what are we going to do about this man's photo?' She waved the faded photo from the letters, in the air.

Cat shook her head. 'You're determined. I'll give you that.'

'I get that from you.'

Cat smiled. 'I'm not sure if that's good or bad. But anyway … as Mum said, we could ask William Lester. Or, as you're now on such good terms with Amias, you could show him the photo and see if he's willing to help.'

'We could show it to him, together. I'm sure he'd love to see you again after all these years.'

Cat raised her brows as a derisive laugh escaped her. 'Oh no. I can assure you, sweetheart, I am the last person Amias Wells would love to see.'

Chapter Seventeen

'We could post the photo on some of the social media sites I'm on,' Kyra suggested, 'and ask if anyone recognises him.'

'I don't think that's wise,' Cat said, glancing at the faded photo they'd found in Granny Viola's trunk of the gorgeous RAF pilot. It now stood in the centre of the dining table, propped up against a vase containing autumn blooms. 'We don't know anything about him. He may not be dead as we now seem to have assumed he might. He may be alive and married with kids and grandkids. I'm not sure I'd like to see a photo of my husband, dad or granddad plastered on a stranger's social media page or whatever it is they're called.'

Kyra sighed. 'I know you dislike the whole concept of social media, Mum, but millions of people love it.' She snapped a shot of the photo with the camera on her phone.

'I agree with Catherine,' Mary said, refilling their crystal wine glasses. She may have been persuaded to leave the precious porcelain in the cupboard, but not serving wine in crystal glasses at their evening meal seemed to be a step too far for her. 'I would be mortified if someone did that to me or a member of my family.'

Cat threw her a sarcastic grin. 'Perhaps I should get Kyra to stick a photo of me on there with a caption or whatever, asking if anyone knows who my dad is. What would you think about that, Mum?'

Mary narrowed her eyes. 'I would think you were being rather mean and selfish, Catherine. But as I don't believe you are either of those things, the question is irrelevant. Besides, you're still a little self-conscious of your scars, although I don't know why. But you would no more post a photo of yourself in a public place than I would.'

'Touché! But you do realise, now the question of my parentage has once again reared its ugly head, I'm not going to let it rest until you eventually tell me.'

Cat reached out and touched Mary's hand. She wasn't cross about her mum continuing to keep the information from her; Mary clearly had her reasons. And Cat had survived for thirty-five years without knowing. She could wait a little longer. She and Mary had come a long way in the few short weeks since Cat and Kyra had arrived in Merriment Bay, but there were still some emotional wounds yet to heal that they had inflicted on one another. But now that she had come home, Cat was determined to finally find out who her dad was.

'I wouldn't expect you to, Catherine. You're a Devon.'

What a typical response from Mary. Cat

grinned at Kyra and flicked her eyes skywards.

Kyra grinned back. 'So what are we *Devons* going to do to find out who this man is? Are you going to invite the Lesters round for dinner tomorrow, Gran? Or shall I show the photo to Amias when I see him tomorrow morning, and ask if he can help?'

Mary stiffened. 'Personally, I'd rather we ask William. Especially as he's the Mayor. If there are records at the museum or wherever, but they're not open to the public, as Mayor of Merriment Bay, William may be able to find a way to work around that.'

'And you think Amias wouldn't?' Cat gave a snort of laughter. 'You clearly don't know him as well as you think you do, Mum. Unless he's changed over the years.'

'I'm pleased to say, I hardly know the man at all. And I'd very much like to keep it that way. His sister, on the other hand, I can't avoid. Horton and Wells are the only Estate Agency in Merriment Bay, so I really had no choice. But as it happens, she is quite delightful. Now that she's married to that lovely Josh Horton, you wouldn't even know she was once a member of the Wells family.'

Cat gasped, unsure of what surprised her most about Mary's comment, that Natalia was an estate agent, that she'd married Josh Horton, that they were the agents handling the sale of Devon Villa. Or that Mary seemed to think that being married to Josh somehow meant Natalia had broken all ties with her family.

'Forgetting for one moment that I knew nothing of Natalia's current status, I hate to point this out, Mum, but Natalia is *still* a member of the Wells family. She always will be. Nothing will ever break that family apart. They're as close as it's possible for a family to be.'

Mary dismissively waved her hand in the air. 'Oh, I know they were all as thick as thieves. And probably *were* thieves. Don't look so cross, Catherine. I've known that family for far longer than you. Mother knew them too. What I meant was her lowly beginnings haven't held her back.'

'Lowly beginnings? Sometimes, you astound me, Mum. They may have lived in a tiny, tumbled down house, but at least it was theirs and they owned the land it stood on. And despite the fact they had nothing but that land and that house, Alwick would never sell to make a quick profit and I don't expect that's changed. He told Amias and Natalia the land would be theirs one day. Although I know you said that Amias has done well and that he now owns a big, new house on the bay.'

'Yes. And Alwick built himself a new house on that land, and one for Natalia, some years ago, so at least they no longer live in that hovel.'

'Did he? Well I'm glad to hear that. But it wasn't a hovel, Mum. Anyway, my point is, it shouldn't matter where anyone comes from. What should matter is what they do, and where they end up.'

'That's what I said.'

'No. You said–'

'Does it matter?' Kyra interrupted. 'Isn't it time we all got along? I'll ask my question again. Are we asking William Lester for help to find the man in the photo? Or are we asking Amias Wells? A. William? Or B. Amias? An A or B answer will do.' She shook her head and grinned. 'In my opinion, we should ask them both. Two heads are better than one, as you're often saying, Mum.'

That was true. Cat did often say that.

'You're getting rather cheeky, bossy and stubborn since turning eighteen just over a month ago, sweetheart.'

The grin grew wider and Kyra raised her wine glass in the air. 'What can I tell you? I'm a Devon.'

Even Mary smiled at that.

'I agree with my cheeky, bossy, stubborn daughter.' Cat winked at Kyra. 'It makes sense to approach them both. They might look at it from different angles.'

Mary sighed. 'Reluctantly, I agree. But I certainly won't be the one asking Amias Wells. And before you ask again, Kyra, the answer is no. That man will not set foot in my house. You and Catherine can have the dubious pleasure of requesting his assistance. But one thing does occur to me. Granny Viola was a WAAF during the war. That's probably how she and this man met.'

'What's a WAAF?' Kyra pulled a face. 'Is that an old-fashioned term for a WAG?'

'No.' Mary frowned. 'It was something to be proud of. The Women's Auxiliary Air Force was set up in 1939 and in December 1941, the government passed the National Service Act, allowing the conscription of women between the ages of eighteen and sixty. Granny Viola became a WAAF on her eighteenth birthday, in January 1942. She worked in the radar control system at RAF Merriment. That was vital work, although more so during the Battle of Britain in 1940, and during the Blitz. She was too young to join up in time for those.'

'That must've been exciting.' Kyra sounded impressed.

Cat nodded. 'Exciting and terrifying in equal measure, I suspect.'

'Yes,' Mary agreed. 'I constantly asked Mother about her life back then but she always said, as I do now, "The past is the past. Let's leave it there." But she told me snippets. Mainly, I longed to hear about her sister, Ivy.'

'Ivy?' Kyra looked from Mary to Cat. 'I've never heard about her.'

'She died in the war, sweetheart.'

Mary sighed. 'I never knew her. She died in January 1945 but her life must have been thrilling. Mother was scared of heights, so she kept her feet firmly on the ground and joined the WAAF. They weren't allowed to fly. But we lost so many pilots that training more in secondary roles to release front line pilots for active service, became paramount.

That led to the formation of ATA. That was the Air Transport Auxiliary, and women were allowed to join. ATA pilots were civilians and that suited the RAF. They didn't like the idea of women pilots flying military aircraft. You must have heard of the famous pilot Amy Johnson, Kyra. Well, Ivy was a pilot just like her.'

'Really? A pilot? But who taught Ivy to fly?'

'ATA. Everyone assumes they only took experienced pilots but that soon changed. Ivy became what was known as an "Attagirl" in 1943. She'd always wanted to fly, apparently, so the ATA motto of "Aetheris Avidi", or in English, "Eager for the Air" was apt. Mother used to become dreadfully upset at the very mention of Ivy's name, so I know little of her except that she delivered new planes from factories to RAF airfields all over the country and took planes back for repairs. She was returning a damaged plane from the former RAF Acklington, in Northumberland when she was caught in a blizzard and crashed into a hillside. She was only twenty-two. Far too young to die.' Mary gave a sudden cough as if realising that comment may have hit a nerve. 'Now I really must dash off. I promised Gladys I would pick her up at 7 p.m. on the dot and it's 5 minutes to the hour now. Bridge club members abhor tardy behaviour. Catherine, may I leave the clearing up to you and Kyra?' She was already getting up from the table and about to head for the door.

'Of course. Woe betide anyone who falls foul

of the bridge club. You go and have fun. Kyra and I will clear up and then we might watch a movie.'

'Um. I meant to mention this earlier, Mum.' Kyra cast Cat an apologetic smile. 'But I have plans tonight. It slipped my mind what with everything earlier. You know I said I'd met Lucas and Marcus Lester?' Cat nodded that she did. 'Well, they asked me if I wanted to go and hang out with them on the beach this evening. Just for a couple of hours. It's still so warm and there's going to be a gorgeous full moon tonight. I promise I'll be back by 10 and Lucas and Marcus will bring me to the door. There're a few other people my age going. It's a chance to make some friends. Is that OK?'

Cat smiled. 'Absolutely, sweetheart. You go. I'll clear up. You had my permission when you said Lucas and Marcus. Not that you need my permission. I hung out with their dads for a while in my youth, and Mum was right about them, even if she is still so wrong about certain other people we won't mention. Will and Stephen were lovely young men. I know you'll be perfectly safe with their sons.'

Kyra beamed and shoved her chair back, kissing Cat on the cheek and hugging her shoulders. Then she raced to the door but stopped and glanced back.

'I may be safe with them, Mum. But I wouldn't bet on them being safe with me. Lucas is a hunk. And Marcus isn't bad either. He just needs more self-confidence and I'm determined to give him a hand with that.'

She grinned, winked, and was gone before Cat had time to reply.

But Kyra was only joking.

Wasn't she?

Chapter Eighteen

Cat already had several unanswered questions, along with her concern for Granny Viola, and far too many memories, both good and bad, vying for space in her head. Now, as she cleared the table and loaded the dishwasher, she had added an interest in Ivy Devon's life, and had squeezed in doubts about the Lester boys and worries about Kyra on the beach, on a sultry night beneath a full moon. She knew from experience where that could lead. Not that she regretted it. None of it. Well. Perhaps she had one or two regrets. But she shoved them to the deepest recess of her mind as fast as she could.

What she needed to do was declutter. Yes. Declutter her mind just as Mary was decluttering Devon Villa. Ivy Devon's life was no doubt fascinating, but did Cat really need to think about it now? And discovering who her own dad was, as important as it may be, had waited this long. It didn't need to be foremost in her mind right now. And Kyle? Perhaps Kyra had been right when she had said that maybe it was time the Devon women put the past behind them. Eighteen years was half Cat's lifetime. If there was any chance of her finding happiness in the future, she would have to let go of the past.

Or lock it up in a large leather trunk and stick it in her bedroom, as Granny Viola seemed to have done with hers. Somehow that was even sadder than carrying the memories around in her heart. Or maybe Granny Viola did that too. If she ever came out of the coma she was in, Cat would ask her.

No. Not if. When.

Granny Viola would wake up. She would. She must.

Cat had left a note when she ran away eighteen years ago, but she had never said goodbye. And now she really wished she had. No. She wished she might get a chance to heal the rift between them first. She wasn't ready for goodbye.

When Isla Presley passed away two years ago, Cat had been devastated. Isla had become a surrogate mum and grandmother. But her death should've made Cat realise that Granny Viola might not have much longer on this earth. She was ninety-five; ninety-three back then. Why hadn't Cat cast aside her stubbornness, her bitterness, her pride and her anger and made this journey sooner? Why had she left it until Mary's letter had arrived? Was she now too late?

She switched the dishwasher on and poured herself another glass of wine. She could go and sit in the front garden and watch the twilight fade into night. She'd missed the sunset but it wasn't yet dark. She could read or watch TV. She could continue with the decluttering of the house. Or begin the decluttering of her mind.

But was she really ready for that?

She was glad Kyra was making friends. Perhaps she should take a leaf out of her daughter's book and do the same. Mary had said that Abigail, William's wife, was about Cat's age, and Mary was intending to invite the Lesters round for dinner. She could text her mum and offer to go and do that now. Perhaps they were free for Sunday lunch tomorrow? But perhaps they wouldn't want her turning up on their doorstep on a Saturday night to invite them. And Mary might not be pleased to have her bridge game interrupted.

Cat slumped on the window seat and stared outside. The shore was deserted and waves lapped hungrily at the shingle on an incoming tide. It would be dark in less than an hour. She could go for a walk beforehand.

Oh to be young and carefree again, like Kyra. But would she want that? Could she go through all of that again? If Kyle had lived, what would the two of them be doing right now? Would they have had more kids? Would they have stayed in Edinburgh as they had planned? Didn't Mary's friend, Annie say that everyone came back to Merriment Bay, one way or another? Would they have come back by now? Would they be friends with Amias and maybe go out as a foursome with him and one of his many dates? What was Amias doing right now?

She swung her legs down and leapt to her feet.

He wouldn't be sitting on a window seat staring out to sea; that much was certain. And neither would she. She could go to The Hope and Anchor for a drink.

Nope. If Amias had a house in the bay, that might be where he was tonight.

She could go to the golf club. He definitely wouldn't be there. Or would he? Maybe he played golf now. She somehow doubted it. Amias didn't do 'slow'; he did everything at breakneck speed as if afraid he would run out of time. Had that got worse since Kyle's death? Kyle had so many plans, but time had run out for him.

Did Amias make love at breakneck speed too?

God! Why had that thought come to torment her? The last thing she wanted to think about was Amias making love with someone.

The Fitness Centre. That's where she could go. A good work out would do wonders for her mind, her body and her spirit. And Amias wouldn't go there. He preferred his workouts in the open air.

And again, her thoughts placed images of him on the beach … making love.

'You're losing your mind, Cat Devon!' She shouted at herself: 'Forget about Amias Wells. That way madness lies.'

With new found determination she rushed upstairs, tossed a few things in a denim rucksack which had an image of one of her paintings on the front and back, changed into the grey leggings she wore for yoga and the matching T-shirt and longline hooded sweatshirt. She grabbed her phone and keys from the hall as she ran out of the front door.

The evening air was warm as she jogged along Channel View Lane, and across Coast Road, trying, as she always did, not to look at the spot where her life had changed so many years ago. It was just a road. Just tarmac and paving slabs. And it wasn't where Kyle had died. He'd died in hospital in the ICU.

She continued into Lord Lane and burst through the double doors of the Fitness Centre. Either everyone in Merriment Bay was extremely fit, or they all came here in the week and had better things to occupy their time at the weekend because when Cat entered the lobby, it was clear this was not the 'in' place on a Saturday night. But that suited her. She could take her hoody off and work out in just her T-shirt without any enquiring looks, furtive glances or whispers behind hands.

Chapter Nineteen

Two hours of a strenuous workout, a soothing sauna and intermittent hops in and out of the cold shower, followed by a final warm shower with her favourite jasmine and vanilla body wash had done wonders. Cat strolled home, more content and at peace than she had been since she and Kyra had arrived in Merriment Bay.

Kyra was right about the moon. It was glorious. A gleaming, ivory ball, low in a sky of black velvet, just above a flat-calm silver sea, surrounded by an explosion of stars. Surely if something as magnificent as this could exist, whoever or whatever created it could make Granny Viola wake up from her coma?

Dots of lights on distance ships drifted slowly across the horizon and a gentle breeze crept in from the sea bringing with it a hint of salt and seaweed as waves lapped at the shore. Cat was savouring the sights, the sounds, the smell of the awe-inspiring vista as she turned into the front garden of Devon Villa. But the sight that assaulted her eyes rapidly removed all traces of her blissful smile.

'Amias! What the hell are you doing with my

daughter!'

'Cat!'

He looked as stunned as she felt as he tried to disentangle Kyra's arms from around his neck. He had hardly changed at all. Just grown a little older.

Cat raced towards them, horrified.

'She's had far too much to drink.'

'What? And you thought that meant you could take advantage of her? Jesus Christ, Amias. She's eighteen! And Kyle's daughter. I didn't think you'd stoop to this.'

She grabbed Kyra by the arm, pulled her away from Amias and hugged her tight.

'Stoop to what?' He glowered at her, fury etched into the fine lines around his intense, dark eyes. 'You thought I was kissing her, didn't you? Seriously? Jesus, Cat! I know you've always had a low opinion of me but I hoped you knew me better than that.'

'Are you saying you weren't?'

'Of course I wasn't.'

'That's what it looked like. And I haven't seen you for eighteen years, Amias. I don't know what you're like these days.'

'I haven't changed. I'm still the same as I was back then. In more ways than you can imagine. And taking advantage of drunken women is not something I did then and it's not something I do now. Especially ones who are half my age.'

'Hi, Mum.' Kyra beamed, and let her head rest against Cat's. 'I've had a lovely time. But I may have had one drink too many.' She giggled as Amias glared at Cat but a slight smile formed at the edge of his mouth when Kyra smiled at him. 'Thank you for bringing me safely home, Amias. And for holding me up. Why is the ground spinning?'

He reached out and grabbed her.

'I'm just making sure she doesn't fall, OK?' He threw Cat a sarcastic look. 'I'm not trying to have my wicked way with her.'

'I'd like to do something wicked with Lucas Lester,' Kyra said, slurring the words just a little. 'And maybe Marcus, too. I like them both. It's really difficult when you like two men, isn't it? You would know that, wouldn't you, Mum? Amias? Did you know that Mum was—'

'Kyra! You're talking a lot of nonsense. Let's get you inside and into bed.' The heat in the sauna was nothing compared to the heat Cat was experiencing right now. 'It appears I owe you an apology, Amias.'

'You owe me nothing.'

She fumbled with her keys as his eyes seemed to burn into her. Why were her hands shaking? Why couldn't she breathe? Why did that bloody moonlight have to throw slivers of silver in the strands of his dark hair lifted by the soft breeze, and flecks of gold in those deep, dark eyes? Why did the tight line of his lips look so kissable? Why did her hand want to reach up and trace the length of his firm, clean-shaven jaw?

With one arm around Kyra, he took the keys

from Cat's hand, lightly brushing her fingers with his.

A bolt of lightning lit up the sky.

Or had she imagined that?

He opened the door and waited for her to go inside.

'Thank you.' Cat flashed him a grateful smile as she switched on the hall light, quickly turning her face away, remembering her scars. But she allowed herself a surreptitious look at him from the corner of her eyes.

He was broader than she remembered and possibly a fraction taller. Maybe a little more handsome, too. If that were possible. He wore faded jeans, deck shoes, a blue T-shirt and a well-worn, leather bomber jacket. No doubt an original, like the sheepskin-lined flight jacket he used to wear all those years ago.

'Shall I take her to her room? I don't think you'll be able to get her up the stairs.' He gave Cat a sardonic grin. 'I promise I'll behave.'

Cat tutted softly. 'Yes please. Her room is next to mine.'

'Er. As I never had the pleasure of being invited inside this house, let alone your bedroom, that actually doesn't help me.'

She met his eyes and quickly looked away. 'Top of the second flight of stairs. Kyra's room is the second door on the left.'

'Come on then, young lady. Let's get you into bed.'

Kyra smiled. 'I like you, Amias. But I think you're a bit too old for me. And as gorgeous as you are, I don't want to have sex with you.'

'I'm crushed. But I think that's wise. Can you walk or shall I carry you? Assuming that's OK with your mum, of course.'

'Oooh. I've never been carried upstairs by a man before. But we lived in a cottage and it didn't have stairs. It was a bungalow really. But Bonniemount Bungalow doesn't sound as cosy as Bonniemount Cottage, does it? This house has *so* many stairs. How many, I'm not sure. Shall we count them?'

'Another time, perhaps.' He looked over his shoulder at Cat. 'It really will be faster if I carry her, but I'm loathe to incur your wrath.'

Cat narrowed her eyes at him. 'If you're trying to be funny, you're wasting your time. I'd be grateful for anything you can do to speed this up.'

'Don't worry. I'll be out of here as fast as I can. I know how abhorrent it must be to have me in this grand house.'

He scowled at her as he lifted Kyra gingerly into his arms as if he were frightened she might break.

'That wasn't what I meant. But you're right. You haven't changed. That chip on your shoulder is still firmly fixed in place.'

He tensed visibly but he didn't say a word and she followed him up both flights of stairs in silence, save for Kyra singing some unrecognizable song into the muscles of his neck.

Kyra's bedroom door was ajar and he used his elbow to shove it open. With just the light from the hall illuminating the room, he laid Kyra gently on the bed.

'Goodnight, Kyra,' he whispered, before shooting a look at Cat. 'I'd offer to remove her shoes, but God knows what you'd accuse me of, so I'll leave you to it. Goodbye, Cat.' His voice had returned to a normal pitch as he strode towards the door.

'Wait! I mean … I'll show you out.'

He looked her up and down and sneered. 'Worried I might take something?'

'Don't be so ridiculous.' She marched past him and removed Kyra's shoes before easing the antique, patchwork quilt on the bed, over her. 'I was trying to be polite.'

'Polite?' He raised his brows and shoved his hands into the pockets of his jeans. 'After accusing me of kissing your daughter, you think telling me you want to escort me off the premises is polite?'

'I apologised for that. And I wasn't going to escort you off the premises. I was going to offer you a coffee.' She hadn't meant to yell and she took a quick, calming breath. 'But I see now that was a mistake. Goodnight, Amias. You can show yourself out.'

He eyed her for a moment and didn't move. She busied herself adjusting the quilt.

Why wouldn't the bloody man just leave?

She threw him a quick smile. 'Thank you again for your help. I suppose it was a good thing you were there. But aren't you a bit too old to be hanging out with a group of teenagers on a Saturday night?'

He gave a derisive snort. 'Aren't you too young not to be?'

Kyra let out a soft snore and Cat ignored his remark as she lovingly brushed a strand of ginger curls from her daughter's cheek.

'She's the image of Kyle.' His voice was soft now but there was a hint of gravel in it, as if the words scratched his throat and were painful.

Cat shot a look at him and her heart skipped a beat. He was staring at Kyra as if he felt genuine affection for her. But he'd looked at Kyra like that once before, eighteen years ago. And then he'd completely ignored them. Cat cleared her throat and looked away.

'Yes. She's got his intelligence, too.'

'But your stubbornness and determination.'

She couldn't look at him now, especially as a shaft of moonlight filtered through the window, spotlighting his frame.

'And my love of art. But she's twice the artist I am.'

'She's as good, if not better than Kyle was on anything on water. He would've been so proud of her.'

Now she did look at him and it was clear he hadn't forgotten Kyle. He hadn't forgotten the pain, either.

'Yes. He would.'

Their eyes met for a moment and she flashed him a brief, empathetic smile. For a second it seemed he might smile back as the corner of his mouth lifted, but he didn't let it form.

'She's got your eyes. And your smile. She's grown into a stunning woman.' He turned away, running a hand through his hair. 'I'd better go. If Mary finds me here, I'll be thrown in the cellar in chains.'

Had Amias just paid Cat a compliment, in a roundabout way? That was a first. And what was more, he must've seen the scar on her cheek in the light in the hall, but he hadn't mentioned it, or even flinched.

'Amias?' She hurried into the hall. He was halfway down the first flight of stairs.

'Yes?'

She gave a small cough, and forced a grin. 'We don't have a cellar.'

He looked as if he wasn't sure if that meant something else. 'That's good to know.' He hesitated on the stair before continuing down.

'I'm sorry,' she said.

He stopped again and furrowed his brows. 'For what? For not having a cellar?' He flashed her a tentative grin.

She shook her head. 'For thinking, even for a second, that you would ever do anything inappropriate with Kyra.'

He sighed deeply. 'Oh that.' He shrugged. 'Not

that kind of a guy. Despite the tail and the horns some people like to paint on me. Goodnight, Cat. I'm glad you've come home.'

He was gone before she had a chance to respond.

Chapter Twenty

For a while, after Amias left, Cat had lain beside Kyra on her bed, one arm wrapped around her as she stared at Kyra's face. Every now and then her eyelashes fluttered. Kyle's used to do that when he slept. Not that Cat and he had ever spent an entire night together; just snatched hours, here and there. At Devon Villa, whenever she knew Granny Viola and her mum would be out and at Kyle's house whenever he knew his parents would be in The Hope and Anchor. She and Kyle spent far more time at his parents' house than they did at Devon Villa.

Where did Kyle's parents live now? She hadn't even thought about them until that moment. But then they hadn't thought much about Kyle when he was alive and they had only seen Kyra once – the day they'd agreed with her mum and Granny Viola that Cat should give the baby up for adoption. They hadn't even held Kyra in their arms. They had left Merriment Bay before she had left the hospital, she knew that much.

Amias had told her that. And he'd said she shouldn't have been surprised, as he'd cradled Kyra on that last day she'd spent in the hospital.

'Some people shouldn't be parents,' he'd said. 'But then again, they did give us Kyle, so I suppose we should thank them for that. Although how the hell those two produced someone as great as Kyle is beyond me.'

He'd looked at Kyra that day, just as he had tonight: as if he had genuine affection for her. But he'd looked at Cat as if he despised her. And that was the last day she had spoken to him. Until tonight. Her mum and Granny Viola had collected her from the hospital and driven her home to Devon Villa and Amias hadn't visited, or called, or written.

'He told us neither you nor the child are any concern of his,' Mary said, when Cat asked if they had heard from him. Despite being allowed home, she wasn't fully recovered and had spent the first week or so in bed.

Once or twice, she thought she had heard his voice. He was angry and shouting her name. But Mary assured her he was too busy having fun in the bay with all the female holidaymakers to find time to call on Cat and her child.

She had considered phoning him, but what would she say? 'Why haven't you come to see us?'

'Why would I?' he would no doubt have replied. 'Kyle was my friend, not you. And he's dead now because of you.'

One week had crawled into two, and Granny Viola and her mum continued their stance; that Cat should give the baby up for adoption. The minute they'd discovered she was pregnant, their bombardment had begun.

'You could have a wonderful future, Catherine. Don't saddle yourself with a child at seventeen,' Mary had pleaded. 'That boy won't stay with you. You'll be completely on your own.'

'We're going to get married and be a family. Kyle loves me,' Cat had argued.

Granny Viola sneered. 'What does that boy know about family? The Morrises and that Wells rabble are all cut from the same cloth.'

Mary sighed and shook her head. 'Do you want to spend your future worrying where the next penny is coming from?'

'Are you saying you'll disown me? That's a bit rich coming from you, Mum. You had me when you were eighteen and Granny Viola didn't disown you. At least the father of my child wants to marry me. Just because my dad, whoever he was, didn't want to marry you, don't paint Kyle with the same brush.'

Mary had been furious and they'd all said things they shouldn't. But the final straw had been the day Mary had told Cat she was the biggest mistake of her life.

'My life would be so different now if I hadn't fallen for your father and had you,' she'd said. 'Don't make the same mistake I did. Don't throw your life away over a man and a child.'

Kyle was getting hassle from his parents too.

'They're not pleased that I'll be moving out, but they'll miss the money I give them, not me. We'll get a little place of our own, Cat. Just you, me, and our beautiful daughter. Because we'll have a daughter, I just know it.'

And the scans had confirmed he was right.

'I've got savings,' he had said, when he brought the subject up again a few weeks later. And I'll get a full-time job. We'll be fine. We'll have a wonderful life, the three of us.'

'But your savings are for you to go to college.'

'And now they're for me to have an even better life. A life with the girl I adore and the daughter I already love. Let's get away from Merriment Bay for a while. Let's go to Edinburgh. That's where you want to go to study art, isn't it? We might not be able to afford that right away, but once I get a job, we can save some money and who knows. And I can study architecture at evening classes, I expect. We won't have your family nagging you, or my family trying to get their hands on my wages.'

'I've got some money, too,' Cat had said. 'But Mum and Granny Viola would never let me go.'

'Then let's not tell them. Let's not tell anyone. Apart from Amias. I couldn't leave without telling him.'

'Run away, you mean?'

'Elope. Let's go to Gretna Green and get married right away. Right now.'

She'd laughed. 'Are you serious, Kyle? Do people still go to Gretna Green to marry?'

He shrugged. 'Who knows? We don't have to go there. But yes, Cat. I'm serious. More serious than I've ever been about anything in my life. I adore you, Cat Devon and I want to spend the rest of my life with you and Kyra. And I want the rest of my life to start right now.'

'Kyra?' She'd smiled her surprise. 'You want to call our baby, Kyra?'

He'd grinned. 'It just popped into my head. I don't know why. But if you don't like it we can call her anything you want.'

'No. I like it. We'll definitely call her Kyra.'

'I'll love you and Kyra all my life, Cat. No matter what.'

She'd looked into his eyes. Those gorgeous hazel eyes of his and she'd made a decision.

'Then let's do this. Let's run away.'

'Let's leave today.' He looked so excited.

'Today? Isn't that a bit too soon?'

'Why wait? Please Cat.' He'd swept her into his arms.

'As foolish as it is, if this is the last time I'll see my mum and Granny Viola for a while, I'd like to spend a few hours with them before we go. Is that OK? Let's leave tomorrow.'

'OK. I'll spend some time with Amias. He's the only person I'll miss in Merriment Bay. But let's compromise. Let's leave at midnight. That's still today, but it's also, sort of, tomorrow. I'll pick you up at midnight.'

Cat laughed at that. Despite the fact he loved her, he liked to get his own way.

'OK. But not from the house. Mum or Granny Viola might hear the engine and try to stop us. Let's meet somewhere else.'

'I'll wait for you at the junction of Channel View Lane and Coast Road. That's far enough away. They'll think it's just traffic if they hear anything. I'll be waiting there for you at midnight. I may even spend the evening there, just in case I fall asleep.' He'd laughed and winked. 'I adore you, Cat, and I can't wait for us to start our new life together.'

He'd kissed her passionately then.

It was the last kiss they had shared.

It had been raining all day but it stopped just after 11 p.m. and by the time Cat left Devon Villa at 10 minutes to midnight, the clouds were tumbling away. She spotted the bonnet of Kyle's car as she waddled along Channel View Lane. At eight months pregnant, running was no longer an option. Whether or not he had been there all evening, she didn't know, but as she drew closer, she could see him through the windscreen. His head was tipped slightly to one side, his eyes were closed and his lips a fraction apart. Then, as if he knew she was there, he opened his eyes and beamed at her.

She heard the squeal of brakes and slosh of water a moment before she saw the oncoming lorry that skidded on to their side of the road, hitting Kyle's car like a wall of metal.

Shock and disbelief glued her to the spot but instinct made her dive for cover as debris flew towards her. Whether she sustained her injuries from that, or from trying to free Kyle from the twisted wreck, minutes later, she didn't know, even though she was sure the doctors had told her. But she didn't care. All she cared about was that they were alive.

Until she was told the following day that Kyle had subsequently died.

She hadn't believed it at first. Yes, his injuries had been horrendous and yes, it was a miracle he was still alive when the ambulances had arrived, but she had been sure he would survive.

Or maybe that had just been wishful thinking.

It had only been when Amias had confirmed it that she actually believed it, and even then, it had taken a while to sink in. When he'd given her Kyle's watch. When he'd told her Kyle's parents had moved away. When he'd cradled Kyra that day in the hospital and told Cat that it would be torture for them, but Kyle was gone, and they had no choice but to learn to live with that.

But what he hadn't told her as he'd cradled Kyra, was that she would have to learn to live with it, alone.

That day had been the last time she and Amias had spoken but it hadn't been the last time she'd seen him.

The last time she'd seen him had been the day before she had run away from Merriment Bay with her ten-week-old baby.

It had been an unbelievably warm, October day, near the end of an unexpected, Indian Summer. In spite of the warmth, Cat had worn a high-necked, long-sleeved blouse, and had also styled her hair to aid in covering her scars. She'd taken Kyra in her pram and walked towards the bay.

It was the first time she had been there since the day before the accident. Her heart felt as if it was tearing itself free of the blood vessels giving it life and she had had to stop more than once to catch her breath, and to force herself to continue on. She wanted to see Amias. To ask him why he didn't want to visit them. To ask him if he would still be in her life. Just as a friend, of course. She knew she would never be anything more to him than that. He'd always made it perfectly clear that he had no interest in her. But didn't he want to stay in touch? At least with his best friend's child?

Her mum had been right though. Cat had watched him, his hands on the hips of some stunning girl, holding her on a surf board balanced on the sand. The girl had tumbled against him. Clearly on purpose. And she'd reached up and kissed him on the lips.

Cat couldn't watch any more. She had turned away and hurried back to Devon Villa. And on the way, as she reached the spot where the accident had happened, she had made another decision. She would leave Merriment Bay just as she and Kyle had planned.

There was nothing in Merriment Bay for her and Kyra anyway.

Chapter Twenty-One

Cat hardly slept a wink. When she kissed Kyra on the cheek and finally went to bed, her mind was alive with memories of the past and she tossed and turned all night. It was still dark when she awoke but she desperately needed coffee.

After peeping into Kyra's room and seeing that Kyra was fast asleep beneath her duvet and the antique quilt, Cat went downstairs, made coffee and thought about last night. Not about the strange dreams she'd had, or her memories from the past, but about seeing Amias again after all these years. And about what he had said.

Amias had actually paid her a compliment. And he'd said he was glad that she had come home. What had that meant?

Did it mean that they could finally be friends?

Or if she went with Kyra down to the bay today, would she find him with his arms wrapped around some new woman?

Annie, from Bella Vista, had said just a few weeks ago that he was back on the market after dumping Lorna Carlton. But men like Amias didn't stay single for long. And Amias had always had a string of women chasing after him. Perhaps he was already dating someone else? Not that it mattered. One thing was as certain now as it was back then. Amias Wells would never, ever, date Cat Devon.

'God, Mum. I feel awful.' Kyra padded into the kitchen, dressed in her pyjamas, although her T-shirt type top was on back to front.

'You don't look too good, sweetheart. Sit down before you fall down. I'll pour you some coffee.'

Kyra slumped on to a chair at the table. 'I don't remember getting home. And I have no idea how I made it up those stairs.'

'Amias brought you home. And he carried you up those stairs.' Cat threw her a teasing grin.

'Did he?' A huge grin spread across Kyra's face. 'I wish I'd been sober enough to have realised. I've never been carried up to bed by a man before. Especially not one as gorgeous as Amias.'

Cat placed a large mug of coffee on the table in front of Kyra.

'Yes. So you said last night. But you also told him that he was too old for you and that you didn't want to have sex with him.'

'I what?' Kyra laughed before grabbing her head between her hands and thumping her elbows on the table. 'Oh dear. Do we have any painkillers? There seems to be a herd of rhino rampaging around in my brain.'

Cat got a pack of tablets from the end cupboard which was filled with remedies for virtually every possible ailment. Except heartache.

'Here.' She placed two tablets beside a glass of water. 'That wasn't all you said last night. You almost told him that I was once in love with him.'

Kyra's head shot up and she winced.

'Oh, God. Did I? I'm so sorry, Mum. Did you manage to stop me in time?'

Cat smiled. 'Just.'

'What must he think of me?' Kyra swallowed the tablets. 'Was he cross? About having to bring me home, I mean?'

'He didn't seem to be. Although I was when I came home and saw the two of you standing on the doorstep. You with your arms draped around his neck. Him with his head bent over you. I thought he was kissing you, and I shouted at him.'

'Kissing me?' Kyra looked astonished. 'Why on earth would you think that?'

'I just told you why. You looked so … so intimate.'

Kyra grinned and gulped her coffee. 'Were you jealous?'

'Absolutely not. I was horrified that a man of his age would take advantage of a girl so young, especially as she was drunk.'

'Oh, Mum. Honestly. As if he would. I haven't known him long but even I know he wouldn't do that. I can't remember much about it. Although this coffee is clearing the fog away. I do remember he came along the beach and told Lucas, Marcus and me that he thought we'd partied enough and that he was going to drive me home. And them too, if they

158

wanted to go. Which they didn't. They wanted to stay with the crowd. And so did I. But he gave me such a quelling look, I remember and said I had two choices. Either he would stay with us all and make sure no one did anything they shouldn't. Or I could let him take me home and then everyone else could do whatever they wanted. Although he did tell Lucas and Marcus that if they took drugs or did anything else equally stupid, they shouldn't ever bother to turn up at his door again.'

'He said that? And he wasn't on the beach with you then? I mean he didn't spend the evening with you all?'

'No. Why would you think he would? I'm sure he has quite enough of us all day. I think he'd rather spend his evenings with people his own age, don't you?'

'Yes.' Cat let out a sigh. 'But who does he think he is? Telling you what you can and can't do. And Lucas and Marcus too.'

Kyra smiled. 'Oh come on, Mum. You're glad he did. You know you are. And to be honest, I think I am too. Some of the people there were definitely getting a bit out of control. I think they were all nice and I'm not saying anything bad would've happened. But I'm glad he played the knight in shining armour and came to my rescue.' She tossed a lock of ginger curls over her shoulder and beamed at Cat. 'And so are you. So did anything happen after he carried me upstairs? Between you and him, I mean. Did he stay for coffee? Or anything?' She raised her eyebrows suggestively.

Cat blushed and turned away, refilling her coffee mug. 'Absolutely not. I stayed upstairs with you and he let himself out.'

'M-um! Honestly. When you get a man like Amias upstairs, you shouldn't let him back down again until you've had a bit of fun. I can see you'll need a helping hand in the romance department.'

'Romance department?' Cat smirked. 'That's one place that's strictly off limits as far as Amias and I are concerned.'

Kyra frowned. 'Why? You were in love with him once.'

'A lifetime ago.'

'You could fall in love with him again. I'd fall in love with him in an instant if I were older.'

Cat shook her head. 'I love you, sweetheart. But please don't try to get Amias and me together. There's been far too much water under the bridge for that to ever happen. Besides, the man was never attracted to me when I was young, and if I say it myself, fairly pretty. He's not likely to be attracted to me now that I'm old and scarred.'

'You're not old and the scars are hardly noticeable. You're more bothered about them than most people are. And any decent man wouldn't give a damn about such things anyway.'

'You think Amias is a decent man? Sorry. Of course, he is. But he can have his pick of women, Kyra. He always has had. And he didn't pick me then, so he certainly won't pick me now. And thank you for saying I'm not old.'

Cat laughed and tried to lighten the mood as she sat opposite Kyra. Her legs were feeling a little weak this morning. It must be from yesterday's workout at the Fitness Centre.

Kyra eyed her for a moment over the rim of her mug.

'But you'd like him to, wouldn't you? Pick you, I mean. You like him, don't you, Mum? In fact, by the way you're trying to pretend you don't and the fact that you've just put sugar in your coffee when you don't take sugar, I'd say you like him a lot.'

'Good morning.'

Mary joined them in the kitchen, a broad smile on her face and a note of excitement in her voice. Cat was thankful for the interruption.

'You look happy, Mum. I take it you won at bridge last night.'

'Better than that, Catherine.' Mary poured herself a mug of coffee but her smile faltered as she cast a look over Kyra. 'Your top is on back to front, and frankly, you look a little green in the gills. Are you unwell, child?'

Kyra sighed. 'Hungover.'

'Hungover?' From the look on Mary's face, Kyra may as well have just said that she'd committed murder.

'Don't make a big deal out of it, Mum,' Cat said. 'She's eighteen. If she wants to get drunk, she can.'

'And you condone this behaviour? I'm sorry.' She held up one hand. 'It's none of my business. All I'll say is that I hope you don't make a habit of it, Kyra. Your father's parents went down that route.'

'Mum!' Cat banged her mug on the table and glowered at Mary.

'What? I'm not allowed to tell the truth in my own home?'

'Please,' Kyra said, closing her eyes for a moment. 'I've got a headache. I can promise you I won't be making a habit of it, Gran. And Amias gave me a lecture too.' She grinned mischievously. 'I think that was before he carried me up to bed. But it may have been after. I can't recall.'

'Before he carried you up to bed?' Mary screeched like a parrot.

Cat sighed loudly. 'She's winding you up, Mum. But frankly, you deserve it.'

Mary's horrified gaze darted from Kyra to Cat and back again.

'He didn't carry you up to his bed then?'

Kyra grinned again. 'Oh yes. He did. But to my bed here. Not his. And not in the way you clearly think. You're as bad as Mum. She thought he was kissing me on the doorstep when she got home and found us together.'

'This doorstep? Your bed here? Are you telling me that man was in this house?'

'He was,' Cat said. 'And he was the perfect gentleman. There was no way I'd have been able to get Kyra upstairs without his help. And if you even suggest you'd better go and check the silver, we'll be packing our bags, OK?'

Mary looked uncertain but eventually she sat down. 'How long was he here?'

'Less than ten minutes. He laid Kyra on her bed. We had a brief chat about how much she looks like her dad and then he left.'

Mary fiddled with the handle of her mug. 'Just about that? Not about anything else?'

Cat frowned. 'What does that mean?'

Mary gave a small cough. 'I just wondered if you'd discussed the past at all. The hospital and such. And about you running away.'

She looked rather nervous. There was clearly some reason for her remarks but Cat couldn't think what it could be.

'We didn't reminisce about the good old days. You know as well as I do that he never particularly liked me.'

Mary shot a look at her and smiled. 'That's true. But I do feel the less you see of him, the better. I know he's teaching Kyra to windsurf and I know you want to enlist his help in finding out about the man in the photograph, but there's no point in rehashing the past, is there? What happened, happened. We all said and did things we regret. It's time we put all that behind us, isn't it? Time we wiped the slate clean.'

'Mum? Why do I get the feeling there's something you haven't told me? Something that happened in the past? Something, perhaps, involving Amias?'

'I don't know, Catherine, I'm sure. But let's forget about Amias Wells and I'll tell you my news. I met a lovely man last night. Gladys and I popped into The Hope and Anchor for a glass of wine with Annie after bridge. And yes, Gladys and I did win. But anyway. I was ordering drinks and a man was seated at the bar as Sybil Lester was asking about Mother and whether I intended to remain in this house if the worst happened. You know Sybil. Dreadful woman. But one has to be polite. I said that I was considering putting it on the market but that I intended to have some work done first. And you won't believe it. The very handsome man at the bar apologised and said he couldn't help but overhear our conversation. He also told me how lovely I looked, but that is by the by. To cut a long story short. His name is Jeremy Stone. He's fifty-nine and divorced and he's staying here for a week or so, as he's considering moving to the area. But the best thing is, he's a builder. Well, actually the best thing is he's asked me out on a date. But the second best thing is his being a builder. He's going to give me a quote for the work I'd like done and he assures me he'll put an even bigger smile on my gorgeous face. Isn't that simply wonderful?'

'Eew. Does that mean you're going to have sex with him, Gran? Because that's what that sounded like.' Kyra screwed up her nose as if the prospect wasn't a particularly pleasant one.

Mary looked surprised but then she smiled. 'I

certainly hope so, Kyra. It's been quite a while since I've met such an attractive and attentive man.'

Cat smiled at her. It was a long time since she had seen her mum so happy.

'That's great, Mum. I'm very pleased for you. But you'll get more than one quote, won't you? And you'll take references and such, especially if he's not local.'

Mary's smile faltered. 'Unlike some people, Catherine, I'm a good judge of character. Jeremy also told me that I should get more than just his quote, but that he'll match any others I might get and I wouldn't find a better deal than the one he would be offering. He's coming round later today and this evening we're going out for dinner to discuss it.'

'Oh. That's quick, isn't it? I was going to suggest that William and Abigail and the boys might come round for lunch today. We were going to ask William about the photograph, remember?'

'Oh that. Yes, of course. But Sunday lunch is a bit short notice. Let's ask them round for supper one day in the week, shall we?'

'Have you lost interest in the man in the photo already, now that you've met a man in the flesh, so to speak?'

Mary tutted. 'Of course not. I'm just as keen to find out all we can about that man as you are. But I think perhaps we should simply open one of the letters. It would be so much quicker and then we might not have to trouble William at all.'

Cat sighed. What Mary was really saying was that now that she'd met Jeremy Stone, she'd rather spend all her time with him. There had been a few Jeremy-types in the past and Cat remembered how Mary had behaved back then. She also remembered how they had all turned out. She hoped Jeremy wouldn't turn out to be the same.

'What time is he coming?' Cat asked.

'He'll be here at 5 p.m. and I was wondering if, perhaps, you and Kyra might like to take a walk while he's here. Or maybe visit Mother. We don't want the poor man to be surrounded by women, do we? It might put him off his stride.'

It might make him wonder if he wants to get involved with a woman who has an unmarried daughter and granddaughter currently staying with her, is what Mary meant. Cat knew that.

She threw Kyra a look and managed a smile. 'No problem. We'll stay out of the way. Will an hour suffice?'

'Best make it two. It is a large house, after all. Or possibly three. Just to be on the safe side.' She beamed at Cat and Kyra.

Cat shook her head and drank her coffee. Kyra was right. Mary and Jeremy would clearly be having sex despite the fact they'd only met last night.

Mary Devon hadn't changed much at all.

Chapter Twenty-Two

'You can tell it's now officially autumn,' Kyra said. 'Since Sunday, it's been raining for three whole days and nights.'

Cat grinned and ruffled Kyra's hair as she placed a cooked breakfast in front of her. 'Beginning to wish you'd gone to university, after all?'

'Nope.' Kyra returned the grin. 'Just wishing the sun would come out, even if it's only for an hour. I was starting to build up a reasonable tan. And windsurfing isn't quite as much fun in the rain, although Amias says it's good for me to be able to sail in all weather conditions. Choppy seas are definitely a new dimension and yesterday he showed me how to use a harness for the first time. I'm going to have a go at kiteboarding too, but only if the rain stops.'

'Has he mentioned last Saturday night at all?' Cat tried to quell the butterflies in her stomach as she poured herself more coffee and sat at the table.

Kyra threw her a teasingly exasperated look. 'As I told you on Sunday evening at the hospital, Monday afternoon whilst clearing out the attic,

Tuesday over lunch and Wednesday at dinner ... no. He hasn't. I promise to tell you if he does. I'll even send you a text. Why don't you just come down to the bay and see him?'

Cat slathered butter on her toast. 'I don't want to see him. I just wondered if he'd said anything, that's all.'

'Nope. Not even yesterday when I told him that Granny Mary and 'no job's too big, Jeremy' are having sex. And what you said about it.'

Cat choked on the bite of toast she'd just taken and had to swallow down several gulps of coffee until she was able to speak.

'Dear God, Kyra! What did you say? And why didn't you tell me last night?'

Kyra grinned. 'I couldn't tell you last night because Granny Mary and Jeremy appeared just after you asked me, yet again, if Amias had said anything. All I said to Amias was that Gran had met a builder in the pub on Saturday night and he was now going to be doing a lot of work at Devon Villa. And that you weren't sure you liked him but didn't want to say anything to Gran in case she thought you were jealous because she was the only one of the three of us who was having any sex.'

Cat screwed up her face and bobbed her head from side to side. 'OK. I suppose that's not too bad. For a minute I thought you were going to say what I'd said about being tempted to grab someone off the street because listening to the pair of them going at it like rabbits was making me feel a bit frustrated.' She laughed but the sound died on her lips as she saw Kyra bite her bottom lip. 'Please tell me you didn't tell him that bit.'

Kyra pulled a face. 'I could tell you that. But I'd be lying. He still didn't say anything though. Not a word. He looked a bit surprised at first and then he just smiled. He really does have the most gorgeous smile, doesn't he?'

Cat let her head drop towards her plate. 'If this was a bowl of cereal, I'd drown myself in the milk. You told him I was sexually frustrated and all he did was smile? He didn't say anything mean or sarcastic?'

'Not a single thing. But later, he did say that he might ask around about Jeremy. That's OK, isn't it? Because I didn't say he shouldn't.'

Cat nodded. 'I think so. As long as Mum and Jeremy don't find out and think we're doing something we have no right to do. It does make me feel a bit of a hypocrite though. I criticise Mum for saying things about Kyle and yet I'm saying I'm not sure I like her latest man and I'm asking someone to check into him.'

'You didn't ask. Amias offered. And you wouldn't have known anything about it if I hadn't told you. Oh. I asked him about the photograph. I said we'd been meaning to ask him for a couple of days but things had got a bit weird with Jeremy here all hours of the day and night. I explained about the letters and that Gran now thinks we should open one after all, but that you still think we shouldn't. He

169

says he agrees with you and that he'd be happy to help if he can. He's going to be at the museum tomorrow, working on his plane, so if we want to drop by then, he'll be happy to take a look.'

The butterflies had taken flight and had doubled in number. Cat put a hand on her stomach in a bid to settle them.

'Didn't you take a picture of the photo with your phone? Couldn't you have simply shown him that?'

'Um. I forgot.' Kyra looked furtive and Cat didn't believe that for a second. 'Besides, the actual photo is clearer. It's best if he sees the real thing, I think.'

'Hmm. I'm not sure I want to see him again just yet. Especially now he thinks I'm sexually frustrated.'

'Why not?' Kyra gave her a wicked smile. 'He might be happy to help with that too. Or is that what you're worried about? That he might try to take advantage of you?'

Cat shook her head. 'I think I'm more concerned that I might throw myself at him and he'd tell me to get lost. I did that once before. It didn't have a happy ending.'

'He might not tell you to get lost this time.'

Cat met Kyra's gaze and held it. 'I'm pretty sure he would, sweetheart. Sadly, life isn't like it is in the movies. Amias Wells isn't going to suddenly fall in love with me. Whether I'd like him to or not.'

'Morning, ladies.' Jeremy Stone strutted into

the kitchen like a peacock. He was wearing pale blue chinos, a pale mauve polo shirt and the sleeves of a white cricket jumper were tied about his neck as the rest of it hung down his back, looking as if he'd spent some time ensuring it sat perfectly. 'That breakfast looks good. I could murder a Full English.' He plonked himself at the table and beamed at them. 'And a coffee. Lots of milk, lots of sugar. Mary's in the shower. There isn't room in there for two but give me another few days and there will be.' He winked at them.

'Sorry, Jeremy,' Cat said. 'But Kyra and I are in a bit of a rush and don't have time to wait on you. There's coffee in the pot and as you can see, lots of pans for you to cook yourself some breakfast.' She gave him a cheerful smile.

His eyes narrowed the merest fraction. 'Never mind. Mary will be down any minute.'

'Yes,' Kyra said. 'So you could cook her breakfast too. I'm sure she would love that. Gran is always saying how rare it is to meet a man who cooks for her and how wonderful it would be if she did.'

His brows shot up. 'Is she indeed? Then she's in luck. Because I'm that man.'

He leapt to his feet, and busied himself with his task, humming some tune or other. Or perhaps strangling a tune might be a more apt description. Cat watched him for a moment before grinning at Kyra.

Footsteps on the stairs told them Mary was on

her way.

'Time to go, Mum,' Kyra said, getting to her feet. 'Morning, Gran.'

'Good morning, Kyra. Good morning, Catherine. Jeremy? What in God's name are you doing? That pan is for rice. And I never use oil to cook eggs. We poach them. For heaven's sake sit down and let me do it. There is nothing worse than a man running loose in the kitchen. What were you thinking?'

'If looks could kill,' Cat whispered, hurrying Kyra into the hall, 'we wouldn't have stood a chance. Perhaps that was a little bit mean of us, sweetheart?'

'He's an arrogant pig, Mum. He actually expected us to cook his breakfast. Who does he think he is? If he'd asked and said please, it might have been a different matter but to plonk himself down and tell us what he wanted was really not on. He deserves everything he gets.'

'We'll no doubt get some flak from Mum when he tells her we suggested it.'

Kyra shrugged. 'That's OK. We can cope with that.' She linked her arm through Cat's and grinned. 'We're Devons, remember?'

Chapter Twenty-Three

Cat changed her clothes at least eight times before she finally decided on jeans, a pale green cotton T-shirt and a matching green and white striped linen over shirt with a high collar. It was still raining on Friday morning so she was wearing boots and also a lightweight jacket as she and Kyra walked into the Merriment Bay WWII Museum.

'Are you sure I look OK?'

Kyra grinned. 'What would you do now if I said you didn't? Turn and run home to Devon Villa and change your clothes for the sixty-fifth time? You look gorgeous, Mum. You always do.'

'I don't think I've ever looked gorgeous in my life, sweetheart. But thank you for saying that.'

'Oh. Lucas and Marcus are here. Hey, you two.' Kyra waved at them and they smiled back.

'Hey, yourself. Hey, Miss Devon. I'm Lucas. I haven't had the pleasure.' He shoved a lock of blond waves behind one ear.

Cat rolled her eyes. 'It's Cat, Lucas. Miss Devon makes me sound like a school teacher or something. And no. But you nearly did when my daughter came home very drunk on Saturday night.

Although it might not have been a pleasure.'

He grinned. 'None of my teachers looked like you, Cat.' He emphasized her name as he looked her up and down. 'And yeah. Sorry about that. We all had a few too many. No harm done though. Amias made sure of that.'

Amias appeared from nowhere and gave him a playful slap on the arm and a reprimanding look.

'Cat's Kyra's mum, remember that.'

Lucas grinned all the more. 'Hey. Enough said. I get it. The lady's off limits.'

Something was going on but Cat wasn't quite sure what. She smiled at the other blond young man. A paler, thinner version of Lucas.

'Hi. You must be Marcus.'

'Hey.' He gave her a sheepish smile and glanced at Kyra who was showing something to Lucas on her phone. 'Yeah. I'm the cousin.'

'Kyra tells me you're off to Oxford University next week to study Mathematics and Computer Science at Balliol. That's impressive.'

He shrugged. 'It's what I'm good at.'

'You must be very good to get in there. They don't take just anyone from what I hear. Not that I know much about Oxford. Your parents must be extremely proud.'

He smiled. 'They are. Even Granddad is. At least he says he is.'

Amias placed a hand on Marcus' shoulder. 'Everyone is proud of you, Marcus. And Maths and Computers aren't all you're good at. You hold the highest score on our simulator for shooting down enemy planes.'

'That'll come in handy if there's another war,' Marcus said, in a self-deprecating tone. 'Although I'd probably be crap at the real thing.'

'You'd be brilliant, Marcus,' Lucas said. 'You're brilliant at everything.'

'No I'm not. But thanks.'

He hadn't taken his gaze from Kyra and when she turned, smiled and winked at him, he immediately brightened.

'And you're taking a year out, Lucas?' Cat was beginning to wish he was the one heading off to university and Marcus was the one staying behind.

'Yeah. I'll be working in my dad's firm for a few months. I'm leaning towards law but I'm also leaning towards bumming around the world with my kiteboard and entering competitions. It's a dilemma.' He laughed and so did Kyra. 'But mainly for my mum and dad. I'm not that bothered either way.'

Amias caught Cat's eye. 'He's trying to make you believe he's a free spirit but deep down he's a lawyer on a surfboard. And he's a good kid.'

Lucas tutted and rolled his eyes. 'Thanks, man.'

Amias grinned. 'You're welcome. Why don't you show Cat how good you are at making coffee?'

Another tut, but he grinned and walked away with Kyra and Marcus following behind him.

'You've got them well trained.' Cat avoided

looking at Amias. 'Lucas is very good-looking. I expect he's a hit with the girls. Marcus seems more reserved.'

'I've been keeping an eye on both of them when Kyra's around. I don't think you've got anything to worry about though. Kyra's got her head screwed on.'

'Is that a not particularly tactful way of saying that I hadn't?'

He frowned. 'What? When? Oh Jesus, Cat. I wasn't talking about the past. But if we are then I'd have to say you definitely had your head screwed on. You knew exactly what you wanted and how to get it.'

'Mum and Granny Viola wouldn't agree. And nor would I. Knowing exactly how to get what I wanted couldn't have been further from how I felt at the time. Or even if I really wanted it. Or what I wanted.'

The frown deepened. 'You're saying you didn't? That you regret it? You regret having Kyra? That astonishes me.'

'No. That's not what I'm saying. Kyra's the best thing in my life. She's the one thing I don't regret.'

'I don't understand. You were crazy about Kyle and over the moon to be pregnant, so I heard. And you wanted to move to Edinburgh. You definitely couldn't wait to leave here.'

'And look where that got us. But that wasn't what I wanted. I hadn't planned that, Amias. On the contrary. Discovering I was pregnant blew my mind. I didn't know whether I was coming or going. I was a convent girl, remember. That first summer on the beach was my first taste of real freedom. I had no idea what I was doing. When I discovered I was pregnant, Mum and Granny Viola were livid and wanted me to get rid of her. But I couldn't do that. And Kyle was ecstatic. It was a snap decision to leave. And it was Kyle who suggested it. Not me. I wanted to be with him by then. That was true. And yes. It had been my dream to study in Edinburgh, but not once I discovered I was pregnant. Kyle suggested it might still be possible.'

'Wait. What? You're saying you hadn't planned to get pregnant? You hadn't planned to leave? You didn't talk him into it? That wasn't what you'd wanted all along?'

She stared at him. 'Of course not. Why on earth would you think it was?'

'Because that's what Kyle told me.' He looked genuinely dumbfounded. 'And that's what Devon women do, according to Dad.'

'What Devon women do?' Cat almost hissed the words.

A horrified expression swept across his face. 'I didn't mean to say that. I was taken aback by what you said.'

'You think I got pregnant on purpose? You think I talked Kyle into leaving? And you're saying Kyle told you that? And what the hell has your dad got to do with it?'

'If this tastes like pee, blame Amias.' Lucas carried three mugs in his hands. 'What's up? Are you two having a lover's tiff, as Mum would call it?'

'Give us a minute would you, Lucas? And take Kyra and Marcus with you.' Amias didn't take his eyes off Cat.

'Mum? What's going on?'

'I'm not sure, sweetheart. But for some reason, Amias seems to be lying about your dad, and insulting our entire family.'

Cat glowered at Amias and he glared right back.

'I don't tell lies. And the truth can't really be an insult.'

Cat's nostrils flared and she clenched her fists. 'You seriously expect me to believe that Kyle effectively told you I'd trapped him into leaving with me? And you seem to be saying that your dad told you that's what my family does? Really?'

'Yes. No. Not exactly.'

'Then what are you saying? Exactly?'

He ran a hand through his hair. 'It was a long time ago. I'm not sure I remember.'

'I think you do. Otherwise you wouldn't have said it.'

He shot a look to his right and scowled. 'Are you three still here?'

'Kyra's staying. I want her to hear what you've got to say about her dad.'

Amias sucked in a breath. 'I'm not saying

anything. Forget it. I must've misunderstood. I must've been mistaken.'

'No, Amias. I'm the one who has been mistaken. Perhaps my mum was right about you, after all. Come along, Kyra. I think we're done here.'

'What? But why? What's going on? Mum! Wait for me.'

Cat stormed out of the museum, shoving the door so hard it thumped against the front wall with a resounding thud.

Kyra dashed after her and jumped into the car. Cat sped off, sending an arc of water into the air behind her.

'Er. Are you going to tell me what the hell just happened, Mum?'

It took Cat a few moments to catch her breath.

'I wish I could. But I'm not really sure I know.'

Chapter Twenty-Four

'That bloody woman.' Amias marched into Natalia's kitchen and stopped in his tracks. 'Why are you always on the damn phone?'

'Er. I'll call you back, Josh. Amias is here and he's in an almighty strop.' She hung up and glared at Amias. 'Firstly, please don't just barge into my house as if you own the place, and secondly, I'm not always on the phone. I assume "that bloody woman" is Cat Devon.'

'What? The door was open.'

'The door was unlocked, not open.'

'It's the same thing.'

'It's not the same thing at all.'

'Why does it matter? Can't you see I'm furious?'

'Are you? I hadn't noticed.'

'I'm not in the mood for humour.'

'I wasn't trying to be funny.'

'For God's sake, Natalia. I need your help. Not your sarcasm.'

'Then perhaps you should knock on my front door and say, "Please may I come in, Natalia? And please will you help me?" And I might think about it.'

'I don't have time for this nonsense. Are you going to help me or not?'

She crossed her arms, tipped her head to one side and raised her brows.

'Jesus Christ. OK. Please?'

'Of course. What's happened now? The last time you were here, was very early on Sunday morning. For which Josh still thanks you, by the way.' She threw him a sarcastic smile. 'Cat had accused you the night before of trying to seduce her daughter but then she'd said she was going to invite you for coffee and you didn't know what that meant.'

'Yes. And you told me I was a complete idiot and it meant she liked me, after all. Which I told you at the time she didn't. And she definitely doesn't. Or if she did, she doesn't now.'

'I assume you're going to explain. I'll make coffee.'

'I'd rather have wine. Or whisky.'

'You'll have coffee and like it.' She switched on the machine and smiled. 'I must've known you were coming. Here's one I prepared earlier. Now start from the beginning. And let's try and make it easy to follow, shall we?'

He tutted. 'She and Kyra came to the museum to show me a photo of a man they want to trace. But that's not important. Everything was fine until Lucas went to make coffee.'

'She didn't want coffee?'

181

He furrowed his brows. 'Yes. She wanted coffee. I didn't actually ask if she did but she didn't say no.'

'That opens up a whole new can of worms, Amias. Just because a woman doesn't say no, it doesn't mean yes.'

'I don't think that's something you should joke about, Natalia.'

'I'm not joking. But carry on. Hold on though. Who's this man they want to trace?'

'I said it's not important right now.'

'I know you did. But I'm curious.'

He sighed. 'I'll tell you later. Um. She said something about Lucas being good-looking and how girls must be attracted to him.'

'He is. They are. And you got jealous?'

'No. Of an eighteen-year-old kid? Give me some credit.'

'You were exceedingly jealous of an eighteen-year-old kid once, I seem to remember.'

'When I was nineteen myself. Yes. Will you shut up and let me finish?'

'I wish you would. Coffee?'

'Natalia! I'm dying here. Bloody well listen, will you?'

She held a hand in the air, grinned, poured them both some coffee and shoved a mug in his direction.

'I'm all ears. We'd got to how handsome Lucas is.'

Amias took a gulp of coffee and nodded. 'I said

she had nothing to worry about because Kyra had her head screwed on and Cat jumped to the conclusion that I was saying she didn't. Cat, that is. Not Kyra. And I said I hadn't been referring to the past but if we were, then I thought she'd definitely had her head screwed on because she'd wanted to get Kyle and she wanted to leave the village so she'd got him by getting herself pregnant. Or words to that effect.'

'Wait. I didn't understand half of what you just said. But you accused Cat of getting pregnant to get Kyle to leave the village with her? Seriously? And you're still standing?'

'Well, that's what did happen. That's what Kyle told me. And when I told her that Kyle had said that, she accused me of lying. Oh and there was also the bit about Dad saying that Devon women get themselves pregnant to get the man they want.'

'Ah yes. Dad and Mary Devon. No conversation about the Devons is complete without bringing up that little gem. You actually said that, did you?'

'Yes. Cat clearly doesn't know about it but that doesn't change the fact it's true.'

'From Dad's point of view. That doesn't make it true, Amias. And Mary didn't get the man she wanted, did she? Dad was right to be angry about the rumours at the time, but to still be bitter now, doesn't help anyone. And for you to bring it up with Cat, was just plain stupid.'

He glared at her but she was right. 'I know. I

don't know why I did. It just all came tumbling out before I realised what I was saying. When I saw how cross she was, I tried to back track. I mean what's the point in going over it all now? It won't change the outcome. It won't bring Kyle back. I said I must've been mistaken and she said she was the one who was mistaken and that her mum was right about me. Then she stormed out and took Kyra with her. So what should I do now?'

'Take a vow of silence? But failing that, I'm not sure there's anything you can do. Either you face the past and tell her the truth. And run the risk of her never speaking to you again. Or you leave things as they are. And she'll probably never speak to you again.' Natalia shrugged and drank her coffee.

He blinked several times. 'That's it? That's the extent of your advice?'

'I'm not a miracle worker, Amias. Look. Let's go over the facts. For the last eighteen years you've carried around a lifetime's worth of guilt because you were in love with Cat Devon and you didn't want to be. When Kyle fell in love with her and they became a couple, you were eaten up with jealously. One day you told him you thought you might be in love with his girlfriend and shortly after that, he told you she was pregnant and she wanted them to run away together. And a few months later, they did. For some reason you think you could've stopped all this from happening by being nice to her when she first went to the beach, instead of turning her away because of the stories Dad told us about him and Mary Devon. But that's just silly, as I tell you every year, including this one. I honestly thought there'd been a breakthrough on Saturday night and that maybe you could both finally put the past behind you and move on. Perhaps you still can. But only if you tell her the truth, Amias. The entire truth. Including the fact that you've been in love with her since that first day you saw her on the beach. OK. Maybe not the first day. I know you didn't fall in love with her at first sight, like Kyle said he did. But you couldn't stop talking about her from that very first day and you haven't stopped thinking about her from that day to this. Even if it is only once every year. Although we both know you think about her far more often than that and that she's the real reason you've never had a lasting relationship.'

He narrowed his eyes, frowned and shook his head. 'But then I'd have to tell her about Dad and Mary. And that I've always known who her dad was. She'd hate me even more for that. Not to mention her dad's family. And Mary would probably kill me.'

'Yes. And as I said, Cat may never speak to you again. But at least the truth would be out and perhaps you could both move on. It's time, Amias. It really is.'

He thought about it for a while.

'Perhaps you're right.'

'I'm always right. Just ask Josh.'

He gave her a half-hearted smile. 'But it won't

be easy. I'll need some time to think about what to say and how to say it.'

'That'll be a first. Now tell me about this man they're trying to trace. She doesn't think he may be her dad, does she?'

'No. The photo was taken during the second world war and the man's in an RAF uniform.' He pulled out his phone. 'This is the photo. Kyra showed Lucas a copy on her phone and he synced it to show William later, so he gave me a copy too.'

'Wow. He's really handsome. Why are they trying to trace him?'

'Because they found the photo in a trunk in Viola's bedroom along with some unopened letters and they want to know who he is, what he was to Viola and why she wouldn't open the letters.'

'The letters are from him?'

'They believe so, yes.'

'Why don't they just open them?'

'Because they're addressed to Viola and she's kept them locked up in her trunk for God knows how long. They don't want to invade her privacy by opening them, but they want to know who the man is and whether they should try to contact him, assuming he's alive, which they're not sure he is, to tell him Viola's in a coma.'

'Dear God. And I thought you pining for Cat Devon and being riddled with guilt over Kyle's death for eighteen bloody years was crazy. But hey. This could be good. If you could find out who he is, you could tell Cat, and she might be so pleased she'd forgive you.'

'Or he could be linked to a whole new tragedy.
And she might hate me even more.'

'There is that possibility.'

Chapter Twenty-Five

'I think you and Jeremy may have got off on the wrong foot, Catherine,' Mary said, as Cat and Kyra were preparing dinner that evening. 'I know he may come across as rather full of himself, but he's kind and caring and he makes me happy. Not to mention the fact that he's good at what he does.'

'Eew, Gran. That's too much information.' Kyra screwed up her nose and grinned.

Mary gasped. 'I was referring to the fact that he's a good builder, Kyra, not … the other thing.' A sudden smile swept across her face. 'Although I'd have to say he's also good at that.'

'Definitely too much information,' Cat said, but she wasn't grinning.

'What's wrong with you today? You've been like a bear with a sore head ever since you both came home from the museum.'

'Nothing's wrong.'

'I may not have seen you for eighteen years but I'm still your mother, Catherine and I can tell that something's happened. Is this about Jeremy? I know it's sudden and perhaps we're rushing things a little but when you're our age, time doesn't wait around.'

'For goodness sake, Mum. You're both in your fifties. That's hardly old. And yes, you did rush into things, but it's your life and if he makes you happy, which he clearly seems to, then that's fine with me. It's your house after all so I can't tell you who can and can't stay here. But this has nothing to do with Jeremy. Well, maybe him being here hasn't helped, but that's neither here nor there.'

'What are you saying? That you don't want him here? Why does his presence upset you so?'

'That's not what I'm saying and I'm not upset about him. It's nothing. Let's just leave it.'

'I don't think we should. You seem to have taken an instant dislike to him and I don't know why.'

Cat turned and faced her. 'I don't know why either, Mum. But I have. And perhaps I'm wrong about him. I was certainly wrong about Amias. All these years I've–'

'Amias Wells? What does he have to do with this?'

Cat sighed. 'Nothing, Mum. Nothing at all.'

'She's cross with Amias because of something he said. Or maybe didn't say.' Kyra shrugged. 'I'm not sure what happened and neither is Mum. That's why she's cross.'

'Excuse me, Kyra, but I am here you know.'

'I know. And Gran's right. You have been like a bear with a sore head. You won't even talk to me about what happened.'

189

'Because I don't know what happened. It's just that man. He makes me so mad. I don't know what it is but we never did get on and nothing's changed in eighteen years.'

'You still love him, don't you, Mum?'

'No! Absolutely not. Well. Maybe just a little. OK, yes. Possibly. But nothing could ever come of it so it's stupid to think it could. And loving him doesn't change the fact I don't really like him. He's still got a chip on his shoulder. He still looks at me as if he'd rather he didn't have to. He still makes it clear he doesn't like me. And now today, he tells lies about your dad and accuses me of being the sort of girl who gets herself pregnant to get a man. Oh. And he said the same about you, too, Mum. And that his dad told him. What did he mean by that?'

Mary paled and dropped on to a chair. 'I have no idea. I hardly know the man.'

Cat sighed loudly. 'Oh come on, Mum. Please don't you lie to me too. You were always telling me how awful the Wells family were and that I should stay away from Amias and Natalia and the whole sorry bunch, not just Kyle and his family. And that day in Bella Vista, Annie definitely said something that was connected with Amias, or probably, Alwick. I asked you if Alwick was my dad and you assured me he wasn't. Was that the truth?'

Mary took several deep breaths. 'Yes. That was the truth.'

'But Alwick knows who my dad was, doesn't he?'

Mary nodded. 'Yes. He knows.'

'And I think Amias may know too. Unless I'm mistaken.'

Mary looked horrified. 'Amias knows?'

Cat shrugged. 'I don't know. It was just the way he tried to take back what he'd said. As if he knew that by continuing, he'd have to say something far worse. And that can't have been about Kyle. So it must've been about his dad. Or something his dad had told him. And I got the impression he's known since before the day I met him in the bay when I was sixteen. I may be completely wrong, but I even think it has something to do with the way he behaved towards me then. It was as if he disliked me before we'd even met.'

'Amias Wells has known for all these years? And he hasn't said a word? He hasn't told anyone?'

Cat frowned. 'I don't know. I can't be certain of anything. But you said that he told Lorna he'd known where Kyra and I were for years but he hadn't told anyone. He may be infuriating and he may now be a liar, but it seems he's a man who can keep a secret.'

'Unlike his father, it seems, if he told Amias about us.'

'Us? About you and Alwick? So there was something between the two of you? Mum, I know you don't want to tell me and I know it may be painful but I really think you should. This family has far too many secrets and far too much tied up in the past. There's Granny Viola and her letters.

191

There's the secret of my dad's identity. And your relationship with Alwick Wells. And there's me and Kyle and Amias. Perhaps it's about time we all came clean. Let's start with you and Alwick.'

Mary fiddled with the buttons on the front of her dress and sighed. 'I suppose you're right. I know you are. But if I tell you about your father, it will impact on other people's lives. I can't swear you to secrecy, like I was. But that's part of the problem. I made a promise. An agreement. Not just me. Granny Viola and I signed a contract. In return for …' She gave a small cough. 'In return for a certain consideration. I'm not proud of it but we had this house to look after and there was just the two of us. Three, including you, Catherine. And we didn't ask for it. The offer was made to us.'

'OK. Now I'm really confused.' Cat pulled out a chair and sat opposite Mary. Her head was spinning even more than it had been when she'd raced from the museum. 'Are you telling me that my dad's alive? And that he paid you to keep quiet about me? That he made you sign a contract to that effect? Bloody hell, Mum!'

'I'll open some wine,' Kyra said. 'I think we're all going to need it.'

Chapter Twenty-Six

Amias drove back to the museum in slightly less of a bad mood than he had been in when he arrived at Natalia's.

His sister believed sarcasm was an art form, and making jokes at his expense seemed to give her hours of enjoyment, but he loved her in spite of that. No. That was one of the things he loved about her. No matter how bad a mood he was in, Natalia had a way of coaxing him out of it with her sarcastic humour. And today had been no different.

She had actually made a lot of sense. Perhaps it was time he admitted his true feelings. If he wasn't yet ready to admit them to Cat, perhaps he was at least ready to admit them to himself.

And what she had said about him finding out about the man in the photo also made sense. If he could do that, then at least he would have a reason to get back in touch with Cat. Or maybe Kyra, if Cat refused to speak to him.

If only he hadn't said the bit about her getting pregnant on purpose, the afternoon may not have turned out as it had. But that is what Kyle had said. He remembered that day as if it was yesterday. The day Kyle had told him that Cat was expecting a child. The day when his own dad's warnings about the Devons had been proved right.

'It's what she's always wanted,' Kyle had said. 'She planned it from the day we met. She wanted us to be together. To have a family of our own. And I want it too. But not here. She doesn't want to stay here. Her mum and her gran will be constantly interfering. My mum and dad will be on my back about money. That's no way to build a future. She's suggested we leave. That we run away together. And I think she's right. She's always wanted to study art in Edinburgh. I've got some savings. But not enough. I was wondering if I could work here between my other jobs. Earn a bit of extra cash. Any chance of that?'

'Sure,' Amias had said, once he had recovered from the initial shock. 'And if I can do anything else to help, you only have to ask.'

'Thanks mate. That means a lot. Especially after what you told me about how you felt about Cat. This can't be easy to hear.'

Amias had shrugged nonchalantly. 'That's life. I wasn't expecting anything to come from it. I was never going to tell her how I felt. Not unless you two broke up. And even then, I probably wouldn't have told her. I only told you because I felt I had to be honest and upfront with my best friend. It's cool. We're fine. Don't give it another thought.'

But Amias had thought of little else, despite the fact that it felt as if his heart had been smashed into tiny pieces. He tried to avoid Cat as much as possible. If they had to speak, he kept things brief. He made sure they were never alone, or if they were, he made an excuse and got away from her as fast as he possibly could. Several times, he had actually turned and walked the other way when he'd seen her coming towards him. He never looked at her, unless he really had to. And sometimes, he just had to. He rarely smiled or laughed when she was around. He dated every girl he could, but never remembered to call them. He knew what hell was, but he had no idea how to get out of it. Even Natalia hadn't been able to help him back then.

And when, just a few months later, Kyle told him they had to leave sooner than he had hoped, but that he still didn't have enough money, Amias had dipped into his own savings and given Kyle two thousand pounds. It had set him back about a year in relation to his own dreams and plans, but Kyle was his best friend, and Cat … Well. Amias would have given Cat the world if he could have done so. But she didn't want the world from him. All Cat Devon wanted was Kyle. And she had got him.

Except, if what she had said today, about her naivety, her surprise at being pregnant, her doubts and confusion, about not having any idea of what she really wanted or how to get it, were all true then what Kyle had said couldn't have been.

Had Kyle lied?

Perhaps Kyle had been the one who wanted a child; the one who wanted to leave Merriment Bay.

He had definitely wanted to leave his family. Amias had always known that. Perhaps it had been Kyle's suggestion that he and Cat should run away together. That's certainly what Cat had said today.

Which meant that Amias had not known Kyle as well as he thought he had.

And it also meant that perhaps he had been wrong about Cat for the past eighteen years.

But it didn't change anything. Kyle was still dead. Cat had still loved Kyle.

And when Cat had left the hospital with her baby, eighteen years ago, she had apparently decided she had no place in her life for Amias. Not even as a friend.

Her mobile number had clearly changed because the one he had no longer connected. His notes through her front door had been ignored. She had returned his letters, unopened. She had refused to see him every time he went to Devon Villa. And finally she had threatened to contact the police and accuse him of stalking and harassment unless he left her and Kyra in peace.

It had taken him a while. But he had finally got the message. Cat Devon didn't want him in her life. She couldn't even bring herself to tell him to his face. She had got her mum and her gran to do it all for her. They had given him her messages. They had delivered her threats. They had probably been the ones to put his unopened letters back in the post to him, on her behalf.

And yet here he was, after all these years, and

more failed relationships behind him than he could count on both hands, still thinking about Cat Devon. Still as much in love with her as he had always been.

And only last Sunday morning, after telling Natalia what had happened on Saturday night, he had wondered if there would ever come a day when, even once, he could hold Cat in his arms and believe for just a moment that somewhere in the dim and distant future they might one day be together.

But he'd been too scared to say those words out loud. Or to let himself think of it again. And when Cat had walked in to the museum today, yet again he'd said the wrong thing. And once again they'd rowed.

What the hell was wrong with him? Instead of getting closer, they were moving further apart.

Perhaps the man in the faded photo in Viola's trunk, the one he'd now got on his phone, could close that gap. Perhaps he could help them heal their differences and finally put the past behind them. If so, the sooner he found out who this man was, the better life might be for all of them. Well, certainly for him.

Chapter Twenty-Seven

'When I was young,' Mary said, after taking several swigs of wine from the glass Kyra had handed her. 'Gladys, Annie, Gina and I, together with some of the other teenagers from the village, some of whom you know, and some no longer with us, all used to hang out together. We often spent our summers in the bay, or at Wyntersleap Reservoir. Alwick, like Amias, loved water sports. And, like Amias, he was rather good to look at. But he was from the wrong side of the river and at first I refused to have anything to do with him. In those days, the only houses there were that awful fishing hut-type place where Alwick lived, and two other semi-derelict cottages. One where Kyle's father was brought up and one in which an elderly couple lived until they died and left it empty.'

'Why was it 'the wrong side of the river', Gran?' Kyra asked.

'Because a couple of centuries ago, there was nothing but a hospital there and it was said that the hospital was for lepers. It was run by monks, who also owned Merriment Farm, but the farm is further up. The hospital caught fire, was razed to the ground and never replaced. Until Alwick's ancestors and a couple of others somehow got the land and built their shacks there. But the villagers wanted as little as possible to do with those people. It was thought the land was cursed.

'But not the farm?' Cat queried. 'Or The Hope and Anchor pub, which has been there for centuries?'

Mary shook her head. 'No. Just the site of the hospital. And those three parcels of land on which it sat and where it had its physic gardens in which the monks grew medicinal herbs and such. Two of the parcels were owned by someone not from around here; the one Kyle's family rented and the one the elderly couple lived on. But they have since been sold and there are three houses there now. The third parcel is still owned by Alwick Wells.'

'I think if the monks grew medicinal herbs on the land, it would be a good place to live, not the wrong side at all,' Kyra said. 'Were there really lepers in the hospital?'

'I don't know. There's nothing wrong with the land though. You're right about that. When the owners of the other two parcels sold theirs, soil samples were taken by the developers for some reason and the land was given a clean bill of health. Alwick was approached to sell his land. But he refused.'

'Good for him,' Kyra said.

'So you and several others hung out together,' Cat said, eager to get to the point. 'And something happened between you and Alwick?'

Mary nodded. 'Eventually, yes. We fell in love. Although, if I'm completely honest, he was more in love with me than I was with him. And if Mother had known then what was going on, I'd have been locked in my room and never let out again. I think for me, that was part of the excitement. Doing something I knew I shouldn't. Being with a boy I knew Mother wouldn't want me to be with. We had a relationship for a while.'

'A sexual relationship?' Kyra asked, screwing up her nose.

'Yes. And I'd be grateful if every time you mention sex in relation to me, you wouldn't pull faces.'

'Sorry, Gran.' Kyra grinned at Cat. 'I don't mean to.'

'What then?' Cat asked.

'Then I met your father.'

Cat sat up straight, took several gulps of wine and one of Mary's hands in hers and prepared herself.

'He was gorgeous. Incredibly rich, or so we all thought at the time, and completely out of my league. He was a few years older than me. And, I'm ashamed to say, married with a young son of his own.'

'Mum!'

'I know it was wrong, Catherine. But I couldn't help myself. I believed him when he said he wasn't happy. I believed he wanted to leave his wife, even though I knew he probably couldn't. Or maybe wouldn't. I believed he loved me. Perhaps he did. I ended things with Alwick and he took it rather badly. I think I said some things I shouldn't. About him being poor and that I wanted more out of life than to live in a hovel. I was very cruel and he never forgave me. He turned to Gina, more out of pain than love, I believe. And when I told him that I would never return to him, no matter what, he married Gina. Whether to spite me or himself, I have no idea. And I didn't care. I was in love and I was happy. Amias was born and Gina, Alwick and I never spoke again. I continued my affair and then, almost two years later, I fell pregnant with you. I was eighteen at the time. Just nineteen when you were born. Not much older than you were, Catherine, when you had Kyra. And all hell broke loose.'

'I know that feeling.'

'Yes. Well. I'm not proud of the way I behaved with you, Catherine when you told us the news. But it brought back so many awful memories of what I went through, that I really thought the best thing for you would be, either to not have Kyra, or to give her up for adoption.'

'So what happened, Gran?' Kyra asked. 'Was Granny Viola furious?'

'Livid. Mainly because he was married. That seemed to be the worst part as far as she was concerned. But also because, when it became apparent that he had no intention of acknowledging you were his, we had to deal with all the talk, and rumours, and such. And we weren't wealthy. We would have had to sell the house. Then his mother came to see us and said that if I would tell people that you were someone else's child, she would give us a fairly large sum of money which would mean we wouldn't have to worry about finances again. I believe she made him sell some properties they owned because it transpired that the family were asset rich but cash poor. Anyway, that's what we agreed. And Granny Viola may have said a few things that made people think you were Alwick's child. I never said it. But people assumed. And he hated that I would never deny it.'

'Bloody hell, Mum! That is truly awful. Alwick was married too. And he had Amias. How could you do that? How could Granny Viola?'

'It was wrong, I know. But a few people knew about me and your father and we had to say that you weren't his. It was part of the agreement, you see. And yes. I know that was also wrong, but we did what we did and we can't undo it now. At the time I harboured hopes that your father would change his mind. That he would one day acknowledge you. I was still in love with him, you see. Deeply in love. I would've done anything for him. Anything at all. Even when I discovered that he and his wife had had another son just weeks before I gave birth to you. They were still very much together, it seemed. But a few years afterwards, she left him. And a few years after that, he died.'

'That's awful. But you still haven't told us who he was, Gran,' Kyra pointed out.

Mary closed her eyes and sucked in a long, slow breath.

'And I can't. I really can't. Not yet. Not while Mother is in a coma. Please remember that once I tell you, there is no going back. We signed an agreement, so this is a serious matter, even now.'

'Wait. So you're saying that you still won't tell me?' Cat was even more annoyed by this than she had been by the injustice to Alwick, Gina and Amias. Or by Mary's sad tale. 'But once Granny Viola regains consciousness, you will?'

Mary nodded. 'Yes. I'll tell you then. Assuming she agrees.'

'Oh come on, Mum. That's so unfair.'

'Life is unfair, Catherine. Haven't you learnt that yet?'

Cat glared at her. 'And what if Granny Viola doesn't pull through?'

'Then I'll tell you. But I hope you'll respect the fact that by doing so, I could bring down a family's wrath upon us all.'

'A family? The mother is still alive?'

'Very much so.'

A sudden realisation hit Cat. 'Wait. You said my father and his wife had two children, didn't you?'

Mary nodded and held Cat's astonished stare.

'So I have two siblings?'

Mary nodded again. 'Who have no idea you

203

exist. And knowing them, would probably like to keep it that way. As I said at the start, Catherine. If I tell you who your father was, it will impact on other people's lives. This is not just about us. I'll have to trust that you won't do anything rash and that neither of you will tell anyone else about this, for now. We signed a legal document, remember.'

'I can't believe you've kept this from me. That I have siblings, I mean. I always assumed I was an only child.'

'To all intents and purposes, you are. And I had no choice.'

'Of course you had a choice. We all have choices, Mum. I don't know if I can make you that promise. I think I have a right to meet them. To tell them who I am and for us all to get to know one another.'

'Why? What difference does it make? You've lived a good life without knowing them and they've definitely lived good lives without knowing you. And they may think you just want to see what you can get. They may not want to know you exist. This isn't just about you, Catherine, as I said. Please, please wait until we see what happens with Granny Viola. Please just wait until then. I'm begging you, Catherine.'

Mary looked genuinely distraught and as hurt and angry as Cat was, Mary was right. This wasn't just about what she wanted.

'I need to think about it.' Cat glared at Mary. 'Because I'm not sure I can make you any promises.

And I'm not sure Kyra can either.'

'I think I can. I don't feel strongly about it. I suppose that sounds weird to you, Mum, but I don't. I've lived without knowing about them until now. And you've never been that hung up about knowing who your dad was either, Mum, so why is it such a problem now?'

'Because now I have siblings, and that makes a difference. Quite a big difference. Once I know who they are, I can't promise I won't want to meet them. If I don't know, it will eat away at me. But the last thing I want is to potentially upset other people's lives. This is a really important decision. And I don't know what to do for the best.'

Chapter Twenty-Eight

'I'm not sure I really want to be here,' Cat said as she and Kyra crossed the bridge and walked towards the bonfire. It was on the piece of common land on the other side of the river, just a little inland from where the hospital had once sat.

'But you have to be here, Mum. This is a big event in the calendar of Merriment Bay, Gran said. The bonfire and fireworks are held to remember all those from the village who died in wars over the centuries, including the first and second world wars and all the earlier ones too. There'll be dancing and food and drink. And it's also Marcus' last night here before he goes off to uni.'

'I know all that. But I haven't seen Amias since that day I stormed out of the museum and I don't want to see him tonight. Are you sure he's going to be flying his vintage Spitfire and that he won't be here for hours?'

'Yep. Because Lucas told me Amias always cleans it after a flight and before he puts it away, or whatever it is you do with planes. And the museum row was over a week ago and I told you, when I saw him a couple of days after that day, he said he hoped he hadn't upset you and that he was sorry if he had. Plus he's been trying to find out all he can about the man in the photo. So there's clearly no hard feelings on his part. If you really don't want to see him, you can make sure you're gone before he arrives but can't you just let it go and try to be friends? Haven't we got enough bad feelings between you and Gran without you and Amias having this ongoing row?'

Cat sighed. 'I'm sorry things are awkward at the house. But every time I look at Mum I feel angry, and hurt and betrayed. And although Jeremy has been all sweetness and light since that day we conned him into making breakfast and falling foul of Mum's wrath, I still get a feeling there's something not quite right about him. I shouldn't have come here tonight. I'm not in the mood for a party.'

'That's precisely why you should be here. A party is exactly what you need. It's what we both need. Visiting Granny Viola isn't getting any easier. There's still no sign of improvement and I'm not an idiot. I've seen the doctors looking at her and at you and Gran and me as if they're saying it'll soon be time for us to make a decision about her. I know that's also playing on your mind. You've got so much going on in your head I'm astonished you can sit and paint as you have been.'

'That's the only thing that keeps me sane at the moment, sweetheart. Well, that and having you here. I don't think I could've coped with any of this if you'd gone off to university in September.

Perhaps you should've gone to Oxford. They seem to have shorter terms.'

Kyra grinned. 'And much harder courses and higher entry requirements. I'm bright but I'm not as bright as Marcus. Nowhere near. I'll miss him when he's gone. But he's coming back here for Christmas. His mum and dad are going to be staying at Lucas'. Well, William and Abigail's but you know what I mean.'

'That's something to look forward to. And in the meantime, you've got Lucas to keep you company.'

'Yep. And there they are.'

Cat walked towards the group and waved at William and Abigail whom she'd finally met during the week.

'Hi Abigail. How are you? Sad to be saying goodbye to Marcus, I expect.'

Abigail laughed. 'Yes. But actually wishing he was taking this one with him.' She ruffled Lucas' hair and although he moved away from his mum, he smiled good-naturedly.

'It's chilly tonight. What a good thing there's a bonfire. I'm surprised the Spitfire will be flying tonight though. The sky's clear but will we see the plane going over or just the lights?'

Abigail gave Cat an odd look. 'The Spitfire doesn't fly at night. As you said. You wouldn't really see it. Unless Amias did one of those vapour trails which he sometimes does in the summer. But no. Not tonight. And speaking of Amias. There he is.'

Abigail waved over Cat's shoulder and Cat froze on the spot. She shot a look at Kyra who shrugged her shoulders and grinned, mouthing the words, 'Sorry, Mum', before walking off with Lucas and Marcus.

Cat was going to kill her later. But first she had to find a way to get out of here before Amias joined them.

'Hi Abi. Hello Cat.'

Too late. Too bloody late.

She shoved her shoulders back and stuck out her chin, turning to face him with a fixed smile on her lips.

'Hello Amias, I hadn't realised you would be here.'

He raised his brows and looked her up and down. Her heart leapt to her throat but she kept the smile firmly in place.

'Really? I always come to village events and I specifically told Kyra I would be here. I was hoping to see you.'

'I'll leave you two to it,' Abigail said. 'I need to check on the food.'

'See me? Why?' Cat hardly heard Abigail and was still dissecting Amias' meaning.

'Apart from the fact that I like seeing you, I wanted to tell you I think I know who your mystery man is.'

'Mystery man? What mystery man? You mean my dad? You've known all along, haven't you and you've kept it to yourself?'

He looked stunned. 'Your dad?' He glanced around as if worried they'd be overheard. 'I wasn't talking about him. I was talking about the man in the photo. The faded photo of the RAF pilot you found in amongst the letters in Viola's trunk.'

'Oh him!' Cat screeched. 'I thought you meant …'

'Obviously,' he said as her voice trailed off. 'Has Mary told you? About your dad, I mean?'

'Yes and no. It's difficult.'

'I can imagine.'

'But you do know who he is? His actual name, I mean?'

'Your dad?' He lowered his voice even more.

She lowered hers. 'Yes.'

He moved closer and whispered in her ear. 'Yes, Cat. I know his name.'

His warm breath made her ear lobe tingle and sent shivers up and down her body. She had visions of him whispering other things in her ear. She dismissed them as fast as she could, coughed and stepped away from him.

'Mum still refuses to tell me. But apparently, I have siblings. Two, in fact. Did you also know about them?'

He held her gaze and nodded. 'Yes. I know.'

Cat sucked in a breath and pursed her lips. So he knew everything about her. Who her dad was. That she had siblings. For some reason, that made her even more cross with him.

'If I asked you to tell me, would you?'

He studied her face for a second and she moved her head a little to one side, in a futile attempt to partially hide her scar. Which was ridiculous. But she suddenly felt self-conscious and more than a little vulnerable.

'No, Cat. I wouldn't. It's not my place to do so. I'm sorry. But others are involved. If I tell you, I'd be no better than a gossip.'

She bristled at his words. 'But it was your dad who told you, wasn't it? He gossiped.'

'Yes. And I dearly wish he hadn't.'

'Why did he?'

Amias shook his head and ran a hand through his hair.

How she wished, even right now, that she could do that too. What was it about this man that drew her to him? It was as if there was a sort of magnetic field or something, pulling her towards him. But she had to resist. She stepped a little farther away and he narrowed his eyes as if he noticed.

'I don't know what Mary has told you about the past, but let's just say that she and my dad weren't always the enemies they seem to be now. But things happen in life that make us do things we normally wouldn't. Dad feels bitter about certain events in the past. He can't seem to let it go. When we heard that you were coming home that summer, all those years ago, he felt … well … That it might be best if I kept my distance from the Devons. All Devons. And he told me a story that involved him and Mary and your dad. And once he'd told me, I couldn't pretend I hadn't heard it.'

Cat stuck out her chin. 'Mum did tell me about her relationship with your dad. She said he loved her very much.'

He met her stare. 'He did. He told me that Mary Devon broke his heart.'

Cat couldn't take her eyes from his. 'But he was quick enough to marry your mum.'

'Yes. And he said that was the best thing he ever did. Mum saved him, as far as he's concerned. And she stood by him when … when things were said.'

Cat's tone softened. 'Yes. Mum also told me about the rumours. I'm so sorry your family had to go through that, Amias. It was cruel and unjust.'

He smiled wanly and shrugged. 'It's a village. There are always going to be rumours. But I'm not sure Dad will ever forgive Mary and Viola for that.'

'I'm not sure I blame him. I'm finding it hard to forgive them myself. It's weird isn't it? We go through life thinking we know people close to us, only to find out we don't really know them at all. Or at least that we don't know them as well as we thought we did.'

'You're right about that. I've just discovered … er … that I didn't know someone as well as I thought I did. And it was a bit of a surprise. But I'm not sure we ever really know anyone entirely. The thing is, if we love someone, we accept the good and the bad about them, don't we?'

Who was he referring to? He'd stopped and given her an almost apologetic look at the start of that statement. Was he talking about Kyle? She wanted to ask. But he wouldn't tell her, would he? Amias was a man who clearly kept some things close to his chest.

'And the man in the photo?' She needed to change the subject. 'You know who he is too?'

'Yes.' His relief was palpable.

'For certain?'

He smiled. 'Yes.'

'Who is he?'

'His name is Bailey Mitchell and he was stationed here in the war. He was a pilot, as we thought and according to the records, and a bit of other digging I've managed to do, he was Canadian. Is Canadian, I should say. His mother was British though and he, like several others wanted to do his bit for England. Quite a few Canadians served with the RAF during the war, but some enlisted directly into the RAF. Bailey did so in 1939. He returned to Canada after the war ended and that's where he still lives. In British Columbia. Vancouver, to be exact. I've managed to get an address for him.'

Cat's mouth fell open. 'How the hell did you manage all that?'

He smiled again, before glancing over her shoulder. 'I have friends in high places, as George Lester would say. Good evening, George. And Sybil, you're looking lovely. You both must be so proud of Marcus.'

George puffed out his red cheeks and smiled as Cat turned to face him.

'We're extremely proud. Good thing the boy's good at something.'

Amias narrowed his eyes a fraction and Cat watched his smile turn to a sneer.

'Yes. And not only is he going up to Oxford but to Balliol. Wasn't that where Dad told me you once applied?'

'I changed my mind.'

'I'm sure you did. But how wonderful to know that they wanted Marcus. Oh, and in case you're interested, he can windsurf now too. Rather well as it happens. Have a lovely evening.' He took Cat's elbow and marched her away from the Lesters. 'God, I loathe that man.'

'You were rude and sarcastic. But he deserved it. Will you please let go of my arm?'

'Sorry.' He immediately released his hold on her and smiled sheepishly. 'I can't help myself. Whenever George comes near me, I feel as if I'd liked to punch that arrogant look off his face. But I don't believe in violence.' He looked her in the eye. 'Sometimes though, I say the wrong things and upset people when it's the last thing I want to do.'

Cat tensed. 'If you're referring to the other day, in the museum, I do the same. Let's forget it, shall we?'

'Yes let's.' He beamed at her.

She looked away but her gaze wandered back. 'You were telling me about Bailey Mitchell. What else have you found out?'

He raised his brows. 'Isn't that enough? It wasn't as easy as I've made it sound.'

She gave a short laugh. 'Sorry. I didn't mean to sound ungrateful. I'm sure it wasn't. Thank you so much for doing this, Amias.'

'It was a pleasure, Cat.'

A firework whooshed into the air and they turned to look at it.

'If you'll give me the details, I'll write him a letter and explain how we found his photo and his letters and ask if he wants to know about Granny Viola or not.'

'Actually, I can tell you a bit more about him. Are you doing anything tomorrow night?'

Her body tensed once more. 'No.'

'Then would you like to come to my place and I'll cook dinner? Nothing fancy. Just pasta and wine. And I'll show you everything I've found out about Bailey Mitchell.'

Was he asking her on a date?

Another firework shot into the night sky, exploding in a shower of red sparkles.

'Bring Kyra too. If she's free.'

Apparently, he wasn't.

Which was probably just as well.

'Thanks. I'll ask her.'

'Great. I'll get my sister, Natalia and her husband, Josh Horton to join us. If that's OK with you? You remember them, don't you?'

A third firework spiralled upwards, this one

hissing as it twirled in tiny, tight circles.

'Yes. And of course it's OK. I'd like to see them again after so many years. I was surprised to hear they were married. I didn't think they liked one another. At least, it seemed that way eighteen years ago. Mum tells me they own the only Estate Agency in Merriment Bay.'

Amias nodded. 'Horton and Wells. Although if you believe what Natalia says, it's really more Wells than Horton.' He laughed and shook his head. 'And they didn't like each other back then. Until they fell in love.' He smiled strangely, as if he had yet another secret. 'Love can take anyone by surprise, Cat. Anyone at all. And there's not a damn thing we can do about it when it does.'

Now several fireworks lit up the sky one after another, flashing, banging and exploding above them in a variety of colours and sizes, each one seemingly larger and more spectacular than the one a second before.

Cat knew all about being taken by surprise by Love. It had happened to her on that first summer day she had walked on the sand in the bay so many years ago. And she hadn't been able to do a damn thing about it ever since.

She cast a surreptitious look at Amias.

He wasn't looking at the fireworks.

He was gazing intently at her.

Chapter Twenty-Nine

'Let me make sure I've got this right.' Natalia poured Amias, herself and her husband, Josh a large glass each of wine, and grinned. 'The stars were aligned. The bonfire was burning, giving off a welcome warmth in the cold, night air. Fireworks soared into a clear, black sky and you and Cat Devon were staring into each other's eyes. Yes?'

Amias nodded. He felt like a naughty child being scolded by his sister. His younger sister, to make things worse. He was beginning to wish he'd stayed at the celebrations on the village common and not walked up the hill to Natalia's house which overlooked it.

'Yes. I told you. It was the perfect night. Everything about it was perfect.'

Natalia burst out laughing. 'Except for you, you absolute plonker.'

Josh laughed too and shrugged when Amias glared at him. 'Hey. I'm with my wife on this one, mate. Even I would've taken the woman in my arms and kissed her.' He darted a look at Natalia. 'Not me, of course. I meant if I were Amias.'

Natalia blew him a kiss. 'I know what you

meant, my darling. And you're right. If I did a survey of every man on this planet, I think I could guarantee that 99.9% of them would say the same. But not my brother. Oh no. Despite the fact he's besotted with the woman, what does he do? After staring into each other's eyes, he says the fireworks are the best he's seen in years then asks if she's hungry and without waiting for her to respond, marches off to get her some food. And when he comes back and finds she's gone, he's surprised.'

'I was nervous, OK? It was just too perfect. I wanted to kiss her. I told you that. I'm not an idiot. And I almost did. But as I moved closer, I could feel myself breaking out in a cold sweat and I just knew I'd make a complete and utter mess of it. When you've wanted someone for as long as I've wanted Cat, the thought that you might finally get to kiss her is monumental. You want it to be the best kiss ever. And that's not going to happen if you start doubting yourself. What if she didn't want me to? What if she slapped my face? What if she stormed off again? What if she called the police and accused me of sexual assault? That happens you know.'

'You could've asked her,' Josh suggested.

'What? Asked her if she'd mind if I kissed her?'

'Yes. That way at least you would've known.'

Natalia nodded. 'Josh is right. It would've taken the edge off the romance a bit but better that than do something she didn't want you to. Although if she was staring into your eyes as you said, then I think it's pretty much a certainty the answer would've been yes. Or if it had been me: "Yes, you bloody moron, of course I want you to kiss me." Or words to that effect.' She gave him a Cheshire Cat-like grin.

Amias furrowed his brows. 'It didn't occur to me to ask.'

Natalia sighed. 'It never does. You burst in here without asking, every single time you visit.'

He was disconcerted by the change of subject, but this wasn't the first time Natalia had admonished him for that. Was she trying to tell him he was getting on her nerves?

'I rang the bell tonight.'

'You did. But did you wait to be invited in? Did it occur to you that we might be doing something? Like kissing, for example. And we may not have wanted to be interrupted.'

Amias glanced from Natalia to Josh and back again. 'Are you serious?' He shook his head. 'To be honest, no. It didn't. I assumed you'd be sitting on your balcony watching the fireworks and celebrations. Which you were. And I've always just let myself in. If you don't want me to do that, perhaps you should lock the door. Or if you're sick of seeing me, just say so.'

'Oh for God's sake, Amias. Don't get into one of your moods. We love seeing you. And we don't mind you letting yourself in. But it might be nice if you waited until we said you could. That's why we've got the video doorbell thing by the front door.

So that we can see who's there and decide if we want them to come in or not.'

He frowned. 'But as, more often than not, you leave the door unlocked, that sort of defeats the object, doesn't it? The whole point of that video doorbell is that you can turn away unwanted callers. They've only got to try the door handle to find out it's not locked and that they can walk right in.'

'Yet no one does. Except you. Not even Dad. Everyone waits to be invited. And I thought I had locked it this evening, but I must've forgotten. Perhaps we should change the door to one that self-locks after entry. That way I wouldn't need to remember. I was brought up in a house where the front door was never locked. Day or night. That's a difficult habit to break.'

Amias grinned. 'Yeah. But that was because everyone knew there was nothing in our house worth taking. Even strangers only had to look at it to see that. People used to bring us stuff because they felt sorry for us.' He shook his head and laughed.

He could joke about it now. He had to. But when he was younger, he couldn't. Being what was referred to as 'dirt-poor' shouldn't be anything to be ashamed of but it definitely didn't make you want to invite friends round for tea. Not that his mum and dad could have afforded to have his friends round for tea. And especially not when his mum became sick, and he, his sister and his dad had to look after not just her, but also his granddad, who was crippled whilst serving his country in the second world war, and his gran, who had suffered with Alzheimer's since Amias was very young.

And yet, for all of that, they were a happy family. A close family. A family who could deal with whatever life threw at them. Most of the time. And whose door was always open to anyone worse off than them. Not that there was anyone worse off than them. Not in Merriment Bay, at least. Or so it seemed to Amias in those days.

His gran died when he was twelve, and his granddad, not long after. And as awful as it was, things actually got better. His dad got a full-time job and was bringing home a good wage. His mum got well and also found a job. She worked in the Spitfire Café and loved it there. Until she got sick again. For the final time.

Cancer is a bastard disease. Why it had chosen his mum, not just once but twice, he would never understand. Gina Wells was the kindest, most loving woman you would ever meet, and yet breast cancer picked her, just a few years after Natalia was born. She'd beaten that after a long battle and a double mastectomy and was given the all clear. And then the tumour was found on her brain, eleven years ago. And this time, she couldn't beat it.

Natalia's laughter brought him back from his melancholy thoughts.

'Those were the days, eh?' She glanced around her lounge. 'Sometimes I forget that I actually own anything worth stealing. You're right. I should lock the door. But I know I probably won't.'

Amias grinned. 'And you're right. I should wait until you or Josh say I can come in. But I know I probably won't. No. I'm joking. From now on that's what I'll do.'

'Yay!' Natalia clapped her hands together and winked at him. 'That just goes to prove that leopards can change their spots. Now, to get back to the subject. As I've said repeatedly for the last eighteen years, it's time you made a change and let go of the past. It's time you dealt with your feelings for Cat Devon. So either tell her how you feel, or make a decision to get over her and make a fresh start with someone else.'

'Someone else?' He sighed and shook his head. 'I've tried. Believe me. You have no idea how hard I've tried. But the truth is, I don't think I'll ever be able to get over Cat.'

Natalia gently placed a hand on his arm. 'Then tell *her* that, Amias. Not us.'

He sucked in a deep breath and squared his shoulders. 'OK, I'll tell her. I'll find a way to get her alone tomorrow night and I'll tell her.'

'Are you seeing her tomorrow then? You didn't mention that.'

'Yes. And that's the other reason I came here tonight straight after the fireworks. Cat and Kyra are coming to my place for dinner tomorrow and I'd like you two to join us.'

'Sorry, mate we're–'

'We'd love to come,' Natalia interrupted her

husband. 'We were going into Eastbourne to the cinema, but we can do that another night. I'm not passing up the chance to see you and Cat Devon spend an evening together. You don't mind, do you darling?'

Josh shook his head. 'Nah. I've only wanted to see this film for six months and I'm sure we can find someone to give the tickets to.' He pulled a face before smiling at her. 'I don't mind at all. If Amias' performance tonight is anything to go by, watching him during dinner tomorrow should be fun.'

'Thanks.' Amias threw Josh a sarcastic grin. 'It's good to know it's not just my sister who finds my love life so entertaining.'

'Hey, don't blame us,' Natalia said, mockingly. 'You're the one who keeps making a pig's ear out of every so-called relationship you've ever had despite the hours of advice we give you. Do us all a favour and make sure you do get Cat alone tomorrow. Tell her how you feel and then say something along the lines of, "I really want to kiss you right now." Then wait and see what she says.'

Amias knocked back his wine and reached for the bottle to top up his glass, but not before refilling Natalia's and Josh's glasses.

'My wife is always right,' Josh said, winking at Natalia before giving Amias a sympathetic smile. 'I know how terrifying it is to tell a woman you feel is way out of your league that you love her so much it actually hurts to look at her. But I managed to summon up the courage to tell Nat how madly in love I was with her and look at us now.'

'Absolutely.' Natalia nodded as a huge grin spread across her face. 'And Josh is right. I was way out of his league.'

She blew her husband another big kiss and waved her left hand in front of Amias, the diamonds in her matching engagement, wedding and eternity rings almost blinding him.

'Yeah, yeah. And if, after pouring my heart out and telling her how much I want to kiss her, she says, "Thanks, but I'd rather kiss fifty thousand frogs than kiss you", do I just say, Oh, OK then. Perhaps we can still be friends?'

'Amias!' Natalia tutted in frustration. 'You're already chickening out, I can tell. But don't you dare. Or I may end up having to tell her for you. You can't spend another eighteen years of your life keeping your feelings locked away. And besides, you're being ridiculous. Where would she find fifty thousand frogs?'

Chapter Thirty

'How's your headache this morning, Mum?'

Cat looked up from buttering her toast as she sat facing the kitchen door, and smiled at Kyra. There was a definite spring in both Kyra's step and her voice.

'My headache? Oh, yes. Um. The walk home helped to clear it and the early night did me a world of good,' Cat lied.

Kyra seemed to accept that as she took a mug from the cupboard and poured herself some coffee.

Cat hadn't had a headache at the fireworks last night. She merely used it as an excuse to leave the celebrations. And the truth was, she'd hardly slept a wink. All she kept seeing was Amias gazing into her eyes, his face moving closer to hers as fireworks exploded in the clear night sky around them and people screamed with excitement and cheered with pleasure. She really thought, for just one moment, that he was actually going to kiss her. He'd clearly come to his senses though and hurriedly said how great the display was, then mumbled something about did she want some food? Then he'd rushed away like someone who had just had a narrow escape.

She had felt so foolish; so despondent; so lost. There was no way she was going to stand there and wait to see if he came back. What if he didn't? She would look even more ridiculous then. She had tried to pull herself together, had searched the crowd for Kyra and having found her had lied about needing to go home due to a headache, when in reality it was heartache she was suffering from.

'Where's Amias?' Kyra had asked, her eyes scanning the happy throng. 'You haven't had another row, have you?'

'No. Um. He's gone to get something to eat but my head is splitting and I really need to go and lie down. Please give everyone my apologies. And wish Marcus good luck at Oxford.'

'Er. Shall I walk home with you? Didn't Amias offer?'

'No one needs to walk home with me. It's only a short walk and I've got a headache, not a twisted ankle. Have fun. Have you got your key?'

Kyra smiled. 'Always a mum, even when you're not feeling well. Yes. I've got it. I hope you feel better. Shall I pop in and see if you're awake when I get home?'

'I'll be fast asleep as soon as my head hits the pillow, sweetheart. I'll see you in the morning. Now I really must go. Don't be too late. And make sure Lucas or Marcus walk you home.'

'Yes, Mum.' Kyra kissed her on the cheek. 'But how come it's fine for you to walk home alone, but it's not for me?'

'Because I'm older and wiser to the ways of the world.'

'Really?' Kyra grinned. 'That's what you're going with? But you're forgetting something. I can run faster.'

Cat grinned. 'Then run home with Marcus and Lucas. Good night, sweetheart.'

All the way home, Cat kept looking over her shoulder, wondering if Amias would have asked Kyra where she was and then come after her. But why would he do that? He was the one who had run away.

This time.

And he had been the one who had cut off all contact eighteen years ago too.

Yet at some stage during those eighteen years, he had tracked her and Kyra down, but hadn't made contact with them. Why had he done that?

When her mum had told her that it was Amias who had, in a roundabout way, disclosed Cat's address, she'd been determined not to ask him about it. What difference would it make?

But now she wanted to know.

She wanted to know so many things.

Like why he'd taken such an instant dislike to her all those years ago. Was it because of the things his dad had said? Because his dad had told him to stay away from the Devons?

She wanted to know why he'd seemed so caring and attentive while she was in the hospital and yet, the minute she got out, he never contacted her again. And yet he'd tracked them down. Why?

She wanted to know why he had said he was glad she had come home. Had he meant that? Or was it just a throwaway line? And why he'd said those awful things about her getting pregnant on purpose to trap Kyle. Was he really suggesting that Kyle had told him that?

But most of all, she wanted to know why, as fireworks flashed and banged around them, he had looked at her as if she was the only woman in the world. And a beautiful one at that. Why his dark eyes had filled with longing. Why he had looked as if he was going to kiss her. And why he'd changed his mind and fled, albeit with some lame excuse.

What exactly was Amias Wells playing at?

Was that it?

Was he playing?

Was this all some sort of game to him?

By the time she reached the front door of Devon Villa, she really did have a headache.

She let herself into an empty house. Mary and Jeremy must have gone to the celebrations too. Or out for dinner. Or to the pub. What did it matter? At least she could be alone with her thoughts.

But she didn't want to be alone. She wanted to be back on the village common with Amias. She wanted to be staring into his eyes and for him to be staring into hers. And she wanted him to kiss her. She wanted that so badly it made her stomach churn.

Or perhaps that was hunger. She grabbed a

packet of crisps, a wine glass and a bottle of wine and went to her room.

She had drifted off once or twice, but she hadn't really slept and was rather tired this morning.

Kyra joined her at the kitchen table. 'Amias said we're going to his place for dinner tonight.'

Cat choked on her toast. She had to swallow several gulps of coffee before she could reply.

'Er. Yes. He's found out about the man in the photograph. His name's Bailey Mitchell and he's Canadian.'

Kyra nodded. 'I know. He told me. But he says there's other stuff and he's also got more photographs to show us.' She tilted her head to one side and grinned over the rim of her mug. 'I can say I've got a headache if you'd rather go alone.'

'What? Absolutely not. Besides, we wouldn't be alone. His sister and brother-in-law will be there.'

'Oh.' Kyra reached out and grabbed half a slice of toast from Cat's plate. 'He didn't mention that bit. Don't frown at me like that. I'll make some more when I've eaten this.'

Cat sighed, got up and put four slices of wholemeal bread into the large toaster, turning around when Mary walked into the room.

'Good morning.' Mary looked excited before she smiled contritely at Cat, as she had been doing ever since refusing, yet again, to tell her who her dad was. 'The bonfire and fireworks were rather good, weren't they?'

'So was the food,' Kyra added, glancing at Cat. 'You missed a really superb buffet, Mum. And that blackberry Pavlova was to die for.'

Mary gave Cat a curious look. 'Didn't you have any food?'

'She had a headache,' Kyra said, 'and left early.'

'Are you unwell, Catherine?'

Cat sighed. 'No. I'm fine.'

'Are you sure? You do look a little peaky.'

'I said I'm fine, Mum.'

Mary darted a look at Kyra before smiling wanly at Cat. 'That's good. Because I have some exciting news I want to share.'

'Oh?' Cat eyed her warily as she poured herself another coffee.

'Is it about Granny Viola?' Kyra asked. 'Has she come out of her coma?'

'Sadly not.' Mary furrowed her brows. 'But you know that because you and Catherine visited her yesterday, didn't you?'

Kyra nodded. 'Yeah. But I thought the hospital might've called you this morning, or something. So what's the exciting news then, Gran?'

Mary beamed at them. 'Jeremy has asked me to marry him. And naturally, I've said yes.'

Cat stared from her to Kyra and back again, her mouth wide open in disbelief.

'You've done what?'

'I knew you probably wouldn't be thrilled, Catherine. You seem to have taken an instant dislike to him, and since I refused to tell you about your father, it seems neither of us can do anything right. But he makes me happy and I'm not getting any younger. I don't want to spend my life alone. He's handsome, kind and considerate. And he's doing a wonderful job on this house.'

'Which is costing you a small fortune. I overheard the two of you yesterday. "Another ten thousand pounds", I heard him say. I assume that means you've already given him one lot of ten thousand pounds. I can't see even one thousand pounds worth of work, let alone ten or twenty.'

Mary stuck out her chin. 'That's because you have no comprehension of the cost of things, Catherine. Or the amount of work that needs doing. The entire house requires rewiring, for one thing, and that's not cheap. Plus a large portion of the money is to pay for goods that are on order. The new marble for my ensuite, for example. That's coming all the way from Italy. You can't get the marble I want from this country. You have to pay for items like that in advance, not on delivery.'

'Isla got some lovely fake marble tiles from the local DIY store for the bathroom in Bonniemount Cottage,' Kyra said. 'It only cost a couple of hundred pounds to do the whole room, didn't it, Mum?'

Cat nodded. 'It did.'

'I don't want fake marble, thank you very much. I want the real thing.'

'I thought you were planning on selling this

house,' Cat said. 'OK, perhaps rewiring is a good and sensible expense, but don't you think spending a fortune on an ensuite is throwing money away?'

'No. Jeremy says it'll add value.'

'And what does Natalia say? She's the estate agent who's going to be selling it, isn't she? Don't you think it might be wise to ask her opinion?'

'No, Catherine. I don't. Jeremy does this sort of thing for a living and he knows what does and doesn't add value. With the greatest of respect to Natalia, she's only handled property in Merriment Bay and the surrounding area. Jeremy has refurbished houses in London so he knows the market there. And that, after all, is where we're most likely to find a buyer.'

'So now you're saying you won't be giving Natalia the instruction?'

'I'm not saying that. I'm simply saying that I'll be strongly suggesting she markets the property in one or two of the upmarket magazines or in conjunction with a London agent, perhaps. Which was always my intention. But it just so happens that Jeremy has a friend who is a partner in a London firm.'

'I bet he does.'

'And what's that supposed to mean?'

'Mum! Gran! Can we stop this please?' Kyra pleaded. She shook her head and sighed as they both fell silent. 'I have to be honest, Gran and say that I'm not sure about Jeremy, either. But if you've just got engaged then we should be congratulating you, not arguing with you. And Mum. I hate to point this out, but for the past eighteen years – well, not eighteen, but ever since I was old enough to listen – you've been telling me that Gran and Granny Viola made you miserable because they didn't like Dad. All you wanted was for them to give him a chance. So don't you think that we should now give Jeremy a chance? If Gran loves him and he makes her happy, isn't that enough for us to be happy for her?'

Cat stared at Kyra, emotion sweeping over her, making her unable to speak right away. She looked at Mary and back at Kyra and eventually smiled.

'I've said it before and I'll say it again. I'm glad you get your brains from your dad, sweetheart. You're right.' She smiled at Mary. 'If you love him and he makes you happy, then I'll try to give him a chance, Mum. I'll try to see what you see in him.'

Mary swallowed hard and blinked several times. 'Oh, Catherine. You don't know how pleased I am to hear you say that. This means the world to me.'

'Congratulations, Gran,' Kyra said, beaming at them. 'Have you got any champagne? Shouldn't we be celebrating?'

'Where is he anyway?' Cat asked. 'I haven't seen or heard him yet this morning?'

Mary grinned. 'He's gone to London to buy me a ring. There's champagne in the fridge, Kyra. Use my favourite crystal glasses.'

'He proposed before he'd bought the ring?' Kyra pulled a face as she got up to get the champagne and glasses. 'That's a bit weird.'

Mary laughed like a teenager. 'He was planning to go and buy the ring today and he was intending to propose next week. But he said last night was just so perfect and that I looked so beautiful he simply couldn't help himself. He got down on one knee as we walked home across the bridge. It was so romantic, with the moon throwing silver sparkles into the River Wynter and the smell of bonfire smoke as the embers slowly burnt away. He took me in his arms and we started dancing on the bridge as he sang 'Moon River' in his best Frank Sinatra voice. He looks a bit like Frank Sinatra did in his fifties, don't you think? He's a big Sinatra fan. What was I saying? Oh yes, we danced on the bridge and then he stopped suddenly, looked into my eyes and got down on one knee and popped the question. I'm not going to tell you the exact words, because I know you, for one, Kyra, will screw up your pretty little nose and pull faces. But it was wonderful.' She gave a long soft sigh and stared dreamily into the distance.

'OK,' Cat said, smiling. 'Perhaps I have misjudged him. That does sound quite romantic. Congratulations, Mum. I hope you'll both be very happy.'

'I just wish Mother was here to share my joy.' Mary slumped into a chair at the kitchen table and Kyra handed her a glass of champagne. 'Although knowing her, I don't suppose she'll be best pleased by the turn of events either. I'd better wait until she's fully recovered before I break the news to her. She is a big Frank Sinatra fan though, just like Jeremy. I told him we used to watch all Sinatra's films together on Sunday afternoons. He did the same with his mother when he was young, so we have that in common too.'

Cat didn't have the heart to say that, the way things stood, it was looking less and less likely that Granny Viola would ever fully recover. If she even woke up at all.

'Congratulations, Mum,' she said, raising her glass in the air. 'Here's to you and Jeremy and your bright new future together.'

Chapter Thirty-One

'This isn't a date,' Cat repeatedly told her reflection in the full-length mirror in her room as she dressed for dinner. She told herself the same thing, but silently, as Mary drove her and Kyra to Amias' house in the bay. Which was a complete surprise. Both because Mary offered to drive them, and because she didn't make any sarcastic or caustic comments about why they would want to have dinner with Amias in the first place.

The next surprise of the evening was Amias' house.

Mary pulled up a short distance from the door. It seemed she couldn't bring herself to pull up on the driveway. She stopped at the end of the private road which led to the three new houses standing above the bay.

They weren't brand new. They looked as if they'd been there for a few years now, but when Cat was last in the bay, eighteen years ago, all that had been here were sand dunes and a cliff overlooking the sweep of sand and sea below.

Even then, as she, Kyle and Amias had sat on that cliff, looking out across the sea to the sun setting on the horizon, Amias had said that one day he'd build a house up here. He'd also said that Kyle could design it and they'd actually drawn sketches of what it might look like, while Cat had drawn a sketch of what she would have built there for her dream home.

None of the three houses looked like those sketches, at least, not from the front.

'That one on the right is his, I believe.' Mary pointed to the largest of the three.

'Wow,' Cat said, 'I know you said this was a posh new house, Mum but this looks like something you'd see featured in a magazine.'

'Yes. Well. I'll say one thing for him,' Mary added grudgingly. 'The man seems to have acquired rather good taste in certain areas. Would you like me to come and pick you up? You won't stay for more than a couple of hours, will you?'

Cat grinned. 'I have no idea how long we'll be. But please don't worry, Mum. You do whatever you've got planned tonight. Kyra and I will either walk home, or we'll call a cab.'

Mary hadn't argued. She was expecting Jeremy back from London at some point during the evening, Cat knew that, and would no doubt be celebrating. And with a sparkling new ring on her finger.

Cat waved her mum goodbye and, linking arms with Kyra, walked across a block-paved area towards the house to their right.

The house stood the farthest away from the

road, on the highest part of the cliff, which meant it overlooked the roofs of the other two houses, and yet it was set a little farther forward, towards the sea, which would give it a 360° view of the entire area.

To the right of it was a small copse of trees, perched somewhat precariously on the undulating grassy slope of the cliff. Had they been there eighteen years ago? Cat couldn't recall. There had definitely been some bushes, which were still there. A fence, made to look like driftwood, enclosed part of this area but the rest was open.

The block paving, on which a Land Rover Discovery was parked with several surfboards strapped to the roof rack, gave way to a pale turquoise wooden decking, the colour of the sea on a hot summer day. The front door was an impressive blue-grey smoked glass affair, set between pale blue, timber cladding boards the length and height of the frontage with only four exceedingly large, no doubt floor to ceiling windows to break up the expanse; two on each level, it seemed, and one central oriel window between the two on the second floor. The oriel had wooden corbels etched with carvings of dolphins leaping from waves.

Kyra rang the video doorbell, and Cat made sure her hair covered the scar on her face.

'Come in.' A cheery female voice greeted them almost instantaneously via the speaker. 'Give the door a shove. It's heavier than it looks.'

Before they had a chance, the door opened and

Amias stood in front of them and smiled.

'Welcome to my humble abode.' He stepped aside to let them enter.

'Humble?' Cat threw him a sarcastic grin. 'I don't think there's anything humble about this place. And that includes its owner.'

He raised his brows and grinned. 'It's just a house made of wood, some bricks and a few concrete pilings. Unfortunately, the pilings were a necessary evil.'

'It's not what I'd imagined.' She glanced around the hall; the pale blue painted wooden floor blended perfectly with the even paler blue walls.

'Oh?' A hint of concern flitted across his eyes. 'Are you disappointed?'

'On the contrary. I'm impressed. Very impressed.'

He beamed at them and laughed. 'In that case, you can stay. Let me take your coats.'

He was helping Cat out of hers before she knew what was happening and, as a hint of his aftershave pervaded her nostrils, inappropriate thoughts invaded her mind.

'Are you hot?' he asked, giving her a curious look as he then took Kyra's coat.

'W-what? Oh.' Her hands shot to her cheeks as the blush spread across her face. 'Um, it's a little warm in here after the cold outside, that's all.'

She coughed and looked away. What a good thing he couldn't read her mind.

He opened a door and hung their coats on

hangers in the closet.

'Natalia and Josh are already here.'

'Was it Natalia who answered the bell? I didn't recognise her voice. I thought it might be…'

'Might be…?' He prompted, frowning just a little.

'Your girlfriend or someone.'

'I don't have a girlfriend at the moment, Cat.'

Why did that sound almost like an invitation? It certainly sounded sexy as he had softly emphasised her name. Or was her imagination running wild yet again?

'Oh? That's almost as surprising as this house.'

Even to her, the laugh she gave sounded a trifle hysterical. As if she was trying really hard to be funny. And failing miserably.

'It's this way.' He nodded towards a glass flight of stairs. 'Would you like to elaborate?'

'No, she wouldn't,' Kyra said, grabbing Cat's elbow and propelling her forward. 'Mum's had a bit of a shock today. We both have. It's taking a little while to sink in.'

'What kind of a shock?' He stopped in his tracks. 'Has something happened to Viola?' He looked and sounded concerned.

'No. To Granny Mary.' Kyra grinned.

He seemed completely bemused. 'Is it serious? God, Cat. Why didn't you let me know? We could've … You're both grinning. Is this some sort of joke?'

'We were hoping it was,' Cat said. 'Sadly it's

not. Mum's engaged to the builder, Jeremy Stone.'

'Who? The man she met in the pub a few weeks ago, you mean?'

Cat nodded. 'The very same.'

'These stairs are a bit intimidating,' Kyra said, stepping on to the first one and hurrying to the top. 'Apart from being a bit frightening by being made of glass, I'm glad I'm wearing trousers. You wouldn't want to walk up these wearing a dress and no knickers, would you, Mum?'

'Kyra!' Cat blushed a deeper crimson than her dress. 'I'm wearing knickers,' she said, stupidly glancing over her shoulder at Amias and immediately regretting it.

The shock and surprise on his face about Mary, morphed into a massive grin.

'Thanks for sharing. But you needn't worry. I don't have hidden cameras. And even if I did, the glass on the other side of the treads has a special coating so you can only see through them if you're walking up or down them, not if you're standing beneath. A few women who weren't ... Um.' He cleared his throat.

Kyra burst out laughing. 'A few women who weren't wearing knickers have mentioned that before, were you going to say?'

Cat dashed up the stairs as fast as the tight skirt of her dress would let her.

'Let's just say, it's been brought to my attention before, that some women might not like them,' Amias said, following closely behind Cat.

'I like them,' Cat mumbled. 'I've always liked glass stairs.'

'Are you discussing those bloody awful stairs?' A stunning woman who looked so much like Amias that you would know she was his sister even if you didn't know he had one, greeted them at the top, grinning broadly. 'Hello, Cat. You're looking lovely. It's been years since I last saw you. I don't think you've changed a bit. And this must be Kyra. I've heard so much about you from Amias. And he's right. You do look just like your dad. Sorry. I'm Natalia. It's great to finally meet you. Oh, and this is my husband, Josh.' She hugged both Cat and Kyra as she spoke, before they had a chance to say a word.

'Hi,' Josh said, clearly unsure of what he was supposed to do. He hung back a little and smiled.

'Natalia. It's so good to see you again. You've certainly changed. I think you still had pigtails the last time I saw you. You've grown into a beautiful young woman. And Josh. You're as handsome as we all knew you'd be. Listen to me. I sound as if I am so much older than the pair of you when in reality, I think there's only about four or five years between us.'

'Four between us,' Josh said. 'Five between you and Natalia. Would you mind if I gave you a hug?' He threw an odd look at Amias as if he was trying to tell him something.

'No. I don't mind at all.'

Cat held out her arms and Josh gave her a brief

hug. He gave Kyra an even briefer hug.

'You definitely do look like Kyle,' he said, smiling at Kyra. 'But you've got Cat's eyes and her smile, I think.'

'That'll be quite enough of that.' Natalia grabbed his arm and linked hers through it, laughing. 'Not that I'm a possessive shrew or anything, you understand, Kyra. But girls as gorgeous as you give us oldies pause for thought. And my husband used to have the biggest crush imaginable on your mum, when we were young.'

Josh went bright red. 'I did not! She's teasing. Oh. Not that you weren't really pretty, Cat, because you were. And I may have said so once or twice. But I've only ever had eyes for Nat and she knows it.'

Natalia winked. 'That's true. I do. That's why I married him. I couldn't let the poor man pine away for me all his life, could I, Amias?'

Amias narrowed his eyes a fraction before a smile crept onto his lips. 'No, sister dear. You couldn't. Let's go into the lounge. I'll get Cat and Kyra some drinks and then, perhaps, you could give me a quick hand in the kitchen? Cat, would you like wine? Or something else? And Kyra? What can I get for you?'

'We'll both have wine, please,' Cat said. 'Red, if that's OK.' She followed Natalia from the spacious hall into a massive room.

'And Mum can give you a hand if you like,' Kyra offered. 'She's really good in the kitchen.'

A gasp escaped Cat. At the same time, a snort of laughter burst from Natalia, who turned it into an odd little cough.

Something strange was going on tonight. Cat was certain of it. She glared at Kyra before darting a look at Amias. He appeared almost terrified.

'Oh. Er. That's kind. But I'm cooking one of Natalia's recipes so I really need her to check I've got it right.'

He walked towards what looked like a large cocktail cabinet and opened a folding door. One side of the cabinet held a shelf stacked with various bottles of spirits and liqueurs with a rack of wine beneath; a central part was shelves and hanging sections for a variety of glasses and the third part was actually a fridge. He took a bottle of red wine from the rack and an open bottle of white wine from the fridge.

'I thought you said we were just having pasta and wine,' Kyra said. 'That's what you told Mum.'

'We are. But with a sauce Natalia makes.' He handed the open bottle to Josh.

'I'm sure Cat will be able to tell you if it's good or not,' Natalia said, grinning. 'And she may be able to make some suggestions to improve your skills, um, in the kitchen. Don't be shy, Amias. I'm sure she won't mind if your kitchen's in a bit of a mess.'

He removed the cork from the bottle of red, retrieved two wine glasses from the cabinet, and having filled them, handed one each to Cat and Kyra.

'But Cat's a guest and it's not polite to ask guests to help you cook.'

'Mum doesn't mind at all. Do you, Mum?'

'Clearly, Amias doesn't want me in the kitchen.'

'He wants you anywhere he can get you,' Natalia said. 'Whoops. Did I just say that out loud? Sorry. Um. It was just a friendly joke.'

'Excuse Natalia, Cat.' Amias looked less than pleased. 'Her sarcasm and humour aren't for everyone. Sometimes she forgets that.'

'He's right. I do. And he's also right about not asking guests to help, so I'll give him a hand. You and Kyra can stay here and admire the view. And I don't mean Josh. I mean the view of the bay and the village.' She nodded towards a row of four sets of French windows along the facing wall which also had a sizeable raised fireplace and brick hearth at its centre. 'There's a large balcony outside, but it's a bit too cold to sit out there tonight.'

Cat turned and looked at Amias.

'You built the balcony? And the terrace from the kitchen? Do you have that too?'

He nodded. A little sadly perhaps. 'Yes. The kitchen is downstairs opposite the front door and the terrace wraps around three sides of the house and into the cliff. There's a snug in which to curl up and watch the sunset on cold winter nights if you don't want to be up here, a study from where you can watch the sunrise, the kitchen, which due to its position jutting out as a wide triangle, benefits from both sunrise and sunset, and a utility room, a shower and loo on that floor.'

Cat stared at him for a moment or two.

'That all sounds very familiar. Is that why you didn't want me to see it?'

He shook his head and ran a hand through his hair, giving a little laugh as he did so.

'No. That's not what that was about. That was something else entirely. But anyway, the house is a little different for practical purposes. There's access to the beach with wooden steps down from the terrace to the sand. And I'm happy for you and Kyra to see it. I'm happy for you to see anything you want. You can go over the entire house from top to bottom. In fact, I hope you do. I'd like to know what you think.'

'I think I should charge you commission.' Her tone reflected her mood. She was more than a little upset.

'What's going on?' Kyra asked.

'Yes,' Natalia added. 'I'd quite like to know what this conversation is about.'

Amias took a small breath, shook his head and forced a smile. 'Basically, the design of my house is very similar to one that Cat sketched many years ago.'

'Of my dream home.'

He met her eyes and nodded.

'Of your dream home.'

'Wow,' Kyra said. 'You both wanted the same dream home. That must mean something.'

'It means we spent far too much time daydreaming,' Cat said. 'And look where that got us.'

'Mum. You're not cross because Amias built your dream home, are you?'

Cat shook her head. 'I'm very surprised. At the time, I seem to remember you criticised it quite a lot.' She narrowed her eyes at Amias.

He shrugged. 'You're right. I did. I was an idiot. I did make a few changes though. Especially in the master bedroom.'

'What? Did you add mirrors to the ceiling? And a secret passage so that you could escape whenever you wanted?'

'Mum!'

'I'm sorry. I shouldn't have said that. I didn't mean it.'

Amias scanned her face. 'That's OK, Cat. As I said. I was an idiot back then.'

'Well,' Natalia said, grabbing Amias by the arm. 'We'd better get to the kitchen before something boils over. Josh, darling, keep Cat and Kyra entertained, will you please?'

'Er.' Josh looked confused, as if he had no idea what was going on. 'Of course.'

Amias glanced at Cat as he allowed himself to be led towards the stairs.

'What the hell was that about, Mum?' Kyra demanded, completely ignoring the fact that Josh was there.

Cat walked over to one of the sets of windows

and peered out across the bay. The view was spectacular. Miles and miles of sea and sky; the lights from the village; the darkness of the surrounding countryside, a few houses dotted here and there, apparent from sporadic single lights; the moon and the stars beyond. All, just as she had imagined it, when she had drawn the sketch of her dream home all those years ago.

'It was about the fact that our dreams are dangerous things, Kyra. We need to share them with people who will keep them safe. Not with people who will steal them away from you without you even realising.'

Kyra came and stood beside her, lowering her voice so that only Cat could hear.

'Are you actually saying that you think Amias has stolen the plans for your dream home? And you're annoyed with him for that?'

Cat shook her head. 'No. He's stolen my dreams and made them his. But he hasn't included me. And somehow, that's the worst betrayal of all.'

Chapter Thirty-Two

'OK,' Natalia said, as she and Amias walked into his kitchen. 'Would you like to tell me what just happened?'

Amias shook his head. 'I'm not sure I can. I'm not sure I know. But I do know one thing. There is absolutely no point in me trying to get Cat alone tonight, and definitely not in telling her how I feel or asking if I can even hold her hand, let alone kiss her. I saw the look in her eyes just now. It's a look I've seen before. Several times, in fact. Lorna had the same look on her face the evening she threw the glass of wine in mine. And I've seen it on the faces of a few women before her, when I've ended things with them. It's a look of disappointment. Disillusionment. Dislike.'

'Why? You've done nothing to disappoint Cat tonight. Is this about some sketch she drew one hundred or so years ago?'

He smirked. 'Nineteen years ago, to be precise. Shortly after she started dating Kyle. And yes. I think it's about the sketch. I loved that house she sketched, but like the jerk I was back then, I criticised all of it. I didn't want her to know that she

249

had just drawn the house of my dreams. Only the gold star version, not the crappy one I'd envisioned. And she was dating Kyle. How could I say, "God, Cat. I want to live in that house. I want to live in that house with you. I want us to sit on that terrace and watch the sunset. And to lie in bed with you in the morning and look up into the skylight and watch dark blue turn to gold as the sun rises in the East." That would've gone down really well.'

'If you'd said that back then, I would've thought you'd hit your head. "Dark blue turn to gold," indeed.' Natalia tutted and rolled her eyes. 'But I still don't see the problem. Surely she should be thrilled that you loved her sketch so much you used it to build your dream home?'

He nodded. 'I stupidly thought she would be. But she's not. Far from it. I think she feels betrayed or something. Almost as if I've ripped the world from under her feet. I don't know. I could ask her, I suppose. But I don't think I'd like the answer. I'm sorry, Natalia. But it looks like I'm going to be pining for a whole lot longer. Perhaps for the rest of my life.'

Natalia slapped him on the arm. 'Don't be so bloody melodramatic. If you're going to let some stupid sketch get in the way of telling the woman you love that you love her, then frankly, you deserve to spend the rest of your life pining. Don't be a jerk. Talk it over with her. Discuss it. Have a conversation. That's what grown-ups do.'

'I don't know. Where would I start?'

'At the beginning, you plonker. That first day you saw her on the beach. Start from there.'

'OK. But not tonight. It just doesn't feel right.'

'You know what? I'm beginning to think you don't really love her at all. Not the real her. I think you're in love with a fantasy. Of some dream you had half a lifetime ago. Because if you really did love her, you wouldn't keep making excuses. Last night was too perfect. Tonight doesn't feel right. Sometimes you've just got to take a chance. And if you're not going to do that, Amias, then there's really no point. Think about that. But in the meantime, add some oregano to that sauce, and a smattering of paprika and let's get this dinner started. Somehow I don't think it's going to be the fun evening we were all hoping for.'

Amias frowned. 'Fine. Wait. How do you know it needs oregano and paprika? You haven't even tasted it.'

Natalia tutted again. 'I don't need to taste it. I know you. Do as I say. I'll grab the plates from the warming rack and the garlic bread from the oven. Is the salad in your snazzy cooler?'

'Yes. I'll bring that.'

He added the oregano and paprika to the sauce and stirred it well before mixing it with the pasta he was draining when Cat and Kyra had arrived. He and Natalia filled separate trays with plates, cutlery, pepper and salt grinders, a bowl of grated Parmesan, a bowl of sliced jalapeno chilli peppers, a mixed green salad and a sliced raw onion and tomato salad.

'I think that's everything.'

'Perhaps you should slice up your heart and serve that on a platter.' Natalia gave him a playful nudge. 'Come on. Smile. Put on a brave face. You can do this.'

'Yeah. What's one more night after eighteen years' worth of nights?'

They took the food upstairs and Amias was relieved to see that Cat, Kyra and Josh seemed to be having a friendly discussion and that Cat was smiling again.

'Dinner's ready,' Natalia said, nodding her head in the direction of the dining room which was next door to the lounge.

Cat met Amias' eye but she quickly looked away. She followed Kyra into the dining room and stood behind a seat as far away from Amias as she could get, he noticed. As if she hadn't made her point so unmistakably already.

Amias took the red wine he had decanted earlier, and the white he had placed in the ice bucket on the table and offered them to his guests. Natalia and Josh were both drinking white this evening so he passed them the bottle and the ice bucket and they served themselves. He poured red for Cat, Kyra and himself.

'It's a casual evening, so help yourselves to the food, or I'll serve if you prefer.'

'No thanks.' Natalia threw him a grin. 'I've seen your portions. No pun intended.' She winked at him. 'We'll help ourselves. You're OK with that

252

aren't you, Cat?'

'Yes. That's fine.'

'So,' Amias said, desperate to get Cat to look at him. 'Mary is engaged. I must admit, I didn't see that coming.'

'Mary's engaged?' Natalia looked astonished. 'Since when?'

'Since last night,' Cat replied. 'She told us this morning. Jeremy went to London today to buy the ring.'

'He proposed without a ring?' Josh was clearly surprised.

'It was a spur of the moment thing,' Kyra said. 'And quite romantic, considering.'

'Considering what?' Natalia asked.

'Considering it was Jeremy.'

They all grinned, apart from Cat. Amias watched her for a moment until she looked up and saw him staring.

'How do you feel about it?' He had to think of something quickly. 'I mean, it is a bit sudden, isn't it?'

'Just because you don't believe in love, Amias, it doesn't mean it doesn't exist. Some people fall in love very quickly. Some people fall in love at first sight.'

'Wait. What makes you think I don't believe in love?'

'Well, do you? Have you ever been in love?'

He swallowed hard, grabbed his wine and swallowed that before looking directly at her.

'As it happens, yes. Yes, Cat. I have.'

'What happened?' Kyra asked.

He dragged his gaze from Cat. 'It didn't work out. It seems my love was unrequited. She didn't love me.'

'I … I didn't know that,' Cat said. She looked as if she was stunned by his admission. 'But then I wouldn't, would I? I've been away for eighteen years. Was it anyone I would've known?' She fiddled with the stem of her wine glass and wouldn't meet his eye.

He wanted to shout out, right then and there, 'It's you, Cat. You were the woman I was in love with. Still am in love with. Will probably always be in love with.' But he didn't.

Instead he said, 'Yes. You knew her. Although perhaps not as well as you thought you did. But it was a long time ago.'

Natalia gave him a questioning look and so did Josh. For some reason, Kyra looked at Cat. Oddly enough, her expression was one of concern. As if Cat might be upset by this revelation. But of course that was ridiculous.

'When's the wedding, Cat?' Josh asked.

'What wedding? Oh. Mum's you mean? I don't know. She didn't say. I think she's hoping Granny Viola will come out of her coma first.'

'Is that likely?' Josh glanced around the table.

'I don't think so,' Kyra said. 'But Mum and Gran still hold out hope.'

'Hope's important,' Amias said. 'Sometimes

254

it's the only thing that keeps us getting up every day.

'Yes. I agree.' Cat still wouldn't look at him. 'But sometimes it's false. And that's the worst kind of hope there is. The doctors don't seem as hopeful as Mum and me. And unless things change soon, we may have to make a decision neither of us wants to make.'

Amias knew how that felt. 'If there's anything I can do, please just say. I'd be more than happy to help in any way I can. Even if you just need a shoulder to … to cry on.'

He was regretting that offer already. If she cried on his shoulder, he would definitely want to take her in his arms and comfort her. And more. Much more. He'd want to kiss away her tears and … No. He mustn't even think about that.

'Is Jeremy moving in?' Natalia asked. 'Now that they're engaged.'

Cat gave a snort of derision. 'He already has to all intents and purposes. He spends more time at Devon Villa than he does at wherever he's supposed to be staying. And he was only supposed to be in Merriment Bay for one week when Mum first met him. He said he was thinking of buying around here and was sussing the place out. But that one week extended without an expiration date once he started doing so much work at the house.'

'Work? What sort of work?' Natalia looked concerned. 'I know Mary said that she was considering a bit of refurbishment in order to get a better price. Is that what he's doing?'

'If you call ordering marble from Italy at some exorbitant cost, and having the ensuite to Mum's room completely rebuilt, along with having the entire house rewired, amongst other things, then yes, that's what he's doing.'

'Marble from Italy?' Amias said. 'Why? I know it's still regarded by many as the best in the world but there are some very good marbles available at half the price. And some incredible artificial stone.'

Natalia raised her brows and pulled a face at Amias.

'Says the man who had to have the timber for his oriel window from a certain firm no one except him and the super-rich has ever heard of because they're so exclusive.'

'Apparently only Italian marble is good enough for Mum. Which is odd, because although she's always been a bit of a snob, she always liked a bargain and if she could get something similar for half the price, she would, regardless of where it came from. Providing it was legal, of course.'

'I'm not convinced Italian marble will add that much to the value,' Josh said. 'Although sometimes it's the strangest things that make a person determined to buy one house rather than another. But it's the view that'll sell Devon Villa more than anything, and its original features. Rewiring is a good move, as is replacing outdated fixtures and fittings from the seventies, like avocado bathroom suites and such, but only if what they're replaced with is either in keeping with the era, or so ultra-modern and luxurious that people simply must have it. Italian marble may fall into that category, but I still think it's an unnecessary expense for Devon Villa. And unless the rest of the fittings are in keeping, it just won't work.'

'Perhaps you could tell Mum that.'

'I'll happily tell her. If she asks. We both will, won't we, darling?'

Natalia nodded vigorously. 'You bet we will. I wonder if perhaps it might be an idea for me to pop round. Just on the pretence of a catch up to see where we are regarding the sale. Would that be useful?'

'Yes. I think it would. Or you could just pop in for coffee and I could say I'd invited you as a friend. That way, Jeremy won't think we're going behind his back and get all defensive.'

'Does he do that then?' Amias furrowed his brow. 'Get defensive, I mean? Because that's an odd thing for a builder to do if he's genuine and above board. I'm not saying he isn't. But the builders Dad used for his house and Natalia's and the ones I used for this, were more than happy to have input from experienced people and other professionals. Obviously, no one likes to be criticised, but ideas and suggestions always went down well.'

'From what I've seen of Jeremy, he seems to decide what he wants to do and then persuades

257

Mum it needs to be done. I've kept out of it, really. It's not my place to come back after eighteen years and start to tell her what she should and shouldn't do in her own home. Well, hers and Granny Viola's. But I heard him asking her for more money. I won't say how much because that would be wrong, but it was rather a lot and I was surprised. But when I brought it up this morning, I got the Italian marble story and when I said I didn't like him, Kyra reminded me – and rightly so, that no one likes the person they love to be criticised by their family members. Mum was so excited about the engagement and I said I'd give the man a chance.' Now she did finally look at Amias. 'Kyra said you might ask around about him. Did you get a chance to do that?'

Damn. He'd completely forgotten about that.

'No. I'm sorry. I was so intent on finding out about Bailey Mitchell that it completely slipped my mind. I'll definitely do it though. And I'll let you know what I find out.'

Cat returned her attention to her plate. 'Thanks. Or you could tell Natalia and she could tell me.'

So that was it. Cat didn't even want to see him again. Was that going to be until she'd cooled off about whatever it was that had upset her? Or was this now a firm decision? She'd cut off all contact with him once before. And he hadn't seen her again for eighteen years. Well, not to speak to, at least.

'Whatever suits you best. Would you like to hear about Bailey Mitchell now?'

'That is why we're here,' Cat said, without looking at him. 'Although this pasta is delicious, Amias. Natalia, you must give me the recipe for this sauce. Unless it's a family secret.'

Natalia threw a look at Amias. 'No. No family secret. I'll happily share it with you.'

'Tell us everything you know about Bailey Mitchell,' Kyra said, grinning at Amias and rubbing her hands together. 'Including any sordid details.'

He smiled at her. 'The RAF doesn't keep those types of details. But luckily for you, I know a man who does. That is, I know someone who knew your Bailey Mitchell.'

'Really?' Cat glanced at him and he smiled but she quickly looked at Kyra.

'Yes. He knew Viola, too. And her sister, Ivy.'

'Ivy? The pilot?' Kyra was very excited. 'That'll please Gran. She said she was always more interested to hear about Ivy than she was about her own mum's life in the war, but Granny Viola wouldn't talk about her sister. Or about any of it much.'

'And I think I may know why.'

'Why?' Cat looked directly at him.

'Because Bailey Mitchell was engaged to Ivy Devon.'

Chapter Thirty-Three

Cat couldn't have heard him correctly. Had Amias just said that Bailey Mitchell and Ivy Devon were engaged? But that didn't make sense.

'I don't understand.' Cat tried to avoid eye contact with Amias. She had been trying to do that ever since they had sat down, but every time she glanced in his direction, his gaze seemed to be fixed on her.

'Neither do I,' Kyra said. 'Both you and Gran said that Granny Viola was always hugging the photo and the letters. Unopened letters addressed to her. If Bailey was engaged to Ivy, why would he be writing to Viola? Unless he was writing about Ivy. You said she died in January 1945.'

Cat nodded. 'She did. I remember seeing her death certificate once when I was searching for my birth certificate.'

'Your birth certificate?' Kyra looked as if a penny had just dropped. 'But, Mum. Doesn't that give the name of your–'

'No, sweetheart. It doesn't. And we're discussing Ivy and Viola.'

Cat glanced at Natalia and Josh and hoped

Kyra got the message. She shouldn't have mentioned her birth certificate. She wasn't going to discuss with Natalia and Josh that Mary was the only listed parent.

It still astonished her that Granny Viola had allowed that. Information on birth certificates could be accessed by almost anyone, if they had a few details. The fact that both her mum and Granny Viola would rather people saw a blank than her dad's actual name, had always made her think that her dad must have been someone very bad indeed. That was one of the reasons she hadn't been that concerned about knowing who he was.

And now, as she had just discovered, they would also have preferred people to think that Alwick Wells might be the father, rather than divulge the truth, that worry was only accentuated. Except her mum had said he had a wife, two children, and apparently a mother who had been willing to go to extraordinary lengths to keep his identity a secret. Cat still couldn't decide whether that meant the man was even worse than she feared, or just some unhappy soul who couldn't stay faithful to his wife and would rather people didn't find out.

'So if Ivy died in 1945,' Natalia was saying, 'when did Bailey write the letters? Was it before or after?'

Cat looked at Kyra and they both shook their heads.

'I didn't really look at the dates,' Kyra

261

admitted.

'Neither did I,' Cat said. 'But I think I recall seeing a 1945 date, so either around the time of Ivy's death, or after. We'll check.'

'And where did he send them from?' Amias asked. 'He was stationed at RAF Merriment and Viola was a WAAF. I discovered that, but I assume you already knew, from what you've said. They would probably have seen each other on a daily basis. Why would he write to her? If, on the other hand, they were posted from Canada, that's a different matter.'

Natalia coughed. 'Perhaps he had something to tell her and didn't have the courage to say it to her face. Could that be it, Amias?'

'Possibly.' He narrowed his eyes at his sister as if her comment had irritated him. 'But why didn't Viola open them? Unless she knew what they said and she didn't want to hear it. Or read it.'

'Wow,' Kyra said. 'Are you suggesting that you think Bailey might have been in love with Viola even though he was engaged to Ivy? I don't know whether to be pleased or annoyed about that. I mean, on the one hand it's really romantic. But on the other, they were sisters. To be engaged to one, whilst writing love letters to the other is a bit crappy.'

'We don't know if they were love letters,' Cat reasoned. 'We're just assuming they are because Mum and I saw Granny Viola hugging them and the photo too many times to count. But perhaps they were letters telling her that her sister had died and how much Bailey missed her, and as she already knew those things, she didn't want to read about them.'

'Nope.' Kyra shook her head. 'That can't be the case. It would've been incredibly rude of her not to reply to her sister's fiancé. From what you and Gran have said about Granny Viola, she wouldn't have done that. She would've opened at least one and replied. And if the contents had upset her, she could've simply asked him not to write to her again. I think he loved them both. And he couldn't make up his mind between them. That happens, doesn't it, Mum?'

Kyra was obviously referring to Cat's confession about being in love with Amias and also with Kyle, and she shot a look at Amias before frowning at Kyra.

'Yes, sweetheart. That does happen.'

Natalia refilled her glass, along with Josh's and pointed at Cat's and Kyra's glasses as if telling Amias he might like to do the same with theirs. He clearly got the message because he picked up the decanter and did so.

'What I don't get,' Cat said, 'is why Viola would constantly hug the letters, and more importantly, Bailey's photo, unless Kyra's right about him loving them both, and Viola loved him back. She wouldn't hug a photo of her sister's fiancé for more than seventy years, would she? Unless she really loved him. And perhaps, felt guilty about it.'

'There's one way to find out,' Josh said. He had been looking thoughtful but hadn't said a word for a while. 'Now that you know who the man is, and that he was engaged to Ivy, you could open the letters.'

Cat immediately shook her head. 'No. I can't do that. Knowing this, somehow makes those letters even more private.' She glanced at Amias. 'You said you have Bailey's address? May I have it, please? I'm going to write to him and tell him we found his photo amongst some unopened letters. I'm not going to say that we know about him and Ivy. I'll simply tell him about Granny Viola and say that we believe they were friends during the war and we thought he might want to know. The rest is up to him. And if Granny Viola ever does wake up from her coma, I'm going to say the same to her. I'm not sure if we should tell Mum about this new development just yet, Kyra.'

Kyra shrugged. 'That's fine with me. Gran can hardly tell us off for keeping secrets.'

'I've got some photos of Ivy and Bailey if you'd like to see them.' Amias pushed his chair away from the table.

'Photos? Photos of Ivy and Bailey?' Cat glanced from him to Kyra and back again. 'When were you going to tell us about these?' She laughed, despite herself and the fact that she was still annoyed with him.

'I was going to tell you when the time was right. Which is now.'

'Really? Where did you get these photos from? Were they in the archives at the museum?'

'A couple were. But most of them I got from men and women formerly stationed here. Now don't get mad.' He gave her a little grin. 'I didn't mention any names and I didn't show Bailey's photo to anyone. I simply posted on the museum website that I was looking for photographs, and details of people who were stationed here, for a project I was working on for the anniversary of The Battle of Britain, which will be eighty years ago in 2020. RAF Merriment played a part in that. An important part. Will and I are going to be holding some sort of celebratory event, so it wasn't a lie. Anyway, the response was amazing. I still haven't been through all the letters I've received, so there may be more photos and more details about Ivy and Bailey. He may even have written to me himself. Although I have been checking the envelopes for Canadian postmarks since I discovered his name and where he lives.'

He handed Cat a pile of black and white photos, some badly faded and some almost pristine, as if they had been taken just a few days ago.

'These are amazing!' Cat carefully looked at one after another.

'Ah. Here are the ones of Ivy and Bailey.' He laughed and gave her a sheepish smile. 'I'd put them somewhere safe.' He also handed those to Cat.

She recognised Bailey immediately, but tears welled in her eyes as she studied each one in turn.

Ivy was beautiful. Far more beautiful than Viola had been in her twenties, from photos she had seen of her. She was almost as tall as Bailey, and she had a perfect figure as she posed in different outfits. They ranged from her pilot's heavy flight jacket and the Attagirl uniform she wore beneath it, to casual trousers, a blouse and cardigan, to a pretty floral summer dress and sandals.

'She's really beautiful. Sorry. She *was* really beautiful. And she looks so full of life. So happy. So excited. As if she had the whole world at her feet. Who sent you these? They must've been a person, or people who knew her well, and clearly liked her enough to take a photo or photos, of her and her fiancé and keep them all these years.'

'Most of those came from one person. Her name is Sarah and she became a photographer after the war. She sent those and lots of others, not just of Ivy and Bailey, but of everyone who was stationed at the base. Strictly speaking, taking photos, other than for official use and propaganda, wasn't allowed. But everyone did. Well anyone who had a camera, that is. Not everyone had one of those. But photography was Sarah's passion. She said in her letter that she has a great many photos from that time. The ones she sent are just a selection, so I was astonished to see so many of Ivy and Bailey. She put her number on the letter and I called her up and she said exactly what you did just now. That Ivy was incredibly beautiful and so full of life that the camera simply loved her. She said she probably took more photos of Ivy than she did of anyone. But that Ivy was only here from time to time because she was always flying here, there and everywhere, delivering planes in varying states from brand new to in serious need of repair and in all kinds of weather. But whenever she was here, she was always with Bailey. Sarah said it broke her heart when Ivy died. And she also said it broke Viola's and Bailey's too. If Viola and Bailey were in love, they were either very discreet, or they hadn't acted on it because Sarah clearly didn't know anything about it. I think she would've mentioned it if she had.'

'That's so sad.' Kyra rubbed her eyes. 'I've got to know what happened. I really need to know. Can't we just open one letter, Mum? Just one. So that we get some idea of what was going on.'

Cat shook her head again. 'No. Would you like someone to open letters that you had kept for years, just because they wanted to know whether or not you did something with someone you shouldn't?'

'No. I wouldn't.' Kyra let out a sigh of disappointment. 'OK. You need to write the letter to Bailey tonight and post it first thing tomorrow. The sooner he gets it, the sooner we can find out. I don't suppose you know if he's on social media, do you?' She looked hopefully it Amias.

'No. I did look but there are no Bailey Mitchells in the Vancouver area. Lots of Mitchells. Some of whom may be related to Bailey, but none that made it obvious. And you can only see a limited number of photos in a general search, unless you're friends with the account holder. You'll have to wait, I'm afraid. Unless, of course, Bailey Mitchell looks at our website and responds directly to my request for photos for the celebrations.'

'This really is amazing, Amias,' Cat said, giving him a grateful smile. 'I hadn't realised you had gone to so much trouble. Thank you. I really appreciate it.'

'It was a pleasure. And I've discovered things about the base, I didn't know. I've even been sent some photos of my own granddad. Photos my dad, Natalia and I had never seen before. So it's been pretty amazing for me too. For all of us. More have been sent by email. It's going to take a while to go through them but I'll let you see any others I find of Ivy or Bailey. Or Viola. And if I find out anything else, I'll let you know. Here's Bailey's address. You'll be needing that if you're going to write that letter.'

She took it from him and as his fingers brushed against hers she felt the usual thrill. How could she be so in love with this man and yet at the same time be so cross with him?'

Perhaps that's how Viola felt about Bailey. Perhaps that's why she couldn't open his letters. Did she feel guilty about Ivy's death? Was that what this was all about? Only two people could answer that question. One was in a coma in Eastbourne District General Hospital. The other lived thousands of miles away and was ninety-five or older. But at least he was still alive. Or as far as any of them knew, he was.

Chapter Thirty-Four

Cat wrote the letter to Bailey Mitchell, with Kyra's input, the moment they got home. It took several drafts and almost two hours but just before 1 a.m. Cat finally licked the envelope and wrote his address on it.

There had been no sign of Mary or Jeremy when she and Kyra had returned from dinner. They had probably gone to bed, but Cat had half expected to find them both sitting up waiting, so that they could all celebrate their engagement.

What a strange day it had been. Cat was still a little irritated with Amias and definitely felt betrayed somehow, but he had gone to so much effort in tracing Bailey Mitchell that she was finding it difficult to be cross, or to justify feeling betrayed. That was the thing with Amias Wells. One minute he was her dream man; the next, he was her nightmare. Well maybe not a nightmare. More of a thorn in her heart.

She didn't sleep. How could she, with so much going on in her mind? But she got up early, showered, dressed and went downstairs for breakfast to find Mary searching through the kitchen drawers.

'Morning, Mum. How are you today? Can I see the ring?'

Mary turned, a confused look on her face. 'Ring? Oh that. He didn't get it. At least he said he didn't. They didn't have the one he wanted. But he's hoping to get one today.'

'He's going back up to London today?'

Mary rummaged through another drawer. 'What? No. He's still there. He went to see that friend of his. The estate agent. They had a few drinks whilst chatting about this house, and before he knew it, he had missed the last direct train. He stayed the night with his friend and he'll come back today.'

'Mum? What are you looking for? You seem upset. Is everything OK?'

Mary glanced over her shoulder and frowned at Cat. 'Yes, of course it is. I've just misplaced something, that's all. I seem to be doing it a lot lately. It's nothing important. It's simply that I don't like forgetting where I put things. Have you been moving things around?'

'No. And before you ask, neither has Kyra. We put everything back exactly where we find it. What are you looking for? Perhaps I can help. Perhaps I've seen it.'

'I'm looking for my cheque book. I always keep it in that end drawer. The one beneath the medicine cupboard. But it's not there. I searched high and low for it last night. And again this morning. But it's nowhere to be seen.'

'Mum? Please don't get cross with me for saying this, but do you lock that drawer?'

'Of course not. Why would I?'

'Because it's important to keep things like your cheque book safe. I know hardly anyone uses cheques these days, but it can still be a problem if they fall into the wrong hands.'

'Wrong hands? What are you talking about, Catherine? How can my cheque book fall into the wrong hands?' She slammed the drawer, crossed her arms in front of her chest and glared at Cat. 'You're suggesting Jeremy has taken it, aren't you?'

'No. But let's be sensible about this. Either you've put it somewhere different and forgotten where that was. Or someone has moved it. I haven't. Kyra wouldn't. That only leaves one person.'

'Jeremy. I knew it. You said you would give him a chance. But you're not, are you?'

'I'm trying to. But if your cheque book's gone missing, and so has he, it's a little difficult to give him the benefit of the doubt. Is it just your cheque book you can't find? What about your bank cards? And credit cards?'

'Jeremy has not gone missing, Catherine. He stayed in London with his friend. He phoned me last night.'

'Has he phoned this morning?'

'Not yet. No.'

'Have you phoned him?'

'No.'

'Then perhaps you should. He may know where your cheque book is.'

'That's actually a very good idea. I'll call him now.' She glanced at her watch. 'He should be up.' She picked up her phone and called him.

To Cat's surprise, he answered within seconds.

'Good morning, darling,' Mary said. 'I'm sorry to trouble you but I'm being rather silly. That's sweet of you to say that I'm no trouble and I could never be silly.'

She glared at Cat, having clearly repeated his reply for Cat's benefit.

'The thing is. I seem to have mislaid my cheque book and I was wondering if you happened to notice where I put it after I wrote the cheque out yesterday. I thought I had returned it to the drawer, but it's simply not there.'

Cat poured herself a mug of coffee and watched the expression on Mary's face change from one of anxiety to one of relief.

'Oh, darling. You have no idea how glad I am to have called you. But I clearly am very silly if that's where I put it. Why didn't you say something? You didn't want to offend me? Yes, of course. I'll check right now. In fact, I'll ask Catherine to check because she's standing right beside it. Catherine? Will you check the Royal Doulton teapot beside you, please? Jeremy says that's where I put my cheque book.'

'In the teapot? Seriously?' Cat turned around

and, shaking her head, removed the lid of the teapot. 'Oh my God.'

'Well?'

Cat pulled out Mary's cheque book and handed it to her, putting the lid back on the teapot and pushing it against the wall.

Mary took it and smiled triumphantly, although she had looked a little perplexed when Cat first handed it over.

'You were right, darling. We've found it. Thank you. But please promise me one thing. That in future, if you see me doing something so incredibly foolish, you'll say something to me.'

He obviously said he would, and he must've said something that made Mary blush, because she was flushed and grinning when she told him that she loved him, missed him, and couldn't wait until he came home. With an engagement ring or not.

'I'm so sorry, Mum. I mean it. I can't seem to get anything right at the moment.'

Mary smiled. 'I forgive you. But you really must give Jeremy a chance.'

'I will. I promise.'

'I mean it, Catherine. He makes me so happy. I love him. I think I love him almost as much as I've ever loved anyone in my life. Apart from you, and Mother, and now Kyra of course. I'll never love anyone as much as I do the three of you.'

'You love us?'

Mary looked shocked. 'Of course I love you. Why on earth would you think otherwise?'

'You have a funny way of showing it.'

'Do I? Well, the same could be said for you, couldn't it? But I've always thought you loved me. And I've always thought you also loved Granny Viola.'

'I have. I do. But we all said and did so many hurtful things in the past.'

'The past is the past. Let's leave it there, as Mother often says. And let's try harder in future. It's been so lovely having you and Kyra here. I know you'll want to go back to Bonniemount Cottage one day in the not too distant future. But, if you don't. There will always be a home for you here. Either in this house, or wherever it is we move to.'

Cat grinned. 'Does Jeremy know this?'

Mary nodded and grinned back. 'He knows. And he agrees with me 101% that you will always be welcome, and Kyra too. No matter what, or for how long.'

'Wow. Thanks, Mum. That means a lot. May I ask you something? Have you told Jeremy about my dad?'

Mary shook her head. 'No. I've told him what I told you in the past. That he was a mistake and that he is dead. Which is another reason I would really rather you wouldn't want to drag up the past.'

'But it's not about the past, Mum. It's about the present, and the future. I almost wish you hadn't told me that I had siblings. I almost wish I still thought I was an only child. But one day, I'm going to have to find out. I'm sorry. But I really am.'

'I know. And as I said, when Mother comes out of her coma, we'll deal with that. But in the meantime, I'm going to put my cheque book back in this drawer and I'm going to go upstairs and have a shower and then see if I can get my hair done. Jeremy says he's going to make sure he catches an earlier train than he had planned, and I want to look my best for when he gets here.'

Cat smiled and watched her go. It must be wonderful to be in love.

No. Cat was in love.

It must be wonderful to be in love with someone who loves you in return.

Until Cat had come back to Merriment Bay, she had believed she was happy with her life. The occasional night with Greg. More platonic than passionate, but at least it was sex. Sex with no strings attached. The few friends she saw from time to time. Her painting: that was her passion. And Kyra, of course. But since coming back, she had felt things she hadn't felt in years. Longing. Yearning. Wanting. Lust and desire. And love. Love for a man she could never have.

But was there someone out there for her? Someone like Jeremy? No. Not someone like Jeremy. Definitely not. But someone who might love her like Jeremy seemingly did love her mum.

Would she, perhaps, walk into The Hope and Anchor, or somewhere similar, or not, and start chatting to a handsome man? A man who would tell her that she was beautiful. Well, not beautiful. Her scars meant she could never be beautiful. But pretty, perhaps? She could still be pretty, couldn't she?

Would she meet a man who would travel to London, or even to Eastbourne, to buy her an engagement ring? A man who would want to share his life with her and, of course, with Kyra?

She wanted that. She wanted that more than anything right now. But to get it she would have to make a choice. She would have to get over Amias. She couldn't go on loving him forever. It was just too foolish. Too futile. A complete and utter waste of time. To love a man who would never love her back.

So that's what she would do. No matter what, she would finally put the past behind her. The entire past.

And that included Amias.

But right now. She had a letter to post. And the post office in the Merry Shopper supermarket opened at 9 a.m. on the dot. If she left now, she could have a cup of coffee and a sticky bun in the Merry Meals café in the store and be at the post office desk the second it opened. How long did airmail to Canada take? And would Bailey Mitchell answer right away?

Assuming that is, he answered at all.

Chapter Thirty-Five

Cat had been told that her letter would take approximately five days to reach Bailey Mitchell in Vancouver and, assuming he wrote back the day her letter arrived, which she knew was probably unlikely, it would be at least ten days or more before she heard from him.

It was probably going to feel like the longest ten days of her life.

She walked along Coast Road and turned into Market Square and the small shopping arcade where the early Christmas Market was in full swing. Only Merriment Bay would have a Christmas Market in October. But as crazy at it seemed, it had become a tradition – and a bit of a tourist attraction. There were rows of stalls selling gifts and some selling cakes and sweets and other festive treats; one with a wide variety of wrapping paper, ribbons and bows; another selling cushions and throws. The stall selling mulled wine and freshly baked mince pies seemed to be particularly popular.

There was a small ice rink that could be erected and dismantled pretty much anywhere. It was only large enough to accommodate around twenty people at a time but everyone was having fun and one or two skaters clearly had talent.

To one side of the rink was an outdoor café selling hot drinks and hot snacks, served by rather attractive men and women, all dressed as Santa's elves.

Christmas music rang out all around, and myriad lights swung, in the chilly wind blowing in from the sea, as if they were dancing to the merry tunes.

Cat returned to Devon Villa loaded with several bags of gifts and goodies, some of which she showed to Mary over a pot of tea and a couple of slices of Stollen that she had bought at one of the stalls.

'I would've joined you for a merry mint hot chocolate,' Mary said. 'I've only been back from the hairdressers for about five minutes. I don't know what I'm going to do when Sandie sells The Mane Event and moves to Spain for good. It's bad enough that she's closing the place over Christmas.'

'Perhaps another hairdresser will buy it. Oh. I saw a gorgeous man today. Well I bumped into him, I should say.'

'Oh? A visitor or someone local?'

Cat didn't get a chance to answer. Jeremy returned much earlier than expected.

He didn't say a word. He simply smiled, got down on one knee and produced one of the most beautiful rings Cat had ever seen.

Mary cried, and so did Cat. Even Jeremy

looked a little tearful. But maybe that was because the ring must have cost him not just an arm and a leg, but probably his kidney and every other useful part of his body. Only really good diamonds could sparkle like that. Or perhaps, really good costume jewellery.

No. Cat had said she would give him a chance, and she would.

Two days after that, Cat received a text from Amias.

'How did he get my number? K-yra? Did you give it to him?'

Kyra buttered her toast and shrugged.

'He asked for it. I couldn't very well say no. Not after all the trouble he went to to find out about Bailey Mitchell. I told him you didn't particularly like receiving texts, but then I thought he might call, and I know that would probably send you into some sort of frenzy, so I told him you preferred texts to calls. What did he say?'

'He said he's got some more information on Ivy and Bailey. I'm texting him back to say that Natalia's coming for coffee today, so perhaps he could give it to her.'

'M-um. That's mean.'

'I know. But the truth is, sweetheart, I need to get over this thing I have for him. I really do. I didn't think I would, but I've started wondering whether perhaps I might one day meet someone. Someone I could have a relationship with. A real relationship. One that's not tainted with memories and history. I want a fresh start. I never thought I'd say this, but I'm actually envious of what Mum has with Jeremy.'

'I'm glad you want a relationship, Mum. I really am. And I want that for you too. I just don't understand why that couldn't be with Amias.'

'Because it takes two to tango, sweetheart. Amias doesn't have feelings for me. Well, not the sort of feelings I'm looking for. I want someone who loves me, for me. Who only sees me when he looks at me. I think there's too much history between me and Amias. I think whenever he looks at me, he sees his best friend. And not in a good way. Perhaps I bring back too many unhappy times for him. I don't know. I just don't think there could ever be anything between us in that way. Even if I want there to be.'

'I don't know, Mum. I've seen him look at you sometimes and it even makes my heart skip a beat. Honestly. He looks at you as if he's in a desert and you're the water that will save his life. As if he's drowning, and you're his life raft. As if he's suffocating, and you're the air he needs to breathe. He looks at you as if he loves you. He does, Mum.'

Cat couldn't answer for a moment. If only all that were true. She shook her head.

'I don't see that, sweetheart. Whenever I catch him looking at me, all I see is hurt, and pain, and bitterness. Guilt, too. For some reason. Dislike, definitely. Contempt, once or twice. I've certainly never seen love. Or any sign that he either wants me or needs me. Although there was that night on the village common. The night of the bonfire and fireworks. That night he did look at me in the strangest way and I really thought for one moment, that he was actually going to kiss me. But do you know what he did? He made an excuse and hurried away as if his life depended on getting as far away from me as he possibly could.'

'Really? It's funny how two people can look at the same person and see completely different things. But OK. It's your life. You must do whatever makes you happy. And if that's not being with Amias, then I hope you find someone who you can be happy with.'

'I hope so too. And in the meantime, I need to avoid Amias Wells as much as possible. Will you help me with that?'

'Of course I will. If I can.'

'Damn. He's just texted back and asked if I'd like to meet for lunch sometime this week. He says he'd rather not give the stuff to Natalia.'

'You see. He wants to see you.'

'Well, he can't. I can't. I'm telling him I'm too busy this week, but that you're free, and that you can pass on anything to me without a problem.'

'Thanks. So now I'm your go-between. That's just brilliant, Mum.' Kyra let out a long sigh. 'Oh, by the way. Lucas and I are dating.'

'What? Since when?'

'Since the night you thought Amias was going to kiss you.'

'But that was days ago. Why am I only hearing about this now?'

'You've had a lot on your mind. I didn't want to bother you.'

'Bother me? Kyra? How can you say that? I knew there was something about you that morning. The morning after the fireworks. You looked so … happy. So beautiful. So full of life and excitement.'

'Hold on. Stop there. Wasn't that what everyone said about Ivy? Look what happened to her. She crashed into a mountain.'

'Don't joke about that, Kyra. Please. Don't ever joke about things like that.'

'Oh, Mum. For God's sake, lighten up, will you? People die every day. Every single day. Global warming will no doubt kill us all if some meteor doesn't demolish the planet beforehand. We need to joke about death. At least, I do. And it's the one sure thing in life. It's coming for us all.'

'I'm going to ignore that. Tell me about Lucas. I bet he's a good kisser.'

Kyra smiled. 'He is. He's a bloody good kisser. I bet Amias is a good kisser.'

'K-yra!'

'OK, OK. But I bet he is. And before you ask. No. We haven't had sex.' She grinned. 'And nor have Lucas and I.'

'Very funny.' Well, this is simply wonderful. My mum's dating someone and my daughter's dating someone. I feel a bit like a soggy filling in a sandwich.'

'Then the sooner you start dating, the better. Got anyone in mind?'

'No. But when I was on my way back from the post office the other day, I did bump into a really good-looking man in the Christmas Market. Literally bumped into him. He had such dreamy eyes and was so polite, with a very sexy voice. I apologised, because it was my fault as I wasn't looking where I was going. He smiled and said, he was probably the one to blame because he was always bumping into people, or things. He said it began when he was three and he bumped into his grandmother, knocking her flat on the floor, much to her displeasure, and as long as I was OK, there was no harm done. Then he smiled and walked away and as I turned around, I also bumped into Constance Raine, the vicar's wife.'

'Constance Raine!' Kyra burst out laughing. 'That's an unfortunate name. Especially for the wife of the vicar. Is she a bit of a wet blanket?'

Cat grinned. 'Very funny. No she isn't. But she does know most of the gossip in the village, so I asked her whether she knew who the man was, and whether he was local or just passing through. She said his name was Adam Wynter. He lives in Wynter House, the stately home on the other side of Wyntersleap village. The village actually gets its name from one of his ancestors who leapt from the top of Wyntersleap Falls. Or was it more than one who jumped? I can't remember exactly. I haven't thought about the place for years. Anyway, he's roughly the same age as me and he's single. The problem is, he lives and works in London and only returns home at the weekends and holidays. Not that he would be interested in me.'

'Why do you always do that? Why do you put yourself down? It's because of those scars, isn't it? No matter how many times people tell you that they're hardly noticeable. To you, they seem horrific. You say you want to find someone who loves you for you. Well I've got news for you, Mum. No one is going to love you unless you love yourself. Because the minute someone looks at you, the first thing you do is try to hide your scars. Natalia and Josh didn't even mention them.'

'That was because they knew I had them. And also, probably because Amias had told them not to.'

'Oh, for heaven's sake. Sometimes you say the most ridiculous things. Learn to love your scars, Mum. And most importantly, learn to love yourself. And forgive yourself for Dad's death while you're at it. It's time to move on. And talking of moving on. I'm meeting Lucas in half an hour. I'll be back this afternoon, and we can go to see Granny Viola together, if you like.'

Cat nodded. 'Have fun.'

She watched Kyra go. Her daughter was right. Cat knew it. She just wasn't sure what to do about it.

But after Natalia came for coffee, she had more important things to worry about. Luckily, Jeremy and Mary were both out for the duration of Natalia's visit.

'I'm not convinced he's very good,' Natalia said, having inspected some of Jeremy's work.

'Are you saying his work is not up to an acceptable standard?'

Natalia pulled a face. 'I wouldn't use him to do any work on any of the properties our firm manages. And I definitely wouldn't use him to do any work on my own home. He's not planning on doing the rewiring himself, is he? Because you have to be qualified to do that sort of work and if what I've seen so far is anything to go by, I seriously doubt that Jeremy Stone has any qualifications whatsoever in the building trade.'

'It's as bad as that?'

Natalia shrugged. 'In my opinion, yes. I would say he has the skills of an average DIY enthusiast. Some of it's OK. None of it's brilliant. If you can find a way to stop him from continuing, I would suggest you do.'

'I was afraid you were going to say that. But what am I supposed to do? Mum is happier than I've ever seen her. They're engaged. He's living here. And she thinks he's a builder. How can I stop him doing any work?'

'You could develop a sudden allergy to dust.'

'Seriously?'

'It's a suggestion.'

'Do you have a better one?'

'Tell her the truth.'

'I'm sorry. Have you actually met Mary

Devon?'

Natalia laughed. 'Yes. And my dad and brother speak highly of her. Oh damn. Sorry. I didn't mean to say that.'

Cat looked at her for a moment and then she smiled. 'I suppose that's fair. Mum didn't treat either your dad or your brother particularly well.'

'I still shouldn't have said that. I am sorry, Cat. I'd like to be your friend.'

'I'd like that too. And don't worry. Let's forget about it.' She grinned. 'Providing you find a way to help me stop Jeremy Stone from dismantling Devon Villa around us.'

Natalia frowned. 'You drive a hard bargain. But I'll see what I can do. I know Amias is planning to ask around to see if anyone knows anything about Jeremy.'

'Yes. It'll be good if he finds something that I can show to Mum. I'm not sure hearsay will convince her. She's very much in love.'

'And what about you? Are you in love?'

'Me? No. No way.'

'Are you telling me that there isn't anyone you're even remotely interested in?'

'No. Well. Perhaps a little.'

'And?' Natalia looked incredibly excited.

'I don't know much about him. I don't know anything about him, to be honest. I bumped into him the other day in the market. But I do know his name. It's Adam. Adam Wynter.'

Natalia's face fell. 'Adam Wynter? Are you

serious? There's no one else? No one at all?'

Cat shook her head. 'No. No one. I was seeing a man called Greg, in Bonniemount. But that was more platonic really. I do want to meet someone though. I didn't think I did, but since being back here, I've realised I do. I want that. I want a relationship. And Kyra thinks it's a really good idea. She's dating Lucas now.'

'Is she?' Natalia suddenly seemed uninterested. It was as if the wind had been taken out of her sails. 'I'd better go. I've left Josh alone in the office and he gets himself into such a mess if I'm not there. Thanks for the coffee. If I think of anything to help with the Mary and Jeremy situation, I'll let you know. And if Amias comes up with anything, I'm sure he'll be in touch.'

'Thanks for coming round. And thanks for your time.' Cat grinned. 'And if you hear of any single men, looking for a slightly worn, single mum, please let me know.'

'Yeah. Of course. I'll do that. There's always Amias.'

She looked a little hopeful, but she was obviously joking.

'Yeah, right.' Cat forced a laugh. 'Could you imagine that? I'm not saying he's not great. Because he is. For someone. Sadly, just not for me.'

'Right. OK. I'll see you soon.'

Had Cat said something wrong? Why was Natalia suddenly in such a hurry to leave? Earlier, she had said that she could stay for as long as Cat

288

wanted her to. How strange.

And now Cat had Jeremy to add to her list of problems.

Chapter Thirty-Six

Cat managed to avoid Amias all week. At first he sent several texts. He even called her once or twice. She took her time to respond to the texts and she sent his calls to voicemail. By the end of the week, there were no more calls and only one text. She felt bad about it. But what could she do? Even listening to his voicemails made her yearn for him. She couldn't keep inflicting this on herself. She had to stay away. At least until she could be near him and not turn into a puddle of quivering goo.

She hadn't found a way to resolve the Jeremy situation either. But since he and Mary had got engaged, he didn't seem quite as interested in work, so any additional damage he might do was actually less than Cat had expected.

Kyra was spending more of her free time with Lucas. Cat was glad she was happy, but she couldn't help but feel a little concerned. And also a little lonely from time to time. She had seen Abigail for coffee at the weekend, but Abigail worked all week, so had very little time.

Painting had once again been Cat's salvation. It had been her art, and Isla Presley, of course that had got her through after Kyle's death. What she was going through now was hardly comparable. And yet in a way, it was. Being in the same village as Amias and forcing herself not to see him, was akin to a slow and painful death, or so it seemed. But she told herself that each day would be easier than the last. One day soon, she might actually believe it. Until then, she had no choice. She would simply have to get on with life.

The following week, Amias didn't call or text at all. Eighteen years before, the same thing had happened, so why was she surprised? And yet she was. A little.

And the week after that, she got the worst news of all. Amias was dating someone. No one knew who she was. And apparently, no one had seen her. Apart from Natalia. She was the one who had told everyone about Amias and his new girlfriend.

'I think this could finally be the one,' Natalia told Cat one afternoon when they met by chance in the car park of the Merry Shopper supermarket. 'But don't tell him I said that. He's trying to play it cool. You know Amias.'

'Oh yes. I know Amias. I hope he'll be very happy. I'm sorry, Natalia, but I must dash off. I've actually got a date myself this afternoon.'

'You have? Not with Adam Wynter?'

'Who? Oh him. No, no. Um. It's a doctor from Granny Viola's ward. We've been chatting for ages. It's just coffee. Nothing serious. Yet.'

Cat winked and dashed away as fast as she

could. She was becoming a pretty good liar. Or at least, someone very good at making up stories and hiding the truth.

Dear God. Was she turning into Mary Devon?

Why had she done that? There was no reason to make up a boyfriend. As if Amias would care either way. Although it wasn't a total lie. She was seeing the doctor that afternoon, and she would be drinking coffee. But it was to discuss Granny Viola's latest tests, that was all.

Back at Devon Villa, she banged the shopping bags on the table and slumped into a chair.

'Amias has got a girlfriend.'

Kyra glanced up from her phone. 'Has he? I haven't heard about that and Lucas hasn't mentioned it.'

'Apparently, he's trying to keep it quiet.'

'Why?'

'Who knows? Who knows why that man does anything? And who cares?'

Kyra raised her brows before giving Cat a sympathetic smile. 'Clearly you do. Although, of course, being a Devon, you're too stubborn and pig-headed to admit it. But you said yourself that Amias is a man who wouldn't be long without a woman. I still think that woman could've been you. But hey. You told me not to go there, so I won't.'

'Natalia thinks this could be the one.'

'The one? What? The one Amias marries?'

'Yep.'

'Wow. Do you think we'll get an invite to the

wedding?'

'I really don't want to talk about it, Kyra. I don't want to hear that man's name mentioned again.'

'Er. You were the one who brought him up.'

'I've got a headache. I'm going to my room.'

'You haven't unpacked the shopping.'

'You've got two hands for a reason, Kyra. And it's not to send lovey-dovey messages to your boyfriend every hour of the night and day.'

'OK. I'll unpack the shopping. But does that mean you don't want to read this letter? The one that's got a postmark from Vancouver.'

Cat stopped in her tracks and turned around. 'If this is your idea of a joke, sweetheart, I'm not going to be amused.'

'No joke.' She waved an envelope in one hand in the air.

Cat raced back and grabbed it, studying the writing for a moment or two.

'It's not the same. The writing's not the same as the letters upstairs.'

'They were written a lifetime ago, Mum. Bailey Mitchell is getting on for a hundred or so.'

'But this isn't the writing of an elderly man. Look.' She held the envelope in front of Kyra. 'This is the writing of someone younger. Oh no. You don't think he's dead do you?'

'Bailey? How would I know? Why don't you open the letter and see?'

Cat tore open the envelope and pulled out two

sheets of paper.

'OK. It says, "Dear Cat. Thank you for your lovely letter. It was addressed to my grandfather, Bailey Mitchell, and he has asked me to reply on his behalf. Let me introduce myself before we go any farther. My name is Ben Mitchell. I'm thirty-six, recently single, and along with my sister, Diana, I run wildlife tours here in deepest, darkest British Columbia. It's not really deep or dark here – except in the woods. And Diana has just told me that this sounds more like my dating profile than an introduction so I apologise for that. Grandfather was very surprised to receive your letter, and he was extremely distressed by its contents. We are all hoping that by the time this letter reaches you, you will have received some good news regarding your grandmother. Grandfather was also surprised that you said his letters were unopened. But then he said afterwards, that perhaps he wasn't. I don't suppose that makes much sense to you. It didn't make any to us. But since then, he has told us a lot more about his life in Merriment Bay, and at RAF Merriment. I'm not sure if you are aware of this, but Grandfather is ninety-eight. I honestly think if he could, he would get on a plane right now and come over there. Sadly, at his age, that isn't really an option. But he would like to keep in touch, and to get updates on any changes in your grandmother's condition. We have a presence on social media, via our wildlife tours company and I'm giving you the details for that, in case you want to get in touch that way. It's so much quicker than the postal service, especially as we live on an island. Grandfather is very keen to hear from you again and he says he will try to answer any questions you may have. With thanks and best wishes, Bailey, Ben and Diana Mitchell." What a lovely letter.'

'Ben sounds interesting. Recently single and thirty-six. Perhaps we should consider visiting Bailey Mitchell and his family in person. I've always fancied going to Canada and a wildlife tour sounds like fun. Especially if there are bears.'

'Let's not get ahead of ourselves. But he has given us the social media handles, or whatever it is they're called, so perhaps we could at least look them up. You're good at that.'

Kyra stretched out her hand and Cat gave her the letter. She typed the details into her phone and placed the phone on the table so that they could both see the results.

'Mitchell Mountain Tours,' Kyra said. 'Do you think that means there's actually a Mitchell mountain? Or does it mean that their tours are in the mountains?'

'Ah, the importance of grammar,' Cat joked. 'It could be either. Hold on. Scroll down again. Stop. Is that them?'

Kyra looked closer. 'It says, "A warm welcome from the Mitchells", so yes. I think we can safely assume it is. Wow, Mum. Ben is my sort of mountain man. Look at him.'

'I am. He's my sort of mountain man too.

Blond hair, blue eyes, gleaming white teeth that only people on the other side of the Atlantic seem to possess. Broad shoulders, strong hands, from what I can see of them, and a rather lovely smile. I think you're right, sweetheart. We do need to take a wildlife tour. So, are we going to message them or something? Tell them we've got the letter and ask a few questions?'

'Should we wait for Gran?'

Cat looked at Kyra and grinned. 'Nah. We can tell her about it later.'

Chapter Thirty-Seven

Cat decided that social media might not be that bad after all. In fact, it might actually be rather good.

Or perhaps it was Ben Mitchell who was the deciding factor. Contact with him, his sister Diana and his grandfather, Bailey was now part of Cat's day; like taking a shower, or having that first, aromatic cup of coffee after she woke up. She looked forward to checking the notifications, so much so that Kyra had helped her set up her own social media presence. Now she and Ben were sending each other messages at all hours of the day and night, despite the eight-hour time difference. Cat was awake when she would normally be asleep, and asleep when she should be awake. Half the time, she wasn't quite sure what day it was. But she was sure of one thing: Ben Mitchell had brought a breath of fresh mountain air into her life.

OK. She occasionally compared him to Amias, and yes, more than once when she was lying awake in bed she wondered whether Amias was lying awake in bed with his girlfriend, and what, exactly, they were doing. But that only made her more determined to develop her friendship with Ben.

There was just one tiny problem. Ben lived almost five thousand miles away.

That was the odd thing about social media. It transcended borders, turned distances into a mere click of a button, or tap on the screen, and made anything seem possible.

'It's done nothing here but rain for weeks and weeks,' she typed on her phone.

'It's snowing here,' Ben replied.

'I love the snow.'

'I love the rain.'

'Perhaps we should switch places.'

'Or perhaps we should share the experiences. I'll visit you. You visit me.'

Cat got excited. 'If only we could.'

'Perhaps we can work something out. How's Viola? Any news?'

'No change. It's so disheartening.'

'Grandfather asks about her constantly. Thank you for the photo. You were right, it was depressing. But he says he's glad he got to see her face again after all these years. Even if her eyes were closed and she's in a coma. He pretended he had popped into her bedroom and that she was simply fast asleep.'

'I wish he could pop into her room. The doctors say that some people know what's going on around them. That's why it's so important to be careful what you say or do. Perhaps knowing Bailey was in her room might pull her out of the mist and fog she's in and bring her back to us.'

'Wouldn't that be something?'

'Well, it's getting closer to Christmas. And that is the season of miracles.'

'I believe in miracles.'

'We made the Christmas cake and the Christmas puddings the other day. It's a tradition in England that if you stir them you can make a wish. I stirred them all and made a wish with each. That's three wishes. I'm hoping at least one of them comes true.'

'We do that here. And my great-grandmother was British. I don't suppose I'm allowed to ask what you wished for.'

'I'm surprised you need to ask.'

Cat typed that sentence, deleted it, retyped and deleted it yet again, and finally decided, what the hell. She had retyped it again and this time she had pressed send. He was almost five thousand miles away. He couldn't see her blush.

But he had seen her photograph. He asked for one a few days after they had connected on social media. She had explained about her accident eighteen years ago, but she hadn't given many details. There was time enough for that if they ever met. Not that they were likely to. And in a way, that made her feel less vulnerable in letting him see her photo. But even so, she covered her scar with her hair a little and made sure she wore make-up in order to look her best.

He had told her she was really pretty. Beautiful, he'd said.

Her heart had soared and she had waved her arms in the air just like Kyra did when she was excited about something.

And yet her heart played tricks on her, and so did her brain. 'How would you feel if Amias told you you were beautiful?' it asked.

'I've sent you a Christmas card,' Ben said, one day during their online conversations.

'I've sent you one too.'

She had. And she had chosen it very carefully. It had the words. 'To a special friend at Christmas' blazoned across an image of a couple snuggled on a loveseat in front of a roaring fire whilst snow fell outside of a leaded light window.

Would Ben get the not so subtle message?

What would his card be like?

'And I've sent you a card for Viola from Grandfather. Will you take it to the hospital?'

'Of course. I'll put it by her bed.'

'And there's a letter inside the card for you. He says it should answer most of your questions. I wrote it for him so I know what it says, but I'll let you read it before we discuss it.'

'Discuss it? Does it need to be discussed?'

'I was surprised by what he told me.'

'Oh come on. You can't leave things like that. I'll have to wait at least five days before it arrives.'

'I could call you. We could discuss it over the phone. I just don't want to type it out.'

'I'd like that. I'd like to hear your voice. To see if it sounds as I imagine it does.'

'And how do you imagine it sounds?'

'Like you look. Strong, sexy, confident and caring.'

'That's a lot to live up to. I hope you won't be disappointed.'

'I won't. I know I won't.'

'And I expect your voice will sound like you. Beautiful, sensual and sexy, confident, a hint of stubbornness, and a great deal of love.'

She wasn't disappointed. And Ben said neither was he.

But she was surprised by what he told her.

Chapter Thirty-Eight

'You talked to Ben?'

Mary seemed as astonished as Kyra, who had already said that she was surprised by how quickly their friendship had developed. Mary was now up-to-date with everything that had happened. Including the fact that it was Amias who had first uncovered Bailey Mitchell's identity.

Cat nodded. 'Yes. And he sounds as lovely as he looks. But I now know what happened between Ivy, Bailey and Viola. There's a letter from Bailey coming in the post with a Christmas card, but Ben told me over the phone, most of what it says.'

'What, Mum?' Kyra was clearly excited.

'We know that Ivy and Bailey were engaged. What we didn't know is that they began dating almost as soon as he arrived at RAF Merriment. Apparently, everyone from the base frequented The Hope and Anchor and the Spitfire Café. Ivy worked as a waitress at the Spitfire, and it seems she was instantly attracted to Bailey and she was the one who asked him out. He said he was both astonished and flattered and immediately said yes.'

Kyra smiled. 'I knew I liked the sound of Ivy.

She was definitely a go-getter.'

Cat smiled too. 'She was only sixteen at the time, but she told him she was eighteen. He says she definitely looked eighteen. And no one in the village told him any different. He thinks she was attracted to him because he was a pilot. She told him she longed to fly and was determined she would. Anyway, as we know, she did, and once Ivy became an Attagirl, they saw far less of one another. But they thought they were in love and he proposed. He says that times were different then. Especially if you were a pilot. Your life expectancy wasn't great. Every time you went up, you had no idea how you would be coming back down. Whether you would land safely on the airfield, or crash, and possibly burn, or drown, or both. He was often on missions, and Ivy was back and forth across the country delivering planes. But when Viola joined the WAAF, he saw Viola constantly. At first they were friends and talked about Ivy. Then, one day, they looked at one another and they knew they were so much more than friends. Suddenly, they couldn't keep their hands off one another.'

'Are you telling me they had an affair?' Mary asked, disappointment etched across her face. 'Mother did that to her own sister?'

'Yes. She did. It went on for a few weeks and they both told one another it was just a fling. But it wasn't. Bailey wanted to tell Ivy and break off the engagement. He wanted to marry Viola instead. But Viola wanted to be the one to tell her. In the end, they agreed to tell her together. And he now thinks that was the worst mistake they made.'

'Bloody hell,' Kyra said. 'I should think so. One of them telling her they were cheating was bad enough. To have both of them stand in front of her as a couple and tell her that the two people she probably trusted most in the world had been lying and deceiving her behind her back. God. How awful.'

'That's what he feels now. That's what he felt afterwards. But it was even worse than that. Ivy told them that their timing was wonderful because she had just discovered she was pregnant. She said she would bring the baby up alone. Quite something in those days. But Bailey couldn't walk away from her and his child and he was torn between his love for Viola and his sense of duty to Ivy. He says he's not proud of his behaviour, but he was young and foolish and in love. And there was a war on. Ivy and Viola were both terribly upset, of course. They all were. But Ivy insisted she would be fine and actually wished them well, refusing to discuss it further. Then she went off on her next flight to RAF Acklington. And on her return, her plane crashed into the hillside and she died.'

'So Mother killed her. She killed her own sister. Ivy was clearly too upset to fly. They shouldn't have let her go.'

'Which is exactly how they felt as soon as they heard the news. But they couldn't have stopped her. Viola ended things immediately and refused to see, or speak, or write to Bailey ever again. She applied for an immediate transfer and it was granted. He says they loved each other desperately. But neither of them could handle the guilt. The letters in the trunk were effectively begging her to reconsider. To grieve together. To see if they could assuage each other's guilt. They were sent here because this was the only address he had for her. But Viola never replied. He was told that she was now part of a team whose work was classified as 'Top Secret', so no information could be given. When the war ended, he assumed she would come back here, but she didn't. He heard she'd gone to stay with friends. He never saw her again and after a time, he had to return to Canada. And yet, even though he eventually married someone else, he never stopped loving Viola. His wife died many years ago, but he said she knew about Viola.'

'But not about Ivy?' Kyra was clearly irritated by that.

'I don't know. As I mentioned, he's sent a letter with a Christmas card and when that arrives, we can read exactly what he says.'

'I'm not sure how I feel about this,' Mary said. 'It's ridiculous, I know. But I somehow feel as if Mother has let me down. I know that sounds rich coming from someone with my past. But we can't help how we feel, can we?'

The Christmas card arrived a few days later and Bailey's letter said pretty much what Ben had said. There were a couple of extra paragraphs saying how

Bailey wished he could turn back the clock. How he wished he'd met Viola first. How he wished he'd stayed and waited for Viola's eventual return, and tried yet again to persuade her to forgive herself and him. The only difference between the letter and what Ben had told her was the final paragraph.

It said: 'We can't help who we fall in love with. Some loves last a lifetime. Nothing can end a love like that. Not guilt. Not distance. Not time. Some loves transcend all of that. It's as if that person is a part of us. Like a limb, or an organ. We might survive without them but that is all we will do. Survive. Only with that person will we ever find true happiness and be at peace with ourselves and feel whole. Some loves define us. They make us who we are. There's no escaping that sort of love. No matter how far we go or how hard we try. I have tried. Truly I have. But for me, there will only be one person I have ever truly loved with my entire heart and soul. And that person is Viola.'

Ben's card had arrived the same day and Cat wasn't disappointed. Like her, he had bought a special card, but unlike her, he had gone much farther. He had admitted that what he felt was something stronger and deeper than merely friendship. And that even though they hadn't met, in his mind, they already had a bond.

His card had a couple strolling hand in hand through a magical snow-laden forest, the woman's head leaning against the man's shoulder. And across the image the words: To Someone Very

306

Special, said so much more than special friend, somehow.

But what really made Cat's heart leap in her chest was what he had written inside.

It read: 'I know we'll meet one day very soon and then I can say things that I probably shouldn't say to someone who, strictly speaking, I hadn't previously met. But I feel as if I know you, Cat, and as if this was meant to happen. I hope you feel the same. Love, Ben xx'

After that, every time they spoke, there was a frisson of excitement. But neither mentioned meeting. It was as if to do so would break the spell between them. That's how Cat felt anyway.

Apart from this, life went on much the same as it had been. More rain than ever had fallen in early December and throughout the month. The nearby village of Wyntersleap had actually flooded on the weekend before Christmas. Thankfully, no one was hurt and news soon spread that the villagers and some visitors were now staying at Wynter House until the River Wynter receded and the cottages could dry out.

The river also passed through Merriment Bay, but there was no danger of the village flooding. Wyntersleap reservoir took most of the flood water and what it couldn't cope with would overflow onto fields long before it would reach the village. Cat wasn't concerned, and nor was anyone else in Merriment Bay, as far as flooding went, but they were all getting mightily sick of the weather. There were storms, showers, hailstones, more torrential rain and finally, the day before Christmas Eve, it actually began to snow.

Chapter Thirty-Nine

Snow started falling on Merriment Bay just before lunch on the day before Christmas Eve and Mary, Jeremy, and Kyra went with Cat early to the hospital that day. They had been invited to a party at Abigail and William Lester's house that night and as awful as Cat felt about it, they wanted to get to the hospital and back without being caught up in traffic jams caused by Christmas shoppers and now, by the weather.

The hospital looked as cheery as any hospital can at Christmas. There were trees and decorations here and there. And the fake tree that Cat and Kyra had placed on the windowsill in Granny Viola's room gave it a little bit of festive feeling. Even if Granny Viola was seemingly unaware of it.

They stayed for almost an hour, discussing their options yet again with doctors, and chatting amiably with the nurses about their holiday plans.

'What's that commotion?' Kyra asked, popping her head around the open door of Granny Viola's private room shortly before they were about to leave. 'Oh. My. God. Mum. You will never guess who is walking towards this door.'

'Amias?' That was the first name that popped into Cat's head.

'Amias?' Kyra repeated, looking at Cat as if to ask where that had come from. 'Why would Amias be here?'

Cat was flustered. 'I don't know. I have no idea why I said that.'

'Well, prepare yourself for an even bigger surprise. Unless I'm very much mistaken. And I'm not. Bailey, Ben and Diana Mitchell have flown five thousand miles and are walking down the corridor.'

'What?' Cat leapt to her feet. 'That's not possible. They can't be. Ben didn't mention this yesterday.'

She dashed towards the door and peered into the corridor, only to be met by Ben's smiling face, certainly more handsome in the flesh.

'Ben! Bailey! Diana! How? When? Why?' She didn't know where to start.

'Hello, Cat,' Bailey said, holding out a shaking hand and offering a beaming smile. 'It's so good to be here. How is she?'

'Viola?' Cat shook her head. 'No change. But it's wonderful to meet you. I can't believe you're here. Am I imagining this?'

Ben smiled. 'You're not imagining it. It's a dream come true for us to visit. I probably should've let you know. But once Grandfather suggested it, we weren't sure whether it would actually come to pass and we didn't want to get anyone's hopes up. Including our own. Then we decided it would be a nice surprise. We were sure you would be here. Although we hadn't accurately calculated the time difference or the transport delays to get here.'

'But we're here now,' Diana said. 'And that's what matters. It's lovely to meet you all. And may we wish you a Merry Christmas in spite of the situation?'

'Yes.' Cat's eyes darted from her to Bailey to Ben and back and forth between them all. 'And you, Diana. And a Merry Christmas to all of you. Um. Do come in. This is my daughter, Kyra. My mum, Mary. And Jeremy, her fiancé. And this of course, is Granny Viola.' She nodded towards the bed where Viola lay, as if asleep, save for the tubes going to and from her frail body.

Bailey smiled and said hello to everyone but it was clear he was impatient to get to Viola's bedside and they all moved aside to let him pass.

'Hello, Viola, my angel.' His voice shook almost as much as his hand had done. 'It's been a long, long time, but you haven't changed one bit. You're still as beautiful as ever. I hope you won't mind if I hold your hand.'

He gently took one hand in his and tears filled his eyes as he squeezed it softly and raised it to his lips.

'Did you see that?' Kyra screamed, pointing to Viola's other hand which lay at her side. 'Her fingers moved. I swear they did. I only saw it from the corner of my eye. But they moved. They did. They really did.'

Cat shook her head. 'We know that sometimes there are involuntary spasms.'

'It wasn't that, Mum. It wasn't. She lifted her finger. I know she did.'

'All right, sweetheart. We believe you. Mum and I will go and find a doctor and see if he can check on her condition.' She glanced at Ben. 'Is that OK, Ben? Do you mind if we leave you all here for a moment?'

Ben smiled. 'Of course I don't. We'll be here when you get back.'

The doctors confirmed that there did indeed appear to be a very slight improvement on Viola's score on the Glasgow Coma Scale. But they couldn't give any promises or reassurances. Sometimes, this could mean the person was coming out of the coma, but sometimes, they had seen this happen before the final gasp. Although they were a little more tactful than that.

Cat, Kyra, Mary, Jeremy and the Mitchells remained at the hospital for several hours, none of them wanting to leave Viola, just in case.

Eventually, Diana said that she needed to get some sleep. They had been travelling for several hours and owing to the time difference, she was suffering from jetlag. So was Ben it seemed. But Bailey was determined to stay as long as he could. When the situation was explained, although not all the details, merely that Bailey and Viola were once very much in love, the staff had pulled out all the stops and arranged for Bailey to stay for as long as he wanted. But they had been very flexible with visiting hours ever since Granny Viola had been moved to her private room.

'We'll come back in a few hours,' Ben and Diana said.

Mary wanted to stay too, but felt that in the circumstances, she and Jeremy would give Bailey and Viola some space.

'We have a party to go to this evening,' Mary said, 'but of course we will simply show our faces, explain the situation and come back here as soon as we can.'

'Should I ask Abigail if Ben and Diana can come to the party?' Cat asked Mary. 'Kyra wants to go to be with Lucas and also to see Marcus. He and his family will be there for Christmas.'

'I don't think Ben and Diana will want to go to a party filled with strangers after a transatlantic flight, but if you want to, then I'm sure Abigail and William won't mind.'

Cat wasn't sure what to do for the best.

'I think perhaps, like you, Mum, I'll just show my face. Then I can spend time with Ben and Diana so that they're not alone in a strange town on the night before Christmas Eve. Perhaps we'll go out for dinner, or something.'

'That sounds like a very good idea.'

Ben and Diana seemed to think so too. Although they said they were fine if Cat and Kyra went to the party. The journey had been tiring and they were happy to simply catch up on some sleep.

It was Cat who would rather they didn't. Ben was definitely even more gorgeous in real life and now that he was here, she wanted to spend as much time as she possibly could with him. She would be perfectly happy if Diana wanted to stay in her room and sleep, but she was hoping that like her, Ben would rather do other things with his time.

Before he left, he managed to get her attention and they found a quiet corner. He smiled as he looked into her eyes.

'You're even prettier in the flesh. When I told you we'd meet soon, I didn't know it would be this soon. But the minute Grandfather said he wanted to take one final trip to England, I was determined to make it happen. Not just for him. But also for us.'

'For you and Diana, you mean?' She smiled up at him.

He shook his head very, very slowly.

'No. For you and me, Cat Devon. As I think you know.' He took her hand in his and moved closer.

There were no butterflies. No doubts or fears or worries like she always had when she was close to Amias. Just the knowledge that Ben was going to kiss her and that she wanted him to. Still holding her hand, he pulled her close and bent his head towards her.

Their lips met in a soft and gentle kiss. No fireworks. No trumpets. No choirs of angels. Just a sweet and pleasant kiss. A kiss she would be happy to repeat.

'That was nice,' she said, when they eased apart.

'It was very nice,' Ben agreed.

A cough interrupted their moment.

'Mum? Gran says we're going to leave now. Are you ready? Sorry to interrupt, Ben, but patience isn't one of Gran's virtues.'

'It's not a problem, Kyra. Your mum and I'll have plenty of time to talk again. Drive safe, now. I'll see you later, Cat.'

'I'm looking forward to it already.'

'Nice?' Kyra whispered as she and Cat walked towards Mary and Jeremy. 'Nice? What does that mean?'

Cat tutted. 'It means exactly what it says. And it also means you shouldn't have been eavesdropping.'

'You were in a corner of the hospital corridor, Mum. If you'd wanted privacy you should've got a room. Nice. Honestly. I bet a kiss from Amias would be a lot better than nice.'

'Amias? Why would you bring him up at a time like this?'

'Er. I hate to point this out, Mum, but you were the one who brought him up when I said that you'd be surprised who was walking down the corridor. Now, I may be young and I may be foolish, but if his name is the first one that pops into your head, I think that tells you all you need to know.'

'If Ben hadn't lived half a world away, I would obviously have said Ben. But I was thinking of someone local. That's all.'

'Yeah. You keep telling yourself that, Mum. But I for one, will never believe it.'

'Well as you said, you're young and foolish.'

'I'd rather be young and foolish than "nice" any day of the week.'

Chapter Forty

Cat made an extra effort to look her best. Not for Abigail and Will's party, but for later, when she had arranged to see Ben and Diana for dinner in Eastbourne. But snow was now falling thick and fast. More so than it had been earlier and roads were becoming a bit of a problem in places, according to the traffic news. She texted Ben, not knowing if he was sleeping or not, and asked him to call her when he got a chance.

She, Kyra, Mary and Jeremy, crunched through the snow to Will and Abigail's, two doors away from Devon Villa. She was surprised at how many people had turned out, especially bearing in mind the weather was so appalling. Cat loved snow, but tonight she didn't like it anywhere near as much.

She spotted Natalia the moment they walked in and her eyes scanned the room for Amias. He stood a little away from Natalia and was talking to Marcus in a corner of the huge lounge. She saw the top of his head and then his eyes as he lifted his gaze in her direction, as if he'd known she was there, or felt her presence in some way. But that was ridiculous.

She smiled and tried to look away but she

couldn't. It was that bloody magnetic field or whatever it was that always drew her to him, even after all these weeks.

He smiled back but a little wanly and he did look away. He looked at some stunning woman who was standing with him and Marcus.

So that was his girlfriend, was it? She was certainly beautiful. But young. Far too young for him, surely?

'Hello Cat. It's lovely to see you here tonight.' It was Josh who was standing beside her. 'I haven't seen you for weeks. Not since the dinner at Amias'. I know Natalia's seen you once or twice. How are things? How is Viola? Any change?'

'There may be actually. We've been at the hospital all afternoon and Viola seemed to move her fingers. We think it might be because of Bailey. Having him there and holding her hand may just be the miracle we've all been praying for.'

'Bailey? Bailey Mitchell? The man in the photo who Amias tracked down? He's here? In the UK?'

Cat laughed. 'Yes, to all of that. Are you swaying, Josh?'

'I think I may be. I went to three parties today and now this one makes four. I might have had just a bit too much to drink. But hey. It's Christmas, right? You were telling me about Bailey. He's here? He's really here? I thought he'd be dead.'

'He's very much alive. He, his grandson, Ben and Ben's sister, Diana all arrived today, much to everyone's surprise. We didn't know they were coming. We've only popped in for a moment to say hello and then we're all back to Eastbourne to see them.'

'In this weather? Are you sure that's wise? After all the rain there's so much ice on the roads and now with this heavy snowfall, it doesn't exactly make for safe travelling conditions. The police are saying that unless you really have to travel, it's best you don't.'

'Well I think we really have to, Josh. But we'll be very careful.'

'Have you seen Amias?'

'Um. Yes. We nodded to one another just a moment ago.'

'Nodded?' He tutted. 'I think he at least deserves a hello, don't you?'

'I didn't want to interrupt him and his gorgeous new girlfriend. They look so cosy over there, laughing together.'

'New girlfriend? What new girlfriend? The last girlfriend he had was Lorna and that ended months ago.'

'No. Natalia told me he's found 'the one'. But if that's her she looks much younger than I expected.'

'I don't know why Natalia would've … No. Actually, I do. But anyway. Amias doesn't have a girlfriend, Cat. And if you're referring to that dark-haired beauty standing beside him, she's Marcus' girlfriend, not Amias'. And yes. We all looked as astonished as you, but not only is she gorgeous, she's also very smart. They're at uni together.'

'Wow. Miracles definitely do happen. I'm so pleased for him. So why did Natalia say Amias had found 'the one' then?'

Josh shook his head. 'It's really not my place to say but I think this whole saga is so bloody ridiculous that someone needs to say something or it'll continue for another eighteen years.'

'Saga? What saga?'

'The saga of you and Amias.'

'Me and Amias? You're definitely drunk, Josh. We may row from time to time but I wouldn't call it a saga. He forgot about me eighteen years ago and only remembers me now because of Kyra.'

Josh snorted with laughter. 'That's the biggest load of turkey droppings I've heard all year. Forgot you. As if the man could bloody well forget you. I understand. I really do. When you love a woman but feel she's far too good for you, it's tough. But you've got to be a man about it and tell her or how else will she know, eh?'

'I have absolutely no idea what you're talking about, Josh. And I think perhaps you don't either.'

'Oh I do. Believe me I do. He's come to our house often enough over the years to ask Natalia's advice on this relationship or that. For someone who seems to have so many women at his feet he really hasn't a clue what to do with them.' He laughed again. 'I don't mean in the bedroom. He knows exactly what to do there, or so I hear. I mean as far as emotions are concerned. You've ruined him for every other woman on the planet, Cat.'

'I've what? I've done absolutely nothing to him.'

'Precisely.'

'OK, Josh. You're talking nonsense.'

'Am I? Am I really? Then tell me this? Did he come running to you to say that he'd made a complete mess of firework night? No. He came to us.'

'Josh!' Natalia appeared at his side, concern etched across her face. 'I think perhaps you need some fresh air before you start talking rubbish. Come with me, my darling.' She linked her arm through his and gave Cat an odd smile. 'Excuse us, Cat. He gets a bit silly when he drinks too much.'

'But it's cold outside,' Josh argued. 'I want to stay here and tell Cat about–'

'About our New Year's Eve party. Yes, I'm sure. But we're sending out invitations, so there's no need. We're having a bit of a do for New Year, Cat. You'll get all the details soon. Save the date though. Now come along, Josh.'

She virtually dragged Josh across the room before Cat had a chance to reply.

How weird was that? And what did Josh want to tell her that Natalia clearly didn't want him to? And why had Natalia lied about Amias having a girlfriend? Or was Josh just drunk and silly as Natalia had said?

Cat watched Amias for a moment or two. He

was still chatting and laughing with the stunning girl. But at least she wasn't his girlfriend.

Not that it made much difference.

Abigail hurried towards her, smiling. 'Glad you could make it.' She handed Cat a glass of champagne. 'I just heard Kyra telling Lucas that the man in the photo is here. Bailey Mitchell. Is that true? I mean. Of course it's true. I know Kyra didn't make it up. What I mean is, I can't believe it. And Ben? Is he as gorgeous as you thought he'd be?'

Cat dragged her gaze from Amias and returned Abigail's cheerful smile. She had told Abigail about her exchanges with Ben and also, that she liked him. They had shared a bottle of wine one evening and discussed Ben's pros and cons, the main ones of which were, that he looked strong, sexy and handsome, but he lived too far away and long-distance romances were a problem.

'I can't believe it either. And yes. Ben is as gorgeous as I expected. Maybe more so, in the flesh.'

'The flesh! You're a quick worker.' Abigail gave a snort of laughter. 'Sorry. I'm being facetious.'

Cat blushed and grinned mischievously.

'You're not. I'll tell you a secret. We kissed.'

Abigail's eyes and mouth opened wide. 'When?'

'Not long after they arrived at the hospital. We went into the corridor for a private word and he kissed me.'

'Wow. And?'

'It was nice.'

'Nice?'

'Yes. Nice. Oh don't you start. I've had enough of that from Kyra. Nice is good.'

'Hey.' Abigail laughed. 'I didn't say it wasn't. But was that all it was? Just nice? Didn't you feel your heart beat faster, or get tingles up and down your spine? Or hear a choir of angels, or even Santa's elves playing violins, or something?'

Cat frowned and shrugged. 'Not really. But I enjoyed it. It was soft and warm and … comforting, somehow.'

'Excuse me for saying this, but that sounds like a kiss from my gran. Those are soft, warm and comforting, although she doesn't kiss me on the lips, I'll grant you that. But even so. Didn't you feel anything? A tiny spark, if not a raging fire of passion?'

'I felt safe. I felt special. I think I even felt loved.'

'Well, that's something, I suppose.'

'That's a lot. It's been a very long time since a man has made me feel like that.'

'Then I wish you more of it. And definitely more of Ben. You deserve to be happy and in love. Perhaps he's a slow-burner. You know? One of those guys who builds up to the main event. Where is he anyway? You could've brought him. I can't wait to meet him.'

'He and his sister, Diana have gone to get some

sleep. I've left him a message to call me later. I was planning to go back to Eastbourne and take him and Diana out for dinner, but this snow may make that difficult.'

'How long are they going to be here?'

Cat shook her head. 'I didn't ask. I was so surprised. Oh! Did Kyra also say that Granny Viola moved her finger?'

'No. Really? That's wonderful news. I'm so pleased, Cat. They say Christmas is a time for miracles and it clearly is. What did the doctors say?'

'That they'll monitor her and if there's more sign of improvement, we'll discuss the next step. Whatever that means. To be honest, I was so astonished by the change after all these months, and by Bailey and Ben and everything that I'm not sure I really took it all in properly. We'll have another chat with them tomorrow. But it's such good news. And we're all convinced it's because of Bailey. We're sure Viola knows he's there because it was after he took her hand that she moved her finger.'

'Love conquers all, so they say.'

Cat shot a look at Amias. 'If only that were true.'

'Mum.' Kyra hurried towards Cat, beaming from ear to ear and grabbed her hand. 'You've got to try this Christmas buffet. It's delicious. This is a fantastic party, Abigail.'

Abigail smiled. 'Thank you, Kyra.'

Cat smiled too. 'I'm sure it is, but I'm not that hungry, sweetheart. Besides, I may be going out for dinner later.'

'If you and Gran and Jeremy drive to Eastbourne in this weather, you're crazy. But anyway, you need to have some food in case the car breaks down or something. Come on.'

'Can't you just get me a plate with a selection of goodies?'

'Nope. There's far too much to choose from. You need to see it all for yourself.'

'I should mingle,' Abigail said. 'I'll catch up with you again later. Have fun.'

Cat sighed at Kyra as Abigail disappeared into the crowd. 'OK then. I'll come.'

She allowed herself to be dragged over to the long line of tables to one side of the massive lounge and was amazed at the spread. Kyra was right. The selection of food was incredible. Platters of turkey, beef, several types of hams and cheeses of all shapes, sizes and varieties vied for attention against platters of prawns, crab, salmon and even lobster. There were canapés of every description, ranging from lobster vol au vents, to smoked salmon and fresh horseradish crostini, to fresh figs stuffed with goats' cheese, and everything in between. It was a cornucopia of delights. And there was an actual cornucopia: a large, white wicker, horn-shaped ornament filled with shelves and trays of individual portions of cakes, trifles, chocolate logs, mini Christmas puddings and brandy butter, tiny meringues with Christmas fruits, tarts, mince pies, and more, surrounded by Turkish delight and truffles.

'I don't know where to start.' Cat laughed as she scanned the festive feast. 'You're right, sweetheart. There is so much to choose from.'

'Start with the figs and goats' cheese.'

Amias' voice made Cat jump. Where had he sprung from? He was busy chatting to Marcus' girlfriend the last time she looked. Now he was standing close to her, with Lucas right beside him.

'What?' She didn't look at him. She didn't want him to see her blushing.

'You loved figs, I seem to remember. And goats' cheese was another favourite.'

'How can you remember that?' Now she did look at him. In astonishment.

He met her eyes. 'I remember lots of things, Cat.'

'Mum. Amias. Look!' Kyra sounded excited.

Cat managed to drag her gaze from Amias and look up. She gasped when she saw what Kyra had been pointing at.

Mistletoe.

Had Kyra done this on purpose? Had she, with the help of Lucas, planned this? Had they got Cat and Amias together on this very spot?

'It's mistletoe,' Kyra said, gleefully.

'So I see.' Cat glared at her.

Lucas had the decency to look a little uncomfortable. 'Mum says it's bad luck if two people stand under the stuff and don't kiss.'

Amias narrowed his eyes. 'Does she? Are you

sure about that Lucas?'

He nodded. 'Hey, man. It's up to you. But even I'd do it.'

'Thanks,' Cat said, throwing Lucas a sarcastic glare. 'There's no need, Amias. I don't believe in silly superstitions like that.'

She turned to walk away but Kyra stopped her.

'Mum! It's Christmas. And it's really rude not to kiss someone you meet under the mistletoe.'

'Amias doesn't care.'

'Don't I? I'm not sure I want bad luck. Is kissing me such an awful prospect, Cat?'

She met his look. There was something in his eyes that unnerved her even more than usual.

'You don't want to kiss me any more than I want to kiss you, but I suppose we'll have to or we'll never hear the last of it from these two.'

Amias stiffened at her words.

That did sound rude, but so what? He didn't really care, did he? And there was no way she was going to admit that she would give anything to kiss him. That she often dreamt of doing exactly that.

But a kiss from him might make her want him even more. If that was possible.

'Thanks,' he said, looking a little hurt.

'Let's get this over with then.' She couldn't look into his eyes. Instead, she stared up at the mistletoe.

He stepped closer and Cat caught a whiff of his aftershave. Butterflies took flight in her stomach. Goosebumps crawled up her arms. Her knees wobbled and her heart pounded.

What on earth was wrong with her? He hadn't even touched her yet.

And when he did, for a split second, she closed her eyes and really wished he hadn't. Her skin felt scorched, her throat felt dry and her head spun as his lips met hers in the briefest kiss imaginable.

But as he moved away, their eyes met and before she knew it, his mouth was on hers again. This time in a real kiss.

There was nothing nice about that kiss from what Cat could remember when it finally ended sometime later. The butterflies went crazy. Her heart was fit to burst from her chest. Her blood boiled in her veins and her legs turned to Christmas trifle. Her mind exploded, her head was like a whirlpool and if Amias hadn't had his arms around her she probably would've toppled over.

Nope. There was definitely nothing nice about that kiss. It was so much more than nice. It was deep and passionate, possessive and demanding, giving, yet filled with longing. It was sensual. It was sexy. It was intense, feverish, almost frenzied. It was all-consuming. It promised so much in just one kiss.

And when they eventually managed to part, they stared at one another in silence, both breathing deeply. Amias looked as astonished as Cat felt. She had reason to be. Eighteen years was a long time to love someone and wait for a kiss like that. A kiss she wanted again and again and again.

Why was he looking so mesmerised? Almost

as if the kiss had felt the same for him as it had for her. But that wasn't possible. Was it?

She was sure Amias did everything at breakneck speed, but that kiss hadn't been fast. It had been slow and tender, then passionate and earth-shatteringly wonderful. It had seemed to go on for ever and yet it was over far too soon.

No. There was definitely nothing nice about that kiss. And she didn't know whether to thank her lucky stars for that, or to curse her bad luck for discovering, in precise detail, exactly what she had been missing. And would never have again.

Christmas might be a time for miracles but it would take more than a miracle for Amias to kiss her like that again.

Several people were looking at them but she didn't care. One or two were clapping but she ignored them. All she could do was stare into his eyes and wish that he would take her in his arms once more.

'Cat.' He looked serious and yet he seemed filled with doubt. 'I think we need to talk.'

A tiny bubble of hope formed inside her. But perhaps he was simply going to say that the kiss hadn't meant anything to him and she shouldn't see it as something other than what it was. Merely a Christmas kiss under the mistletoe.

'About what?'

He opened his mouth but Mary's excited shriek as she hurried across the room towards them made him stop whatever he was about to say.

'Catherine! Catherine. It's a miracle. A nurse from the hospital has called. She's awake! Mother is awake. We must get back to the hospital without delay. Come along. Jeremy has gone to get the car.' Mary turned back towards the door.

Cat glanced from Amias to Mary and back to Amias.

He smiled. 'That's wonderful news.'

'You wanted to talk.'

She was grasping at straws but some instinct told her that if she left right now, she might not get this chance again.

He nodded. 'It can wait, Cat. It's waited eighteen years. One more day won't hurt. You go. I'll see you soon.' He reached out his hand and gently touched her arm.

Heat seared through her. She hesitated for a second but Mary called her name once more. She had to go.

'I'll see you soon then.' She forced herself to turn away but she glanced back at him and grinned. 'By the way, Amias, that was a pretty good kiss.'

He frowned momentarily before a devilish smile swept across his face, lighting up his dark eyes. 'Just pretty good? Next time I'll try to do better.'

A thrill of excitement shot through her. 'Next time? What makes you think there'll be a next time?'

'There'll be a next time, Cat, if that kiss was anything to go by. And I'll make sure there is.'

'Catherine! We can't wait all night.' Mary was clearly growing impatient.

Should Cat say anything more to Amias? He had just said he'd make sure there was a next time. What did he mean by that? Was there any chance at all that he did feel something for her? Any chance he did want to kiss her again?

Or, like Josh, had he had too much to drink?

She didn't have time to ask him now. She'd have to wait until the 'next time' as he had said. And that couldn't come fast enough for her.

The sound of the Christmas bells ringtone that Kyra had downloaded to Cat's phone trilled loudly. Cat pulled it from her bag and glanced at it. It was Ben Mitchell and his smiling face shone out at her from the screen, reminding her of the kiss they had also shared.

With a final, slightly guilty look at Amias, Cat hurried after Mary, answering Ben's call as she went.

Chapter Forty-One

'Have you heard the amazing news that Viola is awake?' Ben asked. 'Grandfather says he's crazy with joy to see Viola's beautiful eyes again after all these years. He's still with her at the hospital and we're going to meet him back there. Will you be coming back too?'

'Yes,' Cat said, glancing back at Amias once more as she left the lounge, and being both thrilled and surprised that he seemed to be watching her leave. As if he didn't want to take his gaze from her. 'We're just leaving the party and will hopefully be there in twenty minutes or so. Although with this weather, I'm not sure how long it may take.'

Ben laughed. 'This is just a flurry compared to the snow we get but I'd heard that everything grinds to a halt in England if you get the wrong kind of snow.'

'It grinds to a halt if we get any kind of snow. At least if we get more than a smattering. And this is definitely more than that. Did you and Diana get some sleep?'

'A little, thanks. But to be truthful, I was too excited to sleep. It was so good to finally meet you,

Cat. And that kiss was really nice. I'm looking forward to doing that again.'

Cat coughed to clear her throat – and swallow her guilt. Should she say something now? Should she tell him that she was in love with someone else?

Her mind was in a whirl. She was trying to fathom what Amias had wanted to talk about after that incredible kiss beneath the mistletoe. Could it be that he did have feelings for her, after all? Surely to kiss someone as he had just kissed her, you had to feel something for them?

Or maybe Amias kissed all women like that. Maybe he wanted them all to know just how good he was. How he could twist them around his little finger, body, soul, heart and mind. That they were putty in his experienced hands.

Was she being ridiculous to even have the slightest iota of hope that there could ever be anything between them?

And what about Ben? Ben had travelled thousands of miles to see her. OK, perhaps it was Bailey's idea because he wanted to see Viola, but Ben had come too.

Then again, so had Diana.

They had both come for Bailey's sake. It had nothing to do with her.

But Ben had kissed her. He'd said nice things to her.

Nice.

There was that word again.

Amias never said anything nice to her. No. that

wasn't completely true. Since she'd come home, he'd said a couple of nice things. But that kiss wasn't nice.

Oh God, that kiss! She would be dreaming about that for weeks to come.

Could Ben ever kiss like that?

Should she tell him about Amias?

Before she managed to find the words, Ben continued:

'Sorry. I'm probably embarrassing you, aren't I? How was the party? I know you weren't there for long but did you have a nice time?'

Nice? Was everything about Ben 'nice'? Even his conversation and the words he used?

'Er. Yes. I had a good time, thanks. I'd better go because I'm just about to get in the car and it'll be awkward chatting with my mum, Jeremy and Kyra listening to every word. I'll see you at the hospital.'

She rang off and climbed into the back seat of Jeremy's car.

Was writing that letter to Bailey Mitchel the right thing to do? Or had she now made her life even more complicated than it had been?

'Was that Ben?' Kyra asked.

'Yes. He phoned to see if I'd heard about Granny Viola. Bailey called him to tell him and Diana. He says Bailey is ecstatic, or something along those lines.'

Kyra grinned. 'I bet he is. He's just performed a miracle. We spend weeks talking to Granny Viola and playing her music, combing her hair and doing everything we can to wake her up and nothing happens. Nada. Zilch. Bailey Mitchell gets off a plane and takes her hand in his and poof! Granny Viola is suddenly and miraculously awake.'

Mary glanced over her shoulder from the front passenger seat. 'It certainly seems like a miracle. But the nurse told me that Granny Viola isn't quite 'with it' as yet and there may be some way to go before she recognises anyone or speaks. At the moment, she seems to be staring into space. But at least she's awake. So there's hope.'

'Hope?' Cat queried. 'Are you saying that this may not be quite as good news as we all think it is?'

'Yes. I'm afraid so. The nurse said that the fact she's staring into the room may be a sign that her brain isn't functioning fully yet. I think she was being tactful. There may be a possibility of brain damage and as awful as that is, we have to prepare ourselves for whatever happens.'

'No.' Cat didn't want to prepare herself for that. She wanted Granny Viola to recover. She wanted a chance to say she was sorry and to tell her she loved her. 'That can't be the case. It can't. That just wouldn't be fair. She's got to pull through. She's got to make a full recovery.'

Kyra took her hand and squeezed it. 'Don't get upset, Mum. She's in good hands. She'll be fine. I'm sure she will. It's Christmas. It's the time for miracles. She's just taking a while to wake up properly. It often takes me time to fully wake up and realise where I am in the morning. Granny Viola's been asleep for weeks. It's just going to take her a little bit longer, that's all.'

Cat smiled. 'You're right, sweetheart. Her brain is simply taking its time.'

'But you do all need to brace yourselves,' Jeremy said. 'Miracles happen. I know that because Mary walked into The Hope and Anchor and fell in love with me.' He threw Mary a huge smile. 'Sometimes though, they're not always what we want them to be.'

Mary sighed. 'Whatever happens, we'll cope. At least having Bailey here will be a comfort to Mother, I'm sure.'

The remainder of the journey was spent in virtual silence, each of them deep in their own thoughts, save for Frank Sinatra singing Christmas songs on the in-car sound system.

The snow was really coming down and it took twice as long as usual to get to the hospital. The roads were treacherous and despite Jeremy's careful driving, more than once, the car skidded on a patch of ice.

But Cat wasn't concerned about the conditions, even though it was a skidding lorry that had taken Kyle away from her.

All she could think about was Amias and that kiss.

It had felt as if her body had been in a coma, and that kiss had finally woken her up.

But as they dashed into the hospital and hurried

to Viola's room, Ben and Diana were standing in the corridor a few doors up from that, concern etched across their faces.

'What's wrong, Ben?' Cat stopped in her tracks. 'What's happened? Has …?'

The shrill cry died in her throat. She couldn't bring herself to say it.

Ben shook his head and sadness filled his eyes.

'It's Grandfather, Cat. He's had a stroke.'

Chapter Forty-Two

Christmas had looked so promising.

Cat had finally been kissed by Amias. And what a kiss!

Granny Viola had opened her eyes. OK, she was merely staring into space, but it was a step in the right direction.

There was even snow. Too much, in fact.

Then Bailey had gone and had a stroke. Why did life do stuff like that?

Thankfully, he was OK. It had been a mild one and the doctor had said he was fine, and would probably continue to be, as long as he took care of himself. But it was a warning. And one that changed things more than Cat expected.

In a way, it dampened everyone's Christmas spirit. But on the other hand, it made them realise how things could change in a second.

'It makes you think, doesn't it, Mum?' Kyra said.

Cat smiled wanly. They were sitting at Granny Viola's bedside, along with Mary and Jeremy, waiting for further news of Bailey – and for Granny Viola to do something other than stare into space.

'What does, sweetheart? Bailey's stroke, you mean?'

'Yeah. But not just that. All of this. The fact that we're all just jogging along and then life throws something unexpected in our paths. I know Granny Viola and Bailey are old, but it doesn't seem right that they've spent most of their lives apart and now they both end up in the same hospital, and both could … well ... you know.'

'Die at any minute,' Mary said, glancing across the bed at Cat and Kyra. 'Don't look so surprised, Catherine. It has to be said. We have to accept it could happen. I think Bailey having a stroke has really brought that home to me. And look at Mother. Lying here, staring at the ceiling. I think I preferred it when she had her eyes closed. At least she looked peaceful. Now she looks … worse somehow.'

'A bit like a zombie,' Kyra said, her voice no more than a whisper.

'Kyra!' Cat gave her a look of reproach.

'Sorry, Mum. But she does.'

Cat got to her feet. 'I'm going to find Ben and see if there's any news about Bailey.'

She trudged from the room and made her way to another, a few doors down, where Bailey was now resting. She tapped on the door, which was ajar, and waited to be invited in. Ben opened the door wider and smiled.

'How is he?' Cat asked.

'He's sleeping now,' Diana said, from inside the room. 'But he's determined to get back to

Viola's bedside as soon as humanly possible.'

'I'm so glad he's OK. I feel this is all my fault.' Cat gave them both an apologetic smile.

'Your fault?' Ben queried. 'How could this be your fault?'

She met his eyes. Kind, caring, lovely eyes, now so sad and yet at the same time, hopeful.

'If I hadn't written that letter, Bailey wouldn't have flown thousands of miles and he wouldn't have had a stroke. He'd be at home, in a chair in front of a fire, drinking whatever he drinks and looking forward to a wonderful Christmas.'

Ben shook his head. 'If you hadn't written that letter, he wouldn't have had the chance to see Viola again. I don't think you realise how much this means to him, Cat. As for the stroke. At his age, it's hardly a surprise, is it? As awful as it is, we're prepared. This isn't his first. He had an episode a year ago. I think that's why he was so determined to make this trip.'

Diana nodded. 'Ben's right, Cat. You've got nothing to be guilty about. Quite the opposite. We're all grateful to you.'

'Diana?' Ben took Cat's hand. 'Would it be OK if I took Cat to get some coffee? I'll bring one back for you.'

Diana smiled. 'Sure thing. If there's a bar of chocolate, could you bring me one of those too?'

'Done.' He smiled at Cat as he led her to the corridor.

What should she do? His hand was warm and

comforting. His smile was full of hope. She should pull her hand away, but she couldn't.

'I didn't realise this wasn't the first time. About Bailey's stroke, I mean.'

She was getting tongue-tied. Bailey's stroke wasn't the only reason she felt guilty.

There was also Amias.

Ben stopped and turned to face her. The corridor was empty, save for them and one or two nurses visiting each of the rooms and the wards, checking on their patients.

'We didn't want to say anything. It didn't really seem relevant. But now there's something else, I'll tell you. And this may sound strange, given what's happened. I'm sure we'll all be going home at some stage, but I think Grandfather may want to stay a while. Possibly longer than a while.' He looked down at their joined hands and ran his thumb along her finger. 'I was with him when he wrote his will and there's a clause in it that says where he wants his ashes to be scattered. It's here, Cat.' He gave a little laugh. 'Not in this hospital, obviously. But in England. And I think you can probably guess where.'

Cat looked down at their hands before meeting his eyes.

'Merriment Bay?'

Ben nodded.

'Really?' Cat was astonished.

'Yes. So you can see how important the place is to him. One way or another, he was determined

341

to come back.'

'But … what about his wife? Your grandmother? Doesn't he want to be with her?'

Ben shook his head, slowly and a little sadly.

'He loved her. I know he did. You could see it when he looked at her. And he was heartbroken when she died. But even so, he loved Viola more. He's always loved Viola. We had a long talk after your letter arrived and he told me that you can love more than one person, but only one person will ever have your soul. For him, that person was Viola. Is Viola.'

'So you'd be coming back to … to scatter his ashes when … I mean if …' she let her voice trail off.

'When he dies. Yes. But your letter, being here, and all this has made me realise something too. Life is short, Cat. It gives us opportunities but it can take them away in a flash if we don't act on them. I know we've just met, and I know the situation isn't ideal, but I really like you, Cat. *Really* like you. And I don't want to waste a minute. I don't want to throw away this chance. This opportunity. If Grandfather wants to stay, I'm going to stay here with him. And hopefully, see more of you. A lot more of you. And if something happens to Grandfather, I couldn't hope for a better person to be with at such a time.'

She should have pulled away. She should have told him about Amias. But how could she do that at a time like this? He was going to kiss her again. That was obvious.

He took her gently in his arms and this time his kiss was better than just nice.

But it was nothing like the kiss she had shared with Amias.

'Cat!'

Oh God. Was she even hearing Amias' voice in her head now? She must be, because it couldn't possibly be him in the flesh. He was at Abigail and Will's party.

'You certainly don't waste time, do you?'

Cat pulled away from Ben and glanced along the corridor.

Natalia was glaring at her.

And unless Cat's eyes deceived her, Amias was striding away from her, along the corridor, as fast as he possibly could.

Chapter Forty-Three

'Natalia!' Cat screeched as the look of contempt on Natalia's face burned into Cat's brain. 'What are you doing here?'

Natalia scornfully raised one brow. 'I might ask you the same question. Except it's obvious what you're doing. Amias and I are here because my darling husband tripped and fell. He gave himself a nasty-looking cut on his head. While they're stitching him up, Amias suggested we should come and see how you were. And Viola, of course. It seems you're enjoying yourself, so I suppose that means Viola's doing well. I'm glad, Cat. But I have to say, I'm a little disappointed in you.'

'Excuse me.' Ben stepped forward, a protective arm around Cat's waist. 'We haven't met. I'm Ben Mitchell. And you are?'

Natalia looked him up and down. 'I thought I was a friend of Cat's. It seems I was mistaken. It seems I was mistaken about a lot of things. Merry Christmas to you both.'

She turned and marched away.

'Natalia!' Cat called after her. 'Sorry, Ben. I need to have a word with her.'

Cat chased after her but Natalia was almost running and it was only when she stopped in the Accident and Emergency Ward that Cat caught up with her.

'What?' Natalia glowered.

'Why are you so annoyed?'

Natalia raised both brows. 'I'm astonished you need to ask. Oh look. Here's Amias. Won't this be jolly?'

Amias didn't even look at Cat. He looked at Natalia. 'Josh is ready to go. I'll get the car and meet you at the front entrance.'

'Amias?' Cat reached out her hand and caught the sleeve of his jacket. He looked down at her hand, but not at her. 'Amias, speak to me. Please.'

'I don't think we've got anything to say. Oh. But Merry Christmas, Cat.'

'I can explain. It was just a kiss, Amias. It didn't mean anything.'

Now he did look at her. 'Like the kiss we shared? That clearly didn't mean anything either. And I was stupid enough to think it did. My bad, as Lucas would say.'

He shrugged her hand from him and walked towards the exit.

'Amias!' She ran after him, taking two strides to each one of his. 'Amias. Stop! Your kiss did mean something. It did. Honestly. You must believe me.'

'Must I? Why? I believe my eyes, Cat. You and that man, who I assume must be the Ben Mitchell

I've heard about, looked very cosy to me. Why should I believe that our kiss meant something but that kiss just now, didn't? I'm not an idiot, Cat. Even if you think I am. You've led me on before and then dropped me stone dead. I thought this time was different. I thought … It doesn't matter what I thought. It's clear that nothing's changed. That you haven't changed.'

'What? I have no idea what you mean by that. I've never led you on in my life. And I certainly would never – and have never – dropped you like a stone. Dead or otherwise. You were the one who did that. You came to the hospital and made me believe you cared. You cuddled baby Kyra as if she actually meant something to you. And then, when I went home from the hospital, you stopped calling me. You didn't bother to come to see us. You told my mum and Granny Viola that you had no interest in me or my child and when I came to see you at the bay to ask you why, you were so busy with yet another stunning girl, that I decided there was no point in asking ... because it was obvious.'

He looked stunned and he blinked several times as if he were trying to comprehend everything she had just said.

'I didn't do anything of the sort. And I definitely didn't tell Mary or Viola that I had no interest in you or Kyra. Quite the opposite. I called you but you'd clearly changed your number. I came to see you but Mary and Viola wouldn't let me in. They said you didn't want to see me. You returned my notes and letters. And then you threatened to tell the police I was a stalker or something. That's what they told me. And I have no idea what girl in the bay you're talking about. But you did the same thing a few weeks ago. Just when I was getting up the courage to talk to you, you ignored my calls. You stopped answering my texts. I got the message. But then that kiss tonight made me think …' He ran his hand through his hair. 'It doesn't matter. I was wrong.'

'I did what? OK. I'll admit that I did that recently, but eighteen years ago I did no such thing. Did you just say that Mum and Granny Viola told you I didn't want to see you?'

'Yes. They told me to leave you alone because you never wanted to see me or speak to me again. And that those were your words.'

'But I said no such thing. They told me it was you. They … oh my God. They lied to me. They lied to us both.'

'They lied?' He stared at her. Incredulity etched across his face. 'Why?'

Cat let out a strangled laugh. 'Because you were from the wrong side of the river. And because they didn't like you.'

He bristled at that. 'I know they didn't like me. And I know what they thought of where we lived, but they were no better than we were.'

'I know.'

'Amias.' Natalia walked towards them and gave a little cough. 'As fascinating as this all is, we seem to be forgetting my husband has a head wound and needs to get some rest. Any chance you and Cat could continue this conversation another time, please? I'd like to get Josh home. Or I'll call a cab and leave you here to sort this out.'

'No.' Amias looked torn. 'I'll take you home. Cat? Can I call you?'

'Yes. Sorry. Of course.'

He frowned and then a tiny grin tugged at his mouth. 'And you'll answer?'

She grinned back and nodded. 'I'll answer, Amias. I can promise you that.'

He nodded at Natalia. 'I'll get the car. Can you manage Josh?'

'Yep. They're putting him in a wheelchair to get him to the door. I'll need your help from there.'

She threw Cat a smile and shook her head. 'Merry Christmas, Cat. I hope you two work it out. Sorry about what I said.'

'Merry Christmas, Natalia. I do too. And it's fine. I hope Josh feels better soon.'

Natalia tutted. 'It's his own fault for getting drunk. But I suppose it is Christmas. The season of goodwill, hangovers and almighty headaches. Especially in Josh's case.'

Amias was still there, looking at Cat.

She wasn't sure what was going on. If all this was true it meant her mum and gran had kept her and Amias apart. They had lied to him and more importantly they'd lied to her. Could she forgive them for that?

348

But it also meant he had tried to see her. He had called. He had gone to the house. He had cared.

But had he cared enough?

More to the point, did he still care?

And if so, how much?

'I've got lots of questions,' he said, when Natalia was out of earshot.

'Me too. Let's see if we can find some answers, shall we?'

'Mum! Mum!' Kyra came running along the corridor. 'There you are. I've been searching everywhere. Come quick. Granny Viola just blinked and looked at Gran. Hi, Amias. Sorry to interrupt.'

Cat darted a look from her to Amias.

Amias smiled at Kyra. 'That's OK.' He shook his head and sighed. 'Fate seems determined to throw things in our way, Cat. You go. But I'd be grateful if you didn't kiss anyone else until we've talked.' He gave her a sardonic smile.

'I won't. And don't find any stunning girls, OK?'

She grinned at him as Kyra grabbed her hand and dragged her away.

Chapter Forty-Four

Viola's blink, and the fact she now seemed to be staring at Mary were apparently more signs that there was some improvement, but tests still showed Viola was unresponsive. The doctor asked her to move her fingers or blink her eyes at his command. She did neither.

'She'll come back to us when she's ready,' Mary said. 'I'm going to stay here just in case it's tonight.'

'You mean this morning, Gran,' Kyra said. 'It's gone midnight so it's now Christmas Eve.'

'Why don't you stay at our hotel?' Ben suggested. He was standing in the corridor waiting for an update on Viola's condition so that he could relay it to Bailey the moment he woke up. 'I know there are rooms available. I heard someone at reception say there had been several cancellations due to the adverse weather.'

That seemed like a very good idea. The snow had been deep and driving conditions dreadful getting to the hospital. If the hotel did have rooms it would make sense to stay, instead of going all the way back to Merriment Bay.

The hotel was only a fifteen-minute walk from the hospital, meaning no one needed to drive, but Jeremy decided he would, and everyone seemed thankful for that. Fifteen minutes trudging through several inches of snow wouldn't be much fun. But while they had been in the hospital, the roads had been gritted and partially cleared so the journey to the hotel wasn't as dreadful as Cat had imagined. Even with Jeremy's driving.

That was mean. He was a good driver. But he did seem to be in a bit of a rush and Mary commented on it.

'I think there are enough people in hospital beds as it is, darling. We don't need to add more by having an accident.'

Ben was right. The hotel did have vacancies. Two rooms on the same floor as Ben and Diana's had suddenly become available.

'It's Fate,' Ben said, smiling eagerly at Cat when he and Diana arrived at the hotel a little later, Jeremy having gone back to get them after Cat, Kyra and Mary had checked in.

'Is it?'

Cat wasn't sure if that was good or bad. She wasn't sure if she trusted Fate. It seemed to be giving her mixed messages. One minute it was throwing her and Amias together, the next, her and Ben. Why couldn't it make up its mind?

Why couldn't she make up hers?

When she was with Amias, she wanted him. She wanted him so badly she felt a stabbing pain in her chest. She had wanted him for eighteen years, from the very first day they met. She was sure she would want him for the rest of her life.

And yet when she was with Ben, she felt calm and comforted.

Amias was like a raging fire. Ben was a cosy blanket.

Cat and Kyra shared a twin room at the hotel but Cat didn't get any sleep. Her mind was racing as images of Amias and Ben drifted in and out of her head.

Infuriatingly for Cat, when she eventually managed to get some sleep around 8.a.m. she missed a call from Amias. He also sent a text asking if everything was OK.

When she remembered to check her phone at breakfast and called him back, it went straight to voicemail.

'We stayed at the hospital and then went to a hotel nearby to get a few hours' sleep,' she said. 'We're staying over here and I don't know when I'll be back at Devon Villa, although we need to come back at some stage to get a change of clothes. We're all still wearing what we wore to Abigail and Will's party. I'll call you as soon as I know anything.'

All morning they missed each other's calls. She left him more messages.

'I'm not avoiding you, in case you think I am. Phones have to be switched off, or at least to flight mode, in Granny Viola's room. It's hospital policy. And I haven't kissed anyone since yesterday, if you're wondering about that too.'

He'd left messages to assure her it was fine.

'I understand. No stunning girls here, either. I wish I could be there with you, but I know that would give Mary a heart attack and neither of us want that. Although, having discovered that she and Viola lied to both of us all those years ago, I have to admit that I would quite like to have a quiet word or two with her. I was really hoping I could see you tonight, especially as it's Christmas Eve.'

'I don't think I can get away,' she said in another message. 'Why do we keep missing each other's calls? This is so annoying. We're seeing the doctor at 3.p.m. so if it's OK with you, I'll call you after that to let you know. And I'm tempted to strangle Mum, myself. I'm going to have it out with her at some stage, but I don't want to do it right now. It doesn't seem appropriate, given the situation. I'm so cross about it though and I think she knows there's something wrong because she's been giving me the strangest looks ever since last night.'

His message in reply half an hour later said: 'That's fine with me. We'll chat this afternoon.'

Just after lunch, Jeremy offered to drive back to Devon Villa and get them all clean clothes and collect the Christmas presents so that they would have them at the hotel on Christmas Day. Cat called Amias to ask him to meet her at the house if he could. But he didn't reply until twenty minutes after she and Jeremy returned to the hospital.

'I wasn't expecting to hear from you until after

3.00 this afternoon so I wasn't checking my messages. Sorry, Cat. I wish I'd known.'

And he still wasn't answering his phone. She left another message. 'I didn't think he'd want to drive all that way and back again in these conditions, but Mum was getting tired of wearing the same dress for two days running. And as it's Christmas Eve tonight, she wanted to wear something different.'

'Will you be at the hospital all night?' Another message from Amias, asked.

Her message in response said, 'Not all night, no. We're having a Christmas Eve dinner at the hotel. There were several tables vacant due to the continuing bad weather, and the doctors – and Bailey, who is now in a wheelchair, sitting beside Granny Viola's bed – have told us they would call if there was any change in her condition.'

'I thought you couldn't get away? Who's 'we'?' A later message queried. 'Does that include Ben Mitchell? I'm pleased to hear that Bailey is recovering well. Perhaps they'll all go back to Canada soon.'

'Please answer your phone, Amias!' Cat replied sometime later. 'I've got a good excuse for my calls going to voicemail. I'm in the hospital. Where are you? Anyway, yes. It does include Ben. It also includes his sister, and Kyra, Mum and Jeremy. And it's just dinner. We all need to eat. We're not staying for the dancing or anything.'

She got a message half an hour later and he

didn't sound thrilled.

'There's dancing? That sounds like fun. I've been giving a friend a hand at the ice rink at the Christmas Market all day. They're short-staffed. I couldn't hear my phone above the Christmas music and screaming kids. Sorry. And I've also been helping Natalia. Josh is still a bit woozy. Dad and I are replacing her front door with one that's self-closing and self-locking, so that's involved drills. Believe me, Cat, I'm not avoiding you. I really want to talk. Perhaps we can schedule a time slot? If you can fit me in between your dinner and dancing tonight.'

So now he was in a mood? She shouldn't have mentioned the dancing.

She sent a text. 'Are you free at 9.30? I'll call you then if you say yes.'

There was no response for twenty minutes then another message said, 'I'll be at The Hope and Anchor with some friends. But yes. Please call me then. I'll set my alarm so I don't miss your call.'

Her call went to voicemail yet again. She was getting sick of this.

'The pub? You're going to the pub on Christmas Eve with friends. That sounds almost as much fun as our dinner dance. I'll set my alarm too. Merry Christmas, Amias. I'll call you at 9.30 on the dot.'

Chapter Forty-Five

Back at the hotel that evening, after a luxurious bath and the added luxury of clean clothes, Cat went down to dinner with Kyra, Mary and Jeremy. Mary looked upset and Jeremy looked cross. Had they had a row?

'It's so good to have a change of clothes,' Cat said. 'Thanks for doing that, Jeremy.'

'It was no trouble. We're family. At least, that's how I think of us.'

'That's how I think of us too, darling,' Mary said, a little apologetically.

That wasn't quite how Cat thought of him but she didn't say that.

'Actions speak louder than words, my darling,' Jeremy said, with a touch of bitterness.

'I don't think this is the time or place to discuss it.' Mary shot a look at Cat.

Something was clearly going on. Cat glanced questioningly at Kyra who shrugged. She had obviously picked up on the tension in the air too.

'Is everything all right, Mum?' Cat asked.

'Of course it is, Catherine. Why wouldn't it be?'

'OK. Please don't bite my head off. You two just don't seem quite as lovey-dovey as usual, that's all.'

'We're fine,' Mary said.

'Are we?' Jeremy asked. 'Where's the bloody waiter? I'm starving. The place is half empty and they still make us wait.'

'I think they're short-staffed,' Cat said. 'I heard the guy at reception say that several people were having trouble getting here in this weather, and not just guests.'

'Why? I drove to Merriment Bay and back without too much trouble.'

'Yes. But your car is built for this weather. Not everyone has a four-wheel drive. Not everyone has a car. Some have to rely on public transport and that goes nowhere when it snows. Ah. Here are Ben and Diana. And the waiter's coming too.'

'About bloody time.' Jeremy scowled as he studied the menu.

This was going to be a fun evening.

'You look lovely, Cat.' Ben took the empty seat beside her.

'Thank you. So do you.'

He did. She couldn't lie about that. But she did feel a little guilty. It was a good thing Amias wasn't around.

The waiter took their orders which were pretty simple. They all chose the Christmas dinner of turkey and all the trimmings. Jeremy told him they were in a hurry to get back to the hospital so insisted they got theirs first and Kyra rolled her eyes at Cat. He really was in a mood this evening.

Kyra smiled at Ben. 'Bailey had some really interesting stories to tell today. I loved listening to him. I hadn't realised how tough it was to be a pilot in the war. When he said that he hesitated over his first kill, I wondered why. But it's not like the video games or the simulator at the museum. He made that very clear. He should give talks at schools and colleges.'

Ben smiled back. 'I think he's a bit too old to do that now. But I agree. He has a way of making the past come to life. You feel as if you're in that cockpit with him. Making the life and death choices he had to make. Watching your buddies being shot down, or worse and not knowing from one day to the next if this was your last day on this earth.'

Diana nodded. 'I think that's why relationships were so intense. And why there were so many whirlwind romances. People lived life on the edge and they took their chance at happiness whenever and wherever they could.'

'But it wasn't like that with Bailey and Ivy,' Kyra said. 'They were together for quite a long time, considering. Or with him and Viola. They fell in love slowly. And didn't realise they were in love until it was too late.'

'It's never too late,' Jeremy said. 'And everyone has choices. Some people don't act on them and others do. But no one should stay with someone if it isn't working. Or if they don't feel truly loved.'

That sounded as if it had nothing to do with the conversation they were having, and when he looked directly at Mary, Cat was sure it didn't. It was to do with them. There was definitely something going on. Had they fallen out of love as suddenly as they had fallen into it?

'Excuse me,' Mary said, an odd inflection in her voice. 'I'm popping to the ladies' room.'

'I'll join you.' Cat got to her feet.

Jeremy frowned and fiddled with his cutlery.

Cat waited until they were out of earshot.

'OK, Mum. What's going on? And please don't say 'nothing' because I'm not an idiot and it's obvious that's something's up.'

Mary glanced over her shoulder but didn't reply until they were safely inside the powder room section of the ladies'.

'I'm not really sure. I thought it would blow over but it hasn't.'

'What, Mum? You thought what would blow over? Have you and Jeremy had a row?'

'Not a row, exactly. More of a disagreement.'

Cat tutted. 'OK. What was the disagreement about and when did you have it?'

Mary sat on the edge of one of a circle of seats in the centre of the room.

'It started after Bailey's stroke. Kyra told us that you had told her that Ben said Bailey had made a will saying he wanted his ashes scattered in Merriment Bay. She thought it was romantic.'

Cat rolled her eyes. 'I must have a word with her about repeating everything I say. It's getting to be a habit. Sorry. You were saying?'

'When Jeremy and I were alone, he asked me about Mother's will. Whether she had made one and if I was the only beneficiary.'

'That's not really any of his business, Mum.'

'It is and it isn't. We're engaged, so it is, in a way.'

'No. But anyway. Did you tell him?'

Mary nodded. 'Yes. I had no reason not to. He seemed a little irritated that you and Kyra were named beneficiaries. Then today, this morning in fact, shortly before you and he went home to get our clothes, and the presents, he asked if I'd made a will. I said I had but that I'd made an appointment with my solicitor to make a new one because Annie told me that marriage invalidates a previous will. Jeremy suggested we should meet with his friend, who is a solicitor, so that we could both make new wills and when I said I'd rather stay with mine because he's been our family solicitor for as long as I can remember, he got upset.'

'Hmm. That sounds a bit iffy. What did you say?'

She shook her head. 'I told him that you and Kyra would be getting most of my estate in any event. I assumed he didn't need my money anyway. But he was rather cross. He said he was very disappointed. That he intended to leave everything to me and had assumed I'd do the same for him.'

'And are you now going to?'

'No. I love him. But there's no question of me leaving the bulk of my estate to anyone but you and Kyra. That will never change, no matter what.'

'And you told him that?'

'Yes. Both this morning and again when he brought it up shortly before we came down for dinner. He's been moody ever since. He says it's clear that I don't really love him because if I did, I wouldn't treat him as if he didn't mean anything to me.'

'Perhaps he does need your money, Mum. Although with all the money you've given him for the work he was doing on the house, he should have a nice little sum.'

'Catherine. That's not nice. I explained what that was for and he hasn't asked for money for a while now.'

'Because he hasn't been doing any work, thank heavens. Do you think he could have money problems?'

'No!' She looked thoughtful. 'At least I don't think so. And he bought me this gorgeous ring so he must have some money.'

'Unless he used some of the money you'd given him, instead.'

'Catherine! How can you think such a thing?'

Cat scanned Mary's face. 'Be honest, Mum. You've been wondering the same thing, haven't you?'

'No. I merely wondered when the marble

would be arriving, amongst other things and when I asked him, he said that there are delays and it's all to do with Brexit and such.'

'But you don't really believe that, do you?'

'I do. I did. Until today. No. I have had one or two doubts, I'll admit.' She sighed. 'Life is very strange, Catherine. One minute everything is wonderful. The next minute we're doubting everything and questioning things that earlier we would have said we knew were true without a shadow of a doubt. It was his reaction to the wills. I can't explain it and I don't know why, but something told me this wasn't quite right. And I haven't been able to shake that feeling.'

'I didn't want to tell you this but Natalia looked at what he'd done at the house and she was less than impressed. She said it's sub-standard work. I'm not sure he's really a builder at all.'

'What are you saying, Catherine? That he's some sort of conman? That I'm his 'mark'. Isn't that what they're called?'

'I'm not saying that. But I think you're beginning to wonder if it's true, aren't you? I can see the doubt in your eyes, Mum.'

Mary hung her head. 'I don't know what to think anymore. I love him. I thought he loved me. But how do you tell if someone is really sincere? How do you know if someone really loves you for you? Or if they love you for some other reason? Or merely want what they can get from you? I've never been good at relationships. Nor has Mother. And let's be honest, Catherine, nor have you. It's the Devon luck with men. It's all bad.'

'Hold on, Mum. I was lucky with Kyle. Until he died. And I might have been lucky with Amias if you and Granny Viola hadn't decided that was not going to happen.'

'What? What are you talking about?'

Mary's horrified expression showed she knew precisely what Cat was talking about.

'I think you know, Mum. I need to have a conversation with you about exactly what happened eighteen years ago. With you and Granny Viola and me and Amias. But that can wait for another day. For now, we need to deal with you and Jeremy.'

Mary shook her head. 'No, Catherine. *I'm* the one who needs to deal with me and Jeremy.' She got to her feet, smoothed down her dress and stared at her reflection in the floor to ceiling mirrors. 'I thought he was the answer to my prayers. It seems I may have been mistaken. It appears I have been wrong about a great many things in my life.'

Despite being cross with her, Cat couldn't help but feel sorry for her. Mary had been so happy since Jeremy had come into her life.

'What are you going to do, Mum?'

'Nothing during dinner. I don't want to ruin everyone's Christmas Eve. But I'm going to ask him to be honest with me. And then I'm going to ask him to move out of Devon Villa for a while. I think we both need time to think. We Devon women are strong, Catherine. Especially when we need to be. You know that better than the rest of us.'

Cat linked her arm through Mary's and they walked back to the dining room. Jeremy's chair was empty and Cat and Mary exchanged glances.

'Where's Jeremy?' Cat asked.

'He went to the loo,' Kyra said. 'About one minute after you and Gran. He'll be back in a moment, I expect.'

Mary let out a dramatic sigh and slumped down onto her chair. 'I wouldn't count on that, Kyra.'

'Mum?' A sudden thought dawned on Cat. 'He's got a car. And he's got a key to Devon Villa.'

Chapter Forty-Six

Amias smiled at Natalia as he and his dad, Alwick were leaving. 'I'm going to miss barging into your home.'

He watched the door glide shut behind him and waited for the satisfying click of the lock.

Natalia grinned and wrapped her long, thick cardigan more tightly around her.

'You do realise there's a real chance of me locking myself out every time I put the bins out, or I go to get something from my car, don't you?'

Alwick laughed. 'Which is why Amias said we had to put one of these key boxes outside. They're normally found on the homes of elderly people so that care workers and emergency service personnel can gain access if the person has a fall. They're not meant for youngsters like you who can't remember to take their keys with them, or put on the safety catch and remember to click it off again the moment they're inside.'

He used the key to open the front door again before putting the key in the box and shutting it as Natalia stepped back inside the doorway.

'Hmm. Thanks for that. Do I have to remember

the combination for this key box? Because you know what I'm like with codes, don't you?'

It was Amias' turn to laugh. 'Which is why both Dad and I have got it on our phones. And so has Josh. If you get locked out and can't recall the key box combo, call one of us. We've put it on your phone, but you'll forget what it is and delete it, knowing you.'

'Oi. I'm not completely stupid, you know.'

'Not completely,' Amias agreed, grinning as he pulled his ringing phone from the pocket of his jeans and glanced at the screen. 'It's Cat.' He beamed at Natalia and turned away as he answered the call. 'It can't be 9.30 already, can it? I'm still at Natalia's. Wait. What? Slow down, Cat. What's happened? Say that again.'

'I said that we were right about Jeremy. At least we think we were. He and Mum have had a row and we think he may be on the way back to Devon Villa. He's got a key and we think he may take some stuff. He can take his own stuff, but nothing else. We've tried to call a cab but there's nothing available and it'll take us ages to get there. Is there any chance that you could go round and see if he's there? I know it's a lot to ask and I know you're going out but I don't know who else to turn to.'

'Of course I'll go round. You're saying you think he may steal something? Seriously? And you think he'll be there now?'

'He left about ten minutes ago, so it'll take him a little while to get there in this weather. It took us about forty minutes earlier, but it was daylight then.'

'And what do you want me to do? Insist on going in with him and waiting while he gets his stuff? I can do that.'

'Yes please. And make sure he doesn't take anything. I'm not saying he will. I'm just saying we're not sure.'

'And you'd rather be safe than sorry. I get that. Er. Does Mary know you're asking me?'

'She knows.'

Amias laughed. 'And she trusts me?'

'This isn't funny, Amias. This is serious. And if I'm honest, no. She doesn't. But at this point in time she trusts you more than she trusts Jeremy.'

'I'm not sure that's a glowing endorsement. But fine. I'll go right now. Where will you be? I'll call you when he arrives. Just one thing though. What if he doesn't? Is there a key somewhere else? Or do you want me to sit outside in the car all night? Which I'll do, if you want me to. But I'd rather be inside in the warm.'

'Annie has a key. She works in Bella Vista. And I'll either be at the hotel or at the hospital, but I'll keep my phone on, regardless.'

'I know Annie. Will you ask Mary if it's OK for me to get it and go inside?'

'Hold on.' There was a muffled sound before Cat spoke again. 'She says, "needs must", which is her way of saying she'd rather invite the devil and his hordes than you, but she has no choice.' Cat sighed down the phone.

'Thanks. She might want to remember that she's asking me a favour.'

'She's not. I am.'

'OK. That's different. I'll call you later. Hold on. Dad's insisting on coming with me. Although I'm not sure he knows where or why. But he clearly thinks I'm twelve and need some help.' Amias laughed again. 'Best not tell Mary that though.'

'I won't. Thanks, Amias. I owe you for this.'

'And I'll ask for payment. But it won't be money, Cat.' He rang off and grinned.

'What's going on?' Natalia asked. 'Did I hear you mention Jeremy?'

Amias gave a brief explanation.

He wasn't sure he believed it. It seemed a bit far-fetched. But then again, there were men who saw women as cash cows and took advantage of them financially as well as emotionally. Was Jeremy Stone one of them?

He had asked around about Jeremy, as he'd promised, but no one seemed to know the man, or anything about him. Amias had even asked his friends in the police but there was no record of a Jeremy Stone. That was a good thing. If Jeremy Stone was the man's real name, of course.

'Can I come too?' Natalia was clearly excited.

'No. You've got to stay here and look after Josh. We'll pop back later and fill you in on the details though.'

'I thought you were going to the pub tonight.'

'I was. But now I'm going to Devon Villa.'

Natalia came outside to give them her usual hug goodbye and the door glided shut behind her.

'Damn,' she said. 'Amias. I've locked myself out. I can see this door is going to be a pain in the proverbial.'

Amias let out a laugh. 'The door is fine, Natalia. You're the pain in the proverbial.'

He shook his head as he let her back in using the key from the key box outside. With a final wave, he and Alwick got into his car and drove towards Devon Villa via the Bella Vista restaurant on Coast Road.

Chapter Forty-Seven

Cat waited patiently for Amias to call, but by the time she, Mary and Kyra, together with Ben and Diana finally got a cab and made it back to the hospital more than an hour later, there was still no call or message.

'It's a good sign, Mum. It means Jeremy may not be going back to the house, after all.'

They had told Ben and Diana as little as possible about the situation and merely said that Mary and Jeremy were reconsidering their relationship. Which was true in a way.

'Or it means something has happened. His things are at the house. He'll have to go back.'

Cat thought about it for a while as they entered the hospital and slowly made their way to Granny Viola's room. Diana and Ben were hanging back just a little as if they knew the Devons wanted a bit of space to talk.

'But he didn't have much, did he? I mean, he didn't bring much with him when he came to stay. I'm sure I only saw a couple of holdalls when he moved in. He told you he was only planning to be in Merriment Bay for a week when you met him in the pub, remember?'

'That's true. And no, he didn't have much with him, you're right.'

'So he would only return to the house if he actually planned to rob it. I'm not sure if I'm imagining this, because of the situation, but when we went back to the house today, he brought three holdalls out with him, and another when we brought out the bags of presents. I assumed you'd asked him to bring several days' worth of clothes, in case you wanted to stay at the hotel for longer, but perhaps he already knew he might be leaving tonight.'

Mary stopped in her tracks. 'Are you saying that he may have already taken his things? That he packed his bags this afternoon, in case?'

Cat nodded. 'And that he may have already taken a few things he wanted from the house. Perhaps I should ask Amias to check the silver.'

Mary bristled slightly. 'Is that a joke, Catherine?'

'Sort of, but then again, not really. I'm serious, Mum. He may have decided this afternoon that things weren't going to go his way and to cut and run. He may have put a few 'goodies' in one of the holdalls he put in the car this afternoon. Oh God. And I left him to bring in the presents. Did he, Mum? Did he take the presents to your room? Are they there?'

Mary shook her head. 'No. He said he was going to take them to your room. And he only brought one holdall up to ours. There was a change of clothes for us both, but nothing else was in it.'

Kyra gasped. 'Are you saying he's stolen our presents? I hope Amias kills him.'

Cat wrapped an arm around her daughter. 'I don't think Amias will see him, sweetheart. I think Jeremy Stone has gone. And yes, he's taken our Christmas presents with him.'

Chapter Forty-Eight

'We've changed the locks,' Amias said, after Cat had called him to tell him the news about Jeremy. 'And we've had a look around, as you asked, but as I've only ever been here once before, when I carried Kyra up to her room, I don't really know if anything's missing or not. But there were jewellery boxes in what I assume must be Viola's and Mary's bedrooms, and both were open and empty, so I think we can safely say he took the jewellery. Your room and Kyra's looked untouched.'

'Oh God. The bastard. Although both Granny Viola and Mum only used to keep costume jewellery in those, so it may not be as bad as we think. Assuming they still keep the good stuff in the safe.'

'There's a safe? I didn't see that. He couldn't have put that in a holdall though. Sorry. That wasn't funny.'

'I think we could all do with a bit of humour at the moment, to be honest. God, this is all so depressing. Mum's putting on a brave face but I think, deep down, she's devastated. She loved him and trusted him. At first.'

'I wish I'd made more of an effort to find out about him. But everywhere I looked and everyone I asked came up with nothing. He isn't even on social media. Maybe that should've warned me.'

'Hey. I wasn't on social media until I started writing to Ben.'

Amias heard the catch in her voice and knew she hadn't meant to say that. He couldn't stop the twinge of jealously rising up inside him but he cleared his throat and forced himself to smile. Hopefully, that would help him sound less irritated than he felt.

'I meant the fact that I came up with nothing and that no one had heard of him, rather than anything about social media. Is Ben taking care of you and Kyra and Mary? You've all had a dreadful shock.'

'Yes. I mean, he's been kind. But we're fine. As Mum's always saying, we Devon women are made of strong stuff. I suppose we should call the police. But then Mum would have to get back to the house and see what's missing. No point in calling the insurance company. I think inviting a thief and conman to live with you probably breaches their terms. I'll ask her about the safe and the jewellery. It's behind the long mirror in the hall. Would you look to see if the mirror has moved and whether or not the safe is open? I don't think Mum would've given him the combination though.'

'I'm in the hall now and the mirror's on the wall. Hold on. I'll check behind it.' He did, and when he checked the safe, it was locked. 'Nope. It's locked, so he didn't get in there. And yes, you should call the police but Mary will have to talk to them. I can call my friends in the force if you like and one of them can come and get her and bring her back here to look around. I'd offer to come myself, but I don't want to ruin her day even more.'

'Thanks, Amias. I'd really appreciate that. I'll speak to her now and let her know that's what you're doing. And thank you for changing all the locks and for everything else. Thank you for being there, especially when I really needed you.'

His heart skipped a beat.

'I'll always be here for you, Cat. Whether you need me to or not.'

She didn't respond right away and he remained silent. Had he said too much? Had he scared her off already? Or was Ben Mitchell being more of a comfort than she was saying?

God how he wished he was at the bloody hospital.

'That means a lot. Thank you, Amias.'

'There's no need to thank me, Cat. Is there anything else you'd like me to do? I'll call you when I've spoken to my friends in Merriment Bay police, so check your messages if you're going back into Viola's room and switching off your phone. I shouldn't be more than fifteen minutes or so.'

'I'll do that. What about the keys?'

'Dad and I will wait here until Mary arrives.'

'Your dad? Is that wise?'

Amias laughed. 'You're right. It's probably not, but as we came in my car, it's either that, or me taking him home and then coming back. Which I'll happily do, if you want. It'll only take a couple of minutes each way, but we had planned to go to the pub together and meet some friends, later.'

'No. Driving in this weather is bad enough. It's silly to do extra trips just because two people hate one another. Perhaps he could wait in the car though when he knows they're on their way. But if you're still going out – and of course you should, it's Christmas Eve – you could leave the key somewhere safe.'

'Er. I think that defeats the object of changing the locks. People always look for hidden keys. I'll tell you what I can do, if it's OK with you. I can give the keys to whichever of my friends comes to get Mary. I can drop the keys into the station on our way to the pub. Unless you want me to stay here.'

'No. That's a brilliant idea. If your friend, or whoever is happy to do that, that would be great. Go out and have fun. You've wasted enough of your Christmas Eve already.'

'It wasn't a waste, Cat. It was a pleasure. I'm not sure what else I need to say or do to convince you of that. But I still think we need to talk. And the sooner the better as far as I'm concerned.'

'Yes. And we will. As soon as possible. But perhaps tonight isn't the best time. My head's all over the place with this business. And you haven't heard the worst part yet. The bloody man even stole our Christmas presents.'

'You have got to be joking! I hope for his sake he has gone as far away as possible because if I get my hands on him, well, let's just say he won't be the only one spending time in jail.'

'Amias! Then I really hope he has scarpered. Because jail is the last place I want you.'

Amias laughed to himself as they said goodbye for now and he rang off. At least she had said she wanted him. In a roundabout way.

He was hurt and sad that she was going to have such an awful Christmas and that he couldn't even be there to share it with her.

He had an idea. The pub could wait.

'Dad. We're going to the police and then we're heading back to Natalia's and after that, if it's OK with you, I'm driving to Eastbourne to the hospital. I'm friends with some of the doctors and nurses there and I'm sure they'll let me in even if it's very late. I'm going to make sure Cat and Kyra and also Mary and Viola get at least one Christmas present each, although I'll have to borrow them from Natalia.'

Alwick shook his head. 'You must love Cat Devon very much if you're prepared to do all this for her. But Mary won't welcome you at Viola's bedside, son.'

'I do, Dad. I always have. And one day soon, I hope I can tell her that. I'm hoping she feels the same about me. Or at the least, that she feels something. I can work on something. Indifference is much harder to deal with. And the beauty of tonight is that, if I time it right, Mary won't be there. She'll be with the police at Devon Villa. I'll be able to see Cat and Kyra and be gone again before Mary knows I'm there.'

'I hope you're right, son. But the Devon women have a knack of breaking hearts. I hope Cat Devon doesn't break yours – again.'

Chapter Forty-Nine

Exhaustion swept over Cat like a blanket of snow. She was cold, she was tired and she was feeling incredibly emotional.

Amias had been wonderful. Without him, she wasn't sure what they would have done. He'd been there for her when she needed him. And he'd said he would always be there for her, whether she needed him or not. That had sent a thrill through her entire body.

But even thinking of Amias was tiring. Not in a bad way, but in a confused, not knowing quite what was happening kind of way. She shifted from ecstatic to nervous, from jubilant to doubtful, from excited to fearful. Their talk, whenever they were going to have it, could go either of two ways.

Either he would say he cared about her and wanted to have a relationship with her. Or he would say he liked her but just as a friend.

That kiss hadn't been the kiss you gave a friend though. Had it?

And now her head was going around in circles again. She felt as if she was on one of those merry-go-rounds they had at Christmas fairs; a carousel going up and down and round and round. One she couldn't get off and wasn't sure if she wanted to or not. At least while she was on it, she didn't have to face the thing that she dreaded. Amias telling her he could never love her as she loved him.

She sighed as she glanced at her watch. It was getting on for 10.30 and it would soon be Christmas Day. Not that they had much to celebrate. The shops shut long ago and there was nowhere she could get even a tiny present for Kyra to open on Christmas Day.

She smiled wanly at her daughter's head. Kyra was resting it on Granny Viola's bed, her hand in Granny Viola's. This wasn't the Christmas either of them had expected. But then again since they arrived in Merriment Bay, nothing had gone as they expected.

Cat sometimes wished Kyra had gone to uni in September. But that wouldn't have changed very much really. And at least Kyra seemed happy with Lucas. He had been calling her and texting every hour or more since they had left the party the night before Christmas Eve. He clearly cared a lot for her.

What did the future hold for them? Would she go to uni next year? Would she travel as she had planned after postponing her place at uni? Would Lucas go with her? He had planned to work in Will's law firm, but that could change. Or would Kyra decide to stay in Merriment Bay?

Cat hoped Kyra wouldn't set aside her plans and follow someone else's dream. Cat had done that once. It had ended badly. She wanted more for her daughter. But she would let Kyra choose her own path. Follow her own star. Providing it was her own and no one else's.

'How are you feeling, Cat?'

Cat looked over at Ben who was standing in the doorway of Viola's room.

She shrugged and gave a small laugh.

'Not too bad, thanks, considering.'

'It's certainly been a hell of a few days, hasn't it?'

'You can say that again. I feel as if the world is spinning out of control. This latest thing with Mum and Jeremy was unexpected. And yet, it wasn't. Sorry. That won't make sense to you. I'm not sure it really makes sense to me. I'm not sure of anything at the moment. I do wish you hadn't had to witness that though.'

'I'm glad we were here. I haven't been any help but if there's anything I can do, you only have to ask, Cat. I'd do anything I could to put that lovely smile back on your face.'

She met his eyes and could tell he meant that.

'Thanks. Having you, and Diana and Bailey here, has been a great comfort to us all. Is Bailey sleeping?'

'Yes. Diana's with him. Why don't you and Kyra go back to the hotel and get a good night's sleep? I'll stay here with Viola until Mary returns. I promise she'll be in good hands. If you go now, there's more chance of getting a cab. I'll call you if there's even the slightest change in her condition.'

Cat hesitated. A good night's sleep would do wonders for both her and Kyra. But could she really leave Ben with Viola? She trusted Ben, that wasn't the issue. But if Mary returned and found Ben there and no sign of Cat and Kyra, would she be upset?

Probably. Almost definitely.

And yet had Mary given a damn about how upset Cat would be when she and Granny Viola had lied about Amias?

No.

So why should Cat give a damn about how Mary would feel over something so trivial, in comparison?

'Are you serious, Ben?' Cat eyed him intently. 'Would you really be happy to do that? Don't you and Diana want to get some sleep?'

He smiled. 'We've been taking it in turns for most of the day. We're pretty good at grabbing catnaps. We're both fine. And if we're tired tomorrow, maybe you'll return the favour and sit with Grandfather for an hour or two, if he's not in here with Viola again for most of the day, that is.'

'I'll happily return the favour. Thank you, Ben. This is really kind of you. Kyra. Kyra, sweetheart, wake up.'

Kyra stirred, looked around the room and yawned.

'Is it Christmas Day?'

'Not yet, sweetheart. But Ben's offered to sit with Granny Viola while you and I go and get some sleep.'

'Oh. OK.' She slowly got to her feet, yawning as she did so. 'I need the loo first.'

She ambled towards Ben and the doorway, smiling up at him as he stepped aside to let her pass.

Cat got to her feet too and, after kissing Granny Viola on the cheek, walked towards Ben.

He didn't stand aside for her. Instead he smiled. A rather sexy smile, in fact.

'It's Christmas,' he said, pulling a sprig of mistletoe from his pocket. 'I stole this from the hotel.' He raised it above their heads and winked.

Cat stared at it and at him. She had promised Amias she wouldn't kiss anyone. But it was Christmas and Ben was holding mistletoe. Hadn't people said it was unlucky if you didn't kiss someone you met under mistletoe?

She smiled up at him, a little sleepily.

This time his kiss was even nicer. And when he wrapped his arms around her, she did the same, almost instinctively but partially because she felt too tired to stand. Slowly. She eased herself away. This was wrong and yet it felt right in many ways. She had promised Amias, and yet it was just a kiss. A kiss under the mistletoe at Christmas. And Ben was nice. So very nice.

'I think Kyra's waiting,' she said.

But when she looked along the corridor, there was no sign of Kyra. She must have imagined seeing someone in the corner of her eye as she eased away from Ben. Then Kyra appeared from the loo and Cat let go of Ben and walked towards her. She glanced over her shoulder and smiled.

'Thanks for this, Ben. We'll see you later. Merry Christmas by the way.'

He smiled back. 'Merry Christmas to you and Kyra, Cat. Pleasant dreams. I'll be thinking of you.'

'You kissed him again, didn't you?' Kyra asked, her voice drowsy and her eyes half closed.

'He kissed me.'

'Is there a difference? A kiss is a kiss.'

'But it was just a Christmas kiss under the mistletoe.'

'Tell that to Amias.'

'Hopefully, I won't need to because he doesn't need to know. I won't get upset if he kisses anyone under the mistletoe tonight at the pub.'

'Yeah right. Tell that to someone who might believe you. You'd go nuts with jealousy. I don't get it, Mum. You've loved Amias for years. You've known Ben for about ten minutes. Are you really prepared to throw away your chance of happiness with Amias just for a kiss under the mistletoe with Ben?'

Cat stared at her. 'I don't know if I even have a chance of happiness with Amias. But no, of course I wouldn't. Ben's been kind though and it was just a little kiss. Nothing more. Please don't tell anyone about it.'

'I won't. But please promise me you won't do it again. At least not until you know for sure which one you want to be with. Because kissing two men and leading them both on is something I never expected you to do.'

'I'm not leading anyone on.'

Amias had said something similar.

'You may think you're not, but I can assure you, Mum, from where I'm standing you most definitely are.'

'Really? You truly believe that's what I'm doing?'

Kyra shrugged. 'That's the way it looks to me.'

'Excuse me. You're Cat and Kyra Devon, aren't you?'

Cat turned to the nurse at the desk at the entrance to the ward.

'Yes. I'm Cat and this is Kyra.'

The nurse smiled, bent down and put two large, glittery Christmas bags on the desk.

'Then these are for you.'

'For us? I don't understand.'

'They were left for you. Just now.'

'Left for us? Just now?'

Cat was having trouble concentrating. Exhaustion was getting the better of her and Kyra's words hadn't helped. Her mind was in a whirl yet again.

'Yes. About five minutes ago. If you hurry you may still catch him.'

'Catch him? Catch who?'

The nurse glanced from Cat to Kyra and then towards the door.

'Amias Wells. He left these for you and Kyra.

I told him he could take them to you, as he's a friend of my brother and he asked so nicely. I thought he was going to but he turned around and left them here instead. Merry Christmas.'

Kyra sighed. 'Well done, Mum. Looks like you've just blown your chance with Amias. He obviously saw that little Christmas kiss.'

She shook her head, grabbed one of the glittery Christmas bags and nodded for Cat to take the other, before trudging towards the door.

Chapter Fifty

What could she do? Cat had now left close to fifteen messages on Amias' phone and sent even more than that number of texts, but all her calls went to voicemail and the texts remained unanswered.

Kyra was right. Amias had obviously seen that kiss.

So much for going back to the hotel to get some sleep. How could she sleep knowing that Amias was clearly annoyed with her?

And he had every right to be. The more she went over and over it in her head, the more she could see that.

She had promised she wouldn't kiss anyone and whether that request was meant in jest or not, she had broken her promise.

Why did he have to come to surprise her at the hospital? Why hadn't he called to let her know he was on his way? She would never have let Ben kiss her if she'd known Amias was going to be there.

But he had brought presents for her and Kyra and even Mary and Viola. That was so thoughtful and kind. So generous and caring. So wonderful.

And he'd been met with the sight of her, yet

again, kissing Ben. That must have been like a slap in his face.

She tried to call him again.

'Amias. Please, please call me back. I don't know what you think you saw but it wasn't what you think. Ben had mistletoe. It's Christmas. And he kissed me. I didn't kiss him. Why didn't you stay to talk? Why didn't you let me know you were coming? Why did you bring us those wonderful presents and then walk away? Thank you, thank you, thank you for those. It's so kind and generous of you. Please, Amias. I'm begging you. Call me. We need to talk. Your friendship means the world to me.'

Her heart leapt in her chest when she got a text a few minutes later but it died when she read the contents.

'Cat. I won't be calling and I'd appreciate it if you stopped calling me. If you ever need my help, I'll always give it, but I can't do this. I'm glad you like the presents. I wanted you all to have something to open on Christmas Day. Merry Christmas, Cat. I hope you get everything you've dreamed of. Amias.'

'That's it?' She screamed at the phone. 'That's all you've got to say? "I can't do this!" You can't do what? Can't be my friend? Can't return my calls? Can't speak to me? Can't see me?'

'Mum!' Kyra turned over in her bed and glared at Cat. 'Why are you shouting at your phone?'

Cat tossed it at Kyra, taking care to make sure

it landed beside her, not on her.

'That's why. Amias has basically told me to get lost and never speak to him again.'

Kyra sat upright, sighed and read the text. She then scrolled through the mass of Cat's earlier messages to him.

'I can't say I blame him. You were kissing Ben, after all. And I have to say, these messages make you sound a little crazy. First, you're pleading with him. Then you're ranting at him about some stunning woman eighteen years ago. Then you're begging him to call you. Did you leave him voicemails too?'

'A few.'

'How many is a few?'

'Ten. Possibly twelve. OK. Fifteen.'

'Fifteen? That's not a few. That's a bombardment. For God's sake, Mum. Are you twelve or thirty-five? The guy probably thinks you're nuts. He can justifiably accuse you of harassment after that lot and these texts. No wonder he's telling you to stop calling him.'

'But I need to explain. I need to talk to him.'

'You need to get yourself under control and get some sleep. Things will look clearer in the morning. Now I'm keeping your phone so you can't annoy him even more. Go to bed, Mum. Or go for a walk. Or take a cold shower. But whatever you do, leave Amias alone for a while. He's angry. He needs time to cool down. Sending him texts like these aren't going to help either of you.'

Cat collapsed on the bed.

'You're right. I know you're right. But I feel so frightened. So lost. So out of control. I can't bear the thought of losing him again, Kyra. I can't.'

'I hate to point this out, Mum. But you didn't actually have him so you can't lose him. You weren't dating. You were merely going to talk and we're both assuming that was about the possibility of being more than friends. But what if it wasn't? And I'm playing the devil's advocate here. What if he'd said he likes you a lot but that's all? Would you be shooting off crazy texts and making loony phone calls if he'd told you that? No. You might've been heartbroken but you would've smiled and accepted it and cried on my shoulder. This is just because of everything that's happened. And because you're tired. Please get some sleep. We'll talk about it in the morning. Come here and snuggle up with me... and Merry Christmas.'

Kyra shuffled down in the bed and held the duvet up for Cat to slip beneath it and join her.

What else could she do? Kyra had her phone so she couldn't call Amias and ask him to reconsider.

Chapter Fifty-One

Amias slumped into a chair and Natalia handed him a large glass of whisky.

'This was officially the worst Christmas ever.' He emptied the glass in seconds.

'Thanks.' Natalia tutted. 'Here. You may as well have the bottle. You and Dad can share it.'

'I didn't mean being here. This has actually kept me from going insane. I meant in general.'

Natalia gave him a sympathetic smile. 'I know. But it just feels that way. We've had worse Christmases before and we'll probably have some awful ones in the future. Life's not all roses, Amias. You know that.'

He sucked in a deep breath and refilled his glass, handing the bottle to Alwick who was sitting on the sofa a couple of feet away.

'If that's meant to cheer me up, it's not working.'

'Nothing will cheer you up right now. I'm pretty pee'd off myself. I was perfectly happy to give away the Christmas presents you bought for me on the basis that it would make Cat and Kyra happy. And because you let me open them first and promised you'd buy them all again for me when the shops reopen. But I should also point out that you used my favourite wrapping paper to wrap them up again and got me to do it. But anyway, once you saw Cat kissing that guy again you should've brought the presents back. She didn't deserve them.'

He shook his head. 'I couldn't. No matter what, she and Kyra had to have something to open.'

'I did warn you,' Alwick said. 'Those Devon women are nothing but trouble.'

'Yeah. Thanks, Dad. Shall I lie on the floor and you can all dance on my corpse?'

Natalia threw a Christmassy cushion at him.

'Oh don't be such a drama queen. You're heartbroken – again. We get it. But whose fault is that? You've had ample chances to tell the bloody woman how you feel. I'm not condoning her behaviour because I do think she's treated you badly, but it's not as if you were dating or anything. And you could just as easily have gone to the pub last night and kissed any number of women. As you usually do on Christmas Eve at The Hope and Anchor. Don't scowl at me, Amias. It's true. You do.'

Josh nodded and pulled a face. His head was clearly still hurting.

'She's right, Amias. You do.'

'OK. But only because it's Christmas Eve. Everyone does. And it's only kissing.'

'Hmm.' Natalia rubbed her chin. 'And it wasn't Christmas Eve at the hospital then?'

'Yes. But that's not a place to celebrate, is it?'

'Why not? I would've thought that's the very place to cheer everyone up by going around kissing and generally having fun. But perhaps that's just me. What I'm saying is it may be exactly what she said in one of her many, many messages and texts. A Christmas kiss under the mistletoe. And one other little point I'll make. If she doesn't care about you, Amias, why the hell does she keep calling and texting you and begging you to talk to her?'

'I wish I hadn't told you what she said.' He glared at Natalia over the rim of his glass.

'So do I, brother dear. So do I. But you did, so I feel I have the right to comment. You're cross. You're hurt. We all understand that. But we all saw the way you were kissing at Abigail and Will's party. That was definitely *not* a Christmas kiss under the mistletoe. That was full-on passion. That was intense, and hot and actually quite titillating to those of us who watched it. And I watched it. Did the kiss she and Ben shared look like that?'

He stared into his glass.

'No. It looked … nice.'

'Nice?'

'Yes. Gentle. I don't know.'

'It didn't look as if they were about to rip each other's clothes off?'

'No.'

'Then what on earth is the problem? Apart from her breaking her promise not to kiss anyone. Which is the most stupid thing I've ever heard. And you only said that to be facetious. You didn't really mean it.'

'But I did hope she wouldn't.'

'And at any other time of year, she might not have. It's up to you. As I said, I do think she's treated you badly but I'm not going to tar and feather her just yet.'

Amias grinned. 'You did that to the turkey.'

'Yay! You're getting your sense of humour back.'

'Who said I was joking? Pass the whisky, Dad. I need a top up.'

'You need a lobotomy, son, if you're even considering for one second giving a Devon woman yet another chance to break your heart.'

'I'm not. I can't do this anymore. I watched her fall in love with Kyle right before my eyes. Their kisses looked 'nice'. I'm not going to watch her fall in love with this Ben guy. Well, not up close, anyway. I'm going to make myself get over her if it's the last thing I do. That's going to be my New Year resolution.'

'I'll drink to that,' Alwick said, raising his glass.

'We'll all drink to that,' Josh added.

'You won't, darling. Not until your head is better. But I will. Here's to you getting over Cat Devon, Amias. It's only taken eighteen years. Well, eighteen years and counting.'

Chapter Fifty-Two

Christmas had not been the wonderfully cosy, joyful time Cat and Kyra had hoped it would. Cat had imagined sitting by the fire on Christmas Eve, opening presents with her mum and Kyra. And even Jeremy.

They had always opened their presents on Christmas Eve. At least they had eighteen years ago when Cat had spent her last Christmas in Merriment Bay.

It was a tradition Cat had continued when she ran away and moved into Bonniemount Cottage, although as Isla Presley preferred presents on Christmas morning, they had changed the tradition to only open two on Christmas Eve and to save the rest for Christmas Day.

Now that Cat was back in Merriment Bay, she had assumed they would open them on Christmas Eve.

But that was before Bailey Mitchell's arrival, his stroke and Granny Viola's signs of improvement. And before that conman and grinch, Jeremy Stone stole all their presents.

Well, not all their presents. They did have the

ones that Amias had given them.

'Apart from the presents from Amias, this has been our worst Christmas ever,' Cat said, when she, Kyra and Mary sat around Granny Viola's bed on Christmas night.

'I wholeheartedly agree with you, Catherine.'

Mary had hardly said a word all day. In fact, she'd hardly spoken since the policeman brought her back from Devon Villa on Christmas Eve, apart from saying that yes, Jeremy had stolen some of the silver, some cash from an ornate box in her bedroom, and a few rather valuable ornaments. But all of the items were marked with some special pen that the insurance company had told her about several years ago, so Jeremy might have trouble selling them. The policeman didn't seem to hold out much hope of Jeremy being apprehended though, and Mary couldn't seem to decide whether she was glad about that or not.

She had said a few words when Cat handed her the present to her from Amias on Christmas morning.

'Why has he bought me a present? I certainly haven't got one for him. Well, none of us has any presents for anyone, but what I meant was–'

'We know what you meant, Mum. He's given us each a present, and more than one to me and Kyra, so that we have something to open on Christmas morning. It's a kind and thoughtful gesture. Don't make it unpleasant for us. I've done that, myself.'

'Why?'

'I really don't want to discuss it now,' Cat had said.

At the time, Cat couldn't face explaining about the kiss with Ben and the fact that Amias had seen it.

'It hasn't been that bad for me,' Kyra said, smiling as crimson flushed her cheeks.

'That's right, sweetheart, rub it in that Mum and I are alone while you have the gorgeous Lucas driving all the way over here in awful conditions to pick you up and take you back to his parents' house for Christmas lunch.'

'You and Gran were invited too.'

'I know. I was teasing.'

'I'm surprised Amias didn't invite you to join his family, Catherine, especially after coming all this way last night to bring us those presents.'

Cat sighed. Now she had to explain about Ben and the kiss, which had resulted in Amias refusing to talk to her.

'And don't you dare say it's not the first time he's refused to talk to me because we both know that isn't true. When we've all recovered from the shock of Jeremy, we need to have a talk about that.'

'Why wait? We may as well get all the unpleasantness out in the open now. Maybe then we can start next year afresh.'

'Oh God,' Kyra said. 'Does this mean more rows?'

'No, sweetheart. It's too late to have a row

about something that happened eighteen years ago. Although I'm cross, I'll admit that. But it won't change anything. I just want to know the truth, that's all.'

'I'll tell you the truth, Catherine.' Mary sat upright and met Cat's stare from the other side of Granny Viola's bed. 'The truth is, you were far too young to have a baby and settle down with Kyle, but you did what you did and we couldn't change that. When he died, we thought you would have a new start but you refused to give Kyra up, which I fully understand, although I tried to make you see that my life would've been easier if I'd given you up.'

'Yes. I remember. You said that more than once.' Cat glared at her.

'But like you, I couldn't give my baby up once I'd held you in my arms. But this isn't about me. We're discussing you.'

'Wait. Do you mean you had the chance? To give me up, that is?'

Mary nodded. 'Yes. I was told arrangements could be made, but like you, that was one thing I refused to go along with. I fully admit that Mother and I signed the agreement concerning your father, and yes, we were amply rewarded for doing so, but I flatly refused to part with you for any sum. And we were offered rather a lot.'

'You've never told me that before. You've only ever said how different your life would've been without me and how having me was a huge mistake.'

'Having you wasn't the mistake. Having a relationship with your father was the mistake. But maybe I did say you were too. I say things I shouldn't when I'm cross. And also things I don't mean. It's one of my faults.'

'I do the same,' Cat said. 'Though I try not to be mean. You were mean with words, sometimes, and with actions too, it seems.'

'I'm sorry if I was. I never meant to hurt you. I think I meant to hurt myself. But anyway. We hoped that, if you weren't prepared to give Kyra up, you might at least be persuaded to pursue your art studies. We would've found a nanny and arranged everything. But we could see the way things were going. Amias was visiting you at the hospital and you were always pleased to see him. We dreaded you telling us that you had fallen in love with him. I know you'll say we were wrong because he's successful, wealthy and clearly a man of integrity, but the nineteen-year-old Amias didn't appear to be many of those things. None of them as far as Mother and I could tell. Although you obviously knew him better than we did. We made a decision to do everything we could to keep you apart. We changed your phone and the number but we blocked his number on your phone without your knowledge. You never were very technologically minded. Nor were we, but we knew a man who was. When Amias sent notes and letters, we returned them. When he called at the house demanding to see you, we told him you didn't want to see him and that you had asked us to contact the police if he continued to call. It took a long time but he eventually stopped. And we lied to you about him. He did want to see you and Kyra. He wasn't seeing other girls, as far as we knew, but we lied and said he was. We did what we thought would be best for your future. And for Kyra's. We were wrong. But in a way, perhaps, we were right. You have had a good life, and you did continue with your art.'

'Bloody hell, Mum. I've had a good life in spite of what you did. Not because of it. Kyra and I have had a good life because of Isla Presley and because my car broke down outside her cottage. Things could've turned out very differently. And if what you're saying about Amias is true, then perhaps we could've had a good life here. In Merriment Bay. With him. And also with you and Granny Viola.'

'I know. I realise that now. I'm sorry. There's nothing else I can say but that.'

'Wow,' Kyra said. 'This is so messed up.'

'I need some air.' Cat got to her feet. 'I'm going for a walk. Kyra, you're welcome to join me or you can stay here. It's up to you.'

'I'll stay here if that's OK. I think you need some time alone to process what Gran has just told you. It doesn't really affect me in the way it has obviously affected you.'

Cat smiled. 'I'll see you in a bit then. And Mum. Thank you, at least, for finally telling me the truth. And for actually admitting that you were wrong.'

'As I have said before. It seems I've been wrong about a great many things in my life. I am truly sorry, Catherine.'

'I believe you. But that doesn't make it any easier.'

She walked from the room and ambled along the corridor, glancing into Bailey's room as she passed.

Ben spotted her and came into the corridor.

'Want some company? You're looking a little out of it, if you don't mind me saying.'

'I've just been told something and I need to think it through. I don't want to be rude, Ben but I really need some time alone.'

'That's fine. You know where I am if you change your mind. Grandfather's asleep and Diana and I are going to go back to the hotel for the night. If you want to share our cab, you're more than welcome. Perhaps we could have dinner together later? Or a drink, maybe?'

'I'm not sure what Kyra and Mum want to do but I'll ask.'

'Cat? I meant you and me having dinner together. Or a drink. Just the two of us.'

'Oh. I see. Er. Can we discuss it later? I really need to get some air and clear my head.'

'No problem. Come and find me when you're ready.'

Cat gave him a grateful smile and turned away.

Why hadn't Amias said that? Why hadn't he asked her to dinner or for a drink? Why had he said they needed to talk?

Perhaps she had got the wrong end of the stick, after all. Perhaps Amias was going to say that he thought they should be friends and nothing more. Because now she thought about it, if he'd wanted to ask her on a date, surely he simply would've done that? Surely he would've suggested dinner or a drink? Not a talk.

He may have been interested in her eighteen years ago, if what her mum had said was true. And now she had no reason to doubt that. But perhaps he didn't feel anything more than friendship for her now. Perhaps that kiss had just been the way he kissed every woman, as she had thought it might. Maybe all her frantic messages and texts yesterday fell on deaf ears because those ears didn't want to hear what she had to say.

Perhaps it was time she got over Amias Wells. Time to start afresh. Maybe Ben could help her do that.

What had Amias said the other day? That Fate seemed determined to keep them apart or something along those lines. Or was it that Fate seemed determined to put things in their paths? She couldn't recall exactly.

But Fate had put Ben in her path.

Perhaps it had done that for a reason.

Chapter Fifty-Three

Cat slept for the first time in a while and woke on Boxing Day reinvigorated and ready for the day, whatever it may bring.

Perhaps that was due to the four glasses of wine she had drunk, or perhaps it was because she had spent such an enjoyable evening with Ben.

She had refused his offer of a romantic dinner for two and had eaten with Kyra and Mary as well as Diana and him but she and Ben had gone to the bar for drinks afterwards and one hour had drifted into two. Before she knew it, the clock was striking midnight.

Sharing a kiss at the door of her room seemed not just nice but natural. She didn't need to concern herself with promises to Amias now and for one second, she even wondered what she might have done if Kyra wasn't already tucked up in bed in their room.

Would she have invited Ben in? Would she have offered him a nightcap? Would she have offered him anything else?

It had been so long since she'd had sex but it wasn't just sex she wanted now. She wanted to be held in someone's arms. She wanted to feel cherished. Ben could do that, she was sure.

And if her dreams were still of Amias, wasn't that understandable?

Mary had only just told her that they may have had a chance to be together all those years ago. Of course she would dream that they were.

The dreams would fade and reality would take their place.

And she would get over Amias Wells if it was the last thing she did.

That was another thing she was sure Ben could help her with.

She showered and dressed and went downstairs for breakfast, feeling happier than she thought she would.

'You're looking cheerful this morning, Catherine.' Mary eyed Cat over her coffee cup.

'I'm feeling cheerful, Mum. The sun is shining. The snow is slowly starting to melt. That means we'll soon be able to drive back and forth to the hospital and won't need to stay at this hotel. Although, as it happens, I'm happy to stay here for a while longer.'

'I assume this has something to do with Ben. You enjoyed last night?'

'Very much. He's kind, considerate and thoughtful. He's intelligent too. And handsome and strong and … nice.'

'You're right, he is. But what about Amias Wells?'

Cat prickled at the mention of his name.

'What about him?'

'I thought you were in love with the man. That you have been for most of your adult life. Has one misunderstanding changed that?'

'It wasn't just one. It was lots of things. And no. It hasn't changed that. I do still … feel the same. But it's pointless holding on to something that can never be. I want a relationship, Mum. A real relationship. Not just a friendship.'

'So did I, and look how that turned out.'

'I'm sorry about that. I really am. But you can't be suggesting that Ben is anything like Jeremy.'

'I'm not. But he does live several thousands of miles away. Have you thought about that? Kyra is dating Lucas. I know she plans to travel and then to go to university next year but even so, Canada is a long way from here and a long way from Edinburgh. Not to mention Merriment Bay.'

Cat ordered breakfast from the waiter and helped herself to coffee from the fresh pot he had just placed in front of Mary.

'I'm well aware of that. And it's a problem, I'll admit. But we could spend a few months in Canada and some in Bonniemount at the cottage and a week or two here from time to time. I can paint anywhere. That's the luxury of being an artist.'

Mary raised her brows. 'Does Ben know about this plan?'

'Not yet. We haven't discussed the future. We've only just met. It's a bit too soon to be making those sorts of plans.'

'And yet you are.'

'No. I'm merely considering my options and trying to decide if this relationship is viable.' She lowered her voice. 'Don't say anything to Kyra. I don't want her to worry.'

'What are you two whispering about?' Kyra took a seat and darted a look at both of them.

'Were we whispering?' Mary said. 'I think we were discussing our plans.'

'Plans?' Kyra took some toast from the rack in front of Mary.

'For today,' Mary added. 'It's such a gorgeous day and we feel it would be good for us all to get out into the sunshine for an hour or two. We could go up to Beachy Head. Although no. The snow won't clear up there for some time. We could go for a walk or to the shops.'

Kyra screwed up her face. 'If you and Mum don't mind, I'd like to go back to Merriment Bay. There's a Boxing Day Dip. It's in the sea. Lucas talked about it yesterday but I didn't think he was serious. Apparently he was. He's already called me to check I'm going. They go every year. Lots of people do. He says the water's freezing but Amias will lend us wetsuits.' Her gaze shot to Cat. 'Oh sorry, Mum. I didn't mean to mention him.'

Cat smiled and patted her hand. 'It's fine, sweetheart.'

'Ah yes,' Mary said. 'The Boxing Day Dip. I've been to that once or twice in the past. It's fun,

I'll grant you that. If you enjoy shivering so hard it makes your teeth chatter, and being unable to feel your fingers and toes for some considerable time after.' She shook her head and grinned.

'That does sound like fun.' Cat smiled at Mary before turning her attention back to Kyra. 'How will you get to Merriment Bay? By cab?'

'No. Lucas says he'll come and get me. So if you and Gran want to come, or simply want to go home to Devon Villa for a few hours, we'll drop you off. He's coming to pick me up at 10.30 and he said the swim is at noon. Then everyone goes to The Hope and Anchor for a glass of hot Boxing Day punch and a buffet lunch. It does sound like fun, Gran. And we'll have wetsuits, so we won't be shivering quite so much. Oh. Morning, Diana. Morning, Ben. Do either of you fancy a dip in the freezing English Channel today? It's probably considered warm to what you're used to.'

'No,' Cat said, a little too quickly and much too loudly. 'I mean, Diana and Ben don't have swimsuits or anything and besides they're visiting Bailey.'

Ben smiled. 'Strangely, we were just talking about that. We've already phoned the hospital and Grandfather's fine so as it's such a beautiful day, we thought we'd spend some time outside.'

'Perfect,' Kyra said. 'You can see Merriment Bay. You'll love it. It's gorgeous. And you'll also be able to see where Bailey was stationed during the war.'

'I'd love that.' Diana looked excited.

'What are your plans, Cat?' Ben smiled at her. 'Are you going on this dip?'

'Absolutely not.'

He looked a little disappointed.

'It sounds like fun,' Diana said. 'The shops are open today, aren't they? I'm sure we can get swimsuits.'

'You'll need wetsuits,' Kyra said, laughing. 'The water will be freezing. Trust me. But you can hire those from Amias at the bay. He's got several. In fact, if I call him and ask, he'll keep some extra back for us for free.'

'We don't need wetsuits,' Diana said. 'We go swimming in icy water back home. As you said, Kyra, this will be like a warm bath for us. Won't it, Ben?'

'Er. I may stay with Cat. If that's OK with you, Cat?'

'Of course. But please don't stay on my account. I'm perfectly happy on my own. You go and have fun in the freezing water if you like.'

She laughed even though the thought of Ben and Amias in close proximity was rather worrying.

He glanced at Diana. 'Would you be happy if I stayed here? I would like to see where Grandfather was stationed, but I can do that another time. I'd prefer to spend today with Cat.'

Diana laughed. 'Of course. I'm a big girl, Ben. I think I'll be fine on my own. If that's OK with you Kyra? If you don't mind me tagging along.'

'I offered,' Kyra said. 'It'll be a good laugh, I think. I'll call Amias right now. What size are you? The same as Mum, I would guess.'

Diana glanced at Cat and nodded. 'Yep. I'd say so. And our Canadian sizes are different from your English ones, so let's go with Cat's size.'

Kyra picked up her phone and made a call. 'Hi, Amias. Yes, I'm fine. We're all fine. Don't worry. I'm calling about today. Lucas said he told you I'd be coming, and I am. But we'll need another wetsuit, please. Mum's size. Amias? Are you there? Yes. I did say Mum's size. Oh, but not for Mum. It's for Diana, Ben's sister. She's the same size as Mum, we think. Yep. That's a size 12, and no, Mum won't be coming. She's staying here with Ben. Oh OK. Sorry. I didn't know you were in a rush. See you later.' Kyra rang off and smiled at Diana.

'Is everything OK?' Diana asked.

'Yes. All sorted. He's apparently in a bit of a rush this morning but he's really nice so don't worry. You'll like him.'

Cat was surprised that Amias had answered his phone within a couple of rings and she was desperate to ask exactly what he'd said because judging from the snippets of conversation she had heard, Amias had at first thought she would be joining them. She could imagine what he'd thought when Kyra told him she wouldn't. And added that she would be staying with Ben. It sounded far more intimate than it was, even to her ears.

Why was she thinking about this? Amias didn't

care. He was annoyed with her, yes. But he had told her not to get in touch. He clearly didn't want to see her or talk to her.

But what would he think of Diana? Beautiful, sexy, fit and single, Diana, who loved the outdoors life as much as Amias. And it showed on every visible inch of her body.

Chapter Fifty-Four

'I should thank Kyra later,' Ben said, as Cat and he walked hand in hand along Eastbourne beach after breakfast.

It was virtually deserted save for a couple of people and their dogs and the tide was low with gentle waves lapping the sand and softly swooshing in and out, like someone breathing.

A bit like the machines connected to Granny Viola.

'What for?'

'For taking my sister off to swim and Mary back home for a few hours. I thought Mary might ask you to go with her.'

Cat shook her head. 'No. She told me she wanted to spend some time with her friends and to fill them in on the Jeremy situation. I think that means several drinks over lunch at Bella Vista, to be honest. But it'll do her good to see them. I'm sure she'll say things to them she wouldn't say to me and Kyra.'

'She seems to be handling that whole thing well. I'm not sure I could put on such a brave face if I were in her shoes.'

Cat laughed. 'It's the British stiff upper lip. And also because she's a Devon, as I'm sure she'll be only too happy to tell you if you ask. We Devon women are made of strong stuff.'

He moved closer and gently spun her round to face him.

The sun overhead was a balloon of pale yellow against a sky of icy blue. Tiny puffs of cloud, like snow-white bunnies' tails were dotted here and there as if Cat had picked up one of her artists' brushes, dipped it in her pristine-white watercolour paint and dabbed it against the wide canvas of the horizon. They drifted so slowly, they hardly seemed to be moving.

A seagull swooped towards the glassy-blue sea then soared back heavenwards.

Ben looked deep into Cat's eyes and smiled. A rather sexy, smile.

'You're made of gorgeous stuff. And I want to explore every inch of you.'

Cat gasped.

'Sorry. I shouldn't have said that. It's too soon, isn't it?' He looked genuinely apologetic.

'No. I mean, yes. It's a bit too soon. But there's no need to apologise. I'm flattered.'

'The last thing I want to do is offend you in any way. This isn't just about sex, Cat. This is me saying I really like you. I like you a lot.'

She glanced at him from beneath her lashes.

'And I like you, Ben.'

He smiled and eased her into his arms.

'That's all I need to know. I'm in no rush. We have plenty of time.'

'Don't you have to get home? Don't you have a return flight?'

It hadn't occurred to her to ask before now. Ben had previously mentioned that Bailey might want to stay on for a while and that if he did, Ben would stay with him, but he hadn't actually said whether they had a fixed return date that they would need to change.

He shook his head. 'No. Grandfather didn't know how long he'd be staying and insisted we get open-ended flights. And yes. We'll need to go home at some stage. But we have staff we trust and this isn't our busy season. That doesn't start until late March to early April and on through the summer until late October or early November, depending on the weather. It means we have December, January and February to do whatever we like, pretty much.'

'You could stay for a couple of months then?'

'If I had a reason to, yes. And I hope I'll have a reason, Cat. I really do.'

'What if Bailey wants to go home?'

'Diana is perfectly capable of getting him home. They don't need me to be there.'

Butterflies twitched in her stomach. Why didn't that prospect thrill her?

A couple of months with Ben, getting to know him. Kissing him. Going to bed with him. All that should have sent tingles of anticipation racing through her.

God. Just the thought of one kiss from Amias had made her insides go haywire.

Surely the prospect of two months of sex with Ben should be doing so much more than making her tummy twitch?

'That sounds lovely.'

Ben tightened his hold on her and leant in to kiss her.

It was a nice kiss, as all his kisses seemed to be, and when it was over he took her hand in his and they continued walking.

They walked some way in silence, hand in hand, both deep in thought, their boots pressing into the sand just a fraction with each step.

At least, Cat was deep in thought. Ben might simply be admiring the serene vista.

After a minute or two, he stopped suddenly again, looked up at the sun and then turned to face her, an expression of confusion on his face but a smile on his lips and a hint of amazement in his eyes.

'I can't believe that less than two months ago, I wasn't aware of your existence. I was happily jogging along with my life, gradually winding the tours down for the end of the season. Then a letter lands on Grandfather's doormat and my whole world turns upside down.'

'I'm sorry, Ben.' She shrugged and smiled.

'Sorry?' He laughed. 'Oh, Cat. Please don't be sorry. There's absolutely nothing to be sorry about. I didn't mean it like that. I meant I'm glad it happened. Getting to know you by chatting via social media brought something into my life that I didn't know was missing. Then when we spoke, that first time on the phone and I heard your voice, it was as if I knew you. At the time, I didn't think we'd meet so soon, but I knew even then that we would. And when I walked into that hospital, the day before Christmas Eve and saw you standing in the doorway of Viola's room, it was as if all my Christmases had come at once. As if I'd just been given the biggest and best Christmas present ever. I know it may sound clichéd, but I think I fell in love with you at that very moment. Forget what I just said. I don't want to take this slow. I love you, Cat.'

She looked into his eyes. Kind, caring, and rather lovely eyes.

'Ben, I ...'

What should she say? What could she say?

'It's OK, Cat. I know you probably don't feel like that about me just yet. But I also know you could. You said you like me. I'm happy to take this one day at a time. To see where it leads. To see if we can have a future together. But I have to tell you, Cat. I already know how I feel. I already know what I want. I want you. I want you more than I've wanted anyone in my life. I said that if Grandfather wants to stay, I'll happily stay with him and that if he goes home, I'll stay behind so that you and I can spend more time together. But I don't need time, Cat. I've made a decision. I'm going to stay, whether Grandfather stays or not. I want to stay with you. I want to stay for however long it takes for you to want to be with me. Just me, Cat. I want to stay until you feel the same. And then I want you to come back to Canada with me, and for us to build a life together.'

Cat blinked several times. 'Ben! I … I …'

God! What was wrong with her? Why couldn't she get more than two words out of her mouth? Ben had said he loved her. He'd said he wanted them to be together. He deserved some sort of answer.

He smiled lovingly. 'I'm not expecting an answer right now, don't worry. I know I'm asking a lot. I'm asking you to leave your home, your mum and your grandmother. I'm asking you and Kyra to move more than five thousand miles away from everyone you know and love. I'm asking you to start a new life with me. But I'm offering you my heart, my love, my home. We'll be a family, Cat. You and me and Kyra.'

Cat couldn't breathe. Suddenly the gentle swoosh of the waves increased in volume until they were thundering in her ears. Seagulls no longer soared serenely; they squawked and their wings flapped against the air like drums. The sun glared in her eyes. Her head swam, her legs felt heavy. Panic filled her heart.

It was as if history were repeating itself.

Kyle had said almost those exact same words to her more than eighteen years ago. Although Edinburgh was closer by about four thousand-five-hundred miles.

But this time she wouldn't be running away.

This time, everyone would know where she was going and why.

Everyone.

Including Amias.

'It's sudden, I know,' he continued. 'But please just think about it. That's all I ask. I wanted you to know exactly how I felt. I wanted you to be aware that this isn't just a holiday fling for me. An exciting adventure away from home. This is real. This is serious. This is something very special. I just wanted you to know that. I love you, Cat. I love you. Now that I've said it, I want to keep saying it.' He shook his head and gave a strange little laugh. 'Grandfather and Diana will tell you I'm impulsive. And I am. That's true. But this feels right, Cat. And I hope, one day soon, one day very soon, you'll agree with me on that. But I can see you're surprised. With everything that's happened, I understand that. So we won't talk about this again until you're ready to. And then all you need to do is tell me you feel the same. That letter landing on Grandfather's mat was the best thing that could ever happen. It brought me here, Cat. And I'm hoping it also brought me, you.'

He slid his arm around her waist again and pulled her to him as if he needed to feel her body against his. And when his lips met hers this time, his kiss was more than nice. It was filled with love and promise. With wanting and desire.

He was offering her his love, his heart, his

home. He was offering her a future. Her and Kyra.

If she said yes, she wouldn't be running away; she'd be walking forwards. Walking into a whole new future. One that she had never imagined was possible. Not even for a second.

Because how could she have ever imagined there could be a future like this for her?

The only future she had ever imagined since Kyle's death, the only future she had ever really wanted, was one with Amias in it.

But she now knew for certain that could never be.

Perhaps it was time she imagined an entirely different future.

And the future Ben was offering sounded so much more than nice. It sounded almost perfect.

Ben deepened the kiss and suddenly Amias didn't matter quite so much.

Ben's kiss was still a spark compared to the fire of Amias' kiss.

But it was definitely getting bigger.

And definitely a little hotter.

Chapter Fifty-Five

Cat had enjoyed a wonderful day and clearly, so had Ben. Since that second kiss on the beach, Ben hadn't mentioned love again, or said anything about the future, but they'd talked about all sorts of things and Cat felt she knew him a great deal better.

Over lunch, they did what other couples often did; they tasted one another's food, shared a kiss across the table, grinned foolishly at one another like teenagers and played footsy under the table.

After lunch, they'd gone to the Boxing Day Sales in Eastbourne shopping centre and when each of them had tried on clothes and asked for the other's opinion, they had laughed and joked, and even whistled at one another.

One of the sales assistants said they made a lovely couple when they went to pay.

'That's what I've been telling her,' Ben said. 'But she's not completely convinced yet.'

'Oh! I'm sorry,' the sales assistant said. 'I assumed you were married.'

Ben took Cat's hand in his.

'One day very soon, if I have my way, we will be.'

Cat blushed and Ben beamed at the woman behind the counter.

They had kissed again in the lift in the hotel and yet again outside Cat's room.

She eased away from him and smiled.

'I'll just put these bags inside and then we can go to the hospital.'

His eyes danced and his smile was oh so sexy. 'Need a hand?'

He stepped forward but she placed her hand on his chest.

His strong, hard chest.

'Na-uh. I thought you said you weren't in a rush. That we could take this a day at a time.' She grinned coquettishly.

'I did. We can. The problem is, Cat, you're just so God-damn sexy.'

She laughed out loud but excitement built inside her as she walked backwards into the room with Ben slowly moving closer.

Ben was pretty sexy too, right now.

'What if Kyra comes back?'

He smiled devilishly. 'Send her a text and ask how long she'll be.'

Cat smiled back and took out her phone, darting looks at Ben as she sent Kyra a text.

'We're back at the hotel and will be going to the hospital later. Shall we wait for you here or meet you there? What time are you leaving Merriment Bay?'

She had backed herself up to the side of her bed

and Ben took the phone from her hand, put it on the bedside table and kissed her.

His arms tightened around her waist and ever so gently, he eased her down on to the bed.

His kisses became more ardent as his hand drifted from her waist and caressed its way up the length of her arm, to the scar on her shoulder.

She tensed instinctively and for a moment his lips left hers and he looked into her eyes, holding her gaze as his fingers stroked the ridges of the scarred flesh from her shoulder to her neck and to her face. Then he kissed her again and his hand slid slowly down towards her breast.

Was she really going to do this? Was she going to have sex with Ben?

Or was this more than merely sex? Was this the start of a real relationship?

His fingers brushed over her jumper as she closed her eyes and held her breath expectantly.

Should she be doing this? Was this really what she wanted? Was this really *who* she wanted?

She heard the click of the door and her eyes shot open, for some reason half expecting to see a dark-haired, dark-eyed hunk of a man glaring at her.

But it wasn't Amias Wells who stood there staring at her, on the one occasion she actually wished it was.

It was Kyra, standing in the doorway. She looked confused and excited and shocked.

Chapter Fifty-Six

'Mum!'

Kyra's voice made Cat and Ben swiftly part.
Ben leapt from the bed and Cat sat bolt upright,
swinging her legs over the side and getting to her
feet.

'Kyra! Sweetheart! I sent you a text. We were
just kissing. Nothing happened.'

Kyra looked from Cat to Ben and back to Cat
again.

'I don't care about that. You're both adults. Do
what you want.'

'What's the matter then? You look upset.' Cat
hurried towards her. 'Has something happened?
Where's Mum? Where's Diana? Is everything OK
with you and Lucas? What's wrong?'

Oh God. Had something happened to Mary or
Diana? To both of them?

A burst of laughter shot from Kyra.

'Take a breath and give me time to speak and
I'll tell you. Gran's in her room. Diana's still in
Merriment Bay. I haven't seen her since Amias took
her to show her around the museum. I think he's
going to bring her back over, later.'

Cat almost choked and she definitely couldn't stop the gasp and strange little squeal escaping.

'Oh? When, exactly?'

Kyra frowned. 'I didn't ask. They're both adults, too, Mum. It's up to them. But I need to talk to you. I need to talk to you right now because the strangest thing happened today and when I mentioned it to Gran, I thought she was going to have a heart attack.'

'Strange in what way? Mum was upset, you say? Er. OK.' She looked at Ben. 'I'm sorry, Ben, but would you give us a moment, please?'

Ben looked flustered. 'Of course. No problem. I'll be in my room if you want me. I mean. When you're ready to go to the hospital. I hope everything's OK. I might give Diana a quick call to see when she'll be back.'

She smiled as he hurried out, Kyra stepping aside to let him pass.

'So what happened then? What was the strange thing?'

'Apart from almost walking in on my Mum having sex, you mean?'

'We were kissing. That's all. And I texted you. Why didn't you answer? You wouldn't have walked in on us doing anything at all if you had.'

'Because I was downstairs, on my way up here when I got it so I didn't think there was much point. I took Gran to her room and came straight here. Is that really all you were doing? Or have you now decided it's Ben you want?'

'I haven't decided anything. But Ben's my only choice. No. That didn't sound right. What I meant was, Ben wants me. Amias doesn't.'

'I still think you may be wrong about that but anyway. We can deal with that another time. I need to tell you about this and Gran's reaction. I didn't want to say too much in front of Ben. But this was really weird and I had to tell you immediately.'

'OK. I'm listening. But I'm just going to get a glass of wine. Would you like one?'

Kyra frowned. 'No. But you have one. I think you're going to need it.'

'Oh?' Cat took a bottle of wine from the minibar and poured herself a glass. 'I thought you said this was about Mum?'

'No. I said the strangest thing happened and Gran nearly had an apoplexy when she heard about it. Sit down and I'll tell you.'

'Now you're making me anxious.' Cat sat on the edge of the bed and took a gulp of wine.

'OK. We all went swimming, as you know. It was bloody freezing by the way, but such good fun. And so many people were there. You've got to go next year, Mum. Anyway. Afterwards, we were all supposed to be going up to The Hope and Anchor but Amias invited some of us back to his house to get showered and changed first. It's far more comfortable than getting changed on the sand or even at the changing rooms at Bay Water Sports. It was really warm in his place. He had that log fire burning and the heating on and although the sun's not that warm today, it was streaming through the windows, so I went into the lounge after my shower, in just my jeans and T-shirt. The one with the crossover back. Suddenly, this rather good-looking guy, about the same age as you or Amias, in his mid to late thirties, comes up to me and asks me who I am and how I got the mark on my back.'

'What mark on your back? Your birthmark, you mean?'

Kyra nodded. 'Lucas was still in the shower, so I'd gone into the lounge to wait for him. Anyway, I told this guy I was staying with my Gran in Merriment Bay and that I was born with the mark and that you had it too. I didn't give him our names at first, because it seemed a bit weird. He sort of smiled but he didn't really look happy, if you know what I mean and although he asked nicely, there was an odd inflection in his voice. I felt as if I was some sort of alien life form or had some terrifying disease or something. I asked why he wanted to know and he said he thought it was unusual and a very interesting shape. He thought it might've been a tattoo.'

'I suppose it does look a little like a tattoo.'

Kyra tutted. 'Mum. It looks nothing like a tattoo. But anyway, I smiled and walked away and then I saw him talking to another guy who looked just like him and it was obvious they were related. They were both staring at me and they came over from the crowd of people they were with and the first man asked if I'd mind if his elder brother took a quick look at my back.'

'How bizarre. Did you let him look? Didn't you ask their names? Or ask Amias who they were?'

'I'd looked for Amias but he and Diana had gone to the museum, so someone said.'

'Oh? Just the two of them?'

'Yes, Mum. I told you that earlier. And I did ask their names but they just skipped over that even though, when the elder brother asked for my name, I told him it was Kyra. Then he asked how I got the mark and I said that I'd already told his brother I was born with it. This guy says, "That's not possible," and then asks for my surname. At that point I'd had enough because although they were trying to be nice they were clearly irritated, so I told them politely that I had to find my boyfriend and I went to find Lucas. When we came back, I couldn't see them anywhere. So maybe they were the aliens.' Kyra laughed but it sounded forced.

'So Lucas didn't see the men? And you did nothing out of the ordinary to make them stare at you?'

'Mum! Of course not. And I just told you. They were staring at my birthmark. I just thought they were two weird guys who were interested in tattoos so I didn't make a big thing about it. Lucas and I went to the pub. Those guys weren't there and that was that. Amias and Diana still hadn't shown and then Diana texted to say she'd be staying on for a while and that Amias had offered to bring her back. We picked up Gran, and on the way back here, she asked if I'd had a good time. I said I'd had a great time apart from the creepy guys at Amias' and when she asked what I meant by that and I told her, she went as white as a sheet and nearly fainted on the back seat.'

'Good heavens. Why?'

'That's what I wondered at first. But now it's dawned on me. When I'd described the guys to Lucas he'd said it could've been anybody based on my description, but when I told Gran about them, and also said they looked so much alike that I knew they were related even before they told me they were brothers, Lucas said I hadn't mentioned the bit about them being brothers and if I had done he would've thought I'd meant... But he didn't get a chance to say who because Gran cut him off and said she wasn't feeling at all well and would we mind being quiet and would Lucas drive faster. Every time either Lucas or I opened our months, Gran had a sort of hissy fit, so we shut up and Lucas dropped us back here. But the more I thought about it, the more I realised it was obvious why Gran was so upset.'

'Really? Why? Because she was concerned for your safety? It does sound very odd. Why would these men think you were lying? Or stare at your birthmark in the first place. Perhaps we should report them.'

Kyra tutted again. 'Mum! You're missing the point. Gran wasn't concerned about my safety. She knew why the guys were staring at my birthmark.'

'Why? How could she know? What are you suggesting?'

Kyra looked her in the eye. 'I think the penny is beginning to drop, isn't it? I'm only guessing, and I suppose I could be wrong, but I think it has something to do with your dad. We've got the same birthmark and these men recognised it. I think they know who your dad is.'

'W-what?'

'And you haven't heard the best bit yet. When I'd made sure Gran was settled in her room and given her the bottle of whisky from the minibar, as she requested, I called Lucas and asked who he thought the guys might be.'

Cat knocked back the contents of her glass and took a deep breath. The thought that someone may have recognised the birthmark was a surprise to say the least.

'And?' Cat fiddled with the stem of her glass.

'It's the Wynters, Mum. Rafe and Adam are their names and they live at Wynter House. And guess what else? Their dad is dead and they live there with their grandmother, Olivia.' Kyra looked excited. 'Well, say something, Mum.'

Cat couldn't speak for a moment or two.

'The Wynters? Why would the Wynters know who my father was?'

'Oh for heaven's sake, Mum. Because he was their father too. We need to ask Gran about this and we need to ask her right now because I'm not having some guys staring at me like I'm some sort of freak, when it turns out we may, in fact, be related.'

'To the Wynters? No. That's not possible, Kyra. It's not. But I suppose you're right that they may know who my dad was, if your assumption is correct and they recognised the birthmark.'

'If you'd seen their faces, Mum, you'd agree with me that they were as shocked as you are now. Didn't Gran say you had two siblings? And that your dad was dead? And that it was his mother who came to her and Granny Viola to get them to sign the contract? Lucas says Olivia is a bit of a tyrant although Rafe and Adam take no notice of her demands and such. But he said he'd heard that in her day, she was terrifying and a force to be reckoned with. She lost her own husband young and turned into a bit of a cow, apparently. And what's more is that they are friends of Amias'. He's known them for most of his life and taught them both to sail and windsurf, according to Lucas, whose dad is also friends with them. Don't you see it all makes sense?'

Cat was having trouble seeing anything. Her head swam and her heart thumped against her chest. The last time she felt like this was when Amias had kissed her. But this was no kiss. This was something else entirely.

'I don't see anything, Kyra. I'm far too confused and surprised and frankly, too stunned to think. Are you actually suggesting that my dad was Olivia Wynter's son and that Rafe and Adam Wynter are my siblings?'

429

'That's exactly what I'm suggesting. And I'd stake my savings on Gran confirming it. If she doesn't have a heart attack beforehand.'

Chapter Fifty-Seven

Mary hadn't had a heart attack when Cat and Kyra went to her room but she definitely didn't look well.

For a while she tried to convince Kyra that her theory was utter nonsense but eventually, she relented and confirmed that Kyra was right. About everything.

'Now do you see why I couldn't tell you, Catherine?'

Cat was still too stunned to take it all in.

'No. But I can see why Olivia Wynter wouldn't want me to know. Why she wouldn't want anyone to know. And the worst part is, if I now say I want to meet my siblings, they'll probably think it's because I'm after their money or something.'

Kyra laughed. 'No need to worry about that, Mum. According to Lucas, they haven't got any. Well, not much. Their wealth is all tied up in the house and the land, and it's really tied up. I mean legally. Lucas has a tendency to overhear things he probably isn't meant to, especially at his dad's law firm. I don't know the details but I do know the Wynter brothers can't sell the house or land or anything. Apart from some cottages they own in the village of Wyntersleap. They owned them all once upon a time but some of them were sold off many years ago.'

'That rings a bell.' Cat stared at Mary.

Mary shook her head and sighed. 'Kyra's correct about the money. They did have some. Quite a lot, I believe, but unfortunately your father frittered most of it away, along with a few earlier Wynters. The only Wynters with any financial wherewithal were Sebastian, who was Olivia's husband, and Rafe. Although possibly Adam, too.'

'My father. That sounds so weird now. My dad's family owns a stately home not more than five or six miles from Devon Villa and I knew nothing about him or his family. What was his name? I don't even know that.'

'It was Phillip. Phillip Sebastian Rafe Wynter.'

'And my half-brothers are Rafe and Adam? Oh my God! I've just realised. I saw Adam in the village one day at the Christmas market and I really fancied him. I asked Constance Raine, who he was. Oh, yuck. I had the hots for my own half-brother. Just imagine what might have happened.'

Cat leapt up and jumped up and down, shaking her arms, hands and head as if she was trying to get rid of some creepy crawlies.

'Catherine. Please sit down. You're giving me a headache.'

'A headache! I could've had sex with my half-brother and you're worried about a headache!'

Mary tutted. 'You're exaggerating. You only

432

saw him once from what you've said so there was little chance of you having sex or anything else. But I appreciate the point you're making and I can assure you I would never have let that happen. What are you going to do now? Now that you know, I mean.'

'Have several stiff drinks. And a shower. I feel dirty somehow.'

'Oh don't be ridiculous, Catherine. The stiff drinks are a good idea but there's no need to shower or feel dirty. You're part of the landed gentry. That's hardly something to feel ashamed of, even if it is on the wrong side of the blanket. The Wynters aren't aristocracy. There are no titles in the family. But they can trace their lineage back to the times of Alfred the Great and beyond, and that's something to be proud of.'

'I don't care if they're not aristocracy,' Kyra said, laughing. 'I'm going to start wearing a tiara, because they do have a stately home.'

'This really isn't funny, sweetheart. This is a dilemma. I want to get to know my siblings but now I feel I can't.'

'Er. I hate to point this out, Mum. But I think they already have an inkling that you may be related. And I suspect this Olivia Wynter is having a similar conversation with them right now.'

'They may get in touch with us, you mean?'

Mary snorted derisively. 'It's more likely that we'll get a summons or such from Olivia's solicitors, for breach of contract and a demand for repayment of part of the money she paid us. I wouldn't wait for an invitation to afternoon tea to drop on to our doormat. Olivia Wynter will do all she can to ensure you are never acknowledged as a Wynter.'

'Ah,' Kyra said. 'But you're forgetting one thing, Gran. Mum and I both have the same birthmark. And from the way Rafe and Adam stared at it and practically accused me of lying about how I got it, so do they. I think it's from the Wynter side of the family. Which is quite apt really seeing as it looks just like a holly leaf resting on our shoulder blades.'

'Are you saying you could use that to blackmail Olivia Wynter?' Mary's voice rose to a shriek. 'For money?'

'Of course she's not, Mum. We're not criminals. She's merely saying that if Olivia threatened to sue you and Granny Viola, we could say that we have proof we are related and that if she'd rather keep that quiet she would need to rethink her position.'

Kyra laughed again. 'But money would be nice. And there's always DNA if she gets pushy. I hate to say this, Gran, but it's a good thing Jeremy left when he did. He would definitely have used this knowledge to blackmail Olivia.'

Mary closed her eyes and screwed up her face. 'That doesn't bear thinking about. What were you saying about those stiff drinks, Catherine? I could do with one right now. The minibar seems to be empty. At least, there's no more whisky.'

'I could do with several.' Cat smiled wanly at Kyra. 'Sweetheart. Phone down to reception please and ask them for a bottle of wine. I need to call Ben and tell him we may not be going back to the hospital just yet and that he should go without us. No. Wait. You'd better make that two bottles of wine.'

'And a bottle of whisky,' Mary added. 'Wine is not a stiff drink, Catherine, and if you think it is, you don't get that from the Devon side of the family.'

Chapter Fifty-Eight

Cat and Mary were slightly intoxicated by the time they made it to the hospital. Although Cat felt more so than Mary seemed to be and she was beginning to wish she had taken Kyra's advice and stayed at the hotel.

Ben walked towards Cat to greet her, but he stepped back a fraction and studied her face intently.

'Have you been drinking?'

'Yes. But it was necessary, believe me.'

'Is everything all right?'

'That very much depends on your definition of all right.'

'You're not making much sense, Cat.'

'Nothing makes sense right now. Not Granny Viola being in here. Not Bailey's stroke. Not you and me and Amias and Diana. Not life. Not Fate. Not anything.'

'I think you need to sit down.'

'I think I need to be held in your arms. And kissed as if I'm the most beautiful woman in the world. And … No. You're right. I need to sit down.'

Kyra shook her head and grabbed Cat's arm as

Ben stepped forward to help. Mary walked, albeit a little unsteadily to Granny Viola's room and Cat watched her, wondering how Mary had managed to stay relatively sober while she herself was having difficulty voicing what was in her head.

'As I believe Mum mentioned when she called you, Ben, she's had a bit of a shock,' Kyra said. 'We all have. I told her and Gran to stay at the hotel but they insisted on coming here. Fortunately, the nurse wasn't at the reception desk or she probably wouldn't have let us in.'

Cat smiled up at Ben as he and Kyra helped her to a chair beside Granny Viola's bed.

'You're very handsome, Ben. Have I told you that?'

He smiled. 'Thank you. And you're beautiful, Cat. Sit down and I'll go and get us all some coffee.

'I'm not beautiful. I never was. Even before I got these scars.' She tapped at her face and neck. 'Diana's beautiful. Diana's stunning. She's a stunning girl. And she's at the museum with Amias. Or at his house right now. His beautiful house. That's my dream home, you know. I designed that. Even the glass stairs to let more light in the hallway. But they may have been better on paper than in reality. Although he likes them. I didn't design the front though. He did that. And it's beautiful. But I'm not beautiful.'

'Mum. I think you should take a few deep breaths.'

Cat did. Loud deep breaths. But they didn't

make her feel better. It took almost an hour, several cups of coffee and a little nap in the comfy chair in the corner of Granny Viola's room to do that.

'Oh God. Why did you let me drink so much, sweetheart?'

Cat sat upright, wiped a trickle of dribble from her mouth, and gulped several mouthfuls of water from the glass, which Kyra handed to her from Granny Viola's bedside cabinet.

'As if I could've stopped you. You and Gran were pretty determined. I stopped after two glasses. You got through almost two bottles and how Gran isn't flat on the floor is a complete mystery to me.'

'We Devon women can take our alcohol,' Mary said, without even slurring at all. But perhaps she'd also had several cups of coffee.

'Where's Ben?'

'In Bailey's room.' Kyra looked Cat in the eye. 'And Diana's back.'

'Diana? Did … did Amias–?'

'Did Amias bring her back? Yes. But he dropped her at the door.'

'Did she have a good time?'

'She did, Mum. And I think you need to prepare yourself for another shock.'

Cat's stomach churned and she felt sick.

'She's seeing him again, isn't she? He's asked her out, hasn't he? Oh God. I knew it. I just knew it.'

'Er. No. He hasn't. But she's hoping he will. She's very keen on him and was asking me all sorts of questions. She was particularly eager to know exactly what your connection was with him.'

Cat couldn't stop the sigh of relief but Kyra's comment made her think.

'What did you tell her?'

'I told her that you'd been friends a long time ago and I told her a bit about Dad. Not all the details, just that he and Amias were friends and that Dad died and we moved away. I said you and Amias were still friends. I didn't want to lie to her but I couldn't tell her the truth. Especially not when, every time I've seen you lately, you're kissing her brother in the corridor of this place or having sex in our hotel room.'

'Who were you having sex with in your hotel room, Catherine?' Mary stared wide-eyed at Cat.

'No one, Mum.' She tutted and looked at Kyra. 'I'd be grateful if you wouldn't go around saying such things, sweetheart. OK, I'll admit that both you and Amias do seem to have a tendency to pop up at the wrong moment but I'm not always kissing Ben. And I haven't had sex with anyone for months.' She let out a sigh. 'Are you sure Amias hasn't asked Diana out? They haven't made plans to see one another again?'

'Not as far as I know. Why don't you call him and ask?'

Cat narrowed her eyes. 'Are you being facetious, sweetheart?'

Kyra grinned. 'Perhaps a little. But at least now you have another reason to call him.'

'I do?'

'Yes, Mum. You now know who your dad was and that you have half-brothers who just happen to be friends with Amias. And he's known that all along. It seems it's not just you he didn't tell. He clearly hasn't told his friends either because if he had, they wouldn't have been so surprised to see me and my birthmark, would they?'

'You're right.'

'So calling him and asking for info about them is a fairly good excuse for you to talk to him. Just don't blurt out anything about Diana right away. OK? Use my phone. That way he might actually answer.' Kyra handed her the phone and grinned. 'And don't start a row, Mum. Not if you want to mend bridges.'

Cat smiled and kissed Kyra on her forehead.

'You're a genius. How did I get so lucky to have a daughter like you?'

'You had sex with my dad. It's not rocket science.'

She winked and laughed and took the seat that Cat vacated.

Chapter Fifty-Nine

Amias glanced at his phone and smiled.

'I was debating whether or not I should call you. Is everything all right? Lucas isn't answering his phone. Where did you two disappear to? Or shouldn't I ask?'

'It's not Kyra, Amias. It's Cat. But please don't hang up.'

He stiffened at the sound of her voice.

'What do you want, Cat? Christ. Has something happened to Kyra?'

'No. Kyra's fine. She's sitting beside Granny Viola's bed. I borrowed her phone. And I think Lucas may be asleep. He apparently told Kyra he was going home to crash and I assume he meant on his bed, not anything else. Oh God. I shouldn't joke about things like that. I've had a bit too much wine and although the coffee's helped I'm not completely with it really.'

Amias let out a sigh of relief and allowed Cat to continue. He couldn't help but smile but he checked it as soon as he could.

'And you're calling to tell me this because…?'

'I'm calling to tell you that two men at your

house asked Kyra about a birthmark she has on her back. A birthmark which I also have on mine. They were two friends of yours, I believe. Rafe and Adam Wynter.'

He dropped onto a chair.

She knew. After all this time, she now knew.

'Did they? I had no idea. Is that why she left before I got back from the museum?'

'Yes. And you know why, don't you, Amias? I know who my dad was. Kyra worked it out.'

He didn't answer right away but he did go and pour himself a glass of whisky. A large glass.

'Did you hear me, Amias?'

'Yes. She's a bright girl. I knew that the moment I met her.'

'She takes after her dad. And I've been wondering if I take after mine at all.'

'Perhaps you should ask Mary.'

'I have. I'm now wondering if I'm anything like my half-brothers. Whether we have anything other than a parent in common. And who better to ask than their friend?'

He caught his breath.

'Asking them might be your best bet.'

'Really? Oh, OK. I'll pop round for coffee and a chat tomorrow, shall I? Amias, I know we've had our differences and I realise I'm not flavour of the month as far as you're concerned. Clearly Diana has that honour. But I think you owe me this, at least.'

'What did you say? About Diana, I mean. What does she have to do with this?'

'Nothing. I was merely astonished how quickly the two of you seem to have become an item.'

'A what? If you're suggesting that Diana and I are dating, you're mistaken, Cat. Not that it's really any of your business. Perhaps I should ask her out. You and Ben and me and Diana could go out as a foursome. Wouldn't that be cosy?'

'Yes. It would. We could all go to Bella Vista and chat about the fact that I'm a Wynter and you've always known it.'

'I haven't always known. Dad only told me when I was a teenager. And he swore me to secrecy so what was I supposed to do? Unlike some people, Cat. I don't break my promises.'

'Oh really. You made some sort of promise to Kyle, or so I've been told. What was that exactly? Because whatever it was, I don't think you kept it, did you?'

'I promised I'd take care of you and Kyra. And I tried. You know I did. We both discovered the other day that it was Mary and Viola who stopped that from happening.'

He was getting cross and he wasn't nice to be around when he got cross. He said things he often regretted.

He took a deep breath and tried to calm himself. Cat Devon always made him mad. He mustn't let her get to him.

'But you tracked us down, Amias. I know it was you who told Lorna where we were. And yet you didn't write, or come to see us, or try to fulfil the promise you made to your dying friend. So don't lecture me about not keeping promises.'

'I did come to see you and I saw that you were happy. I couldn't pop in for tea, could I? Because don't forget, I was under the impression that you had threatened to call the police and accuse me of stalking a few years before that. To admit I'd spent time and effort, not to mention a lot of money, trying to find you wouldn't really be a good defence against a complaint of stalking, would it?'

He took a few more deep breaths while silence hung between them.

'But why did you track us down if you didn't intend to see us?'

'Because as I said, I keep my promises. And because I needed to know you were both safe and happy and had enough to live on. It was obvious you were and when I spoke to Isla Presley I knew at once that you were in good hands and that's what really mattered to me.'

'You spoke to Isla? When?'

He hadn't meant to say that. Damn his temper.

'I arranged to bump into her in Bonniemount. I made up some excuse to talk to her. I think I asked her for directions or something. I don't recall. It was a long time ago. Fourteen years or so. And we chatted about family and she said she had a granddaughter of sorts and a great granddaughter, whom she loved very much and she hoped would live with her or nearby until the day she died.'

'She said that? To a total stranger?'

'I told her I was visiting a relative – a distant relative and that my mum was dead and about my sister. We had a conversation. I opened up to her and she opened up to me. She was a very friendly woman.'

'You don't need to tell me, I know how lovely she was. But I can't imagine you opening up to her. Or to anyone for that matter.'

'Really? You might be surprised. I pour my heart out to Natalia and Josh on a virtual daily basis. Not that it helps.'

'Perhaps you should check that you have a heart. Or that it's working as it should.'

'What's that supposed to mean? It's working fine. No. That's a lie. It's been defective for the last eighteen bloody years. What do you want from me, Cat? I mean. Why have you called?'

'I told you. I want to know about my half-brothers, Rafe and Adam Wynter.'

'I don't think I can help you. Talking to you about them would feel like I was gossiping. And I don't gossip, I told you that. They're my friends.'

'Fine. So much for saying I could call you if I ever needed your help. And some friend you are. You've not only lied and hidden the truth from me for all these years, you've lied and hidden the truth from Rafe and Adam too. Friends don't do that, Amias. Or haven't you heard? Friends look after one another. I should've known it was pointless to ask you.'

'I don't think that's fair, Cat. I've gone out of

my way to …' He let his voice trail off. He wasn't going to remind her about changing the locks at Devon Villa on Christmas Eve, or giving her and her family most of the presents he'd bought for Natalia. Or about how he'd helped Kyle, financially all those years ago by giving him extra hours and then the additional sum of two thousand pounds. For all the good that did. That extra two grand had vanished on the night that Kyle died. And shortly after, so had Kyle's parents. But at least he'd stopped them from taking Kyle's watch. The one that Cat had given Kyle. At least he'd been able to give that back to Cat. But he wasn't going to tell her that he'd had to buy that back from Kyle's parents, too. He wasn't going to tell her all the things he'd said and done to try to make her happy. Even though she was still ranting at him.

'To what, Amias? To be nice to me? To be my friend? Friends don't keep secrets from each other. Friends don't hurt their friends just because they can.'

'I've never done anything to hurt you. Not intentionally at least. I may have acted like a jerk sometimes when we were teenagers, but I never meant to hurt you. If I hurt anyone back then, it was me.'

'You hurt Kyle. You warned him against me. You told him we shouldn't be together. You told him I got pregnant to trap him.'

'No I didn't. He was the one who told me that.'

'So you say. But why would he?'

446

'I've been asking myself the same question, believe me. Over and over. The only thing I can come up with was that he wanted me to think badly of you. He wanted to prove my dad right. He wanted me to dislike you.'

'Why? That makes no sense. Are you saying he felt threatened by you? That he thought you might try to steal me away if you liked me?' A burst of hysterical laughter shot down the phone. 'Yeah right. He didn't need to do that, did he? You never really liked me, even though you said the other day you did. You made me think you might care about me, but you don't. You've never cared about me. Ever. Even though you've just told me that you promised your best friend you'd look after me and Kyra. He asked for your help and you didn't give it.'

'Don't ever accuse me of not caring about you and Kyra. If anything, I care too much. Far too much for my own bloody good. And I helped Kyle in every way I could. When he asked me for extra work, I gladly paid him even though my fledgling business couldn't afford it. And when he asked me for money just before you both ran away, I gladly gave it, just to make sure you and your baby would be OK. Kyle wasn't exactly the best friend a man could have, as I've discovered. He lied and deceived me too. And I think…'

Oh Christ! He had done it again. He'd blurted out the very things he'd been so determined not to.

'You gave Kyle money? When? Just before we

ran away? Just before he died, you mean?'

Amias shook his head and rubbed a hand across his forehead as he let out a deep, heavy sigh. He walked to the French windows and stared out across the bay. The sky was black, shimmering with twinkling stars, above a flat calm sea.

'It doesn't matter, Cat. It was a lifetime ago.'

'It matters to me.'

'Well, it needn't. It wasn't a loan or anything. It was a gift. For all the good it did.'

He forced a laugh.

'If you really gave Kyle money for me and Kyra then I'll repay you.'

Now he did laugh. A bitter laugh.

'So you don't even believe that? But it doesn't matter. And you certainly won't repay it. I know for a fact you didn't get it. Not that I'd let you repay me even if you had. I didn't mean to say it. I say things I shouldn't when I'm cross. And I seem to be cross almost every time I talk to you.'

'Actually. I think I do believe you. How much did you give him?'

'I said it doesn't matter.'

'And I say it does.'

He grinned suddenly. He was glad she couldn't see his face.

'And you think you'll win this argument?'

'It's not an argument now. It's a discussion.'

'Oh, I see. What? Like a kiss isn't really a kiss if it's under the mistletoe at Christmas?'

'For God's sake, Amias! Stop going on about

that bloody kiss. You may or may not believe this. At this point in time I'm not sure I really care anymore, but Ben's kiss meant nothing then. Yours meant the world. And the second time he kissed me meant nothing, either. Since then though, his kisses have got a whole lot more meaningful.'

'What?'

He clenched his jaw. What a fool he was. He should've hung up the minute she had said it was her and not Kyra calling.

He'd said he wasn't going to give her another chance to break his heart.

And yet he had. Cat Devon had done it again.

'You heard me.'

'So that's it, is it? You and Ben are having a relationship. Thanks for letting me know.'

'Don't pretend you care. You've never been interested in me in that way, so don't get angry just because someone else is. Because someone wants to kiss me and sleep with me and make me feel warm and safe and loved.'

'Sleep with you? You've slept with him? Already?'

'Already? If I remember correctly, you slept with more than one girl you'd only known for a day. So don't lecture me about that. But no. We haven't. Yet.'

'Yet? So you're going to?'

He heard her clear her throat.

'Mind your own business. Have you slept with Diana?'

449

'Diana? I only met her today.'

'As I said, that never stopped you before.'

'That was a long time ago. A lifetime ago.'

'So have you had sex with Diana or not?'

A burst of derisive laughter escaped him.

'Let me get this clear. It's none of my business if you've had sex with Ben, but you feel you have a right to know if I've had sex with Diana?'

'I'd like to know, that's all. I take an interest in people I think of as friends.'

'I'm not sure if that means I'm your friend, or Diana is, but no. I haven't had sex with her. Are you suggesting I should?'

'No! I mean. That's entirely up to you. I don't care either way.'

There was something in her tone that suddenly made him wonder if perhaps she did care. The shriek of 'No!' sounded very much as if she would rather he didn't have sex with Diana.

'I may be an idiot. In fact, I know I am. But it sounds a little as if you do. Do you, Cat? Does it matter to you who I take to bed?'

'No!' She coughed down the phone. 'I don't feel well. I think my hangover is kicking in. I need to go. You're obviously not going to tell me anything about Rafe and Adam, which is why I called you in the first place so we may as well say goodbye.'

'Is it, Cat? Is that really why you called me? Or was it to find out if Diana and I had had sex?'

She gasped down the phone.

'Goodbye, Amias. Have sex with who you want. I don't give a damn.'

'Cat? Cat?'

She'd rung off.

He frowned. Should he call her back? Did she care? Was she jealous?

He smiled to himself and stared out into the darkness. The lights of the houses in Merriment Bay and the Christmas lights along Coast Road twinkled and flashed and danced in the cold night air.

Perhaps Natalia was right, after all. Perhaps Cat Devon did care about him. And more than just as a friend.

He pressed speed dial and waited for an answer.

'Don't tell me,' Natalia said. 'Something's happened concerning Cat Devon and you want to know if you can come and talk about it?'

'How did you guess?'

She laughed down the phone.

'This may come as a surprise, Amias. But a two-year-old could guess that's why you've called. Cat Devon is all you ever want to talk about these days. You haven't even asked how Josh is but at least you haven't come round and simply burst in. So that's a step in the right direction, I suppose.'

'I was going to ask about Josh. You didn't give me a chance. How is he? And I can't burst in now we've given you your fancy new door.'

'Come round and bring some of your expensive wine and I'll tell you. And you can use the key in the key box to let yourself in if you like. Assuming you remember the combination. I've forgotten it already.'

He laughed down the phone. 'I'll be there in five minutes.'

Chapter Sixty

Cat was furious. Not just with Amias but with herself. She'd made it pretty clear that she did care if he was having sex with Diana. That it mattered to her a lot. And now he was probably having a good laugh about it and about how stupid she was.

Damn the bloody man.

'Mum! Mum! Come quick. It's Granny Viola!'

'Has she woken up? What's wrong, sweetheart? Oh no! Please God, no!'

Kyra had tears in her eyes as she shook her head.

'They're working on her now. The doctors. But it's not good, Mum.'

Cat ran to her and hand in hand they raced to Granny Viola's room just as the doctors and nurses who had been with Viola, pronounced her dead.

'There was nothing we could do. We're sorry,' one of the doctors said.

Mary crumpled to the floor in the corridor. Cat fell back against the wall a few inches behind her and Kyra burst into tears.

Bailey sat in his wheelchair, tears trickling down his cheeks but an odd sort of smile was sitting on his lips.

Ben and Diana helped Mary to a chair. Ben went to Cat and put his arm around her but she shook her head and eased herself away, wrapping her arms around Kyra instead.

Tears came thick and fast and the smile on Bailey's lips was actually annoying her.

'Why are you smiling, Bailey? She's dead. You didn't even get a chance to speak to her. What is there to smile about?'

He looked at her as if he was coming out of a trance.

'I'm so sorry, Cat. I truly am. But you're wrong. I was with her just before she passed. Sitting beside her bed and holding her hand. It was just me and my Viola. I was talking about old times and telling her how much I missed her and suddenly, she looked at me and smiled. That gorgeous beaming smile I've longed to see for so many years. Then she got up from her bed and walked to the door, swaying her hips as she walked, just the way she used to. And at the door she turned and smiled again and do you know what she said?'

The man was clearly delusional. Viola's death had affected him even more than it had anyone else.

Cat shook her head as Ben looked concerned and squeezed Bailey's shoulder. Cat wiped her eyes and forced a smile.

'No, Bailey. What did she say?'

'She said, 'I've missed you, Bailey. I hoped you'd come. Don't sit there all night. I'll be waiting for you to join me.' And she winked as she left. Just like she always did when we'd arranged to meet.'

Everyone stared at him but no one said a word until Diana let out a sudden shriek.

'No! She didn't say that. You're imagining it. Ben! Tell him it's all in his imagination. He's in shock. Doctor! Doctor. Please take a look at my Grandfather. He's not feeling well.'

'Shush, child,' Bailey said. 'I'm fine. I'm better than I've been for a long time. I feel like I'm young again. Like I'm about to get into my Spitfire and fly off on some new adventure. Don't worry about me, Doctor. Make sure Viola is comfortable. That's all that matters now.'

The nurses were unplugging the machines.

'We'll be a few minutes,' one of the nurses said. 'Then you can come back in to sit with her. You can stay for as long as you like.'

They waited in stunned silence, all dealing with the grief in their own way, Cat glancing at Mary and Kyra and Bailey every so often, until the nurses opened the door once more and said they could now go back in.

Bailey looked at Mary and Cat. 'Do you mind if I stay with her awhile?'

Mary shook her head, a dazed expression on her face.

'No. I think she would want that. I need to get some air. I can't be here right now. Catherine? Will you help me?'

'Of course.'

Cat and Kyra helped Mary to her feet.

'Take care of Mary, Ben,' Bailey said. 'And you, Diana. I'd like to be alone with my Viola for a moment.'

Diana hesitated. 'Don't you go anywhere. I mean it.'

'Where am I going to go, my dear sweet child? I'll be here with my angel when you get back.'

'Come on, Diana,' Ben said. 'It's what he wants.'

Cat smiled wanly at Diana as she, Mary and Kyra walked past and Diana and Ben followed them as they all trudged along the corridor, not knowing what to say or do. It was as if they were all in limbo.

'Let's go outside for a while,' Cat said. 'It's cold but it's such a beautiful night. Despite what's happened. There are so many stars in the sky, I noticed earlier.'

'Yes,' Mary said. 'Let's do that. Mother loved starry skies. She would sit in the window and stare out at them for hours, or sit up in the attic with the telescope. She said she used to do that to watch for planes returning in the war. But it was obviously for one plane that she was really watching out. It was for Bailey's plane.'

It was freezing outside and they could see their own breath in the air, but none of them spoke. Perhaps this wasn't such a good idea.

'I'm going back,' Diana said, after about a minute. 'I've got to, Ben. I've got the most awful feeling that something's not quite right. I think–'

'You think he's going to join my mother, don't you?' Mary gave her a small smile. 'But in a way, nothing could be more right, although it may not feel that way for us.'

'No!' Diana's horrified expression proved she was thinking exactly what Mary had said.

Ben smiled sadly at Cat. 'I'd better go too. Just in case. Are you OK?'

She nodded. 'I'm fine. You go.'

She watched as he and Diana hurried back inside.

'He's dead,' Mary said, once they were out of earshot. 'I don't know how I know that but I do. He's gone to be with the love of his life.'

'Oh God,' Kyra sobbed. 'I don't know if that's wonderful or awful. I don't know if that would make me happy that they're finally together, or sad that they're gone and they never got to speak. Do you think Granny Viola really knew Bailey was here?'

Mary nodded. 'I'm certain of it.'

'And do you believe he saw what he said he did? About her getting out of bed and walking out of the room and asking him not to be long?'

Mary nodded again.

'I didn't,' Cat said. 'I'm not so sure now. And if Ben comes back and says ... well, you know. If he says Bailey's dead, then I think I will believe it. Whether or not it's actually true. Because I think I have to. It's the only thing that makes this better. Not that anything can really do that. I never got to tell her I was sorry. I never got to say I loved her.'

Mary hugged her tight. 'She knew, my darling girl. She knew. And she loved you too. Probably far more than you could imagine.'

'I wish I'd got a chance to say hello to her,' Kyra said, shivering as she wiped her eyes. 'Can we go back inside? It's freezing out here.'

Cat shivered too. 'Yes. Yes we should. It's colder than I thought.'

'Perhaps it'll snow again,' Mary said, turning to go back inside and glancing up at the sky. 'It's strange how life goes on, regardless. When you lose someone you love, you expect the whole world to stop because it seems to have stopped for you. It doesn't stop though, does it? It keeps on turning.'

Cat nodded. 'I remember when the hamster died at boarding school. I was about eight, I think and I was so upset. I loved that little hamster. His name was Mr Dickens. Granny Viola told me to look out of the window and up at the sky and I'd see a new star there, twinkling. That would be Mr Dickens. I asked if the stars were all hamsters and she said that there was a star for every person and creature on the planet. So perhaps there's another star up there in the sky tonight.'

'Or two,' Kyra said, 'if Bailey's gone with her.'

As the door closed behind them and they walked along the corridor, Ben appeared before them, his eyes filled with sadness and a deep catch in his voice as he spoke.

'He's gone. I thought you'd want to know. We found him holding Viola's hand, his head resting on their entwined fingers. He looked so peaceful.' His lips quivered and it was clear he was fighting back his heartache.

'Oh Ben, I am so very sorry,' Cat said, unsure if she should go to him or not.

He shook his head. 'Mary is right. They're together at last and that's all he wanted. It's just tough for those of us left behind. I should get back to Diana. She's taking it badly. The nurses are with Grandfather now and he'll soon be back in the room he was occupying earlier if you want to see him.'

Cat nodded sympathetically. 'We'll be in to pay our respects but we'll give you both some time. We're going back to be with Granny Viola now.'

He smiled sadly as he turned back and walked beside them. 'I didn't think our trip would end like this,' he mumbled. 'I thought it would have a happy ending.'

'Perhaps in a way it has,' Cat said. 'For them, if not for us.'

He met her eyes. 'For us?'

'I meant for those of us left behind. For all of us who'll mourn them.'

'Oh I see. For a minute I thought …' He let his voice trail off and none of them said anything else, even when, several minutes later, they went into the separate rooms of Bailey and Granny Viola.

Chapter Sixty-One

Clearing Viola's room of the cards, and the little Christmas tree they had bought her, was depressing but they waited until after Granny Viola was taken to the funeral home in Merriment Bay the following morning. Then, after everything they needed to do at the hospital was done, and they'd checked out of the hotel, Cat, Mary and Kyra went back to Devon Villa.

But it didn't seem the same now they knew Granny Viola would never be coming back.

They had invited Diana and Ben to come and stay at Devon Villa but both of them said they didn't want to intrude on the Devon's grief and would remain where they were. Cat and Mary assured them they wouldn't be intruding, but Diana in particular remained adamant. Perhaps they wanted to grieve for Bailey separately.

'We should let people know,' Mary said, almost as soon as they walked in the door. 'I'll do that now.'

'It can wait, Mum. You need to get some rest. There's been one shock after another the last few days.'

'No. I need to keep busy. I don't want to have time to think. And it's what Mother would want. She wasn't one for weeping and wailing, you know that, Catherine. Life happens. Smile, whether you want to or not, and get on with it, she always said. So that's what I'll do. I'll get on with it and maybe in a day or two, I'll smile.'

'Is there anything you want me to do? Can Kyra and I help?'

Mary looked at them both for a moment.

'You could make us a pot of tea. And use the good china. Mother wouldn't want us drinking from mugs on the day she died. And then you can both make me a promise.'

'Oh? What's that, Gran?' Kyra asked.

'You can promise me that you'll both live your lives to the full. That you'll follow your stars wherever they may lead. That you'll chase your dreams, however out of reach they may seem. And that, when you know you're in love with someone, you'll throw caution to the wind and you'll tell them. If they don't reciprocate, then walk away and hold your head high but don't live your lives wondering what might have been. If you do something wrong, apologise, but don't let guilt or regret be a part of your lives. If you fall, get up again. If your hearts break, do what you can to mend them. I love you both. I want you to know that. I love you more than anything in the world. And Catherine, if you want to meet your half-brothers, then do so. Do what feels right for you. We'll face whatever that may bring. We'll deal with it together. Promise me all that and I'll be happy.'

'Gran? You're not going to go and die now, are you?'

'Kyra!' Cat looked at her in astonishment.

Mary smiled wanly. 'No, my darling. I'm not. I'm going to get through this and I'm going to practise what I preach. I'm going to live my life to the full. But first. I'd like a cup of tea and to sit in a comfy chair for a while.'

'I'll get that right away,' Cat said. 'I'll bring it to you in the sitting room.'

'I'll make up the fire,' Kyra offered.

She was good at that and although the heating had come on via the timer while they were away, the house felt cold somehow. Although that was probably more to do with their grief and lack of sleep than anything else.

Cat went to the kitchen and as she waited for the kettle to boil, she pressed speed dial on her phone.

Astonishingly, Amias answered right away.

'Good morning, Cat. Thought of something else you want to argue about? Or are you calling to see if I've had sex with anyone?'

He was being flippant and it made her smile. The sound of his voice made her smile. The fact he'd answered the phone after their row yesterday, made her smile.

'Neither. I'm calling to tell you that Granny Viola, and also Bailey Mitchell, died last night.'

462

'Jesus Christ, Cat. I'm so, so sorry. Are you OK? That's a stupid question. Is there anything I can do? Do you want me to come over? I'll stay out of Mary's way so she won't be more upset. Just say the word, Cat. I'll be there in a second.'

'No. We're back at Devon Villa. We can't do anything for the moment. And I think we need to get through this on our own. The three of us. Diana is taking it harder than the rest of us. She's devastated.'

He didn't comment.

'Thanks for the offer though. I really appreciate it.'

'I said I'll always be here for you, and I meant it. Do you want to talk about it? About Viola and Bailey, I mean. It's incredible that they both went during the same night.'

'I know. It was so strange. But in a wonderful way. Granny Viola passed away while I was arguing with you.'

'Oh God. I'm so sorry.'

'It's not your fault. Bailey was with her. Mum and Kyra had gone to get some coffee and when they came back, the doctors were working on her. Kyra came to get me right away but Granny Viola was gone. Bailey said she'd woken up and smiled at him and told him that she'd missed him and was glad he was there. Then he saw her get out of bed and walk across the room to the door where she turned, winked and told him not to sit there all night because she'd be waiting for him.' Cat fought back tears and caught her breath. Amias remained silent, as if he knew she hadn't finished. 'Bailey asked if we'd give him a few minutes alone with her and within fifteen minutes, he was dead. That's incredible, isn't it? It's as if he just decided it was time to die and he did.'

'I've heard things like that before. They say that sometimes, when you really love someone, you literally don't want to live without them. At their ages, it's not difficult to see how that could happen, I suppose.'

'Kyra and I, and even Mum and Ben, think it's romantic and somehow ... right that they went the same night. That they'll be together now. Is that ridiculous?'

'No. No it's not. Er. How is Ben?'

'He seems OK. Upset, obviously. But he's strong.'

'What will they do now?'

'I don't know. I haven't asked. But Bailey wanted his ashes scattered in Merriment Bay. Actually in the bay itself. It's in his will. And Mum told me earlier that it's what Granny Viola wanted too. That's also weird, don't you think? That they both wanted their ashes to be scattered in exactly the same place.'

'I can think of far worse places to end up. Perhaps it's because that was the last place they were happy together. This may seem a bit of a weird offer, but if you all want, I could take some of the ashes together in my Spitfire and fly over the museum and the bay before scattering them over the water. It's not really legal but we can get around that. It's just a suggestion and it would depend entirely on the weather and there not being any snow or ice on the runway.'

'Oh, Amias! I love that idea. And I know Mum will. I think Ben will too. I'm not sure about Diana though. I'll need to ask her.'

'Of course.'

'I'm not sure when the funeral will be. We're going to the funeral home later this morning to finalise that. I know this is awful but I wish it could be before the New Year. The thought of starting next year off with two funerals is so depressing somehow. But I don't suppose there's any chance of that. These things usually take a week or so to arrange, I believe. At least I know Isla's did. And then it's the time of year. I did hear one of the guys from the funeral directors tell Mum that this time of year was one of their busiest periods. Can you believe that? He and Mum are friends so they were just chatting, but even so. What a thing to say!'

'It's a sad fact, but statistically I believe that's true. But Cat, if you all feel the same about the funeral taking place within the next five days, it could be possible. I know people, and more importantly, Will Lester does. We could make some calls. Some religions require cremations to be carried out within a couple of days, so it can be done.'

'Thanks for the offer, Amias. I wish we could.

But Granny Viola deserves a proper send off, not something rushed. And so does Bailey. The kettle's boiled. I'd better go. Mum's waiting for her tea.'

'OK. Just let me know what you decide. About the scattering of their ashes, I mean. And anything else. And Cat?'

'Yes?'

'If there's anything I can do for you, just call me. I promise I'll answer my phone.'

'You answered it just now, Amias. You were there when I needed you to be. It seems you always are. I'm sorry for the things I said yesterday.'

'So am I, Cat. All I've ever wanted is for you to be happy. For you and for Kyra. I hope you believe that.'

'I do, Amias. I do.'

She did. Even if it was just as a friend, or if there was the slightest chance it could ever be anything more, Amias would always be there for her; she was certain of that. And she was sure he wanted her to be happy.

The question was, did he want her to be happy with him? Or did he want her to be happy with someone else?

Chapter Sixty-Two

After much discussion with the funeral directors, and with Ben and Diana, it was settled that the funerals for both Viola and Bailey would take place at the end of the first week of January but as none of Bailey's friends, or of Ben's and Diana's could be expected to fly thousands of miles for the funeral, Bailey would have a fairly simple cremation followed by a Memorial Service back in Canada.

Mary, along with Ben and Diana also agreed that Amias' offering to scatter the ashes from his Spitfire was exactly what both Viola and Bailey would have wanted.

It was arranged so that, weather permitting, there would also be a little service at the Merriment Bay WWII Museum over which The Reverend Bartholomew Raine would preside and after that, Amias would fly Viola and Bailey over the museum and do a little lap of the village of Merriment Bay and Devon Villa, along to Eastbourne Hospital where they died and back again to finally scatter the ashes over the sea.

But that was for next year. They all had to get through the last few days of this one.

And Cat had a decision to make.

Now that Bailey was gone, the only reason for Ben to remain in Eastbourne was to spend more time with Cat.

Just a few short hours before Granny Viola and Bailey died, Cat thought that was what she wanted. After all, if Kyra hadn't arrived so unexpectedly that day, she and Ben might have actually had sex by now.

But Granny Viola's death, and also Bailey's made Cat consider her future. Perhaps it was also because of the promise Mary had insisted she and Kyra make about living their lives to the full.

Yes. The idea of moving to Canada and of being with Ben and becoming a family, possibly even having more children, appealed to Cat greatly. But the fact remained that no matter how hard she tried, she still couldn't get Amias out of her head. And how could she start a new life with Ben if her old life was still holding her back?

She was determined to put the past behind her. Determined to have a real relationship. Determined to find love again. But something deep inside her told her that she wouldn't truly find that five thousand miles away.

Even if she didn't find it here, at least she wouldn't be running away again. Because although she thought that being with Ben wouldn't mean running away, she knew that in reality, it did.

And besides, as ridiculous as it might seem, Amias was always there for her. If that was just as a friend then so be it. But he definitely did care for her, she was certain of that. And who knew what might happen given time. Friendships often developed into something more. Some friendships developed into love.

Perhaps if she sold Bonniemount Cottage and moved back permanently to Merriment Bay, spent more time with Amias and maybe now, finally persuaded him to teach her to windsurf, there might be the smallest chance that their friendship could develop. And if it didn't, at least she would know that she had done everything she could to try to make it so. She would have followed her star. She would have chased her dreams.

The only thing she wouldn't have done, and couldn't see herself doing because she just didn't have the courage yet, was to tell the man she loved that she loved him. Perhaps one day she would. But in the meantime, she would have to tell Ben that unfortunately for them both, that man was not him.

He took it far better than she thought he might, but perhaps that was partly because he was still in shock over Bailey's death. Thinking you're prepared for such things was one thing; having to deal with the reality of it was a different matter entirely.

'We can still be friends, I hope,' she said.

He smiled somewhat sadly but nodded as he took her hand in his and kissed it.

'Definitely. We'll keep in touch, of course we will. And if you ever change your mind, you know where to find me. Just send me a letter,' he said, with a smile.

Chapter Sixty-Three

It was New Year's Eve and Cat had yet another decision to make: should she go to Natalia and Josh's party, or should she stay at home?

'I think you should go,' Mary said. 'Gladys and Annie are coming here to see the New Year in, and Kyra wants to go to the party with Lucas. You know she'll feel guilty if she leaves you here with us. Go, Catherine. Have fun. Mother would want you to. You know that. She would be cross if she thought you were sitting here feeling sad when you could be out there having a good time.'

'You're right, I know. But you've been invited too and you're not going. And I'm nervous about seeing Amias. He might be there with someone else.'

'Don't be ridiculous. Why would he be there with someone else? The man has called you every day since you told him about Mother. He's sent cards and flowers. He's arranged to scatter the ashes from his plane against regulations. He's gone out of his way to let you know he's there for you. I may not have always liked the man but he's definitely reliable and thoughtful and kind. And he's handsome too. You could do worse than spend your life with him, you know.'

Cat almost fell off her chair.

'What? Who are you and what have you done with my mum?'

'Don't be sarcastic, Catherine. I'm not in love with the prospect of having Amias Wells in my family, I assure you, and it's probably just as well Mother's not here to see this, but even I can see the man is good for you. You bloom every time he calls. Your eyes sparkle when you talk to him on the phone. Do I have to hit you over the head with a heart-shaped hammer? You're in love with the man, Catherine. Completely and utterly and unless I'm mistaken, he feels the same about you.'

Cat tutted. 'I'll admit I'm crazy about him. I always have been. And I probably always will be. But he's not crazy about me. I do believe he cares for me. And possibly a lot. But I'm not sure if that's out of some old promise he made to Kyle, a sense of duty, or just friendship. But if he actually loved me, he'd tell me he did. Or at the very least, he'd ask me out. And he hasn't. He's sort of hinted at it and made me think he might. But then he doesn't. I'm hoping that in the future, there's a chance he might, but he's not going to suddenly do that on New Year's Eve.'

'His father was the same. He couldn't tell me he loved me. Although he did eventually. But I could tell he did. And I think, deep down, you know Amias loves you. For some reason it's as if you're frightened to take that final step. To open your heart to him and tell him how you feel. You did make me a promise that you would live your life to the full and if you loved someone you would tell them, no matter what. You love Amias Wells. You need to tell him that before someone else sees what a catch he is and does it before you.'

Cat laughed. 'You're saying Amias is a catch! God, Mum. I'm getting seriously worried about you.'

'He is. I'll admit it. But this isn't about money or the fact he's got a profitable business. It's about the fact that I believe, like his father, he's a man you can trust, not just with your secrets, but with your heart.'

'Wow. Are you saying you think better of Alwick now too?'

'I've always thought highly of Alwick. As a man, not as a husband. Gina turned out to be the love of his life. Alwick and I were never meant to be. You and Amias are. I'm sure you're the love of that man's life and I just wish the two of you would stop wasting precious time and get on with it. You had the strength to tell Ben that there would never be a future for the two of you. That you loved someone else. Now it's time you tell Amias that it's him.'

Mary was right. She had told Ben. And it was hard especially after he'd lost Bailey. But it was the right thing to do. But telling Amias she loved him was a massive risk if he didn't feel the same.

But was it a risk worth taking now? She and Ben were still going to be friends. Perhaps if she did tell Amias and he didn't return her love, they could still be friends too and she could still hope that maybe one day, he would change his mind and say the words she desperately wanted to hear.

Lots of the things Mary had said made sense. Perhaps he did love her, after all. Perhaps it was time she found out, once and for all. If he wouldn't ask her out, perhaps it was time she asked him.

'I'm going to the party, Mum. Will you help me choose what dress to wear? Kyra is in the shower.'

'With pleasure, my darling. With the greatest of pleasure.'

Chapter Sixty-Four

Cat eventually walked into Natalia and Josh's at 11.30, having changed her mind several times about coming. She had insisted Kyra go ahead with Lucas and that she wanted to spend some time with Mary but would definitely get to the party. It had taken a bit of persuading but Kyra had finally believed her.

The truth was though, she wasn't sure she would go. She tried on so many dresses that she'd actually run out of things to wear. She wished she'd bought something new but it was far too late for that. She wanted to look stunning but every time she thought she was ready, she got a bout of nerves and needed to have a sip or two of wine to calm them.

'At this rate you'll be drunk before you get there,' Mary admonished, taking away her glass and replacing it with a cup of coffee – in one of the posh porcelain cups. 'Don't look at me like that. It's New Year's Eve. A time to bring out the best china and the best crystal. Now come with me. I think I have the perfect dress. It's actually one of mine that your father bought for me.'

'What? I can't wear an old dress, Mum. And certainly not one my dad bought for you.'

'Don't be so ridiculous. It's a gorgeous dress and it's in pristine condition. I only kept it because it's so lovely. And I know it will suit you perfectly. It's deep purple and that will bring out the green of your eyes.'

Mary was right. The dress was gorgeous. It was velvet, plain and hung off the shoulders. It was tight in every place it could be to show off Cat's figure. It made her feel beautiful, even though it didn't hide her scars which were visible on her cheek, her neck and her shoulder. Make-up made them less so but as Mary said, if Amias did love her, he wasn't the sort of man to be put off by a few scars. Especially as he knew they were there and how she got them, and he'd seen them more times than they could count and hadn't once looked at them as if they were ugly. In fact, they both agreed that he didn't even seem to notice them.

But as she finally walked into Natalia and Josh's lounge, she did pull her hair over her cheek for one brief moment before pushing it away again and taking a deep breath.

Several people gave her sympathetic smiles and said how sad they were about Viola but how well she looked and how pleased they were to see her but as she scanned the large room there was no sign of Amias.

'Lovely to see you, Cat,' Josh said. 'Sorry, once again, about Viola. You look beautiful tonight. We were beginning to think you weren't coming, but Kyra said you'd promised.'

'Thanks, Josh. You look good too. Are you sober tonight? The last party I saw you at, you weren't?' She laughed.

'Yep. Natalia has given me strict instructions that I must watch my drink tonight especially as we're the hosts. And it's not that I drink much usually. That's half the problem. I've never been one to regularly drink to excess, but when I do, I do it in style.'

'Yes. How's your head?'

'Good, thanks. Have you seen Amias?'

'Not yet. No. Is he here?'

'Yes. He was in the kitchen just now. Shall I go and find him for you?'

'Thanks. But I'll do that for myself. I want to have a word with him.'

'You're not going to have a row, are you?'

'No. At least I hope not.'

'Good. Because I really think it's about time you two worked it out and damn well got together.'

She turned to face him. 'Got together? You think Amias and I should be together?'

'Of course I do. And so does Natalia. And probably everyone else who knows the pair of you.'

'Why?'

'Why? Because the man's besotted with you and always has been.'

She gasped in surprise.

'Not always, Josh. But I hope that's true now.'

'Always. For the last eighteen or more years, at least. And I'll tell you how I know. Because he

477

comes to us to ask for advice. He came to us when he made a complete mess of firework night. When he was desperate to kiss you but he broke out in a cold sweat and was so terrified he'd make a mess of it that he made some stupid excuse and dashed off to get you food. He came to us every time you had a row on the phone. He came to us after that kiss under the mistletoe at Abigail and Will's party. Well, we were there. But he always comes to us. He's done so for years and he'll do so for years to come unless you finally put him out of his misery. Because although he keeps saying he's going to tell you how he feels, he never does. He's even more terrified he'll scare you away. So he'll go on pining for you for the rest of his sorry old life.'

'Pining for me? Wait. Did you say he said he was desperate to kiss me at the firework celebration?'

'Completely and utterly desperate. Because he's been head over heels in love with you for eighteen years and there's not a damn thing he can do about it, no matter how hard he tries. And I'll give him that much. He does try very hard to get over you. But every time he fails, and we're back to Cat this and Cat that and how much he hates you but also how much he loves you.'

'Loves me? You're honestly trying to tell me that Amias has loved me for eighteen years?'

Josh looked worried. 'I think I may have had a couple of drinks too many, as it happens because I probably shouldn't have told you all that. But what the hell. Someone needs to. Yes. You broke that man's heart when you fell in love with Kyle Morris and it's never mended since.'

'Now that *is* nonsense. Amias never liked me back then. He made that obvious.'

'Oh, he liked you. He liked you a lot, but that silly dad of his told him all sorts of tales about you and the Devons and you know Amias. When he gets something into his head you need to drill it out. But even for all the stories, he couldn't help himself and he fell hook, line and sinker in love. He tried to act as if he wasn't because he didn't want to be. And he does that even now. He doesn't want to love you, Cat. He simply doesn't have a choice. And he loves you more than anyone or anything he ever has. Possibly even more than Natalia. And he loves her a lot. But don't tell him I've told you. Happy New Year, Cat. I'm going to find my wife and tell her how much I love her because it's almost midnight and I'm going to be the last man she kisses this year and the first she kisses next. And if you've got any sense, you might go and do the same to Amias because I think you love him too, Cat Devon. And I think you're as bad as he is. You try to pretend you don't. And that gets no one anywhere.'

Cat watched Josh march across the floor, grab Natalia around the waist and plant a huge kiss on her lips. He said he was going to do it and he did.

He'd just said that Amias was in love with her. That he had been for years. That he always would be. Could that be true? Could any of what Josh had just said be true? It certainly explained firework night. Amias had done exactly what Josh said he had. And then, apparently, he'd gone to Natalia's and told her all about it. That meant, if this were true, Natalia knew that Amias was in love with her.

Was it possible? Was it at all possible that Amias really loved her? That he had been in love with her for all these years? Even Mary seemed to think so. But it didn't make sense. Why wouldn't he say so? He was outspoken enough about everything else.

But then nothing about her relationship with Amias had ever really made sense. And yet it had. It made complete sense. And she had loved him from the very first day she saw him on the beach.

What was it that Bailey had said in his letter? That we can't help who we fall in love with and that some loves last a lifetime. That nothing can end a love like that. Not guilt. Not distance. Not time. That some loves transcend all of that. He'd said that it's as if that person is a part of us and only with that person will we ever find true happiness and be at peace with ourselves and feel whole. He'd said that some loves define us. They make us who we are. And that there's no escaping that sort of love. No matter how far you go or how hard you try.

Cat could never usually remember things she'd read, even just after she'd read them, but those words had remained with her since the moment she'd first read his letter. The fact that she had read it more than twenty times might also have

480

something to do with why she could remember what it said.

Was that the sort of love she felt for Amias? And, if Josh had been telling the truth, Amias felt the same about her. Was that possible? Was it really possible?

She had to know right now. And as Amias had just appeared, now was the perfect time.

She took a deep breath, squared her shoulders and swept her hair from her face, revealing her scar in all its glory and she marched across the room and stood in front of Amias.

'Hello, Amias. I've just had a very interesting conversation with Josh.'

Amias looked surprised and the colour drained from his face along with his beaming smile. He darted a look at Josh and so did Cat. Josh raised a glass in the air and winked at them.

Amias closed his eyes for just a moment. 'Josh is drunk again, isn't he?'

'He says he isn't but yes, I think so.'

'And he's been telling you some ridiculous story, hasn't he?

'A story, yes. Ridiculous or not remains to be seen. Shall we go somewhere to discuss this?'

He furrowed his brows. 'Discuss what, exactly?'

'Discuss how you feel about me and how I feel about you.'

He made a sort of choking sound, as if he couldn't breathe.

'I think you've made it clear how you feel about me on several occasions, Cat. You don't particularly like me. I get it. Although sometimes you do. But from the look on your face I'm not sure if this is one of the times you do, or not.'

'You're right, Amias. Half the time I'm not sure if I do like you. But I am sure about one thing. I can't seem to get you out of my head. No matter what I do or where I go or how hard I try. Josh just told me you feel the same. And oddly enough, so did Mum, earlier. I can't believe it's true, but if it is, then now's the time to say it. Is it or isn't it?'

He held her gaze and adjusted the collar of his shirt although the button at the neck was open so it was in no way restricting his breathing. He swallowed several times. Ran a hand through his hair and glanced around the room before once again, meeting Cat's stare.

'Er …'

'Oh for God's sake, Amias. It's a simple enough question. A yes or a no will do. I need to know. Right now.'

'Yes.' He sounded as if he was choking. 'Yes, Cat. It's true. But I bloody well wish it wasn't.'

'Seriously!' Cat was astonished. And was actually a little cross. They'd wasted so much time. 'You could've said this years ago.'

'I could've done a lot of things years ago. But I didn't. And when I made up my mind to do so, I thought you didn't want to know me. I thought you had refused to take my calls. That you'd returned my notes and letters and threatened to tell the police I was a stalker. And then when you ignored my calls and stopped answering my texts a few weeks ago, I thought you were doing it again. Then I saw you and Ben kissing at the hospital and despite what you said, and discovering that it was Mary and Viola who had lied about everything, I didn't know what to think.'

'I admit I did ignore your calls and texts after dinner at your house, but that was before I knew that, eighteen years ago you didn't stop calling me and that you did come round. Before I knew my mum and Granny Viola had deceived me. Deceived us both. I believed them when they said you had no interest in me or Kyra and when I came to see you at the bay to ask you why, and saw you with that stunning girl, I realised I had to get away from you. From here. From everything. If I was ever going to get over loving you.'

'But at the hospital at Christmas, we both realised that we'd been misled. And yet you continued seeing Ben. How was I supposed to tell you I loved you, that I've always loved you when you were with someone else? I couldn't bear the thought of getting my heart broken all over again. Not that it ever really healed. Wait. What did you just say?'

'What did you just say? That you wanted to tell me you loved me?'

'Yes. But did you just say you had to get away to get over loving me?'

'Yes.'

He looked stunned. 'You loved me?'

'Yes, Amias. From the first time I saw you. And is it true that you loved me? Really true?'

'Yes. Maybe not from the first time I saw you but very soon after that. And I've loved you ever since.'

'I've loved you ever since.'

'You have?'

'I have.'

He shook his head and stared into her eyes. 'Is this a dream? Or is this real? Am I drunk? Or is this happening?'

'It's happening,' Natalia said. 'Believe it. And it's about bloody time.'

She and Josh had come and stood close by, and only then did Cat notice that a large section of the room had fallen silent and all eyes were on her and Amias, including Kyra's who gave her a thumbs up and a massive smile.

'Oh, for God's sake,' Natalia tutted as she continued: 'Will you just bloody well kiss the damn woman, you moron? It's almost midnight.'

Amias laughed. He simply threw back his head and laughed.

Cat laughed too.

Everyone else began to laugh. A little nervously at first but then they really got into it.

'Amias! Cat!' Natalia screamed.

'All right, all right,' he said, suddenly becoming serious. 'Um. Will you come with me please, Cat? There's something I need to say to you.'

'Say to me? What more is there to say? But if there is anything else, then I'd rather you said it here. Where I have witnesses so that I can check with them later that I didn't imagine any of this.'

He looked into her eyes once more. 'OK. If you want witnesses that's fine with me.' He took her by the hand and eased her into his arms. 'I've wanted to say this for more than eighteen years and I'm not going to risk losing another chance to tell you. I'm going to say it, right here, right now and I don't care who knows it. I love you Cat Devon. I love you with every fibre of my being. I always have and I know I always will.'

To cheers and whistles and fireworks exploding in the distance, and the sound of people counting down the seconds, he pulled her closer and stared into her eyes. Then on the chime of midnight, he kissed her.

Just like the previous kiss they had shared at Abigail and Will's party, it was deep and passionate, possessive and demanding, giving, yet filled with longing. It was sensual. It was sexy. It was intense, feverish, almost frenzied. It was all-consuming. It promised so much more than just a kiss.

It promised days of joy and laughter.

And nights of passionate sex.

It promised an end to doubts and sorrow and guilt.

But most of all, it promised a lifetime of love.

And it promised a bright new future.

And when they eventually managed to ease apart and he took her by the hand, wished everyone a Happy New Year and walked towards the door, she wasn't sure whether she was leading him, or if he was leading her. Or if they were both walking hand in hand together … as quickly as they could.

'Are we going to your house?' Cat asked, laughing with love and excitement.

'We're going to our house, Cat. To the dream home you drew and I've always wanted to share with you. I want you to see the bedroom.' He stopped for just a second and looked at her. 'If that's OK with you?'

'Oh, that's OK with me, Amias. That's more than OK with me. But there's just one thing you should know.'

'Oh? What?' He looked a little anxious.

'That once I'm there I won't want to leave. I'll want to stay. Possibly for … Oh, I don't know … let's say … forever.'

He beamed at her. 'Just for forever? OK. That's good. I like the sound of forever. But I want you there for eternity. How do you feel about that?'

'That we should run, not walk. Because I don't want to wait for one more minute to get into your bed and start our eternity together.'

'God, Cat. I've been waiting more than eighteen years to hear you say that. And to tell you how much I love you.'

'Me too, Amias. I love you with my heart and soul.'

'Happy New Year, Mum!' Kyra said, as Cat stopped briefly to kiss her. 'And Happy New Year to you too, Amias.'

'Happy New Year, sweetheart.' Cat beamed at Kyra and at Lucas, who was standing beside Kyra, his arm wrapped tightly around her. 'I'm going to Amias', so don't wait up. I'll call you in the morning.' She didn't need to check how Kyra would be getting home. Lucas would clearly take care of that.

'Happy New Year, you two,' Amias said to Kyra and Lucas before calling over to Natalia and Josh, 'Happy New Year, Natalia. Happy New Year, Josh. And thanks for everything.'

Natalia grinned. 'Same to both of you. And Amias. If you need advice, feel free to call.'

He laughed heartily, pulling Cat tighter to him. 'Thanks, sis. But I think I can handle things from here. And you probably won't be hearing from me for at least a day or two.' He smiled lovingly at Cat as they hurried on towards the door. 'We've got eighteen years to make up for.'

'I love you, Amias,' Cat said.

'I love you too, Cat Devon. You are – and always have been, and always will be – the only love of my life. There will never be anyone else for me. I want you to know that. I should've said this years ago.'

'You've said it now. That's all that matters.'

'And I'll be saying it every day from now on. That's something I can promise you.'

Cat thought her heart might burst with joy.

If there was one thing she knew about Amias Wells, it was that he always kept his promise.

A Note from Emily

Thank you for reading this book. A little piece of my heart goes into all of my books and when I send them on their way, I really hope they bring a smile to someone's face. If this book made you smile, or gave you a few pleasant hours of relaxation, I'd love it if you would tell your friends.

I'd be really happy if you have a minute or two to post a review. Just a line will do, and a kind review makes such a difference to my day – to any author's day. Huge thanks to those of you who do so, and for your lovely comments and support on social media. Thank you.

A writer's life can be lonely at times. Sharing a virtual cup of coffee or a glass of wine, or exchanging a few friendly words on Facebook, Twitter or Instagram is so much fun.

You might like to join my Readers' Club by signing up for my newsletter. It's absolutely free, your email address is safe and won't be shared and I won't bombard you, I promise. You can enter competitions and enjoy some giveaways. In addition to that, there's my author page on Facebook and there's also a new Facebook group. You can chat with me and with other fans and get access to my book news, snippets from my daily life, early extracts from my books and lots more besides. Details are on the 'For You' page of my website. You'll find all my contact links in the

Contact section following this.

I'm working on my next book right now. Let's see where my characters take us this time. Hope to chat with you soon.

To see details of my other books, please go to the books page on my website, or scan the QR code below to see all my books on Amazon.

Contact

If you want to be the first to hear Emily's news, find out about book releases, enter competitions and gain automatic entry into her Readers' Club, go to: https://www.emilyharvale.com and subscribe to her newsletter via the 'Sign me up' box. If you love Emily's books and want to chat with her and other fans, ask to join the exclusive Emily Harvale's Readers' Club Facebook group.

Or come and say 'Hello' on Facebook, Twitter and Instagram.

Contact Emily via social media:
www.twitter.com/emilyharvale
www.facebook.com/emilyharvalewriter
www.facebook.com/emilyharvale
www.instagram.com/emilyharvale

Or by email via the website:
www.emilyharvale.com

Acknowledgements

My grateful thanks go to the following:

Christina Harkness for her patience and care in editing this book.
My webmaster, David Cleworth who does so much more than website stuff.
My cover design team, JR.
Luke Brabants. Luke is a talented artist and can be found at: www.lukebrabants.com
My wonderful friends for their friendship and love. You know I love you all.
All the fabulous members of my Readers' Club. You help and support me in so many ways and I am truly grateful for your ongoing friendship. I wouldn't be where I am today without you.
My Twitter and Facebook friends, and fans of my Facebook author page. It's great to chat with you. You help to keep me (relatively) sane!
Thank you for buying this book.

Printed in Great Britain
by Amazon